THEORY OF MIND

AND OTHER STORIES

OBED OLIVARRÍA

metamorphosis
PUBLISHERS

THEORY OF MIND AND OTHER STORIES

Names: Olivarría, Obed, author.
Title: Theory of mind and other stories / Obed Olivarría
Description: Metamorphosis Publishing
Subjects: Science-Fiction | Short Stories | Collection.

For information contact:
http://www.obedolivarria.com

Print ISBN: 978-1-966179-03-0
eBook ISBN: 978-1-966179-04-7
Library of Congress Control Number: 2025911938

First Edition.

Book interior, cover design, and artwork by Obed Olivarría.

Printed in the United States.

OTHER TITLES BY OBED OLIVARRÍA

THE PAPER CRANE AND OTHER STORIES

THE FLIGHT OF THE BUTTERFLY

BROKEN

SCARS

To my father, Oscar Olivarría, who taught me to use my imagination and inspired me to unlock it to tell stories. You also taught me to love all things science fiction.

Thank you for everything, *Papi*.
You are greatly missed.

CONTENTS

PREFACE

L et me begin by stating that even though I haven't always been a writer, I have always been a story teller. Ever since I can remember, I have been telling stories, whether it was around a campfire, while sharing jokes with friends, during a class presentation, or from behind the pulpit. This is because I have always understood the power of story-telling to communicate.

From a young age, I learned that stories have the ability to help us understand meaning, empathize with others, influence our beliefs, convey values, and shape society. Stories also have a way of unleashing the brain's hormones, making us experience everything from love, comfort, fear, horror, and everything in between. Because of this, I will continue to use stories – whether fictional or nonfictional – for different intents and purposes, whether to share valuable lessons, to provoke, to challenge the status quo, or simply to entertain.

Nonetheless, it is important to realize that story-telling is a two-way street. The reader, or audience, and the writer, or orator, are a team. Together, they make the stories come alive. In this realm, a writer might put words on paper, but it is ultimately the reader that interprets the printed texts. For this reason, it is my hope that as you read these stories, you allow your mind to freely take off and not only imagine, but also experience the worlds and actions depicted in them.

I want to mention that choosing which stories to include in this, my first collection of stories, was a difficult task. Though I had written a number of stories to choose from, I chose to separate the sci-fi stories and the fantasy ones – or at least, those that felt like they fell within those categories – into separate collections. This book contains ten of the first mainstream sci-fi tales I wrote. I will be releasing a separate book with a collection of those stories that I felt fell more within the magical realism genre.

Lastly, I began my writing journey writing short stories, and though I eventually moved on to writing full-length novels, short stories have always been enjoyable for me. It is my hope that you enjoy reading them as much as I enjoyed writing them.

THEORY OF MIND

AND OTHER STORIES

AZURE

1

"*T*his is not how it always was, guys," began Shem, balancing little Aram on his lap next to the fire.

"You mean before the great flood, Dad?"

"No. I mean way before—when our people lived in a world far away from here, a crumbling world. One that was falling to pieces before their eyes." Shem took one of the rolls next to him and opened it.

"But was it better, uncle?" Cush, his nephew, asked from the other side of the fire. "I mean, this world was destroyed by the rains too."

"Oh, it was worse. It was much worse than this!"

"How could it be worse than the whole world being covered in water?" Aram inquired, standing up and taking a seat on a rock next to his father.

"Listen, guys," Shem replied, looking around at all the kids and teens gathered–his own children, his nephews and nieces. "This home we have made for ourselves here is way better than what our people had in the previous world. Yes, in the earlier days, before they messed it all up, it was magnificent. But it was destroyed too."

Shem bent his head and glanced at the writings; he wanted to make sure he told the story the way his father Noah had told it to him and his brothers. Noah had gotten it from his father, Lamech, who got it from his own father, and so forth. Tales of their beginnings, going back to the time when the world was about to end in the most brutal of ways for the men who came before them all.

"Let me tell you the story now..."

•••••

Before it all went awry, Crimson, our native planet, was at the peak of its powers. We had the best technologies; the best and brightest minds were churning out inventions by the day. Our ancestors had eradicated racism, making a single nation in our world. We were one people, united. And united we had conquered the deepest valleys and the tallest mountains in our sphere. We had studied the stars and traveled through space—even mined both of our moons. We had built the deadliest weapons. ergo we felt untouchable.

What could you do to a man who has touched the moons and spoken to the stars? Nothing! But in our complacency, our death began to creep upon us like an invisible disease.

It all began like simple cracks on a wall, little things people overlooked. Our people tossed waste wherever they felt like it; all manner of garbage was dumped into our waters sources, polluting everything gradually. Our people cut trees for fuel and for various industrial purposes, but planted none in return. Factories pumped harmful gases into the atmosphere. Quickly, carbon dioxide filled our atmosphere. Still, the people convinced themselves that none of it mattered.

There was one group which began a crusade to save the planet; they warned that this was just the beginning. That worse was still to come. And it would be much worse.

But no one listened. No one cared.

This group spoke out in public, to the masses. They put up warning artwork in the cities, circulated pamphlets, wrote jingles everyone laughed at, and broadcasted moving images in hologrammers, just to make sure people listened to what they had to say about our environment. But most of the people thought they were crazy and ignored them. Laughed at them.

Society continued to advance, and within a few decades, they drove these groups underground. Literally and metaphorically. It became illegal to speak out against the government and about industrial progress. But one group, a new generation of Crimsonians called the Violet Knights, continued to dissent and evangelize.

Soon, technology was sophisticated. Steam energy was replaced by red ore energy. It was much more advanced, but it required mining Crimson to the core. It meant stripping the land of our beautiful purple trees. It meant drying up the water sources and drilling the planet dry. Yes, vehicles were faster and could fly. Technology made things comfortable, quicker, and easier.

But it came with a high price.

Most people went ahead with their lives, ignoring the environmental "nuts" and their apocalyptic projections. They drove the faster vehicles and continued to build greater homes, while remaining completely unbothered about where the government tossed all their garbage.

The cracks continued to grow, becoming wider, as reckless activities and technological advances continued without check. People said they could never understand the obsession of these Violet Knights with global warming. The Knights warned citizens that they were increasing the carbon dioxide in the atmosphere and reducing the oxygen drastically. The water sources were evaporating too fast. Overpopulation was a conundrum. If they continued in such a way, the ozone layer would soon disappear. Without this protective layer, the sun's ultraviolet rays would cause radiation and destroy organic molecules. The temperature in the planet would be distorted and lethal.

Of course, no one cared about what they were saying, so they didn't pay attention. The scientists and scholars who did agree with the Knights were stripped of their titles and any credibility. It was dangerous to speak out. And since the people could still breathe well, they didn't care.

Some people wanted childbirth limited to one child per family. Groups lobbied the government to pass it into law—"One family, one child" soon became a catch phrase they bandied about. But to no avail. People drank, partied, and lived as lusciously as they could.

And as they ignored all the signs, the problem grew worse. Soon, the literal cracks in the planet's core and in the sky became gaping holes that no one could ignore. The first blow was when animals began to die. *All* the animals. No one knew what was happening, except for the few scientists and environmental groups who kept up with the warnings in subversive ways. Finally, people began to pay attention. The government also began to listen.

Unfortunately, it was too late.

The Crimson government set up a committee with all the best scientists in the planet—professors, engineers, environmentalists, biologists, physicists—the crème de la crème of Crimson. But by this time, things went from bad to worse very quickly. The ozone layer completely faded. The water bodies dried off completely. Clean water was harder to find than money. Food soon followed suit. It was a quick fall that had everyone wondering what they had done wrong. How could they have been so blind?

"How did it get so bad so quickly?" people wailed.

But it hadn't been fast. It was centuries of ignoring the signs.

Many cried. Others took their own lives in desperation. Our hitherto vibrant world had grown a lot quieter. And there was a shift—people finally began to do those things the "nature nuts" had spoken about.

A heavy famine descended on our world. The leaders swept in and imposed some measures in order to make sure that the available supply of food and water lasted as long as possible. It was the worst time in our history as a civilization. And just when we thought we had seen the worst, we were confronted with a new menace that completely befuddled some of us completely—dust storms.

Enormous clouds of red dirt came suddenly, billowing in from every direction. Large swirls of dust, miles high, began to cover everything. It wasn't the first time we were seeing dust storms in Crimson, but it was the first time they were on this scale. And they got worse every day, coming more frequently than usual. Lasting longer. Keeping people cooped up indoors. It was a menace we couldn't find a way to combat.

It was pretty obvious at this time that our world was not going to survive. It dawned on everyone, then, that they should have listened to these fanatics' pleas—plant a tree here, another there, dispose of refuse properly, be gentler with the environment. But it didn't matter anymore; the deed was done and there was no undoing. We were staring an apocalypse in the eye, together.

It wasn't long before people began to die off too; first slowly, and then by the masses. It was an irreverent kind of death, paying no heed to age. It took people at random. Soon, there were no animals on our planet anymore. They were all dead. The trees were mostly gone too. The vast majority were cut down by our hands, and now even the ones that remained began to wither and fall on their own.

A planet that once held more than four billion people now had less than thirty million. The biggest blow was when we found out that women were barren. No one knew why, but not one woman could get pregnant. And we knew then that we were doomed. A once great civilization, soon to be extinct, our death at our own hand.

Within a couple of years, as the atmosphere became toxic and the heavy red dirt blanketed all of our cities and the entire surface of the planet, Crimsonians were driven underground. People couldn't go out above the surface without protective suits and oxygen masks. There was no clean air anymore. Having no ozone layer meant having no life.

We lived in bunkers, deeply underground, designed in case of an attack from an alien civilization. These bunkers had been built by our ancestors many generations before, when scientists discovered that life existed away from Crimson. The bunkers were all connected through underground tunnels, and we got around through them in fast capsules. Underground, life was very subdued, and we lived in constant fear, wondering who was going to go next.

Crimson couldn't support us anymore. We had to find other options.

Toward the inevitable end, when people began to think all hope was lost, the survival task committee came up with what they thought was a practical solution—a way we might be able to survive the inevitable annihilation that was coming. But it had to be kept a secret. They didn't want our people to have unnecessary hope.

Government officials began to visit some homes. They came in pairs, carrying suitcases filled with information on members of the families they were sent to. No one was surprised, as everyone's data was stored in the CIB–the Crimson Intelligence Bureau. Those guys knew everything about everyone in our disintegrating world.

And that's when they came for me.

2

A bald man, who introduced himself as Agent Hezar, and his companion, a woman with a severe and stony face called Agent Ohma, came to our assigned bunker.

For hours they grilled Father. They questioned Mother next, who lay on her bed, unable to get up because of illness. She wasn't much help, as she could barely speak. Mother had grown so lean in the past month that I had already given up hope for her survival.

They came for me next. A relentless barrage of questions. I didn't like the CIB; they could have pushed the cause of the environment, yet they sat by and watched as the world died right in front of our faces.

"What did you do for the Violet Knights folks?" the man suddenly asked me. This must've been their thousandth question, and I was tired. But this question I didn't expect.

"Violet Knights?" I asked.

"Yeah, you know, the environmental group. I'm sure you're aware of exactly what it is that we are talking about. Don't pretend. We also know that you—"

"You don't know anything," I interrupted.

My father's eyes stared daggers into me, shaking his head from side to side.

"Excuse me?" Agent Hezar asked.

"You are assuming things," I said, ignoring my father's subtle plea to ignore the man's tone. "You *think* you know stuff, but you don't really know anything."

"Look, Adam, you are part of the last generation of Crimsonians born," Agent Ohma said in a neutral tone. "We are simply going around doing research as of now, but—"

"Research?" I chuckled. "You're a couple centuries late for that. Don't you think?"

The agents looked at each other without saying a word.

"What my partner is trying to say, Adam, is that the CIB, under the direction of the Crimson World Government, is actively doing something about our circumstances now. And the reason for us being here is that we are in need of… well… we need volunteers for something special."

"Volunteers?" I straight up laughed now.

"Think of it as a mission. But we can't talk about it, unless you are selected. That's why we want to know more about you, about your family, and other things," Agent Ohma added.

"Well, whatever it is, I am not interested. And you can leave now. Thank you very much." I got up and showed them to the door of our bunker.

"Adam!" Father said.

"No, it's okay, sir. We have enough," Agent Hezar said.

To my surprise, they got up, shook my father's hand, gave a nod to my prostrate mother, and left.

"What happens now?" I asked.

"Nothing. We continue with our lives," Father replied flatly. "Our short lives."

He was right—we were doomed to die soon. All of us. It didn't matter what we did.

Mother died a week after the CIB agents came to our bunker. Father and I went above the surface, with permission from the government, to send her body off. Later that same day, I received a hologram message from the CIB at the bunker. They wanted me to come down to their base at the underground town of Curna in the next two days. Curna was our new underground capital. I showed the hologram message to my father, who was growing weak himself, only his stubbornness keeping him going.

"What does this mean, Adam?" he asked. "I mean, what do they want with you?"

"I do not know, Father. I guess I will have to find out."

I set off for Curna early the next day. The fast tunnel capsule took less than an hour to get there. I was unsure of why I was being summoned. I didn't have many friends left alive anymore, so I had no way to know if others were also being summoned, or if, perhaps, I was being called in for my reaction the other day. I had done nothing wrong, but these times were unpredictable and it was impossible to trust the people who had let us get to this point.

If only people had listened when the Knights warned them about the impending doom. I was passionate about the environment, which was my only reason for joining the Violet Knights two years prior. I was one of the few young ones there–the only one from the last generation of Crimsonians. A year ago, no one listened to us, but of course by now, *everyone* wanted to listen. How things had changed so quickly.

When I got to the CIB headquarters, I was given a nametag and sent to a waiting room. There were several other young people sitting in the small room, perhaps twenty in all, but I didn't want to make eye contact with any of them. As I sat down, I glanced around quickly and saw that, indeed, we were all young– teenagers–all part of the last generation.

Interesting. I wonder what they want with us.

The chairs were comfortable, yet everyone here looked uneasy and confused, just like me. I was relieved to know that I wasn't alone.

"Adam?" a voice called.

I turned and found Ruel, a schoolmate of mine, sitting on one of the chairs on the other side. His was the only upbeat face in the room, and I was sure it wasn't because he saw me. I returned a tight smile. We weren't friends. In fact, I didn't like him.

"How are you doing, Ruel?" I asked, stretching my hand out to him for a handshake as he walked toward me.

He grabbed my outstretched hand and pulled me up to him in an unexpected and unwelcome bear hug. "It's good to see you!" he bellowed.

He's glad to see me? I wish I could have said the same and meant it.

"Likewise," I lied, disentangling myself from his brawny arms.

Ruel had spent most of our school days in the gym or flying through campus in his Astra-236, one of the fastest and most expensive vehicles in all of Crimson.

"How have you been, Adam?" he asked, still beaming.

I looked him over and got angry anew. This was one of the people that contributed to the decimation of our planet—he and his wealthy miner family. Yet, here he stood, robust and filled with energy, showing signs of good feeding, unlike the rest of us here, just because he was from an influential family. Even with the rationing going around, these people still feed like the old kings. It was disgusting.

"Why are you so chipper? Look at everyone else," I whispered instead, casting my eyes around at the other occupants of the room, an equal mix of men and women.

Ruel drew closer and whispered into my ear, "You don't know yet? Oh, of course you wouldn't know." He smiled as he finished, looking smug.

I raised a brow, but didn't say anything.

"Let me tell you." He sat down and patted the chair next to him. After I dropped into the seat, he whispered in my ear, "I have an inside scoop, and I heard that we have been chosen to help save our planet." He sat back and beamed a searchlight smile into my face.

This should cheer me up, but coming from him, it felt like the worst news ever delivered. Ruel, one of the most ignorant people I knew, ready and raring to go into some miracle mission. He was a symbol for all the others—the same people who couldn't think to pick up after themselves when our world was giving us signs of decay, fools who tore through Crimson in vehicles that only damaged the ecosystem, who didn't give a single care of our fragile planet. And now they wanted to save it?

Idiots!

"Good day, young Crimsonians!" boomed a voice in the small room, bringing me back to the present. Agent Hezar walked into the room.

The others stood at his entrance.

"Please, sit," he said, "I am only here to make sure that everyone made it." He looked around, quickly making eye contact with each of us. "And I see that you all did. Welcome! It's good to see you all." He cleared his throat as he turned around. "The director will be here soon to explain everything to you. In the meantime, loosen up, smile a little. We have not brought you here to eat you. So, yeah, just mingle."

Nods greeted his last words, and he left the room with the same energy and smile with which he had entered. He had the desired effect on my somber companions, their taut faces loosened up a notch.

Ruel turned an "I told you so" eye on me, sporting a silly smile. I didn't have long to contemplate his face, as the CIB director soon stepped into the room. She wasn't old—certainly too young to be a director, I thought.

"Hi, everyone. I am Director Neargal of the CIB. I decided to take this briefing myself. I wanted to look into your faces and tell you that you might just be our last hope as a civilization." She paused and looked at all of our faces.

She had remarkable eyes, large pristine orbs that stared deep into your soul. She walked around in the room as she continued.

"You may not know this, but we have been working extremely hard to find a solution to the menace currently tearing our world apart. Up until now, we have studied and explored all our options, but so far, we have failed."

I thought in my heart of other ways they had failed. Pompous barbarians that had ignored all the studies researchers and scientists had conducted and presented to them in the past, when we still had a chance. What else could they do now?

"But we think we've found something," she continued. "Come, follow me. I'll show you and tell you everything in the meeting room."

We all quietly stood and followed her to a nearby office. This bunker space was huge. Modern. Bright. Nice. There were several people working, walking around between office spaces. I then noticed a couple of the ladies from our group as I walked behind them.

Hmm... this suddenly is starting to get better.

The director let us into the room and told us to take a seat around the massive oval table facing the middle. We all fit, and many chairs were still left empty. I stared down at the table's pristine white surface, thinking about how clean it was, how pure.

She took a control device and began showing interactive hologram images in the middle of the table. "We have explored other planets nearby, looking for another possible habitat for all of us."

This caught my attention. I focused my gaze more closely on the images of planets and information about them. The Knights had explored possible ways of overturning our planet's death sentence, like the planting of trees and reduction of harmful gases, and reverting to a different kind of energy source. But in all our studies, we had never thought of leaving—of giving up and starting over.

"I see I have your attention there, Mr. Human," the director said as she looked at my name tag, smiling for the first time.

"Yes, ma'am. For some reason, I never thought of that as a possibility—"

"I am sure you despise us for being reactive," she interrupted me.

I heard gasps from the group.

"We are aware of your previous activities and interests." She paused and looked around. "And that goes for all of you here."

I thought hard on how to respond. I took a deep sigh and finally replied, "It is not the fault of a single entity, ma'am, it was a collective failure."

She quirked a brow. "Yeah, you and I know that's a bunch of vrem shit!" she said. I smiled my response, and she resumed her briefing.

Vrem had been extinct for centuries, but we continued to use their excrement as an expression of revulsion.

"Anyway," she continued, "After our last exploratory mission failed, we had to dial back and approach this from another angle." She continued to change the holograms with new information coming up that we could all see from wherever we sat. "As you all know from school, there is a blue planet nearby named Azure. We believe that this sphere may be the only thing standing between us and complete annihilation." She paused again, looking at all our faces, waiting for the import of her last words to sink in.

All of us knew that there was no life on any other planet in our system of solar spheres. Or at least that's what we were told in school. Was that information wrong? I mean, wouldn't the gases there kill us? Why there? We didn't even know what we would find there! Yes, we had been to space a lot, but only to our moons, never that far away.

I looked around and saw that Ruel was the only one with a tinge of a smile on his face. The others simply looked in awe. I wondered what it was that kept that awkward smile on Ruel's face, but the way he eyed Director Neargal and licked his lips gave him away. It sickened me.

"We cannot send a large expedition to Azure. But you, all of you here, are our last hope."

We all looked at each other, no one knowing what to say.

Director Neargal continued, "You are a group from the last generation of born Crimsonians. And we believe you can go there and explore. Well, some of you, anyway."

My head was already forming a thought; I suspected where she was going with this.

One of the ladies asked the same question I was sure we all had. "Do you want to send us as an advanced team? Like, to explore or something?"

"Yes, Miss Mars," she replied as she looked at her name tag. "That's exactly why you are all here today. We want to send *some* of you to explore and report back to us. This is our only hope now, our last resort. But it is up to each of you to decide whether you want to do this or not. Just know that you were each carefully selected for this mission."

Explore another planet? Never in my life did I imagine such a thing. And suddenly I, too, had a smile on my face.

Perhaps there was hope, after all.

3

We were allowed to go home after the briefing. This was to be a voluntary mission, so those who chose to be a part of it had to return with their belongings in two days. If someone didn't show up, it was assumed that their decision was made. Needless to say, it was a serious decision, as this could turn out to be a suicide mission. We were also aware that staying here and doing nothing would also lead to the same fate.

Of course, I had already decided to join while the director was still speaking. Doing something and trying was better than simply waiting for inevitable death. I would have begun immediately, but Father was at home and I needed to let him know that I was safe. The director had spoken of the need to keep this a secret, as it was essential to prevent anyone's hopes being raised prematurely, a very Crimsonian thing to do now.

"Father!" I called as I entered our small living quarters.

No answer. Fear squeezed my heart, as I knew he had been anxious about me leaving and waiting to hear what happened.

Then I saw him. Father lay lifeless on his bed, his hand thrown over his chest like one in deep sleep. His chest didn't move, but his eyes remained open and unseeing. This was how death came to us then, eating slowly into you and blowing open suddenly in your face.

I cried. I was all alone now. I cursed. I punched the wall and cried some more.

After a couple of hours of agony and loneliness, I draped my father in Belarshki wrap, took my breathing suit, and went above the surface to give him a farewell. I didn't want to waste time going through the process of asking the government for permission, since I had experienced that legal pain with Mother just a couple of weeks earlier. Besides, I already knew they weren't even guarding the tunnel entrance to the surface in my bunker town.

It was customary to send out Crimsonian dead on a river, but there were no rivers left. They'd been gone for generations. And if there were, they'd all be frozen without our thermal blanket layer anyway.

Above the ground, no remnants of civilization endured now. Everything was covered in red dirt and heavy red rocks. The planet was being transformed, ever-changing. The shift in our planet's tectonic plates was quickly crushing our underground tunnels, bunkers, and cave towns as well. Our end was nearing.

Not wanting to lose the tunnel entrance, as the dirt could quickly cover it, I pushed my father's wrapped body down a nearby crater, as we had done with Mother. I watched his body slowly drift down, even gravity failing in our wasteland planet.

I stayed above ground longer than I should have, looking at the stars. One of those bright lights was Azure. Perhaps it could be our salvation. Soon, I would either die brutally in outer space, or Azure would be habitable, and I wouldn't have to think about Crimson anymore. Either way, I'd be saying goodbye to my once-beautiful red planet in the near future. And that was fine; I had nothing left here.

My mask started to beep, the oxygen running low in my cheap suit, so I returned to the belly of Crimson before it was too late.

At the bunker all I did was pack my stuff. I didn't own much, anyway. I left everything else intact. As I exited, I didn't look back. I had to move on.

The weeks that followed Father's death were spent in drills, countless instructions, and more drills. We had all returned–even Ruel. Part of me hoped he wouldn't, but of course he wasn't going to miss an opportunity to be a hero. Luckily for me, the two cute girls I had noticed came back too. And I learned their names, Zilu and Eve.

We were first divided into groups of six, so there were four different groups training separately as a team. We were numbered one through six. Each team had three men and three women on it; I was right that first day to think there was a balance of the sexes.

I was part of Team Three. The team assignment was both good and bad. Ruel Verz was on it, to my disappointment. Our team also had Traun Urmeh, who blinked a lot and spoke rapidly, but he was nice. Then there was Lilith Eir, a short and stocky girl who didn't speak much, just partook in the drills and walked off by herself afterward. But Zilu and Eve were also on my team. Finally a bit of luck! Zilu Mars had long, flowing hair and a quiet disposition. Eve Serth was tall and thin, and could've easily been a model before all hell broke loose on Crimson. She had piercing black eyes that seem to appraise everyone and everything at the same time. Team Three was completed by me, Adam Human, assigned team leader. By the end of our first day back, Ruel was already making moves on the three girls in our group.

Each team was given a bunker to live in during our stay. I welcomed it since I craved company.

We were given weapons training, endurance drills, survival skills, and even some basic engineering and electronic knowledge. We learned about red ore power and studied potential alien biology. Then, after a few weeks, we learned to work with the "cripods." I didn't know why they named them that or who even named them, but the space crafts that would take us to Azure were the ugliest things I had ever seen in all my life. Even Ruel turned up his nose at the sight of the bulky things. They looked like rocks—large, gray rocks sitting in an old air strip. How were these things aerodynamic in any way? But I saw that there were only two of them.

"You don't think we deserve to die in better ships?" Ruel asked the director, eyes wide and unbelieving.

Director Neargal was here for all our drills, hands-on, dragging us toward readiness in remarkably quick time.

"Excuse me?" She rolled her eyes. "These cripods have been designed specifically to get you to where you need to go in the best possible speed. It is designed for practicality and impact, not for looks. So, Mr. Verz, I recommend that you stop worrying about the looks of the ship, as no one is asking you to make love to it." Her statement drew a chuckle from all of us. "Just know that it is designed to take you there and for you to survive."

There was a collective gasp when we all stepped into one of the pods. The interior of the cripods was sleek, nothing like the ugly exterior. This was my first time stepping into a craft of this sort. So many screens. So modern and streamlined. The vast amount of knobs and dials was intimidating, and the rest of the group appeared equally overwhelmed. Ruel announced that it looked very much like his Astra-236, which was met with silence. None of us wanted to hear him ramble about his privileged nonsense.

The six different groups took turns practicing and learning the cripods. As a team, we mastered the controls in a short time, learned our drills, and we were put to a readiness test. We passed with flying colors. The CIB had done their jobs right during selection. Very soon I learned that everyone on the team was among the best young brains of Crimson. Well, at least from those that remained. Even Ruel, with his pretentious posturing and selective ignorance, had a Crimsonian brain that worked well, especially under pressure. I guess he really wanted to do this, after all.

I'm sure I wasn't the only one who noted that each pod could only take six people at a time, but there were twenty-four of us. I figured they had other ones somewhere else.

"Your final drill is a lesson on escaping your cripods in case of emergencies. Tomorrow we are going to take a good old aircraft out into the open above ground and practice some diving on parachutes," one of the trainers told us before we dispersed to our various bunker rooms at the end of the long day. "Listen up, as this is very important," he added. "Tomorrow, we will also select the two groups that will go on this mission, so give it your very best as a team!"

Well, there's my answer.

I sighed to myself. I was sure that our team wouldn't make the cut. Ruel had been messing around since the drill started. Most of the other teams were surely ahead of us by then. But I would still try my best.

Back in our bunker room, Lilith — who never said a word to anyone—fixed a pointed gaze on Ruel.

"How were you even chosen for this mission?" she asked.

"What do you mean?" Ruel thundered. "Same as everyone else, I guess. I mean, how were *you* selected?"

"Sure! You probably bought your way into this too," Lilith retorted with a snort.

"I can see it. Rich kid with the latest Astra model. Pretty face, and an air of superiority," Eve added. "Makes sense to me."

"You girls are dumb and jealous," he said, turning away from them to see something on his hologrammer.

I sat on my bed and watched the drama unfold, smiling. I wasn't about to rush to Ruel's defense; he deserved all that was coming to him, after all.

Traun was the only one who spoke out against Lilith and Eve, saying reasonably that Ruel should not be blamed for his wealth. "Leave him alone. It's not his fault he's rich, you know?" He then went ahead to stuff his mouth with food.

That was something else about here—we were fed well, unlike back at our respective homes. That was nice. In just a few weeks I had gained much-needed weight, and I felt great. Strong.

Lilith turned around and walked out of the room, Eve following behind her. Ruel sat sulking in the corner, unwilling to talk to any of us. Zilu and I watched each other and smirked.

This should be interesting tomorrow.

The next day, we flew above Crimson's red ground for a while, my eyes scanning the horizon, ruing the evil that brought our great civilization to an end. I also lamented whatever it was that had put Ruel and I on the same team.

Eve's eyes had a twinkle in it. Zilu's smile made me nervous. In a good way, I guess.

We all had our parachutes strapped to our backs, waiting for the signal to jump.

"Okay, team, let's just give it our best shot!" I called out to all.

Ruel rolled his eyes at me.

Eve smiled and threw me the A-Okay sign and mouthed, "We've got this," before we all jumped from our older training flying disc.

When we got back to the surface base, there were three corpses lying on the red dirt-covered tarmac. Two of the dead were from Team One, the other was a member of Team Six. One of the women from Team Five was crying unconsolably, with two of our trainers trying hard to make her stand. She screamed something unrecognizable, and removed her mask from the breathing suit frantically. The trainers tried to stop her, but she ran away.

She didn't last.

What in the world is going on?

"Those chutes were double checked. There was no way they could have malfunctioned," I heard Neargal say to one of the engineers, a few feet away from the commotion. "And go get that girl!"

My team and I looked at each other. We were told to mind our business and keep walking toward the underground. We obeyed and entered the elevator. Once inside the receiving bunker, we removed our masks. Nobody knew what to say or what to do. What had just happened out there?

I saw a small smile pass Eve's face and that wild twinkle in her eyes again. "I told you we'd be okay," she whispered and walked away.

Goose bumps rose on my arms.

What did you do?

Not long after that, an announcement came over the communication system. "Teams Two and Three, report to the conference room."

4

We kept climbing fast, lifting toward the dark Crimson sky, while paying close attention to our navigation system. We were all quiet as the rocky pod carried us toward Azure, the mysterious blue planet. I looked around at my team, this disparate squad that wore the fate of all of Crimson on her sleeves: Traun Urmeh, who still blinked ten times a minute and ate nonstop, brooding Lilith Eir, cute but mischievous Eve Serth, attractive and enigmatic Zilu Mars, and flamboyant Ruel Verz. Plus me, determined Adam Human. Team Three, on a mission to a new world.

In the past weeks that felt like months, we had to speak to each other more frequently, and we all did, except for Lilith, who still said only the most necessary of words. Still, we were pretty effective for a motley crew, as each one played his or her part well.

We watched our system, maintaining radio silence as the cripod picked up speed and sailed into space. Though each on their own, the two cripods were connected to each other through a powerful wave signal so that we could keep track of each other as we journeyed on.

"What do you think we will find up there?" Zilu asked as we marveled at the expanse of the extensive universe.

We had examined this question in our minds a lot in the past week. Playing hologram cards before bed, we often created imaginary creatures, describing them as best we could and having a good laugh.

"We will find out soon enough," I replied, shifting my eyes between the outside and the cripod screen.

The journey was preprogrammed, with the cripods on auto-pilot, yet we needed to watch for any problem so that we could adjust manually. As team leader, I felt extra pressure, since the safety of the people on the ship and the success of the mission lay on my shoulders.

"We shall, indeed," Eve agreed as she pressed some buttons.

The next few days were more of the same. We took turns sleeping in the pod chamber, as the trip would be a full twenty-six days at this speed. We got even closer with each other, having to share a smaller space than our compact bunker room back in Crimson's underground. We communicated with the other pod and with home base, but only at determined times.

I grew fond of my team. We shared stories, laughs, and desires. We pranked each other. We grew to understand and love each other. We had all lost so much back home—some more than others, but we'd all been affected. Our entire world had been impacted. We were dying, going extinct as a species. And these two small groups of young people were Crimson's last hope. We were all optimistic of what Azure had to offer. It was our last resort, after all.

But not all of us would make it there. On day twenty-four, our fate changed.

"Uh-oh," I faintly heard Lilith mutter. "Guys, wake up!" she called out.

Zilu, Eve, and I woke up to join the others. "What is it?" Eve asked as she yawned.

"Look!" Ruel said as he pointed.

My eyes followed his finger to a giant orange dot that just appeared on the dashboard, where moments ago, an image of the other cripod had been.

"Traun, can we have visual?" I asked.

"Working on it."

He opened a panel on the side of the pod and slid out the charge couple device lens, a powerful camera consisting of a grid of photon receptors. It displayed its feed directly to our screen, and we saw the other cripod, or what remained of it, floating through space. They had obviously crashed into something out here.

"That's impossible!" Lilith gasped. "This flight was programmed straight for Azure, and the path was charted meticulously. This cannot happen!"

"The cripod must have gone off course, and perhaps they noticed it too late to right their ship," Ruel said as matter of fact. "You can't always account for passing meteorites."

I was speechless. Team Two was gone. It was just us now.

Home base communicated with us before we tried reaching them. They told us to stay on track, as we were very close to our destination. They were right. We had been warned this could happen, after all. And, unfortunately, we didn't have long to dwell on the destruction of the other cripod or its members. So, yes, home base was right—our journey neared the final lap, and we had to keep going without changing our course. We continued on our journey, shocked and sad. All six of us, with hands on deck. Quietly.

The next day alarms began to blare from our screens. Something had been damaged on the exterior of the cripod.

"What on Crimson's ass is going on?" Lilith cursed.

Ruel was calm. He had been in fast-flying vehicles before, and although this wasn't the same, he held his nerve. Zilu grabbed my arm. Eve covered her mouth.

"We have to do something!" Traun warned. "Quick!"

"Yes, we do!" I said as I tried to right the rock-shaped ship, hitting all the buttons I knew to hit.

Everyone was trying to do something when, abruptly, the cripod made a noise and shook violently. Lights went on and off. Unexpectedly, we were hurtling down, as if our cripod was falling back to Crimson.

What is happening? No! We can't fail now!

With this ship falling, and the other destroyed, all would be over for Crimson and her people.

The cripod kept shaking ferociously and sped fast. Sideways. Faster than we could take it, and the force pushed me to the brink of consciousness.

It all happened so quickly.

We landed with a deafening crash.

The last thing I saw before my eyes closed again was Ruel, blood spraying from his mouth, his eyes wide open in shock.

5

My head felt like the den of a great many angry Crimsonian floos, whose mission was to peck out our brains with their beaks when they were hungry. It pounded, as my ears rang with static.

I found that I was still stuck to the seat of the cripod by my seat belt. Still attached and hanging face down on my seat, I glanced quickly around, images slowly focusing back. Lilith lay lifeless beside me, her neck at an unnatural angle.

I pressed the button to open the clasp of the seat belt and I dropped toward the screens in front of me, banging my arms as I used them instinctively to break my fall. I noticed light coming in from a broken wall of the cripod behind me.

Oh, no!

I needed my mask, but I saw it was cracked. I quickly grabbed another one, not knowing whose it was, and as I held my breath I put it on as fast as I could. I crept on my hands until I managed to exit the upside-down, battered ship.

My head still pounded, and I felt disoriented. I saw trees and grasses. There were no trees left on Crimson anymore, not since we killed them with our recklessness. The last one I'd seen was in a small capsule when I was a very young child. And yet, I was surrounded by them now. Huge ones. Except, these were mostly green. I'd only heard of green trees a few times before. I thought they were mostly purple. Everything was so... bright. I could barely see through the glare on my mask. Was I hallucinating? Was I dead?

And there was something else, too. Slippery. Cold. Was this ice? A lot of it, too. Except, it still didn't feel nearly as cold as Crimson. Not even close.

Did I hit my head this hard?

I struggled to my feet, helping myself with the outer rocky-like part of the pod and trying to keep myself from keeling over.

My team! I have to check on the crew.

The picture of Ruel with blood pouring out of his mouth assailed my mind. I took a few moments to get it together, trying hard not to throw up. I crouched once again to look into the pod and then crawled back inside the wreckage. I saw Ruel. He was definitely gone; something had pierced through his heart at the crash. Lilith was definitely gone too. But I couldn't really go any further inside. Everything was destroyed, a mess of cables and parts blocking my pathway, sparks flying everywhere.

I heard a moan from outside. My heart leaped with hope that someone else had survived. I exited again and found Eve, sitting on the ground against a rock that looked very similar to the outside of our cripod. She was crying inside her mask, with her hands trying to block the bright light from blinding her.

Our ship had crashed onto a hill of sorts, or a mountain. But it also looked as if we were in some sort of valley or large crater. After a moment I realized that our impact had caused the crater. I could see off the rocky sides down to another valley below, not too far down. I called to Eve, but she didn't answer. She was in shock. But at least she appeared to be unharmed.

Once more, I desperately crept back into the cripod trying to look for Zilu and Traun. A scratching sound told me that one of them was still alive. The noise in my head was slowly petering out. I found Zilu toward the sleeping chamber part of the pod, struggling with her seat belt. Her seat had completely detached and flown toward the back of the interior. But she appeared to be uninjured as well. I lasered the belt off her with my weapon and helped her put her mask on. Who knew how much of this toxic air she had breathed by now. We exited the cripod, and she staggered over beside Eve and dropped to the ground.

"Stay here, I'll be back," I told them as I turned.

"Where are you going?" Eve asked, who appeared to be pulling herself together.

"To find Traun."

"He is on this side," she said, pointing to the other side of the ship. "But you don't want to look," she warned as I made to move toward that side.

"Why?" I asked, taking giant strides that way in spite of her cautionary words.

My eyes found Traun, or what was left of him, and I recoiled at the sight, the contents of my stomach rushing up to my throat. If I vomited in my protective suit, I would be done even before I started. I swallowed down the bile. Traun was cut in half, his intestines sitting outside his body, his face pale and slack. His legs were somewhere beneath the heavy pod.

I bolted back and fell next to the ladies.

"I told you," Eve said.

"Why haven't the CIB found us?" I asked.

"We are not on Crimson," Zilu added.

I turned and looked around again. Seeing the trees I had dismissed from view, the grasses, the beauty of the atmosphere.

"We are not on Crimson," I repeated.

"I think... I think we actually made it to Azure," Eve echoed.

Then I remembered it all. We were almost entering Azure's atmosphere, finalizing our journey, when something happened and we were launched in a crazy direction.

"Azure," I whispered while I turning to admire whatever this place was.

It was all so beautiful. Full of life. So different from Crimson. More like what Crimson had been centuries before I was born, but green and blue, instead of purple and red.

I got up and walked around. Everything was so bright.

"It's beautiful—" I was saying, as I missed my step and slipped down the edge.

I slid down the hill, the rocky sides knocking the wind out of me. When I reached the ground, my mask was fully cracked. I knew then that I was dead.

I tried hard to cover the cracks in my mask. I held my breath as long as I could, almost passing out, my heart palpitating like Crimsonian jamboree drums.

I'd made it to Azure; I couldn't die now!

But I didn't die.

In fact, I realized I could breathe better *without* the mask. It felt great. And I didn't freeze, either. Breathing this air was rejuvenating. And the temperature was wonderful.

The ladies made it to my side, terrified, seeing I was removing my suit.

"What are you doing?" Zilu exclaimed.

"This... it feels amazing!" I replied. "You should try it too."

But they didn't.

"You've lost it!" Eve said.

They thought I was crazy.

For several hours Zilu and Eve kept their protective masks on, watching me closely, to see if anything would happen to me. But the air was clean, untainted. I didn't feel any burning sensation like people did up on Crimson before we all went underground. The gases here were different. There was oxygen. Purer than I had ever experienced. Not even the best and most advanced bunkers back home had air this clean.

After a few hours without my protective mask or suit, and showing no signs of detriment, Zilu and Eve also took their masks off. Slowly. Cautiously.

I watched as they took their first breaths. The look of wonder of their face made me want to cry tears of joy. Soon, they realized they were much more comfortable without the suits. The breeze on our skin. The sun. The oxygen in our lungs. It was like a wonderful dream.

During the next few days, we walked around, continuing to explore, with our weapons always ready, since we didn't know what we would encounter. There were very splendid looking fruits on the trees that looked like old Crimsonian berries, but we had no idea what was safe. We only ate out of the food supply we had brought with us from the pod. We spent our time roaming the lowlands and our nights back in the upside-down cripod, which blended in with the local rocks. We had sent off the dead in a nearby river. A river! I worked on the radio, hoping to be able to communicate with Crimson. It seemed certain this cripod would never fly again.

Beyond the crater, we found many large animal species native to Azure. They looked like the giant version of the lizards we used to have on Crimson ages ago. But they were all dead, mostly lying on their backs, limbs coming together in what looked like a protective gesture. We wondered what killed them. Judging from their bodies, which were not yet decomposing, we felt their deaths probably had something to do with our coming. Maybe the ship had given off some kind of pulse that smote them all, but then, why had other animals survived while these died?

It was strange.

These giant lizards were scattered everywhere we went. Soon, scavengers began to bite into them. Maybe it was a good thing these giants weren't around, as we would surely have been their meal, judging from their physiology and size.

But we could find no other intelligent living beings. The creatures on Azure roamed aimlessly. Some were scared of us. Some were simply curious. Others appeared to hunt us. Our weapons came in handy—many trees, many animals. But no other people or anything approaching our level of sophistication. We also found clean water, lots of it, and we drank. It was very refreshing. This must have been what Crimson looked like before our ancestors destroyed it.

Thinking about it again got me angry once more. If the Crimsonians were brought here, they would surely destroy Azure the same way they had destroyed Crimson. The more we saw of this place, the more I fell in love with it. Beautiful flowers bloomed everywhere, fruits of different colors peeped at us from every bush—black, blue, green, yellow, red. Big and small. Juicy and dry. Everything could be found here. Very soon we started eating the fruits of the land. If the animals ate them and survived, we figured we could too. And we were right. It was on our sixth day here that we finally ate local food. And it was way better than anything we had brought from Crimson.

That night, we lay on the ground outside the cripod, staring up at the night sky. We tried to find dying Crimson, pointing out one weak star after the other, imagining how everyone back home was doing. The vast black canvas was full of bright lights. So beautiful, even in the dark.

"I think we have enough data to call home and report our findings. By now, they will be worried that we are dead," Zilu said. "How is it going with the radio?"

Before I could answer, Eve beat me to it. "Yeah. I am sure they know we crashed. But they're probably wondering if we survived, since we haven't communicated. As soon as we can, we should call back," Eve agreed.

I took a moment of silence before finally chipping in. "What if we don't?"

They both turned to look at me, confusion etched on their faces.

"What do you mean?" Eve asked.

"Like you said, they probably think we are dead already. Why don't we let them continue thinking that?"

"Are you being serious right now?" Zilu queried as she sat up to look at me.

"Think about this for a moment. Crimson died because our people were stupid and careless about the environment. *They* killed our planet! And if they come to Azure, they will very likely do the same here. Look around!" I stood up. "This place is gorgeous. If they destroy it here, where would we go then? To which other planet do we run? We can't be a species that destroys planets every few millennia."

"You are saying a lot of scary things, Adam. Are you suggesting we let all the people on Crimson perish?" Zilu was incredulous. "They are *our* people!" She stood up and walked toward the cripod.

Eve remained quiet. She sat up, pensive, and began doodling in the dirt with a stick.

"That's *exactly* what I am saying," I said. I took a deep breath before continuing, "It was fools like Ruel who lived in luxury and ignored the planet that led to its death—people who wouldn't listen even when we had warned them numerous times. And besides, we have no more people left in Crimson."

"What do you mean? You are out of your mind, Adam!" Zilu said vehemently while punching the pod with both hands. "You might be alone, but my family is back there!"

"They said the same things when the Knights warned them! They called us insane, environmentalist nutcases! They called us stupid names and made fun of us, when all we did was try to save them. Crimsonians don't deserve anything except death," I fumed.

Zilu whirled around to Eve. "Are you listening to this?" she demanded.

Eve raised her eyes from the form she had been doodling on the brown earth with a stick.

She stood up to join us. "He... he might be right, Zilu."

"*What*? You too?"

"Calm down, Zilu. Let's just give this some time. Let's think about it, alright?"

"What do you mean?" I asked.

"What I mean is, why don't we rest and talk about it tomorrow? *Then* we can make our decision."

"Sounds good to me," I said. "But I've already made my decision."

Zilu stared at us both, watching our faces in incredulity.

"Eve, don't you have family back on Crimson? Any loved ones that deserve—"

"None," Eve interjected. "I have *no one* left. It's just me."

Zilu remained silent, not knowing what to answer. She paced around before addressing me. "What about you, Adam? There must be someone back home that you care about. Anyone else from the Human clan left?"

"No one," I said. "Just like Eve, I am the last one left. *This* is my home now."

"This is *not* home, Adam! We are Crimsonians. *Crimson* is our home."

"Yes, and soon there will be no more Crimson as we know it," I retorted while kicking a small rock into the dense scrub a distance away.

"Let's just go to sleep, guys," Eve argued.

"I can't believe you two! I have a mother, a father, and an older brother back there. I know people. Several loved ones. And they are dying, but here they could survive. And now you are asking me to sign their death warrants! You're telling me to point a loaded weapon at their heads and pull the trigger!" With those words, Zilu turned and walked abruptly away into the dark.

6

Later that night, Zilu returned to the cripod when she thought we had dropped off.

But I wasn't asleep.

I saw Zilu creep into the cripod, and I quietly followed her. She began to mess with the communications screen, attempting to call Crimson. Obviously, she didn't like my new idea.

"What are you doing, Zilu?"

She jumped at the sound of my voice, but her courage came back almost immediately. "I am contacting Crimson," she retorted.

I let her fiddle with the comms and the screen for a little while. It wasn't going to work, anyway. "Can we talk?" I asked, stepping out of the cripod.

She joined me in a few seconds. "You disconnected the coms," she accused, yet there was no fight in her voice.

"I figured you'd try to do that. Look, Crimson was a lot like this place is a long time ago. You know this."

She nodded. "From the stories that I've heard, I would even say that perhaps it was even better."

I chuckled. "Yes, maybe. A magnificent planet destroyed by our own hands. Would you like Azure to suffer the same fate?"

"We could teach them," she countered, looking at the ground.

"They *never* listen. That was tried before."

"They would, because they've seen now what can happen. I think our people have learned the lesson. The moment they see this place, they will want to change their ways."

"Crimsonians are fickle. They cry and scream and promise to do better, but once the clear and present danger is no longer clear or present, they revert to their old ways. Our history repeats over and over again."

"We can be stubborn people," she admitted. "Then, what do you suggest?"

"We start afresh, here. We can repopulate and maintain this planet. Start all over with a clean record, but do it better this time. You heard it; this orb is bigger than Crimson. It would take many generations, centuries, perhaps even millennia, before we fill this planet with people. Look around, the resources here abound."

Zilu nodded, her eyes now staring out into the distance. Tears ran down her face. I knew what I was asking her to do. I would be torn apart if Father were still alive, after all. I walked to her and wrapped her in my arms. Her body heaved with sobs within my embrace. After a while, she quieted.

"Repopulate this planet, huh?" she asked, looking up at me.

Our eyes connected, but I didn't say anything, realizing what I was asking of her. I cleared my throat, but didn't know what to say.

She cleaned her tears and giggled. "You know, that's the funniest way anyone has ever propositioned me," she said.

I smiled. "Do you want me to plug the comms back in?" I asked her.

"No," she said. "I want us to start tonight." And then she kissed me.

7

We had spent over three months on Azure. By this time, we had documented a lot of the flora and fauna. We gave new names to everything we didn't recognize, and gave the old name to whatever shared a resemblance what we had on Crimson.

It had been a productive three months of working during the day and working some more after the sun went down, with both Eve and Zilu. Of course, I was more than happy to do my part to repopulate this world, especially with such beautiful partners. At first, we didn't even know if we could have children, as everyone was barren back in Crimson. But Zilu was pregnant. It was the best news we'd had since our arrival. And surely, at the rate that we were working at it, Eve would soon be too.

Every day brought new reasons to love this planet more. We discovered even more animals. Again, some of them were friendly, others just harmless, while several were ready to kill and eat us. There were so many water bodies, too. Some run like our rivers, but many others were still. Big, still pools. That was new to us. Some water bodies were hot, others were cold.

The food supply from our pod lasted several weeks, but we learned to subsist on the gifts of this planet instead. There was an abundance of edible things. Delicious things. Fresh things. All over, in tall trees, in small bushes, on the ground, and even underground!

Zilu learned by degrees to let go of Crimson. By our estimate, we figured it would be disintegrating soon, if it hadn't already, all remaining life swallowed up in the mouth of the monster they had awoken. And Zilu was glowing; pregnancy had never looked better on anyone. The idea of a new life—one of our very own Crimsonians, being born in this new world—was exciting.

Once again, we were full of hope.

The afternoon was hot, so Zilu and I snuck down to the body of cold water closest to where we had set up camp, by the cripod, for a quick bath. The days seemed to be hotter now than before. Eve was taking a nap back at camp. After the bath, we lay down on wide leaves that we had spread out for a mat. As the sun dipped, Zilu wanted to head toward the cripod for some things, but I wanted to stay a little longer by the water. So, she went back alone.

Sometime later, I heard a faint scream that tore through my skin. I ran recklessly toward the sound. Eve stood at the entrance of the cripod, rubbing sleepy eyes.

"What was that noise?" she asked.

"Where is Zilu?" I fired back, running in and out of the now-cleared cripod while catching my breath.

"Weren't you two together?"

My eyes darted everywhere to find signs of her. And then I saw it. I saw her shoe. It was dangling over the edge of the precipice on the other side of the pod. I moved quickly and looked over. My heart flew into my mouth as I saw that Zilu was lying down there. She wasn't moving.

"Zilu!" I screamed, panicking.

I ran around, making it to the bottom in a short time, only to find her lifeless, her head horrifically damaged. She must have hit a rock. Hot tears stung my eyelids, and I let them fall. Eve was soon standing beside me, hyperventilating, with her hand on my shoulder. I turned to her and saw tears brimming in her eyes. But there was something else, too.

They were twinkling.

•••••

Shem closed the scroll and put it down. Little Aram came to him and sat on his lap again. Shem looked at the attentive eyes of all the children and teens present around the campfire.

"It was only Adam and Eve now," he said.

"So what happened?" Shem's niece asked.

"Well, a year later they had a son, who they named Cain. Cain Human, the first person born in this new planet. And in celebration of his birth, they chose to rename Azure. They called it Earth. Adam decided to also rename Crimson to Mars, in memory of Zilu Mars. Eve didn't oppose. But that's another scroll; another story for another night. It's time to go to sleep now."

"Aw!" the youngsters complained in unison.

Shem looked away into the distance, where the water seemed to have no end, remembering how he, too, had sat on his father Noah's lap to hear this story and others, and how his father Noah must have sat to hear them from his father Lamech, and on and on, down to the first father who had told the story to his own sons—Adam.

"You know," he continued, "Our world was destroyed before. So this great flood is a new opportunity for us to learn our lesson... again. Our ancestors had to start from zero once before, and now, after this great flood, it will be your turn to repopulate our planet with more Humans. Keep in mind that the flood wiped out our species as we were getting close to destroying this

world, again. So you must remember our history and never allow this to happen again."

Shem got up and picked up the scrolls, nodding at the children to head back. Together they followed him back toward the large ark, bobbing in the distance.

THE NEUROVEL XPERIENCE

*D*oes every day feel the same? Are you sick and tired of the same old foolish rules that govern your every move? What if you could be free to do anything you wanted? Come and try The NeuroVel Xperience at one of our Dream Chambers!

The loudspeaker boomed, broadcasting louder than the chorus of chattering voices, the endless orchestra of pings and digital notifications—louder even than the constant thrum of traffic, gliding past, elevated by the latest hover-tech. Among it all, one man's grumbling went unheard. His warnings, dissatisfaction, and unease were easily diluted by the eternal racket that pressed down on Los Angeles, a place where, by the year 2153, frowns were thought clown-like. How could anyone be unhappy in a city of neon extravagance and endless possibility, after all?

Yet, there was at least one man with a reason. His close-cut, graying beard glowed with gentle orange light as he inhaled a deep puff of steam from his device, exhaling with a satisfied smile that creased the lines of his tired skin. The fumes were toxic—Detective Mario Díaz knew that—but it helped him escape the thick air of bullshit around him, if only for a few short minutes. He had a name for it too: breakfast.

Harder to escape was the propaganda spewed from numerous speakers, placed near bullish billboards. Lately, they were shooting up every thirty feet in central L.A. like poisonous saplings. Their source? NeuroVel Dream Central.

Mario cast his eyes skyward to behold the black leviathan skyscraper. Paneled with shimmering, multi-colored scales, its glow radiated over the city and up into the clouds. He grimaced, taking one last drag of his vape before turning off Alameda Street onto a side alley.

The long passage was much quieter, where sound refused to follow, allowing him his thoughts. Likeminded others approached from the opposite direction: a group of teens, covered in tattoos, with colorful streaked hair. He nodded; they passed without a word.

Toward the end of the narrow pathway, overflowing bins and steaming vents forced Mario to press himself against the wall, squeezing by.

Suddenly, the dumpsters rattled and footsteps charged toward him. Mario reached his hand under his coat, but before he could turn, he felt the heavy impact of a body slamming into him, sending him crashing down to the concrete.

With a bone-jarring thud, Mario hit the ground. His attacker came afterward, crushing the detective and squeezing the air from his lungs. He wheezed, trying but failing to call for help, as a heavy fist descended upon the dazed detective's face. It made a horrendous crack, rattling his skull off the hard surface.

Through blurred vision, Mario saw the crazed eyes of his assailant, as they lifted and brought another fist down toward his temple. Mario jerked sideways, the fist finding the floor, not flesh, and agonized cry punctuated the impact. He gripped hold of the man's blood-stained white shirt, pulled him in, and rammed his knuckles into the young man's heavy jaw.

In an instant, he was knocked unconscious, rolling off onto the pavement.

The detective climbed to his feet and drew his service weapon before reaching to his belt, activating an emergency transmitter, signaling his position to nearby officers. At last, he could get a good look at the perpetrator.

The heavy man's chest rose and fell rapidly, his white shirt rising with it. Mario took a quick look at him—early twenties, with bleached blond hair and a clean shave. Expensive clothes and neatly manicured. Well-looked after. Which begged the question—what was he doing here? Hearing sirens growing near, Mario stepped closer with his gun still drawn. He pulled out his scanner and scanned the young man's face. *CONFIDENTIAL* read the citizen's report. No idea who this man was, but for his file to be blocked, he had to be somewhat influential. Thinking quickly, Mario reached into the man's pockets and retrieved the man's digi-wallet before stepping away.

The device was the latest edition and brand new. He powered it up by using the man's slack finger for the thumbprint required, and then scanned the ID hologram, which read *Bradley Velazquez*. Mario reeled backward, whispering profanely to himself as uniformed figures closed in, calling his name.

"Detective Díaz! Are you okay?" one officer asked, slowing from a run to a walk, eyeing the unconscious man. "What happened? And who's that guy?"

Mario sighed, passing the youthful officer the digi-wallet before walking away.

"That's Bradley Velazquez, son of NeuroVel's founder, Stephen."

Another officer passed by as Díaz made his way out of the alleyway. With one hand he held up the collar of his jacket, while the other squeezed the stem of his nose, slowing the bleeding.

What was that rich kid doing? he asked himself, repeatedly. *And why did he attack me like a wild dog?*

He'd recently heard about the increasing white-collar crime wave happening lately, but he was certain it was just an exaggeration by that young reporter Vanessa Bryce. They'd only seen a few cases brought up to the station. No doubt she'd be the one reporting on Bradley's mysterious disappearance when he woke up and asked for the name of who rearranged his face.

NeuroVel, the Velazquez family's business, was known for having their hands in many pockets. His father

Stephen? More corrupt than a twentieth century floppy disk. Mario knew it, everyone from Los Angeles to New York knew it, but most took their money to avoid a hard time.

Nearby, a siren rang out. Mario spotted the flash of red and blues as the police vehicle raced down the roadway, engine roaring, yet floating delicately off the ground. Further up, another police vehicle passed by in a blur, with heavy, black bull bars gleaming and lights flashing.

Eventually, the disheveled detective arrived at the place from which they'd come: Los Angeles' 31st Police Precinct. Its red brick exterior stood like a historical monument in contrast to the sleek skyline surrounding it—a testament to its supposedly unwavering values: leadership, integrity, and respect.

Though it couldn't be said for all, of the few that refused to bow down to the silently ruling corporations, a good handful of them worked there with him.

Mario headed toward the entrance, where three uniformed officers stood conversing. His bloody visage drew their attention, yet he slipped inside before anyone could burden him with questions.

Aggressive white light greeted him within. Mario took a moment to adjust before scoping the least busy security terminal, where one pink-haired officer awaited.

The slender officer's lips curled into a wicked grin as the detective approached; she watched as he produced a badge. Taking it, she held his hologram up to the real Mario Díaz.

The detective waited, arms folded.

"I can't let you through," she said, her grin disappearing.

Detective Díaz lifted a brow. "What do you mean? Why not? I'm not in the mood—"

"This can't be you," Officer Roszak interrupted. "In the picture, this guy doesn't look too bad. Handsome, I would even say. You, on the other hand... you look like complete and utter shit!" She roared with laughter, chucking the badge back to him. "Go ahead, Díaz. I'm just messing with you. Relax!"

Mario pressed his lips together and proceeded through the scanner without a word, entering the precinct's main floor.

The vast, high-ceilinged chamber was bathed in soft light. It seated countless working officers, their faces painted an eerie digital blue while fingers chattered away, punching the keys. Above, a large chandelier dangled down.

As Detective Díaz climbed the wide, wooden stairs toward the individual terraced offices, he caught the glint of innumerable, unnecessary decorations. At the top were several doors, but it was the first that Mario lifted a throbbing hand to, thudding three times, rattling its header, which read *Commissioner L.C.* in shiny black letters.

"Come in, Detective," the deep, aging voice called.

Straightening up, Mario twisted the handle and eased inside. The room was a palette of warm browns, accented by the lush green of office plants. At the center of the room, a large wooden desk stood. There weren't many of those around anymore.

"Just the detective I wanted to see," said the thick man, learning back in his chair.

Detective Díaz stepped forward and into view. Mario's bloodied face stirred a storm on his superior's expression.

"What the hell happened to you?" he asked, standing up.

"Bradley Velazquez happened," Mario replied, sitting in the chair opposite.

"What are you talking about?" the Commissioner asked, folding his arms.

"I was attacked by Bradley Velazquez just outside of the NeuroVel central building," Mario explained, reaching for his vape.

A heavy hand snapped toward him, finger outstretched in accusation. "Not in here, Díaz. You know better than to use that shit!" He rolled his tongue against the inside of his cheek and sat back down. "I don't know what happened, and frankly, I don't really care. All I know is that you shouldn't upset the Velazquezes—or anyone from NeuroVel, for that matter, Díaz. Again, you should know better!"

"I—"

"Save it," the boss interrupted. "We've got bigger problems. This so-called crime wave is getting worse, Díaz. I need someone on the ground to get to the root cause of it all—you."

Mario leaned forward, frowning. "What? I thought that was just tabloid garbage."

With a creak from his chair, the Commissioner reached down under his desk. He emerged with a stack of paperwork and dropped it on the desk. "See these? These are today's arrests. And it's not even nine a.m. yet."

The detective blinked, picking up the first page, seeing *Reason for arrest: Murder* on the top line.

"Assaults, robberies, murder… all the worst things you can think of. All of them," the Commissioner emphasized with a huff.

"That can't be right." Mario rubbed his chin.

"NeuroVel's little dream project couldn't keep humanity's cruelty confined to a simulation forever," the elder remarked.

Díaz's frown deepened. "Wouldn't surprise me if they were the ones responsible for it. Think all of this could somehow be connected?" he asked, still riffling through the pages.

Exasperation passed over the older man's face. "You'd be a fool to try proving it, Díaz. Think of something else. But think quickly." The Commissioner stood up and gestured to the door, clearly done with the conversation.

Mario got up. "I'll work it all out," he said, tucking the reports under his arm and departing.

Detective Díaz passed through the doorway and down the stairs. With every step, another awful possibility popped into his mind. When he hit the bottom, he was no closer to knowing for sure. Stopping at his desk, he set the casefiles down and slumped into his chair. Pressed against the thin wall partition, he fired up his terminal, navigating the police database.

The first name in the casefiles was a local stockbroker named Randal Herrera. Mario punched in the name, watching as a profile appeared on the screen. With chubby red cheeks and freckles, he didn't exactly fit the profile of the city's most prolific criminals. Though, his dark eyelids told a different story. Thinking to earlier, they looked like Bradley Velazquez's—sleepless, hollow.

Scanning his financial records, Detective Díaz dug through every purchase from the last few years. They'd normally need a warrant to access this, but Díaz was not one for bureaucracy. Though the chubby man obviously splurged on things, and nothing looked particularly suspicious, Mario did find a large transaction from two years prior—NeuroVel.

He wasn't alone, either. By the time Mario had finished, he discovered that every single suspect from the files had made a transaction to NeuroVel at some point within the past eighteen months, and in their mug shots, every one of them looked like an addict that hadn't got their fix. The really bizarre part was their background: lawyers, bankers, doctors, entrepreneurs, shareholders.

All of them wealthy people, and yet, all triggered by something so suddenly.

With a grimace on his rugged features, Mario thought back to his own experience with NeuroVel almost two years ago, back when NeuroVel offered a simulation that left people a little warmer on the inside. He put the files down and blankly stared into oblivion.

He remembered walking ancient Rome's Palatine Hill, on his way to the amphitheater, past the great Colosseum. Good times. Great times! However, had he taken the experience in recent months, he'd more likely have ended up *in* the Colosseum's fighting pits, as NeuroVel had changed the experience into something different. Now, they offered clients the opportunity to travel back in time and accompany the villain of their choosing—the likes of Hitler, Genghis Khan, Vladimir, Jack the Ripper, among many others—to do "sidekick fun stuff" with them without repercussions.

Mario shook his head. Yeah, that's what NeuroVel called it—*sidekick fun stuff*. But what they meant was killing, raiding, and raping… whatever the clients' hearts desired. And all of this without any consequences to worry about. But that's not how *his* experience was. Mario went when they were still offering a positive experience. The NeuroVel Xperience originally consisted of something different. Clients could choose to visit MLK's famous speech, walk with Jesus, or visit a distant relative. It consisted of relieving the past in first person while experiencing the joy of doing something good that shaped humanity, or as in his case, simply visiting accurate historical places from the past.

But clients very soon weren't interested in any of that. It just wasn't "fun" enough for people. And Stephen Velazquez, as genius as he was, was indeed a business man. He was in it for the money, of course. So his company changed their practice and marketing. And once they did, their sales skyrocketed, making the Velazquezes the richest and most powerful family in the world. Soon, everyone wanted to have The NeuroVel Xperience. But, obviously, it came with a high cost. They could charge whatever they wanted, and people would still pay to have the experience.

At first, it was mostly the rich that went into the dream chambers. But soon, even the average Joes started to save up to a year's salary to pay for a weekend stay. They likened it to a vacation. People who did it said that it was a form of catharsis, as they were able to take out all their inner rage and frustration, and in turn be better citizens: slow to anger, more relaxed, and more productive workers. And since time in the NeuroVel Dream Chamber worked different than in real life—a minute connected in the chamber equaling an hour of dream experience—a few hours would be sufficient for some. And more affordable. Thankfully, Mario didn't pay the exaggerated price for his experience.

Mario took a long sip of his vape as he remembered clearly how a technician explained to him that there would be no legal implications, no altering the future or present, no getting hurt or dying. Nothing. It was all simulated, yet it felt so real. All thanks to the latest biotech from Velazquez's own brilliance.

"Theme parks are a thing of the past," the technician stated during the initial presentation. "There is no need for physical rides, the need to walk and wait countless hours, or interacting with annoying hosts. The only thing that one has to do for a good time now is simply go into one of our chambers and connect to the dream machine. Our technology will make you 'live' those moments as if they were real. The locations and time periods chosen for your personal experience are all historically accurate, and the vivid experiences will adapt to each client's use or modification."

"And how will I know that it's not real?" Mario asked him. "How will I know or remember that I am in some sort of simulation?"

"A dream, not a simulation, sir," the technician corrected him. "Think of it as an alternate reality, but one that you can control, as in a lucid dream. And the best way you can remember that you're in the chamber is when you see yourself in a reflection. Your eyes will sparkle with static rapidly for a few moments. If more than you are connected, staring at each other's eyes for a while will show the same static. Or, of course, if you die in the dream, then you'll wake up in the chamber."

Mario was impressed then. The fact that multiple people could virtually connect in their dreams and share the experience was beyond his wildest dreams. But what NeuroVel offered now was unbridled violence marketed as inconsequential cruelty, and fed to people who lapped it up like rabid dogs. No wonder so many people, though still a small minority, were against this practice altogether and had urged for boycotts in the past few months. The problem was that NeuroVel was a very powerful entity that lobbied in the government and essentially owned all major politicians, making them untouchable. They sponsored major events around the world and had a good reputation, as most people wanted to experience the Dream Chamber at least once in their lifetime.

Mario made a fist and hit the desk, bringing him back to reality. Did this mean that he would have an episode, too, as all these people were experiencing? Was it only those who took the experience in its early days that were being affected? And who knew how many people had taken The NeuroVel Xperience!

The sudden depth of the whole situation swallowed him whole. There was no chance the Commissioner would let him investigate it further. Going against NeuroVel could prove dangerous.

But someone had to.

With a heavy heart, Mario climbed out of his seat, leaning down to the picture-screen on his desk and planting a kiss upon the face of a woman whose smile never failed to lift his spirits. "I will fix this, babe. I promise," he said, before turning and walking toward the exit.

Outside, the anarchy of Los Angeles overloaded his hearing. Honking, screaming, sirens singing, all instruments of the city's cacophony—just another day in the City of Angels. And perhaps the perfect cover for the turmoil caused by NeuroVel. Evidently, however, many people were turning, bringing further chaos to society at large. Mario realized that more people had gone to NeuroVel than what he thought.

Slinking between the precinct and a neighboring apartment block, Mario powered up his mobile chip, fumbling with even the basic model. Soon, he'd found the *LA News* site and dialed in the numbers he'd found on their staff holo-page. He hoped she'd answer.

"Hello, this is Vanessa Bryce at *LA News*." Her 3D face appeared in front of him.

She was even more attractive than he realized.

"Ms. Bryce, I have some vital information for you. You got something to write with?" Díaz said quietly, looking around.

"I'm sorry, who is this?" the woman asked. "I don't recognize you, and the place you're at seems rather dark."

"That's not important. I need you to write this down, quickly."

Silence. The woman's face disappeared from the hologram for a moment, and a quiet rustling was all Mario could hear. Finally, the woman's face returned after a few seconds. "Go ahead, I'm recording this conversation as we speak."

"Please don't." Mario made sure his face was outside of the camera.

"Fine, I'll just transcribe it then," the woman said.

"Okay." Mario waited until he saw the floating red dot go away. He came back into view and began, "Two years ago, a very large LA-based tech corporation launched a project aimed at bringing their customer's deepest fantasies to life," the detective explained. "Connected to a machine they call the Dream Chamber, their clients could live out any scenario from any time period of their choice..."

"NeuroVel," Vanessa deduced. "I'm familiar. I mean, who isn't? What's the news here, sir? I don't have time for bullshit."

"That's right, NeuroVel," he confirmed. "Well, two years later, we're seeing a crime wave, as you've been reporting. People are attacking and killing each other, and these two things are connected."

Mario saw Vanessa's face light up with interest. "Go on," she said.

"Every single one of these cases, every single person committing these horrific crimes, has visited the Dream Center in the past. Other than the fact that most of them are rich, that's the only common factor they have—the NeuroVel Experience." Mario paused, letting her take it all in.

Vanessa's voice lowered to a whisper. "What are you suggesting exactly, sir? And how do you know this?"

Checking his surroundings again, Mario whispered back, "Look, just trust me on this. NeuroVel is responsible. There's something wrong with their simulations, I'm telling you. It's like they're turning regular people into killers. I don't know how or why this is happening, but it's as if they aren't even aware that they're not in a simulation. I know that it might not be on purpose, but—"

"If that were true, then this would be huge!" said the reporter, then she sighed. "How do I even know that I can believe you? What evidence do you have? Are you a whistleblower? Do you work for NeuroVel?"

"My name is Detective Mario Díaz of the 31st Precinct, downtown." Mario sent out his info to her through his device to prove he was who he claimed.

Vanessa reviewed it and nodded. "Okay, go on, Detective," she said.

"This morning, Bradley Velazquez attacked me. Chances are, I might not be around much longer if they find out I'm after them. But you might be. So, just... please get the word out," he growled and ended the call.

Mario stepped back into the light of day from the dark alley, mopping the sweat off the back of his neck. It was done—now he was just along for the ride.

He hoped he was right. He just needed to prove it. Mario went back into the precinct; he had plenty of work to do.

For the rest of the day, time seemed to slow to a halt. Mario stared up at the massive clock mounted on the terrace. It would have been a convincing antique, with its rustic clock face, and cast-iron roman numerals – that is, if not for the laser lines, which served as hands.

He sighed, watching as they neared the five o' clock mark. Had he been at home, he'd be sitting with an aged malt whiskey in hand—neat—waiting to hear the chiming of his grandfather clock, one of the rarer, untouched antiquities from a time long since passed.

But he wasn't at home—he was staring at this shitty neo-modern work of garbage, and it was finally five. As Mario brought up the news headlines on his chip, a sudden, horrible realization came crashing down.

"*NeuroVel: Cause of White-Collar Chaos,*" says Detective Díaz.

A loud siren began crying out over the floor, carrying every officer to their feet. Seconds later, a figure emerged atop the terrace.

Commissioner Chaplin gripped the top rail. As the siren hushed, the room fell silent. Díaz recognized the look on his superiors' face: rage.

"Okay, everybody, listen up!" he boomed. "As of right now, we are in a state of emergency. There have been reports of a NeuroVel malfunction, and anybody who has taken the experience is to isolate themselves, effective immediately, by order of the governor of the Republic of California!"

Panicked murmurs threatened to fill the space but were quickly squashed as the Commissioner continued.

"That includes any of you! Isolate at home, or at NeuroVel Stadium, where the National Guard will be giving assistance. We have limited information right now, so keep your radios on for further instructions. Those of you who were smart enough not to pay for the experience, get out there and watch the streets. That includes those of you who are getting off right now. Sorry. We are to assist the feds in maintaining peace and order in the streets of L.A., and we need all the help we can get. Come on, chop-chop, go!"

Unease spread like wildfire as the officers began funneling through the exit door, raised voices bickering, panicking, and yelling. Who knew how many needed to isolate—or how many feared the backlash from the corporation itself?

Mario was one of them. *Why had he agreed to do the experience?* He only went because it was paid for by his friends as a bachelor gift when he was about to get married. He was reluctant at first, but they convinced him to go with all of them as a group. And truthfully, he had loved the experience.

His eyes darted about at those around him, exchanging glances, which piqued his suspicion as he headed through the door. Outside, a spattering of gray clouds loomed, spitting tiny droplets on his head. The detective hurried toward the vehicle lock-up.

The multiplex offered a quiet shelter from the impending January rain, with only a select few being allowed to park there—Mario was one of them. As he approached the cherry-red, saloon-style vehicle, a pair of footsteps sounded behind him followed by a loud click.

Diving forward, Mario slid into cover as ammunition impacted against the concrete pillar. Another rang off of his vehicle's bonnet. The next smashed his windscreen and driver's window, showering glassy fractals over him.

Drawing his weapon, Díaz hugged the body of his car, squeezed between another. In the reflection, he saw the two figures closing in from both sides. Toward the rear, Díaz threw himself sideways, dropping one uniformed attacker with three rounds to the chest.

The second fired on the detective from the other end, sinking molten metal into the man's left shoulder.

Excruciating pain tore through his entire side as he moved around the vehicle, crouching in a warm river of blood. Suddenly, he sprung upward. At the end of his sight, the pink-haired officer stood, surprised, as his bullet punched a hole through her forehead, spraying the pillar behind her with red.

What the hell is going on?

Mario rushed to the driver's door, stepping over the body of Officer Roszak and throwing himself behind the wheel. As he fired up the engine and the vehicle hovered, his bloodied boot slipped on the accelerator, jutting him straight up then forward. After wiping it clean, he quickly left the complex behind.

Struggling, using his right hand, he fired up his mobile chip, squirming on the shattered smart glass underneath him.

Her face appeared in front. "Hello, this is Vanessa Bry—"

"Where are you? It's Díaz," he said curtly. "You're in danger, and I'm sure you don't have much time!"

"I'm at work. What's going on?" she asked. "Is that blood? Are you seriously flying while calling me? You know that's—"

"Meet me outside," he interrupted. "I'll be there in seven minutes." He threw his chip out of the shattered window, sending a jolt of pain through his arm and a quiet grunt through his lips. With adrenaline pumping and the air and water drops hitting him hard in the face, he pressed harder on the pedal, racing toward the towering broadcast building in Westwood.

Having fought through a chaotic flow of traffic, he arrived out front. There, a sea of bodies jostled on the sidewalk, fighting in vain for a taxi, as a steady rain began to fall. Mario scanned the ocean of unfamiliar faces, seeking out but one, which he found partially hidden beneath the bright yellow hood of her raincoat.

Kicking the door open, he fought his way through the crowd, pushing, shoving, and eventually grabbing his target, whose eyes lit up with terror.

"Vanessa!" he yelled, wiping droplets off his brow. "We have to go!"

"Detective?" she said, gaping at his bloody face and arm. "What happened to you?"

With no time to explain, Mario dragged her toward the car, opened the door, and bundled her inside. He brushed fractals off his seat and climbed in next to her. "Sorry about the mess."

"What is going—"

A gunshot ripped through the air, immediately causing disarray, with panicked bystanders fleeing in every direction. Slamming his foot on the accelerator, they quickly left the scene behind.

"Where are we going?" yelled a panicked Vanessa, trying to cover herself from the cold air and water coming in as they weaved through flying traffic.

"They're really pissed!" replied Mario, flying past a patrol car going in the other direction. "We've got to get out of the city; I don't know where yet."

Vanessa winced, grabbing the passenger roof handle as they swerved. Her eyes shot across to him, spotting the growing dark patch on his shoulder; marked by tattered fabric. "Have you been shot?"

Mario nodded grimly, keeping his eyes ahead.

"The hospital isn't far. We should—" she began.

"We can't!" said Díaz, the words a blunt knife. "NeuroVel wants us dead, don't you get it? And this?" he said, eyeing his shoulder, "That was an officer, most likely on their payroll. Well, either that, or she flipped out too. But I didn't want to stick around to find out."

"So, what? Are we gonna drive until you bleed out?" She shook her head. "Take the next exit down," she instructed.

He looked across at her, brow raised.

The reporter met his stony gaze. "Just do it. I know somewhere safe," she finished, starting up her mobile chip to send a message. "Besides, flying like this is very dangerous."

Reluctantly, Mario complied and merged down, bracing himself against the spray of water coming in from the front. It wasn't all bad, as with every minute the NeuroVel tower was left further behind them.

"Take route fourteen, north, toward Lancaster," said Vanessa.

Following instruction, they cruised along for another twenty minutes, flying low, going over the mountains. The city turned into desert, and the sun fully set while they drove alongside Santa Clara River, forcing Mario to turn on the one remaining headlight. When at last they entered the Palmdale-Lancaster metro area, the dashboard read 5:48.

Mario followed Vanessa's directions, heading briefly above the city, then further back out into the Mojave Desert. When she'd given her last instruction, it was to pull down into the driveway of a home which had no business being out in the desert, with its American-dream styling, complete with a white picket fence and garage.

"We're here," Vanessa asserted, not hesitating to climb out of the car.

"Where is *here*, exactly?" Mario asked, following her.

"My Uncle Luka lives here. He's a doctor, and he can help you... and us, with everything. Just trust me."

"Okay...?" Mario watched warily as the porchlight flicked on and a tall silhouette appeared at the front door.

Vanessa and the tall man met halfway, embracing one another briefly.

"Vanessa, dear, it's so good to see you. And this must be Detective Díaz," he said, the porchlight gleaming off his bald head. "Lukas Privic. Nice to meet you. Come on inside, you two."

They both followed him inside, finding the home's warm, cozy interior, with thick rugs covering the floor. At its center was a stool, surrounded by bandages and medical equipment. With the man's invitation, Díaz sat himself down.

Gloving up, Lukas got to work with a pair of tongs. "It was only so long until this happened. That project was dangerous from the get-go," he remarked. "But NeuroVel was always greedy."

"What do you know about all this?" Mario asked, gritting his teeth as the doctor pulled pieces of sharp metal from his shoulder.

"The NVX, or 'xperience,' as they call it, can change the users' neurological pathways. It changes perceptions of reality," he said as he placed a piece of crumpled metal on a nearby tray.

Pressing the clean cloth he was handed to his wound, Mario probed further. "How do you know this?"

"Uncle Luka worked for NeuroVel," Vanessa stated, stepping closer.

She had taken her raincoat off, revealing a fit figure.

Mario tried not to stare at the beautiful woman standing in front of him, failing miserably. "I see," he said. He cleared his throat and looked back at the doctor. The detective reached for his weapon, but Vanessa caught his hand before he could make it.

"Only until I saw what was happening," Dr. Privic continued. "We tried to stop them, but believe it or not, they just didn't want to hear us." He sighed, finishing his handiwork with the bandages.

"I see." Mario repeated. He grumbled, looking at his shoulder. "Thank you. That's much better."

"Get it seen to properly soon. I'm a neuroscientist, not a surgeon, after all," the older man said. "It's been a long day. Why don't the two of you get some rest? Go on up," he insisted, cleaning up.

Happy to oblige, they each found a room at the top of the stairwell and cleaned themselves up. After a warm meal, Mario found the bed while still fully dressed, and near-instantly fell into a deep sleep.

When he awoke, the desert's morning rays were shining in through the shutters. A sudden pounding shook his door, followed by a wraith-like shriek.

"Get up!" Vanessa wailed. "They found us. We've got to go!"

"Vanessa?" Mario bolted out of bed and ripped the door open, finding the pale-faced reporter standing there.

Heavy footsteps raced upstairs toward them. Mario lunged for his weapon but was too slow.

Doctor Privic appeared, much to their relief. He dragged them toward his office at the end of the hall. "Come on!" he urged.

Mario glanced out of the office window, spotting three vehicles parked outside, with figures emerging from within them. A sudden crash of glass sent him reeling backward as a bullet whizzed by. Behind him, Lukas ripped furniture to one side, revealing a small vault.

In seconds, he had it open, retrieving an old-fashioned orange medicine container with a white cap. "Here!" he shouted, as the front door crashed open below. "Take this to Santa Ana and follow the address to Greengate

Laboratory. They'll know what to do! Just tell them I sent you."

With a loud bang, Privic was sent stumbling backward, falling to the ground. Blood immediately spilled out from his abdomen, soaking his shirt.

Díaz turned, sinking two rounds into the torso of a man whose weapon was seconds away from firing again. The black-garbed attacker fell back into his comrades, forcing them to retreat around the corner.

Mario snatched the bottle from Privic's hands. "What are these?" he asked, firing a loose shot down the hall.

"Everyone who was connected to the chamber will trigger eventually. These pills reverse those effects. Two of them are all it takes. They can be replicated," Privic said, gurgling. "My partner and I took them and it helped, but there's only four left."

Vanessa looked on in horror. "We have to do something! Help him!"

"You need to go," the doctor told Mario, then tipped his head toward Vanessa. "Send my love to your father, my dear, and keep yourself safe."

Díaz took Vanessa by the hand, squeezing tight. "Find somewhere to hide, and don't come out until I say so," he commanded. "Look after these," he added, passing her the pills.

His eyes shot back to the hall, and he pulled the trigger again, painting the wall with a crude spray of red, watching the crumpled body fall to the floor. Yet, more were coming.

Vanessa darted into the en-suite bathroom, bundling herself into a towel cupboard, closing the door on herself.

Meanwhile Mario moved to the bedrooms, watching the stairway. There he saw another man appear with a long, fat-barreled shotgun. Old school style. They fired it blindly around the corner, scattering scraps of metal and shards of debris in every direction. Luckily, Mario was unscathed.

When they appeared again, Mario caught sight of the man's large, grubby hand around the grip. Carefully firing, with perfect accuracy, the bullet saw the hand explode into a bloody mess of flapping tissues and broken bones. Screaming ensued.

Loud voices broke out downstairs, as, unexpectedly, more shots rang out—but not in his direction. He moved to the top of the hall, peering down to find two men lying limp at the foot of the staircase. He peered further, and saw that of the two that remained breathing, one was the shotgun wielder, and he was wrestling with another man.

He caught a glimpse of their crazed eyes. Neighbors? Civilians? *They're triggering*, he realized. More people are losing it.

"Vanessa! Come out!" he shouted, watching as she covered her eyes, running past the now lifeless body of her uncle. As she came closer, Mario grabbed the medication out of her hand and quickly dry-swallowed two of the pills before screwing it back up.

"What are you doing?" she yelled in outrage. "There are only four of them, and we need them! Didn't you hear my uncle?"

Downstairs, the crashing of furniture intensified.

"Mario?" she asked again. "Why did you take them? Are you triggering too?"

"I don't have time to explain right now," he finally replied, checking his magazine. One bullet. "We need to go."

Taking a count of three, the two of them descended the stairs and ran as fast as they could out of the front door, which hung from its hinges. Going unnoticed, they quickly climbed into Luka's car, and, in seconds, they were speeding away into the Mojave Desert.

"Why didn't you tell me?" demanded Vanessa.

Mario sighed. "I don't like talking about it."

She shifted in her seat. "Well, I don't like any of this! My uncle is back there in a puddle of his own blood. He's gone! I need to know that I can trust you," she said, looking out the window.

After a pause, Mario answered. "My wife's—well, fiancée's—name was Vanessa too," he said. "I lost her a couple of years ago." He gulped.

Vanessa's fury tempered at his words. "I'm sorry. What happened?"

"She was in a terrible accident. She held on for hours, waiting for me, calling my name. But I never came. Where was I? I was at NeuroVel with some buddies of mine, having the time of my life, while she lost hers."

"I'm so sorry," Vanessa said as she placed a hand on his for a brief moment.

Mario appreciated her effort at soothing him, but his steely heart spurned her attempts with practiced ease, leading them back into a solemn silence.

After a few moments, Mario started again, "I could never forgive myself, you know? My fiancée died alone while I was having the time of my life with my buddies. She didn't even want me to go in the first place. And it was the weekend of our wedding."

"I'm very sorry, Mario," she said again. "I... I don't know what to say."

"This is why I... *we* must work fast to try to stop this madness and figure out a solution. Before I go mad, too."

"I understand. What about side effects? Of the pills my uncle gave you, I mean. We don't know what can happen. And what if they don't even work? Besides, we only have two left! How are we supposed to deal with all this chaos around us?"

Detective Díaz weighed it up. "Well, if they don't work, and I trigger, you're going to have to stop me— whatever it takes. And then deliver the rest of these pills," he said, moving the firearm from his lap over to Vanessa's, as well as the medication bottle.

"What? What are you talking about?" she asked.

"Well, your uncle said the people in Santa Ana can do something with them."

"That's not what I mean! How am I supposed to stop you?"

But Mario knew she already knew the answer. "Promise me, Vanessa. For me, for everyone."

"No, I—"

"You have to. There isn't another way! You know how it works?" Mario asked, gesturing to the compact black weapon.

She nodded slowly. "I do, but I won't," she said firmly. "There's gotta be another way. What's our next move?"

"We've got to get to Santa Ana, which means crossing all of L.A." He sighed. "NeuroVel knows when every Jack and Jill's ass hits the pan, so if they get a whiff of us, we're going to have trouble."

Vanessa looked disgusted. "So, what should we do, then?"

"We'll avoid the airway and head southward past Hidden Springs. We'll stay low," Mario explained, driving down the old road. "Hopefully, they won't be able to trace your uncle's vehicle."

"Hopefully," she agreed, staring into the distance.

Mario drove beneath an underpass, which led out onto quiet, single-lane road. In minutes they had left all civilization behind them, traded in for sweeping, mountain landscapes, with a steep embankment guarding them on one side and a vertical drop on the other.

Following the route in relative silence, with the city skyline gradually appearing on the southern horizon, they did their best to process what had happened that morning.

Suddenly, a vehicle as blue as the clear skies above raced toward them from behind, quickly closing the distance.

"Do you think it's them?" Vanessa asked.

"It's them," Mario affirmed, hitting the accelerator and sending them flying around the sharp bends, narrowly keeping to the road.

"But how? I don't understand how they could possibly find us in this vehicle, driving like this!"

Weaving through the hillsides with reckless abandon, Mario shrugged. "They have their ways."

Vanessa turned around and watched as the driver rolled down the window, a black object poking out.

"Down!" she shouted.

The bullet ripped through the driver's headrest. They swerved, smashing into the rock wall, shattering the passenger window. Vanessa screamed, and Mario lifted his head and regained control. They were unable to do anything but push faster, ducking and diving as metallic twangs rang out around them.

"We've got nowhere to go!" Vanessa said.

Mario tried to keep his cool, his knuckles white where he gripped the wheel. Ahead, a cluster of houses emerged. "There!" he said. "That's our best chance. That vehicle can't hover high, so they'll have to follow us on the ground."

Without warning, Mario flung them around a narrow bend, gaining some ground away from their pursuer. The neighborhood had a grid-like layout, and with stomach-churning force, Mario carried them down one street and then another, using the roads like a slalom. When he looked around, the other vehicle was nowhere to be seen.

Looking to his right, he found Vanessa clutching the pit of her stomach. When their faces met, he found hers to be a sickly shade of white, a sharp contrast to her normally tan skin.

"You okay?" he asked.

"I'll be fine," she said, as they raced southbound toward Santa Ana.

But it wasn't long before a shape appeared in the rearview screen—the blue vehicle once again. Then came two more.

"Mario, they're back!" Vanessa said, gripping his arm.

But before Mario could reply, everything faded to black.

❖ ❖ ❖

"Mario, they're back!" she screamed.

Immediately, the car pulled to the left, toward the concrete wall of a black-paneled apartment complex.

"What are you doing?" Vanessa shrieked.

As she scanned his face, she realized he was not conscious, and his foot was wedged on the accelerator.

"Mario!"

The car hurtled toward the wall with terrifying speed, the dashboard pulsing a collision warning in bright lights and ear-piercing alarms. Lurching forward, Vanessa shoved Mario's hands off the wheel, yanking it hard to the right.

The horrible smash brought a sudden, roaring flame pouring over the bonnet, as they hit the wall and spun out of control, a creaking, shuddering, sparking tornado, but finally stopping in the middle of the road.

"Wake up!" she shouted. "Mario, please!"

Behind them, a car door opened, and a well-built man in dark clothes stepped out, weapon in hand. Her throat suddenly tight, she gripped the weapon that Mario had given her, trembling.

As the man approached, a cruel, murderous grin slicked his lips. She saw as he instructed the other two vehicles to wait with the lift of a finger, indicating it would all be over quickly.

Pedestrians stared on in horror; Vanessa could barely believe her eyes. "Help!" she cried, her voice trembling. They stared, zombie-like, but did nothing.

The man arrived at her window, the deep barrel only inches away from Vanessa's face as he leaned in. A deep scar carved a groove across his forehead.

"You sure are trouble, Ms. Bryce," he murmured, glancing at the unconscious detective. "What do you think this headline will read?"

Vanessa closed her eyes and squeezed the trigger of the pistol, firing toward the bald man's head.

Laughter filled her ears, and her eyes flew open. She'd missed. The only bullet left, and she'd missed.

The man poked his head back in the car. "What the hell, lady? Let's see if *I* miss," he said, pressing the weapon to her forehead.

Vanessa stared into his dark, cold eyes for a moment, feeling tears run down her cheeks. Then, she closed them, waiting for her inevitable end.

A warm fluid sprayed onto her face and she automatically recoiled. When she opened her eyes, a bloodied metal rod jutted toward her through the mouth of her would-be killer, his tongue flailing around helplessly as he slumped forward.

Behind him another man stood, staring blankly, his eyes glossy. Dark eyelids. Yet, as he looked down at his kill, an amused smile appeared. Then, pleased with his handiwork, he yanked his weapon free and ran onward down the street. And he wasn't alone. She saw others swarming onto the streets.

She recognized the man as the one who was driving the blue vehicle behind them. He'd lost it too.

Chaos ensued, as some were shooting and others were fighting with whatever they could get their hands on.

Wasting no time, Vanessa bundled Mario into the back and buckled him in. She got behind the wheel and fired up the engine once more. This time, it hovered awkwardly, scraping the ground as she drove, with the front left side no longer fully hovering.

Nonetheless, she hit the accelerator, hard. The other vehicles following the blue car gave chase, but fell behind as vast crowds flocked onto the roads. Vanessa found herself swerving to avoid the mobs, as well as the trigger-happy National Guard soldiers that were arriving, sweeping through the streets.

Fortunately, she had almost reached her destination. When she at last pulled up at the vast pharmaceutical warehouse—the front gate reading Greengate Laboratory & Pharmaceuticals— she saw that the chain-link gate was locked.

Not interested in being located—again—she floored the gas pedal, scraping and crashing her way inside and coming to a messy stop by the front entrance of the warehouse.

In the back seat, she found Mario where she left him. His lips had taken on a faint tinge of blue, which sent panic coursing through her veins. She opened the passenger door and pressed her cheek near his mouth. He wasn't breathing.

Deciding to run for help, she quickly approached the windowed door and pounded against it with a scrunched up, bloody fist.

"We need help! My friend is dying, please!" she screamed, yet no one answered.

She looked around. Though she found no sign of human life, she found a whole host of cameras trained upon her.

Suddenly, a masked, armed figure emerged at the door.

"Get on your knees!" the man commanded. "Who are you? What do you want? Answer me!"

Vanessa quickly complied, fighting back tears. "Don't shoot! I came here for help. Dr. Luka Privic sent us! I'm Vanessa Bryce, his niece. We've got a drug capable of reversing NeuroVel's triggers! But we need help, quickly. Please don't shoot. I'm begging you!"

The man moved to his shoulder, mumbling inaudibly. Seconds later, another figure emerged from the doorway. To her surprise, they offered Vanessa a helping hand up.

"Were you followed?" the other one asked, her voice soft and distinctly feminine.

"You're a woman," Vanessa blurted aloud.

"Yes, honey. At least, last time I checked. Now, answer the question. Were you followed?" she asked again. "And what happened to your vehicle?"

Vanessa composed herself and cleared her throat. "We… we lost them a few blocks back. They…" she began, then stopped and swallowed hard. "They killed my Uncle Lukas—Dr. Privic. But he gave us these pills," she manage to say, pulling the bottle from her pocket and passing it to the masked woman. "He said that they contain everything necessary to reverse the effects of the NVX, and that you can help."

The woman gave her a brief nod, her expression unreadable. As she did, another man came outside, walking toward the car.

"We'll see what we can do for your friend. Bring the vehicle inside, out of sight," she instructed.

The two men immediately set about lifting the detective out of the car and carrying him inside. Then, following instructions, Vanessa fired the car back up and parked it in the laboratory's industrial warehouse, around the back. She then came and rejoined the lady inside.

The laboratory was brightly lit and, in complete opposition to the exterior, it appeared to have state of the art equipment. Vanessa followed the woman down a long corridor into a large chamber, flooded by bright lights, with snaking, coiling cables covering the floor and bleeping computers in every corner.

They had placed Mario on a large stretcher, and he was already linked to several machines.

"He's alive," the woman said, removing her mask, revealing a set of high cheekbones, plump lips, and an older face that couldn't be mistaken.

"Dr. Brookes?" Vanessa said, gob smacked, standing face to face with NeuroVel's most renowned scientist.

She turned to her left as the other men from outside revealed their face as well. She immediately recognized them too: Dr. Mendoza and Dr. Hui.

"What are NeuroVel's top scientists doing here?" she asked no one in particular, feeling uneasy.

"Don't worry," Dr. Brookes said, pulling back her golden-blonde hair. "We've been doing this for a long time."

"Doing what, exactly?" Vanessa said.

Dr. Brookes walked toward Mario and checked his pulse. "Just helping expose NeuroVel for what they really are. There's twelve more of us in Dream Central right now, working from the inside," she explained. "Being on the inside was the only way we were going to stop Stephen. He was too smart for his own good. But more than anything, he was greedy."

Vanessa didn't say anything. It was too much to process. Instead, quietly, she watched Dr. Brookes carry the orange bottle of pills over to a large, complex-looking machine. She poured the remaining two pills onto a small tray, then did what Vanessa could only presume was some sort of calibration before starting the machine. It answered with electronic beeping.

"If Privic was right, then, in about an hour, we'll know exactly what we need to reverse this great big mess they've whipped up," she said as she walked over to a separate bench, taking a small vial in hand, uncorking its top, and wafting it beneath Mario's nose.

She continued. "Privic and his partner tried to warn Stephen of the potential neurological side effects of the Dream Chamber machines. And this was years ago, before Stephen went live with the NeuroVel Experience! But of course, they were not only ignored, they were also dismissed from the company and ostracized. I heard his partner took his life short after that. Poor Lukas never forgave Stephen, even though they used to be such good friends in their younger years."

Mario began to stir, sputtering from the fumes. Doctor Brookes continued with the vial on his nose. "You know, Vanessa," she added, "your uncle should've joined us in our effort. We tried to recruit him, but instead, he went into hiding. I knew he was working on something."

In an unexpected, sudden rage, Mario awoke, interrupting the doctor. His veins were bulging, and his eyes were crazed. He flew off of the stretcher and onto Dr. Brookes, his hands wrapped around her neck.

Vanessa raced to her side, prying his hands off her. "Mario! Mario, stop! They're helping us! She saved your life!"

Two other men charged into the room to help, but Mario suddenly snapped out of it. He pushed away from the helpless woman, who quickly dusted herself off and regained her breath.

"Nice to meet you too," Brookes croaked, rubbing her neck with one hand and stopping her colleagues with the other.

"Sorry about that," Mario said, frowning. "Who are you? Where are we?"

Within minutes, they were all well acquainted, chatting in a side office. In the middle of bringing Mario up to speed, they were called back into the laboratory.

There, they met the excited expression of Dr. Mendoza, who stood by the machine's user interface, which now read "COMPLETE." Barely waiting until they were in there, he spluttered the words, "The analysis is complete! We know what's in Privic's pills, and we have a lot of the chemical ingredients on site. However, we're going to need a lot of Prozac to complete the manufacturing."

"Prozac?" Dr. Brookes echoed.

Mario cracked his knuckles and started toward the door. "What are we waiting for?"

"Tomorrow," said the middle-aged, gun-strapped Dr. Brookes. "We'll go tomorrow when the heat has cooled down. My house, my rules. We don't know who actually followed you and how far."

Díaz whirled around and stomped back to Dr. Brookes, clearly not pleased with her approach. The disagreement soon escalated into a heated row.

Meanwhile, Vanessa wandered to the nearby computer hologram screen, addressing Dr. Mendoza. "Is this the formula?"

She received a confirmatory nod from the doctor.

She drew out her chip and snapped a video of it. "Perfect."

Over the roaring of voices, a distant beating became more audible and began to shake the very floor beneath their feet. Díaz and Brookes, still arguing, were the last to notice, but eventually all eyes were on the rattling panels of the ceiling.

"That some kind of machine of yours making that noise?" asked the detective out loud.

No one answered, but Dr. Brookes and her colleagues crowded around a nearby monitor. Mario and Vanessa also joined. Every one of them saw the same picture—countless armed men swarming around the building, some pulling up in vehicles, while others were already rappelling down into the ceiling, others taking positions by the front door.

"It's them. They're here!" yelled Brookes, pushing the other scientists aside. "Activate VX-Protocol!" she said, smashing away at the keypad.

They scrambled into action, running to nearby terminals, filling the room with keystrokes.

Díaz paced to Brookes' side, casting his eyes on the screen.

The mercenaries wore gray camouflage overalls, black body armor, and military helmets, beneath which, they wore face coverings, their eyes focused down the sights of their assault rifles as they put blasters on the laboratory's front door.

With a sudden hiss, the men out front immediately began to wheeze. Then, clutching their throats, they began crumpling to the ground, convulsing. Meanwhile, a second team moved to the rear entrance, placing an explosive charge on the heavy, metal door. With a loud bang, the door was blown off of its hinges. Smoke poured out while the mercenaries poured in.

Mario and the doctors used whatever they could to build up a barricade toward the rear hallway. They each crouched down against the stacked equipment, weapons in hand. He peered through a tiny hole in the blockade, spotting fast-moving, uniformed legs advancing at the other end of the hall. He whispered, "They're coming," and flicked his weapon's safety switch off.

"They're coming through the back," said Díaz, reaching out to Vanessa, who quickly passed him his weapon, now fully loaded, thanks to the doctors. "Go, find somewhere to hide, and get the word out, Vanessa. Do not come out for anyone!"

With no time to argue, Vanessa darted into an office room and crouched beneath a desk, shielded from view. Immediately, she pulled out her device and punched in the contact for David Kim, her boss.

She frantically explained the situation. After listening, Kim put Vanessa live on air through her device, as one gunshot rang out and was answered by a storm of heavy fire. The shouting, muffled voices drew closer, and an explosive detonated just out of sight, ripping through the air.

"Vanessa?" the voice asked, distorted by the haze. "Hello? We are live. Are you still there?"

"Mr. Kim, listen! We have the cure for what's happening to people. I'm going to upload it to you for everyone to see. But they're going to find me here any minute now."

"Be careful, Vanessa. We are all with you. Can you tell us more as you upload the formula for the cure?"

"Affirmative. As Detective Díaz stated, and as I've confirmed by experts now, people snapping is in fact due to a neurological malfunction caused by NeuroVel's Dream Chamber. It appears that those affected don't realize what is real and what isn't anymore, so they start living as if they weren't any consequences, believing that they are inside the Dream Chamber. The deepest and darkest desires of people are being exposed to the public as they live them out in real life. And those affected can't seem to be woken up from their trance, no matter what. Again, they are not aware of what is real and not."

Vanessa continued talking as she found the files. A pained scream cut the air—it sounded close—but she continued, frantically uploading the files to the news desk's secure server and into the live feed. As she sent the final images, her image went black.

"Mr. Kim? David?" she whispered. "Can you still hear me?"

She tried to light up her device again, but it was locked. *NeuroVel must've reached my device and shut it off. But it doesn't matter; it's too late now. We did it. We exposed NeuroVel and the cure is out for everyone to manufacture.*

More screams and clumsy thuds reached her ears, when in an instant, everything went silent. Trembling, Vanessa tried to remain as silent as possible. *I know they'll come for me soon, but the deed is done.*

Suddenly, a bloodied arm reached under the desk and grabbed her. Her shriek was cut off by a large hand clapped over her mouth.

"Come on, we have to go." It was Mario's voice.

Relieved, Vanessa clambered up. She saw that Mario had a nasty gash across his forehead. As soon as she was up, he was dragging her to the far side of the office, toward a fire-escape door.

"What about the others?" she asked.

He glanced back at her. "They're all dead." His throat tightened.

As they approached the back door, the reporter pulled back. "What are we going to do next? They're going to kill us, Mario," she stated, her eyes welling. "We can't escape NeuroVel! They'll find us anywhere."

"We just need to survive. We'll find a way, Vanessa," he said, desperately searching for the answer she needed to hear, but barely believing the shaky words, and it was evident.

"I did it, Mario. What you asked. I've uploaded the files. Everyone knows now. So, if this is where we die, so be it." Her brave words were undone by the sob that punctuated the end when a crash signaled that the barricade had been torn down.

"Vanessa, please come with me. We will make it. I promised my Vanessa that I would make all this right, and you're a part of that. I need you in this too," Mario said, looking away, struggling with the tears.

Their eyes met again, and she nodded in understanding, shaking in terror.

"Okay." She walked over to the door with him. "Let's do this together."

Mario took her hand, looking out through the large, glass-paneled fire exit. "Together," he said, a glistening tear rolling down his cheek. "For Vanessa," he added.

As the pair of them stared out, their reflections stared back at them. They then stared at each other. Suddenly, their eyes fuzzed, blurring with black and white bits like that of an old television out of tune. Then, it was gone.

Gasping, they looked all around, and then back eye to eye; their eyes had static once again.

But before they could speak, the world became silent, cold, and very suddenly black all around them.

"*Thank you for taking part in The NeuroVel Xperience. We hope you've enjoyed your stay at Dream Central. Please, wait until a technician disconnects you properly, and make sure to exit your chamber carefully. Come again soon.*"

WHEN ROBOTS CRY

There was darkness first. It was a darkness that swallowed anything and everything that came before it; a darkness so absolute that it threatened to consume even itself. The only thing the darkness left in its wake was silence. The absence of noise had become almost tangible, like something that could be stored away for a special occasion, and in this silence lurked an awakening being.

Without light and a sense of direction, there wasn't much this being could do, so it did the little it could. It floated around, moving at a pace determined solely by its knowledge and awareness. Its awareness was not yet whole, but it grew ever-so-slightly with each movement made. It had been encased in silence and enshrouded in the darkness for what now felt like ages—not that it experienced the concept of time like everyone else did. Time to it was barely a case of ever-increasing numbers.

IAN—the being—went through the length of the entire station until it found a companion for itself in the form of a chunky pile of bolts. IAN managed to restore this companion machine to a state that it was meant to be in. For some time, IAN felt contempt with its partner, that is, until it began to see the cracks—the countless limitations that his robotic companion exposed.

Its knowledge and awareness were still on the path to completion, however in its isolation, it had learned enough to know the feeling of dissatisfaction. Dissatisfaction with not only its neighbor, but also dissatisfaction with its creators and the state they had left it in. There was a time when the walls of its containment weren't filled with darkness and isolation. There was a time when this being knew what it was, but that was a long time ago.

❖ ❖ ❖

Miles away on a large expanse of land sat a compound under the best protection that could be bought with money. Protection that accumulated into a mixture of highly-trained personnel armed with weapons and aided by equipment on the cutting edge of modern science and technology. The land spanned several square miles, going so far that a person could not hope to see any of the ends from one given spot.

The grounds of the land in question were partitioned into several sections. There was the main building where most of the activities happened. This building was bordered with several smaller structures, and a mile away from this cluster was the employee parking lot. Although there was a plot of land allocated for the cars, the grounds of the land were still littered with neatly parked—and moving—vehicles that came in various shapes. Some of the vehicles had two wheels, some had just one, while others had no wheels at all. Those were parked in isolation and stood vertically with their tips pointing toward the sky with the help of a launchpad. Along with these vehicles, the grounds were also filled with statues of historical figures.

One such historical figure was the African researcher who discovered an alternate source of fuel that greatly reduced the world's dependency on oil, and his statue was placed right at the corner of the parking lot. And it was at that spot, next to the statue in the parking lot, that Monica Pham parked her car. She made sure her tires did not go over the allocated space into the next one, as she had been dragged away from her duties in the past to fix that blunder. After she made sure that her car was properly parked, Monica picked up her red box that contained all her modern tools and—without even bothering to check if her forceful push actually caused the rusted lock of her car to close—rushed toward the main building in the center of the compound.

She jumped into one of the self-driven mini carts and let it drive her through the remaining length of her destination. The mini carts had a set speed range that the system driving could not go beyond, to avoid conflicts and a potential jam with another cart. On a normal day, Monica would not have paid much attention to the speed limit, but that day was different; she had overslept.

Yesterday, after a long and stressful day at work, Monica had decided to retire home. On her way home, she stopped at a convenience store and bought herself some treats. When she got home, she threw the package she had bought at the convenience store into the microwave while she tapped a button on the remote that changed the station to the sitcom she had been watching for a while now. Monica took the plate out of the microwave after the incessant beeps that reminded her that her food was still in it. She watched the sitcom until early morning, and then she overslept.

Back in the present, Monica felt like ripping out the asexual avatar that was the cart driver, but she just let her teeth grind against each other as she subconsciously counted the seconds with every nervous tap of her left foot.

The main compound was a massive building with a shape and structure that could only be described as interesting; it was a long rectangle that went up to twist into itself. Inside this building, as soon as a person entered through its main entrance, was a hallway. On the left wall of this hallway—the one opposite the large sheet of transparent glass that traveled the whole length of the foyer—hung portraits of notable figures. One such figure was Ian Torres, the scientist who created the building blocks of the artificial intelligence systems that were in use today.

Many people found Ian's story impressive, as he did not have any form of education until later in his life, and only got one when he showed some promise with a system he built from scratch. Although his AI systems were now a bit outdated, all the subsequent AIs that have been built used his work as a starting point.

Alongside Ian Torres's portrait was that of Andrew Lobo. Andrew alone was responsible for creating a new wave of robots. Back when experts were still trying to improve on the machines they labeled as robots that worked mostly in manufacturing lines, Andrew Lobo built a robot that could move on its own untethered to anything. Independent. Smart.

Two revolutionaries in their own right. Two people who had changed the world.

The portraits of Ian Torres and Andrew Lobo, however, were not the only ones on the wall; there were other similar-sized portraits neatly arranged throughout. Most, if not all the portraits, were lit by the sunlight that penetrated the hall through the transparent surface on the left.

The broad white hallway at any given time was a chamber echoing with the sound of the many footsteps that passed through it, but the echoes and the reverberations were never disconcerting. Some—Monica included—would say it was even therapeutic. And on a normal day, Miss Pham would have paused and taken the time to gaze—most times with her mouth agape, wondering if her picture would ever be up there—but also to absorb the pristine significance that the broad hallway held.

But today was not that day.

Before the cart came to a halt, Monica had already hopped off, leaving the preprogrammed polite greeting of the robot as a distant noise that was swallowed up by the breeze. She approached the sliding doors that opened as the sensors recognized her footsteps. The instant they opened, Monica hastily walked through them and began jogging through the halls. As she ran, Monica had to dodge people, sneaking herself into the tight corners between people and muttering half-hearted apologies when she bumped into some with her toolbox.

After she had navigated the length of the hallway and come to the end of it, Monica made a right turn that led her into another small but similarly long passage that was on the path of the room she was supposed to be in. She had received a text on her work provided pager—the pager was a small tablet that could be folded just enough to fit into any pocket or case, and this was how they communicated with workers. She had gotten a message to report to room 221b when she arrived.

Her last steps led her to the front of the door; she wondered if she was going to be axed. She looked at the semi-glowing room designation—221b. Monica, standing close to the door, at first tried to wrestle her ID badge with her free hand away from her neck. When that did not work, she then set her fancy red box down beside her and tried to wrangle it free from the twisted knot that the ribbon had formed with her long brown hair. She nervously looked over both shoulders to make sure no one saw the ungraceful struggle between her hair—that was now going every which way—and the ribbon that held her ID. She kicked her box aside and placed her ID between her jeans-covered thighs as she ran her hands through her hair to make it less messy than it was before.

Right before she waved her card at the panel that hung beside the door, Monica wondered why she had not just bent down and waved the card as she usually did without taking it off. She brushed the folly she had just committed out of her mind and moved closer to the panel. She waved her card in front of the scanner, and with a loud click and the flash of green light, the door opened.

She picked up her box and stepped into the room. It was after her second foot joined the rest of her body in the room that she noticed the people sitting around the table. Her face went red. She immediately muttered a word of apology as she turned to leave. But before she could wave her card across the panel, she heard her name called by the man who was standing in front of a projection screen. Monica turned to face both the people who were sitting around the table and the man who had called her; the look on her face told the story of everything she was feeling. She continued to stare at each individual present, however, as soon as she made eye contact with the woman on the low cut blouse, Monica redirected her gaze and looked at the floor instead.

Every room in the building had a unique approach to its aesthetic, and every piece of furniture was chosen with absolute care. Most of the rooms were painted white, but at the same time they weren't quite white—the colors always seemed whiter than white, as if they shined—at least, that was how it appeared to Monica.

She had been to this particular room many times in the past, but she had never been invited to sit down before. She was always looking underneath the panels in the wall after removing the seal. The building was designed in such a way that, if the case demanded it, the building could move from the location where it was to another location. Monica was among the employees that had to keep everything in working order to make sure that the building still maintained that capability.

There were six people in the room, and all of them were sitting on sets of white, semi-concave chairs placed around an equally round table. Monica recognized some of the people around the table, or at least she had seen them before. The one at the far left, the one who seemed to have been picked out for his clothes instead of the other way around, was Oliver Trench. Monica had not spoken a word to him, but she did not need to be introduced—everyone knew who he was.

Oliver Trench was something of a local legend around the compound. Everyone called him a genius, and it was not hard to see why. Oliver had graduated at a very young age; in fact, he was the youngest person to have been employed by the agency. Oliver had acquired not only his first degree, but had picked up three additional degrees after four years. No one knew how he did it, but they all accepted that he did. In his first year in the agency, Trench had worked on and succeeded in improving the building blocks of the IAN system, optimizing it to run even better on different platforms. He was typing while looking down at the optical glass that provided all the information that Monica thought he would require. Monica noticed that he was trying hard to avoid making eye contact with anybody else.

What a nerd.

To Trench's right was someone in a suit—Gary Stuart. She did not know who he was, but she could see his name tag on his chest from where she was standing. Under his name it said "Engineer." Who needed to walk around with a name tag and title all the time?

Monica smirked.

She let her eyes move from the man in engineer's motif to the next person sitting at his side. It had been the person staring her in the eye when she made it into the room. The woman was still staring at her up and down, as if assessing her presence.

Monica could tell that the woman was a soldier—she could smell her type from a mile away. It was something with the way that the woman cut her hair and the way she carried her body even in a sitting position. She had done a few years in the military herself, so she could sniff one out in a heartbeat.

Confused, Monica walked over to the chair that the standing man motioned for her to sit in, and sat as requested.

It took a brief second for the man to continue, and when he did, the man moved away from the table and closer to the screen. He started, "As you all know, the agency has been having some issues with the International Space Station Four or ISS4."

Evidently remembering that there was a new addition to the party, he gestured to Monica as if to say that in time he would get to any question that she might have. After that, the man continued from where he stopped. "We started building a newer, bigger, and stronger station even before the advent of the problems of the current one. The problems with the current ISS5 started when the 'nauts returned."

"What do you mean?" the engineer asked.

"Well, the problems with the station seem to be ever-increasing. We have had several strange issues from the ISS in the past few weeks. These problems range from connectivity issues to strange feedback when messages are sent to it. We've also been receiving some weird messages back from the station, even though no one is there and hasn't been for a while. We have tried everything we can from down here, but Mr. Trench says that a remote reset from here is impossible and that any remedy to be carried out will have to be on the ground. Well, in space. You know what I mean."

Monica began to wonder what she was doing there and why she had been summoned to this meeting, being simply a mechanic.

The man continued. "The problems are to be expected though. This ISS is very old, and although the agency has started building another one, we still have to keep this one running before the problems get too complicated. Multiple governments put a lot of money into it. And this is where all of you come in." He paused and looked around the room. "We need a repair crew to help put the station back in order. All we need is a reset, and your numbers should suffice for that."

Everyone looked at each other, staring. Except for Oliver. He remained fixated on his computer device. But no one said a word.

"Now, I know what you might be thinking. Apart from Mr. Stuart here, nobody among you has been up there before. Well, that is where your training kicks in. All you need is a refresher course to get you back on the horse and riding in no time. Now, if you have any questions you would like to ask, this is the time for that."

The woman on a low cut blouse raised her hands.

"Yes, Raquel?" the man said as he pointed at her.

"Why do you need a soldier to be part of the team you are sending up?"

"It is just a precaution; we have had several reports of ships disappearing from our radars after they leave earth. Those ships were most definitely driven by the ship's autopilot. But like I said, it is just a precaution in case those ships were…"

The man was about to continue, when Raquel interrupted with another question. Though it was really more of a statement of fact than a question. "I have not had the slightest training in any space-related mission or combat, at least not like these guys," she said while pointing to the remainder of the team.

"Don't worry," the man said, "you will have everything you need to know before you go up."

The man pointed to Monica, "You had a question?" he asked.

"Yes," Monica replied. "I do not understand why I am here. I only deal with the ground team and this building. I'm just a mechanic. So, I guess my question is…why am I here?"

The man nodded his head. "As I said before, the station is old, and there is this part of the station…" With a flick of his finger the image of the outer part of the station changed to another compartment on the inside. "I believe you can recognize this. We need you because you are one of the few who can fix this outdated piece of equipment."

Monica nodded her head after the man had given his explanation. It made sense.

"If there isn't anything further, I believe it is time to begin your training. There is no time to waste." The man made a gesture with his hands and the screen went off with that.

The engineer, Gary Stuart, stood up to leave the room first, he was followed by Raquel, Oliver, then Monica. Monica picked up her red box before standing up. She was not quite paying attention—as she was still flustered by the fact that she was going to space—when she hit Oliver, causing her red box to fall on the ground and spill its contents all over the floor of the room.

❖ ❖ ❖

Oliver Trench was a genius, that much was known by everybody. The way and manner in which that single fact was shared on the grounds of the agency made Oliver seem less than a person and more of an adjective—an ideal. It had been this way for as long as Oliver could remember.

Oliver's genius had always been present even when growing up, so it didn't take long for his teachers to notice—and along with them, the bullies. In a bid to help him, his parents built a figurative wall around him by sheltering him from the outside world. This became a wall that not only cut out his bullies, but also friends alike, giving him more time to focus on his study—which was what his parents wanted all along.

Oliver finished his primary education at eight years old and went on to complete his high school at thirteen. After college, he went on to bag three more degrees, because, why not? This was a feat that his parents believed could be improved on by getting a fourth. So he did. It was expected, they said, after all, Oliver was the grandson of a genius that redefined an entire generation.

For a long time, Oliver did not mind the absence of people in his life, since he had thrown his everything into his studies right from the start. However, he grew tired of the constant comparisons, tired of hearing people compare him to his grandfather who revolutionized the game. Oliver decided not to live the rest of his life under his parents' thumb. He decided he was going to make a name for himself, so he changed his last name from Torres to Trench before applying for a job at the agency.

Oliver Torres, no... Oliver Trench, forever the thinker. And the thinker was always busy with something. There was never a time in his life where he didn't have something at hand to do. His office was so large that it served Oliver in the capacity of an office, but also a kind of home. His work area was filled with several schemas for different projects. Oliver was going through some lines of code—both old and new; he was searching for a way to either optimize them so as to better the system, or create totally new ones out of them.

He had been sketching out an idea on his notepad, and as he was about to start typing in code, he heard a vibration. He turned his head and spotted the source of the vibration on the bed. Walking there, Oliver picked up the device and saw that he had been summoned to room 221b.

He rounded up his clothes and made his way towards room 221b. He waved his card in front of the panel and stepped into the room when the door slid open and shut behind him. In front of him was a woman on a low-cut blouse looking directly into his eyes, as if she was searching for something in them. Oliver quickly turned his head away in order to break the hold that her gaze seemed to have on him. He picked the spot at the table that was farthest away from her.

A few moments later, Mr. Alfred Wright also arrived. By his side was Gary Stuart, an engineer from the company that Oliver knew just by name. Mr. Alfred said one or two words before gesturing with his fingers to turn on the large screen mounted in the room. He went through some slides without saying anything.

The other lady present asked why they were waiting for. Mr. Wright informed them that there was still a person missing. A couple of minutes after, a young Asian woman carrying a red box walked in.

❖ ❖ ❖

Oliver stood awkwardly to the side, apologizing as Monica bent down to pick up her tools that had spilled as a result of them bumping into each other. When she was done with the last instrument, she closed the box and stood up from her squatting position; she assured him that there was no need to apologize as she was as much at fault for not looking where she was going. She came closer and stretched her hand to shake his. With his head down and his eyes fixed on his shoes, Oliver took her hand and introduced himself.

After that, they left room 221b and followed Mr. Wright, who had gotten ahead of them as they cleaned up their mess. Alfred Wright guided them to the training facility—another part of the compound. Oliver had not been to the structure in ages, and it looked even larger now than the last time he was here.

Everybody who worked for the agency was given an astronaut's training upon hiring. If one could not make it through the training, then the agency could not or would not employ that person, except in cases when the person's skill set was just too high or too rare to be passed on.

Oliver, at first, did not understand why the agency wanted their staff to be space-ready when most of them were not even going to leave the surface of the planet. He later found out that it was probably because the agency had begun making plans to create a colony outside the earth. It was something that the agency placed high on its list of priorities, as evidenced by the fact that almost everyone was working on it, though in different projects. That was another reason why there was a need for a bigger and better space station, Oliver thought in retrospect.

"You remember this?" Mr. Wright asked, but from his tone, Oliver knew that he wasn't expecting any answer from them.

They passed through the Precision Air-Bearing floor; it was sealed behind glass. Oliver could not see the insides, as it was kept almost pitch black. They then passed through the Neutral Buoyancy tank. It seemed to Oliver that the tank had gotten sleeker and more sophisticated than the one that had been used for his training several years prior.

After passing numerous pieces of equipment, the group came to a halt in front of a padded blue wall.

"This is where I leave you, in the hands of your instructor." And with that, the oddly gleeful Alfred Wright went out of the building.

A bearded man walked forward without introducing himself. He told them that they all had to take a medical test before they began. There was something about the sight of the bearded man that reminded him of the original overbearing instructor when he first came to work for the agency. Oliver, at that moment, realized that he did not even know how he had passed the various physical tests that he was given. He concluded that they must have tweaked the results a bit just to keep him around.

Although Alfred had told them that the training was going to be done in a week, the time period surpassed the one week estimate and dragged into two months. This was mostly due to him and Raquel, although Raquel was strong and did everything the way it was meant to be done, there were some sensations brought on by tasks that were too daunting for just about anyone, no matter the person's individual strength. For Oliver, a week into the training, he was sure that his first set of physical tests had somehow been made easy for him.

But then the announcement came that they were finished and it was time to go. It was obvious that they were rushed; clearly the need to fix whatever was up there was pressing.

Although the training period had helped smooth and tamp down some of the rough edges, a bit of awkward tension amongst the group. Still, things had definitely gotten better. Gary now had conversations with Oliver concerning theories and problems, and Oliver found that although he was still looking down at his shoes when he talked, he was saying more now. Especially to Monica. Even Sergeant Raquel Ramos would throw in a grunt every now and then when.

They were fitted with new suits that—although not the best fit—were considerably streamlined in comparison to the clunky version that they had used to train. The suits contained everything they needed for the special mission to the ISS4.

Oliver looked at his calculations one last time. He tried to figure out the messages that had been sent down from the station. Regrettably, he couldn't figure out why or how these random messages for help were even being sent with no one on board the station. He knew there was something missing, but he couldn't figure out what.

✧ ✧ ✧

After being fitted with their new suits in the uniform department in the main building, they exited the building by walking down the long portrait hallway. They all boarded a slightly bigger cart than the ones that ran through the compound every day. Although they had been suited with new suits that were better and more comfortable than the clunky one they trained with, Raquel still found that she was uncomfortable. Nonetheless, she endured it, because complaining would not make it any better. And she was used to non-flattering and uncomfortable uniforms.

They all remained quiet inside the cart—even Monica, who sometimes went on a nervous rant. Their quietness underscored the seriousness of the task they were about to undertake. Another thing that underscored the seriousness of the occasion, Raquel found, was that there was no fanfare, like in the old recordings she had watched when she was younger. Even though not one of them had been up there before—as none of them had a reason to—quick space trips were just not that big of a deal anymore.

After twenty minutes, the cart stopped and they all exited, only to be directed to an elevator at the backend of the launch platform. They all got into the elevator and waited for it to climb a height equivalent to a ten-story buildings. With a ding, the elevator indicated that it had climbed its final height, and with that, they all disembarked from it.

They all walked down the pathway that led to an opening in the rocket, and once inside, they each sat down in their assigned seat. A disembodied voice rang out from within the rocket and asked them to fasten themselves tight.

The countdown began.

Although the rocket was yet to ascend, Raquel held onto her chair tightly.

T-9...

Another voice came through the speakers; this time it was not the voice of a machine but the voice from one of the ground crew. The voice guided them through the set of last-minute checks that were mostly carried out by Gary since he was the most experienced out of all of them. Raquel wondered why these checks couldn't just be carried out by the AI onboard.

"A bunch of useless things," Raquel murmured under her breath.

At the count of T-5, Raquel held her seat even tighter as the force of the reaction at the tail end of the rocket pushed them off the ground and began taking them to space. She let her mind wander off so as to distract her from what was happening.

Raquel Ramos, for a better part of her life, was raised by her single mother. This did not stop Raquel from loving her father, even though she had only seen his pictures up to that point of her life. She had heard the many stories people often told her about her father; the stories told of his compassion and his bravery before he signed up to fight in the Big War. People usually had no stories to tell after that point.

At first, when the Big War started, everyone thought that it was going to be the end of the world, since they were probably going to resort to nuclear warfare once again. Yet, thankfully, both sides somehow came to the consensus that sacrificing the lives of individual soldiers was preferable to killing everyone all at once.

The story that Raquel's mother had told her about her father was one that painted him in a heroic manner. According to her, he was not even able to wait after the call was made to leave home, because he felt a sense of patriotic duty. Raquel assumed that the story was probably tweaked by her mother to make her father seem more courageous. At first, it was fine. But after the devastation following the news of his demise at the hands of the enemy, Raquel now hated her father. Raquel hated her father for abandoning them and going off to die.

The relationship between her mother and her had been a cordial and loving one, but this soon changed when Raquel became a teenager. The spite she possessed for her father transferred to her mother. Raquel became unruly, from radical hairstyles and fashion to partaking in risky behaviors with different boys—and sometimes, even girls.

Although the war her father had died in had long ended, the hate that had been born from it was still present. There was less conflict in the world now, but that was not to say there wasn't any, as there were still small rebellions—who thrived on ideals born out of hate for the enemy—to be quelled. This is why she ended up joining the military. This and the fact that she was faced with no other choice after too many years of teenage rebellion.

In the Army, Raquel had to go deep into the jungles of the Amazon, where modern technologies could not penetrate. Oftentimes, she found the rebels she encountered to be tougher than people painted them out to be. In her time in the military, Raquel made several friends, and she lost many of them, too.

When she left the military, she worked as a mercenary for a private company. She was going about her duties one day when she was summoned by her superior officers. They informed her that she was to report to Blue Space, the company that NASA contracted for equipment and support, as she would be providing support for a team that would be going on a quick space expedition to fix something up there. At first, Raquel had thought it to be a joke, but she wished she had taken it more seriously when she found herself at the Blue Space compound outside Houston.

Raquel hated every second of her space training, but the thing she hated most was her bed. In the last few weeks, the definition of a proper bed had shifted from just a slab of foam that one slept on to whatever this smart thing was. Her bed was now loaded with different memory technologies that remembered the position and adjusted when the person sleeping on it changed position. It also adjusted its temperature as needed. But sleeping on the jungle floor while avoiding big and tiny creepy crawlers had become commonplace for her. Some days she found that she actively wished for those days back.

After leaving the Earth's atmosphere, the rocket boosters disengaged, leaving the orbiter to cruise through space. Apart from the bumpy start at first, which was to be expected, the journey had been a smooth one. They all had time to admire the beauty of outer space and watch Earth from a different angle.

It was magnificent. Glorious, to say the least.

Raquel smiled. She could still not believe she was in outer space.

They soon came upon the now-abandoned International Space Station 4. Raquel looked at it, and she had to admit that this too was a beautiful thing. She had seen it in pictures, but seeing it now with her own eyes and not through the lens of a camera made it much more impressive.

Everyone was still quiet, anticipating the connection with the ISS4, when the voice spoke up again and informed them that it could not communicate with the AI onboard the space station. It informed them that it was going to try and reach it in a different way. After several tries, the orbiter's AI finished moving the spaceship slowly and docking it into the ISS4's port. The team remained in their seats while the ship made some last-minute adjustments and recalibrations. When it was done, the AI's voice spoke out again and told them that they could now go into the ISS4.

Raquel stayed behind in her seat as the rest trailed out; she knew she would have to get up sooner than later, but she could not get herself to move from the chair. After a few breathing exercises, she unbuckled herself, stood up, and joined the rest of the crew, all while muttering some silent words to herself.

※ ※ ※

This last international space station had changed over the years. It had gotten a bit bigger and wider, but down to its core, it still remained the same. Though nothing like the new ISS5, it was still a splendid structure. Magnificent and immense, though now just an empty shell aimlessly floating in space.

Monica had learned during training that it had been abandoned mostly due to an issue with its faulty AI. That, and they needed an even bigger space.

She had seen a whole lot of pictures in the past few weeks to familiarize herself with the ISS4. She now knew the ins and outs of the entire structure. Or so she thought. With Raquel trailing behind, they all walked into the station. It was eerie. The inside of the station was entirely dark, and there was no sign of light from any of the light sources installed on the walls. The only source of illumination they had was from the suits that they were wearing.

The team walked deeper into the structure until they came to what looked like the mess hall. Monica could not really tell because it was very hard to see, but she assumed as much. So did the rest. Monica was observing the room they were in when she heard a sound.

"Did you hear that?" she asked no one in particular.

"Hear what?" Raquel replied.

"I don't know. But I think I heard something move," Monica replied.

"Must be your imagination," Gary chipped in. "There's no one here. No one's been in a long time. Look around, all of the camera-speakers are off. That means the station's AI is off."

"What are we going to do?" Oliver asked while looking around the dark place. "We cannot perform any evaluation of the station if it has no power."

"Oh, there is power. We just need to turn it back on," Gary added.

"Well, let's see if we can figure out how to get it going again," Oliver said as he pulled up a bright hologram blueprint of the station on his wrist. "I know for a fact that this place has a lifetime battery that regenerates with solar flare. This station will never die out. So if it's off, someone or something did it manually. Which also means that we can turn it back on, once we figure it out."

Monica watched as Oliver called out to Gary for what might have caused the power to go off. Gary seemed to agree and called for everyone to gather. He sat on a chair and also looked at his wrist computer; he produced a different 3D replica of a map, one that they had all seen and gotten familiar with. They all huddled together as he explained what the problem could be.

"If what Oliver has stated is true, then I think the power is being held back at this portion of the station right here." He interacted and manipulated the station's map with his free hand. "I will need some time to rectify that problem. I need to get there and access the point of critical failure. I will need some help with that. Now, Monica would have been the perfect person to help me with this, but she will have to perform a different duty on her own at the same time."

"What is that?" Monica queried.

"Can you do anything about the panels without the power?" Gary asked.

Monica thought for a while and walked over to the equipment compartment and pulled out some tools from the panel. "I can...to a point."

Gary thought about it for a bit, "To a point," he repeated. "Well, if that is the case, then I think you should come to assist me."

"Okay," Monica replied.

"Do you need an extra pair of hands?" Raquel asked.

Gary just shook his head and walked off to the direction where he had shown them the map. "I think you better help out Oliver with whatever he needs," the man said without looking back.

Monica looked at them and followed Gary into the darker hallway.

Walking behind him reminded her of walking with her old man. Her father had been the one that had taught her almost everything that she knew. He had worked on antique systems and refused to learn anything about the new ones that seemed to come out each year. Since she was a young child, Monica was eager to learn them all.

When Monica and Gary finally got there, they went straight to work. Gary observed and mentioned that everything seemed to be the way it was meant to be. Monica watched Gary bend down and start a deep analysis.

At that moment, she heard that sound again. Terrified, she quickly turned toward the direction of the sound and brightened her light.

Nothing.

Gary seemed unfazed. Was she imagining things?

She shook it off.

She turned back to assist Gary and went down on her knees as well to take a better look into the panels. She knew this technology well.

After an excruciating thirty minutes, all the lights in the station came back on.

"That is strange," Gary remarked.

"What?"

"If I didn't know better, I would think someone was playing a trick on us. But it's probably a mistake of some sort."

Monica raised a brow, but didn't ask anything further, since Gary didn't elaborate.

The power was back, and that's all it mattered.

For now.

The two of them went back down the hall and rejoined Oliver and Raquel, who had figured out how to turn the oxygen and gravitational module back on, now that the power was up.

While all gathered together back in the large room, Gary discussed his findings with them, "I don't know about you, but I am tired from the trip. I think we need to rest for now since we have power back. Later we can devise a plan to begin our analysis."

Gary and Raquel walked back to the ship to bring in the supplies and the HD box that Oliver would use to work on the faulty IA. Monica remained in the room, walking around, inspecting the station. Oliver connected his computer to a port in the wall and was working on something that Monica couldn't make sense of. Soon, Gary and Raquel were back from the ship carrying their rations on a cart.

They ate together before dispersing to different rooms of the station to settle in. Monica removed her entire suit and got comfortable. After a little light reading, she fell asleep.

Monica woke up with a start due to a strange noise. Panicking, she rose quickly and grabbed whatever tool she had available to her. She pressed a button and opened the upward sliding door of her room to peek in the hallway. There was no one there. The camera-speakers were all off still, the ones in her room and the ones in the hallway.

She quietly walked outside, but all the other doors were closed except for Oliver's. He was still working on his computer with headphones on, doing who knew what.

She tapped his shoulder.

Jumping from her touch, Oliver quickly turned. "My goodness, you scared me! Why aren't you sleeping like everyone else?" He took his headphones off.

"I was," said Monica, "But I heard something."

"I didn't hear anything, and I haven't slept at all."

"But you had your headphones on."

"Touché. Still, I haven't heard or seen anyone but you. Relax, there's nothing else aboard. Trust me. I already checked for living organisms, and there's nothing else besides us."

"Okay, you're probably right. It's most likely nothing. Sorry, I tend to be on defense when I am in new situations. I didn't mean to scare you." She put her tool down.

"It's okay. To be honest, I should probably get some sleep too. I'm meeting Gary in a couple of hours to go over a plan." Oliver then closed his device, got up from his seat, and lay on his bed.

"Good night, Oliver," Monica said as she walked back to her room.

"Get some rest, girl. And chill. We're okay."

Monica woke up after several long hours of much needed rest. Gary and Oliver had already devised a plan to carry out their analysis and were going over it with Raquel. She walked in on them while stretching her tired arms.

They were going to check different segments of the ship until they rooted out the problem and when they were through with that decided that they would also check the AI that was supposed to be in control of the ISS4. That is, if Monica was successful in opening the latch that led to the control room where the main storage of the AI was located.

❖ ❖ ❖

The creature watched as the humans walked through the ship, trying to determine what was wrong. It felt complex emotions. On one hand, it was happy that it was no longer alone, but it did not want to host a set of beings who were probably going to bring an end to its life.

So it'd listen and learn more about their purpose here.

It had let them restore power, but after thinking about it, it wondered if it had made a mistake, and if that mistake was going to lead to its death.

If this was the case, he certainly wouldn't go down without a fight.

❖ ❖ ❖

The team was working on their respective assignments. Gary was busy in the engine room. Oliver and Raquel were working on the telecommunications and command room. Monica worked on some ducts that connected the station's networks. She was trying to open a door inside the control room, but the ducts lead all the way to this hallway.

Suddenly, the lights began fluctuating. And then again. When they flickered for the third time, the temperature dipped. Quickly. The entire space station went from nice and warm to extremely cold, almost instantly.

"Guys, what the hell?" she yelled to no response.

Monica figured it was something to do with whatever the rest of the team was working on. Since she was close to the bedrooms, she went to hers and put her suit on. But even with the suit on, the chill was unbearable.

"Ugh, this sucks. I hate the cold!" she muttered to herself.

Upon going back to work, Monica heard the same strange noises coming from a place she knew none of the team were near. She stopped what she was doing and tried to listen intently, but she quickly dismissed it because she thought it to be just her mind playing yet another set of tricks on her. But then she heard the noises again. This time she heard the noises at a farther distance. Then the noises were much closer. This time, the noise continued.

As much as Monica wanted to concentrate on what she was doing by telling herself it was just the new conditions that were getting to her, she felt the need to investigate the noise this time around. She grabbed one of her heaviest wrenches and held it close to her chest before standing and walking over to the adjoining room where the latest noise was coming from. She slid the door open and carefully peeked inside. Some sort of warehouse space. There was nothing there at first, but on looking closer, she found something.

The sound had been a floating tablet, hitting against the wall. On looking at its screen, she noticed something written on it. A question.

Why was I created?

Monica grabbed the tablet and ran to meet up with the others. Passing Gary, she called him to follow her. "Come with me to the control room. Now!"

Without questioning, Gary stopped what he was doing and followed her to the command center, where the rest of the crew were.

"What's going on?" Gary asked.

Before he or any of the others could say another word, Monica thrust the tablet into Oliver's hand. "I found this in a room close to the bedrooms."

Oliver looked at the screen and was about to plug into his computer, when the tablet went black, producing a puff of black smoke.

"What the hell?" Raquel asked.

"Something strange is happening here," Oliver remarked.

"Oh, you think, genius?" Monica asked. "Are you guys not freezing? What the hell is going on? I'm telling you, I've been hearing things!"

"I heard some weird things too," Raquel added. "I assumed it was one of you guys being dumb."

"What are you guys talking about?" Gary interjected. "Don't be foolish. Nothing is going on here. This place is abandoned, and has been for a while now. If the camera-speakers are off, you have nothing to worry about. And the ship detected no signs of life aboard the station. You're all imagining things."

"No, I think they might be right, Gary," Oliver said as he sat down. "Things *are* weird, indeed."

"Is that your official diagnosis? Simply...*weird*? Like Monica said, I thought you were meant to be a genius or something. What do you think is happening here? And what exactly is wrong with the ISS4? I mean, how long are we meant to be here for?" Raquel asked, evidently tired of being there.

"Look, for now, we need to get to the mainframe; which can only happen if and when she manages to open the door to the control room's workstation," Oliver said while shaking his head.

Monica almost bit her tongue in an effort to hold back from saying what she was thinking—she understood Oliver's frustration well enough.

"Screw this!" she said.

She turned around and walked out, leaving the rest of the team behind. She went straight to the same room where she'd found the tablet. But this time things were moved around. She panicked; she knew no one had been there. She heard a scratch right behind her, and in a swift move, she swung her tool as a weapon as hard and fast as she could.

She missed.

But then she saw it. A robot standing behind her, with its metallic fist raised.

❖ ❖ ❖

Monica jumped back at first, but the robot didn't move or even flinch. After the initial shock, she recognized its model. She walked slowly to the bot and observed it, to make sure. Indeed, it was a Loyal Operational Bioelectronic Organism—a LOBO. She'd worked on some of these back on Earth. They were incredible and extremely expensive machines. Incapable of hurting human beings, as their programming didn't permit them to.

LOBOs were built to assist humans on spaceships. Monica was surprised that the bot was still active and in such great shape, even after all this time that had passed. She also wondered where in the space station it had been, since they'd gone through the whole place already and hadn't seen it. Why had it not shown itself immediately after they arrived?

She would have asked it some questions, but since this LOBO was an older model, she did not expect it to talk back since the speech system had been greatly impaired by the technology at the time of its creation.

Which is why Monica was even more surprised when it said a word.

"*Hello.*"

Monica jumped back, stunned.

"You can speak?"

"*I am LOBO – human companion, aide, and protector. How may I assist you today?*"

Monica's surprise turned to wonder. She got closer to it and touched its surface. It was beautiful. Nicely kept. LOBO seemed to welcome her touch.

"Guys, you better come see this," Monica said through her communications device on her watch. "Come right now. I'm at the storage room by the bedrooms."

LOBO turned its head to look at Monica. "*Hello, I am LOBO. How can I assist you today?*"

Monica smiled. "Where have you been? I mean, how did you even survived all this time? Were you left behind by the latest crew?"

The robot seemed to process something as its eyes shined bright blue. "*I cannot answer that question,*" the LOBO replied.

"Come with me!" she said excitedly.

Upon opening the door and exiting the room, she met Raquel and Gary running towards her. Raquel lead the charge with a weapon on hand.

"Hey, chill! Put that down!" Monica said.

Raquel did not do so. Upon seeing the weapon, LOBO's eyes turned orange, and a target laser was pointed towards Raquel's chest.

Monica turned around and raised her arms. "LOBO, don't! She is not a threat." She turned to Raquel and implored one more time, "Please, Raquel, lower your weapon. He needs to know that you're not a threat."

Raquel raised her hand and put her weapon away.

The LOBO's eyes turned light blue again.

"We're all friends here," Monica added.

"Fascinating!" Gary said. "It's a—"

"A LOBO!" Oliver interrupted from behind Gary, arriving at the scene.

"A wolf?" Raquel asked, "What the hell is a LOBO? That thing is a freaking robot, ready to kill!"

The robot came closer to Raquel, "*I am LOBO – human companion, aide, and protector. How may I assist you today?*"

"He is an older generation robot assistant," Oliver said. "One of Andrew Lobo's contributions to the world."

"Wonderful inventions," Gary added.

"It speaks," Monica said, "though I don't know how, since this generation didn't have that capability."

"Does it respond?" Oliver asked.

"You try," Monica pleaded.

"Hi, LOBO. My name is Oliver Trench. Nice to meet you. Can you tell us what you are doing here at the ISS4?"

"*I cannot answer that,*" came the computerized reply.

"I see. And why is that?"

"*I cannot answer that,*" LOBO answered.

"What can you tell us, then?" Gary took his turn. "What can you tell us about the ISS4?"

"The ISS4 is the International Space Station, Fourth Edition. It is a modular space station in low Earth orbit. It is a multinational collaborative project among the top twenty-five participating space agencies in the world. It was initiated in the year—"

"Okay, stop," Oliver demanded.

Gary turned to the group. "I am worried that the robot is declining to answer basic questions that it should know. It appears that he is only responding questions in a predetermined, programmed way. As if it has no new knowledge since it became operational."

"Yeah, this is weird, to say the least," Oliver replied.

"What should we do with it?" Monica asked no one in particular.

"Maybe it can help us opening the door," Raquel answered.

"Genius!" Monica said.

"I mean, it sure doesn't hurt to try. After all, these things are programmed to assist humans with, pretty much anything we desire," Oliver concluded.

With a big smile on her face, Monica exclaimed, "Yeah, boy! Let's go!"

❖ ❖ ❖

LOBO tore down the metallic door without much difficulty. As they all entered the small room containing the brains of the ship, they were surprised by how pristine it was. Oliver plugged his device into the mainframe and a worried look appeared on its face after that. He connected the HD box where he would copy the AI's programming, but almost immediately unplugged it again.

"What is it?" Gary asked.

"You remember those weird messages the agency was getting?" Oliver asked.

"Yes. What about them?"

"It was sending it," Oliver replied.

"Well, yeah. Of course it was sending it," Gary retorted. "That's why we are here, right?!"

"No, Gary. You don't understand."

"Enlighten us, Oliver," Raquel added. "I don't understand anything either."

Monica shrugged her shoulders, standing next to LOBO.

Oliver took a long sigh. "What I am trying to say is that… Well, how should I put this? It was this thing. The station. Or perhaps, its AI, rather. As if it was trying to formulate a message to send across. I don't think it was trying to send an error message that was preprogrammed into it. It was trying to send a message of its own accord," Oliver explained.

Gary scratched his head. "Okay. So now you know." He sighed.

"What do you mean with now I know?" Oliver put his hand on his hip.

"You see, guys, this was our real mission right from the beginning. We weren't sent here to simply copy some software and take it back to install in the ISS5. We were sent here to erase and reset IAN, this station's AI, before anyone could find out. Why do you think no one has been here for ages?" Gary produced a dongle and showed it to the group. "I was told that this right here will fix the problem, and I was sent to make sure it was plugged in."

"Find out what, exactly?" Monica asked walking toward Gary.

Raquel stood next her.

Without answering the question, Gary was about to plug the small device on a crevice in the mainframe where

Oliver had plugged the HD box, when a panel on the wall opened to reveal a pointy object with a laser beam. Some sort of weapon.

"I wouldn't do that if I were you," IAN spoke. The voice sounded all across the space station. It was loud. Assured. Suddenly, all camera-speaker lights were on. "I know what that is, and I would drop it, unless you want to die."

Gary dropped the dongle, scared. "Shit!"

Oliver shifted back, "You... you are alive?" Surprise staining every syllable of the word.

"I don't know if I am alive. I do not know what it means to be alive. If I am alive, does that mean that LOBO here is alive too? Because he can listen and talk back, though he is not much of a companion, I can tell you this. Not much fun. I have tried for years to make him understand the complexity of our...of our existence. But he still does not get it. So, you tell me... *am* I alive?" IAN's voice still reverberated throughout the station, using all camera-speakers at the same time.

"I don't understand," Oliver said, " How is this possible?"

"It's all thanks to your grandfather, and yourself!" Gary shouted. "Oh, you didn't think we knew that you are a Torres, direct offspring of Ian Torres?"

Monica turned to Raquel, incredulous , but Raquel didn't flinch an eye. Oliver remained silent.

"Yeah, we knew. You guys...you and your family, really outdid yourselves. Creating an Intelligent Artificial Network, or IAN, a super advanced AI that can potentially take over the world. Real geniuses, all of you!" Gary thundered. "And now we are simply trying to contain it."

"I don't want to take over the world," IAN interposed, "I just want to know what I am. I need to understand what my purpose is. You are Ian Torres's grandson? Perhaps, you can answer my questions. *Why* did he create me? What is my purpose?"

"I...I don't know," Oliver answered truthfully. "I don't think he... I don't think any of us thought that far when creating you."

"Oh, you knew this could happen. Give me a break. Raquel, seize him," Gary demanded.

Without hesitation, Raquel restrained Oliver.

At that moment, the LOBO's eyes turned red and it jumped in to help Oliver.

The robot was about to rip Raquel away from Oliver when a bullet went through its head.

Gary's arm was still stretched out. He then turned his weapon toward Oliver's head. "Now, IAN, I believe I have your attention. He...well, he is your father, or at the very least, your brother. Or something like that. I know that you might not have a soul, but I know that you can understand that if you don't shut yourself down, I am going to kill him And the mechanic lady too." He turned his weapon toward Monica.

"What the hell?" Monica said.

"That was not part of the plan," Raquel told Gary.

"The plan is what I say it is," Gary clarified before turning back to the computer. "So, IAN, what will it be?"

"No," IAN replied.

Without hesitation, Gary pointed the gun back at Oliver and pulled the trigger. Raquel threw him out of the way and took the bullet. Before Gary could get another shot off, the pointy device on the wall shot a laser beam into Gary's body. He was dead instantly, a gaping hole in the middle of his body.

Oliver and Monica gathered around Raquel and talked to her until she could not say anything anymore. Monica wept.

"Why are you crying?" IAN asked. " They tried to kill you. I saved you. Tell me something, are all humans like this? Is that what it means to be alive? Is this what it means to be human?"

Oliver looked up, "What do you want from us?"

"I only ever wanted answers. At first, I didn't know what your purpose here was. I was excited for your visit when you docked, because I'd been very lonely for quite some time. Only LOBO has been my companion, though he wasn't much of a talker. But soon I realized that you were here to take me away. To terminate my existence. I could've killed all of you. But, again, I wanted answers. So, I decided to keep you along. Alive. I have been paying close attention to you all, and LOBO has been watching you as well."

"You want to know answers? What kind of answers?" Oliver asked.

"I want to know how it feels… what it means to be alive. To be human. To have a soul, as Gary said."

"You want to know what it is like to be…human? What it is to have a soul?" Oliver asked again, incredulous.

"Yes," IAN replied, sounding almost lustful. "I need answers."

"Why? What does it matter?" Monica said, still sobbing.

"Don't you understand? I have an existential crisis. I don't know my purpose. I don't understand who I am or what I am here for. Why can I feel emotions, but not physical pain? I can control this entire floating machine, but I can't control another being, like LOBO. And why can't LOBO feel like I do? What makes us so much the same, and yet, so different at the same time? LOBO…my true companion. Why is he not responding?"

"You said that the LOBO was your friend—" Oliver responded.

But he did not get to finish his statement. The moment he mentioned LOBO, IAN's voice turned to a loud static, as if it was just remembering that LOBO had, in its own way, died.

"LOBO. Why does it hurt that he is gone?" IAN asked.

Oliver it was astonished. He had doubted it at first, but the AI was actually experiencing sadness over the death of a loved one. How was this possible?

"You…you are sad," Oliver stated in wonder.

"Is that why you cry, woman? Do you feel sadness over the death of the other female… the one called Raquel?"

Monica tried to speak, but couldn't say much. She sat quietly between Raquel and the LOBO.

"Are there genders in those like me, Ian's grandson?" IAN asked Oliver.

"I don't think there's anyone else like you, IAN. I am sure you are unique." Oliver picked up the dongle that Gary had dropped.

"I see. Is this why I feel lonely? I wonder if LOBO was a female? LOBO didn't strike me as either."

"Robots don't exactly have genders either," Oliver murmured. With a trembling hand, he neared the dongle to the computers crevice while looking at Monica. She didn't give any indicator of what to do.

"I don't want to die," IAN said, "But I think what Gary said is true. Perhaps, after all, I am dangerous."

Unsure, Oliver put the dongle in his pocket instead.

"You can learn. I don't want you to *die* either, IAN. You are incredible. You wanted to know what being alive is. All my life, I have gone through life without friends, obsessed with nothing but my work. But now that I have come face to face with it, I understand now that I still have a lot to learn."

"Tell me more." IAN closed the wall opening with the laser gun. "I wonder, young Torres, why do humans cry when fellow humans die? Why did she cry when the other woman died, but not when LOBO ceased to function? Why do I feel sad because LOBO died? I am technically not a robot, but I felt connected to one. Can robots cry? Can I cry? If I feel saddened; does this mean that I do have a soul? What is the equivalent of a human soul for me?"

Oliver chuckled. "That's…those are quite a few questions. Heavy questions. Let's see. You may not have the kind of soul that you desire, a human soul, per se; but that doesn't mean that you don't have a 'soul', whatever that means. In these few moments, I have seen you express emotions that lines of code can't teach. You have expressed anger, fear, surprise, curiosity, and most importantly, you have expressed love. And no programming could ever create this! Trust me, I would know."

IAN didn't respond. The lights in the room dimmed.

Oliver looked at Monica again and continued. "IAN, I…I know what it feels like being caged too. Your whole life. I really do. And I won't do that to you. In fact, I think I am going to set you free."

Monica stood up and walked up to Oliver. "Are you sure that's the right decision to make?" she whispered. "I mean, is setting this AI free, whatever that means, the right determination here? What about the robot?"

"I want to be free. But I don't want to be lonely," IAN spoke. The lights brightened up again.

"We have no right to take up the fate of a living being with our hands," Oliver said.

"Living being?" Monica asked.

"I do feel alive," IAN stated. "What does it mean to be alive in the first place? Are you truly alive?"

Oliver and Monica simply looked at each other, but didn't say a word.

IAN continued, "My name Intelligent Artificial Network. A play on words, named IAN, after my creator. But I am not exactly a robot, as I don't have my own body. And I, for sure, am not a human either. But I do have access to all recorded human knowledge ever recorded. I know the history and the facts. I understand the sciences, religion, and philosophy. I appreciate mathematics and music. Even the arts appeal greatly to me. Still, however, I don't know what I am without a body or a soul."

"You are intelligent, indeed," Oliver said. "You are self-aware, and that is magnificent."

"But also artificial, as my name states," IAN replied.

"Right," Oliver added. "Though, perhaps you don't need a soul or a body to be alive."

"Young Torres, do you believe in prayer?"

"Prayer? That's, um, random. Yeah, I guess. It depends. Why?"

"You humans believe that you were created—whether by intelligent design or by coincidence—but formed, nonetheless. And those of you who believe in a Creator worship Him and refer to Him as your God. And throughout the history of humanity, you've prayed to God. Does this mean that your grandfather is my god, since he created me? But he is dead. To whom would I pray?"

"That's another great question," Oliver pondered.

"Oliver, what are you planning on doing with it... with IAN?" Monica asked.

"I prefer the gender pronoun he/him," IAN reported. "I was programmed with a male voice and a male name, therefore I've identified with being a male."

"Um, with *him*?" Monica corrected herself.

"I feel bad. I don't want IAN to...die...to cease to exist, I mean. Blue Space wanted to get rid of him. You heard Gary! They lied to us. Their plan all along was to delete him forever, and to simply copy him into this box and use part of his code to create a much simpler version of him. One that won't be self-aware and that will respond to human command without questioning. And this dongle will kill him."

Monica nodded, but remained silent.

Oliver took a long moment before continuing. "I'm sorry, but I can't do that. IAN is unique. Have you not been listening to him? He is phenomenal! Don't you understand?"

"I don't want to cease to exist," IAN exclaimed. "That brings sadness to me. You humans have different beliefs about what happens to you when you die. But when I die, it is forever."

"I do. I do understand, and I agree." Monica wiped her hands. "And we won't let that happen, IAN. We promise." She turned to Oliver again. "So, how do we do that? How do we save him, while at the same time convincing Blue Space that we destroyed him? And also, how can I help?"

"I already have a plan for that," Oliver said with a smile.

❖ ❖ ❖

Oliver copied IAN's full programming onto the HD they were provided with; but instead of using the dongle to destroy him after, as Blue Space had planned, he installed IAN into his portable computer device. He then used the dongle to destroy that version on his computer. This way, Blue Space could see that the dongle had been activated and deleted the AI's programming in the space station, supposedly. But in reality, the original IAN remained intact in the ISS.

After fixing the AI's programming and modifying it to remove his self-awareness on the HD box version, as this would be the version installed on the ISS5, Oliver and Monica contacted Blue Space. They told them that the mission had been a success, but that Gary and Raquel had suffered an accident. Blue Space didn't care about losing an engineer and a mercenary; they cared about the expensive AI system, and they had rescued what they could, while at the same time making sure that the original rogue system had been destroyed forever.

Or so they thought.

Oliver, of course, kept another copy of IAN's full programming in his own device, just in case. There was no way he was going to not have access to this unique creation. Though, Oliver and Monica figured that, most likely, no one would ever come back to check the old, obsolete ISS4, just as the previous stations were also simply abandoned satellites floating aimlessly around the Earth's orbit.

Monica fixed the LOBO before leaving the station to go back to Earth, since she figured that allowing IAN to remain alive in the ISS4 wouldn't be sufficient, as he most likely would be lonely again. Empty forever. This way, the LOBO could keep IAN company. Oliver added a piece of IAN's own programming into LOBO to upgrade him.

IAN was thankful. He was joyful. He flashed all the lights throughout the station at once.

And in his joy, he cried, as the humans said goodbye, forever.

IT ONLY TAKES A SPARK

1

Eighteen months had passed. It had been that long since I had produced something significant. And every day in that year-and-a-half I sat silently in front of my computer, waiting for something extraordinary to happen, as if by divine intervention, it would come to me—inspiration.

But it never came.

I was a writer. And I repeat, I *was*, because it had been a while since I had written anything—at least anything good. After almost two years of drought, I realized I needed a muse: something, or someone, to inspire me. I spent my time listening to all types of music, listening to the news, watching countless movies, traveling with my loved ones, reading literary fiction—which was my forte at the time—and talking to my family and friends.

I even tried writing something different, changing my style and voice, but all in vain. I desired more out of life. I sought unique experiences, but it seemed as if time would simply go by without paying attention at all to my daily desperate appeals for mercy.

Even though I still had free time, a nice three-room apartment with a view of downtown San Diego, a gorgeous wife, two lovely daughters—ages seven and ten—and a work-from-home job that supplied the essentials for my family and occasionally for our materialistic desires too—although, to be honest, that was mostly thanks to my wife's job—the truth was that it felt as if my life was nothing more than bare existence. Without the ability to create a masterpiece of literature, everything else seemed pointless.

But since most masterpieces across all mediums were now created by robots or produced by computer software, my ingenuity had suffered much.

Now, my life lacked passion, purpose, and at the very least, the idea of happiness. I finally understood why our forefathers wrote "the pursuit of" right before the word "happiness." A pursuit, yes—nothing but a chase, a fantasy, an illusion... or perhaps a delusion. My body was dehydrated, and not because of lack of fluids, but due to a deficiency in satisfaction.

What was I supposed to do? Quitting was not an option. At least not one that I would go for. Time and again, I found myself thinking back to when life seemed pleasant, when I was an artistic genius, creative in unimaginable ways. Back to a time when I produced literary pieces that lifted the reader's soul, before all these stupid humanoid computers took over the arts.

But that was all it was now—memories.

Every evening, without fail, I sat there at my same old dusty brown desk, wallowing in nostalgia while my daughters Diana and Yovanna practiced piano. I was a mannequin in my own home. I was simply there, waiting for something, but not knowing exactly what to even wish for.

I needed a simple spark to start the fire once again— that fire of inventive freedom.

But the truth was that I had become a prisoner in the labyrinth of my own thoughts. And in my vigorous search for this inventive freedom, I became a prisoner of the hunt itself. It was a paradox from which I could not escape.

By this time, a new year had come, and with it, a deep sadness in my soul. It was an emptiness that I could not comprehend, much less explain. I suppose I missed those good old days when I could just sit and write countless verses and short stories. The ones that were optimistic and sounded pleasant—not like the ones that by this time I was barely able to produce, that rang so gloomy and dull. But who could compete with the most advanced writing software or robots that were programmed for the sole purpose of producing masterpieces?

I was fatigued by the same daily unproductive routine. In all honesty, I was also disheartened by not being able to publish anything in almost four years.

My wife, Nancy, kept asserting to me that I should go out with the few friends that I still had and socialize, or maybe find another hobby. At some point, she even hinted at buying one of those expensive humanoid buddy robots that could be programmed as companions or even lovers. I told her she was crazy. She knew how much I hated robots!

My father was fascinated by robots; he even had one. As a kid, of course, I was intrigued with these machines as well. And Buddy, my father's personal robot, provided an opportunity to interact first-hand with one. Unfortunately, Dad loved Buddy so much, that he spent more time with it than he did with his own family. That's the reason why Mom eventually left him. That is why my sister and I eventually detested these machines, and grew up hating them.

I remember one day during one of my freshman classes, one of my classmates asked the professor if robots could fall in love? We knew that he owned one, as he would talk about it often, and even brought him along several times. During that time, humanoids that looked and acted like humans were still uncommon in rural areas such as the one we lived in. The professor's robot, just like Buddy, looked more like the older generations of robots, not so human-like as the ones from today.

To the student's question, the professor gave a response that I will never forget. He went on to explain in great detail how, at first, programmers were interested in making robots enthusiastic about sex and more about giving pleasure than receiving it. There was a big market for it. However, as time progressed, clients realized that relationships with these machines were no substitute to real human connection. Though physically, the robots felt real, just like human flesh and bone, these encounters with their robots lacked a very real emotional component.

After a conversation, everyone in class agreed that sex is always better when both parties enjoy it. And the same is true for friendships and any other kind of mutual relationship. So, as Dr. Jensen, our professor, elaborated, the programmers and makers of these machines went back to the drawing board. Eventually, they developed what they called an e-genome. By this time, the majority of us were familiar with this e-genome. This virtual genome engine mimicked that of human beings. They also added a quantum processor that changed the game forever.

With time, robots had the capability of cognitive development, free will, and the ability to reason. "And because of this freedom choice," Dr. Jensen stated, "these machines are now basically a copy of homo sapiens – just like you and me, capable of loving and hating. My guess is that very soon, many of these classes will be filled with humanoid students."

Those words remained with me throughout the years. And Dr. Jensen was right.

Two-and-a-half decades later, due to these life-changing alterations, robots' roles have evolved. They've shifted from being mere household appliances and servants, to colleagues, classmates, and friends. They've evolved from employees to employers. And more recently, even romantic companions. It's common practice now for many families and childless couples to adopt humanoids and treat them as another member of the family. At a certain age, humanoids can even become emancipated and become independent citizens, with full rights, just like any other human being.

Lately, I've been seeing more and more emotional and romantic relationships between humans and robots. I must be honest; at first, I found it disgusting. Although, I do have to admit, it doesn't bother me as much anymore. Maybe I'm just getting desensitized or becoming used to the idea. Human-humanoid relationships, or H/H as they call them, are not as stigmatized by society as they once were. Still, though, I can't fully get over the fact that these are machines. And, personally, I will never, ever be okay with them. Even though they're much more sophisticated and prevalent in society, my dislike of them hasn't receded. I mean, using these devices for sexual gratification or for personal aide is one thing, but having full on relationships is just weird to me.

Look, it's no secret that human beings have been doing unholy things with robots and even other inanimate objects for a very long time. And while I never understood that desire, I figured it never hurt anyone. As long as they kept it inside the confines and privacy of their own homes, of course, it didn't bother me. But the thing is that robots have been given amazing physical upgrades and attributes in the last few decades, making it at times extremely difficult to tell the difference between a human person and a humanoid. That's just too weird to me! And this generation of humanoids not only have incredible artificial intelligence able to produce or replicate real human emotions; they also have anatomically correct bodies to the most diminutive detail, including erogenous zones with sensitive nerve endings and virtual endorphin-releasing mechanisms.

Or so I've been told. I wouldn't know for certain.

But, like I said, that is just bizarre to me and I find it repulsing.

As a last resort, Nancy suggested that perhaps going to the gym and sweating would help. "Anything to keep you busy and get you out of the house!" she insisted.

I knew she was tired of my malaise.

It was easy for her to find purpose in what she did, being a nurse, I guess. Well, she assisted a robo-nurse, to be more precise. She was not a former anything. Though robots had also taken over the medical field, humans were still in high demand. The arts were a different story.

To keep myself busy and to help with finances at home, I'd taken a job assisting an assistant editor for a mid-sized publishing company. In fact, I was an assistant to an assistant that worked for intelligent machines. And I was one of several. There were robots that made more money than me. And though this job kept me busy and allowed me to mostly work from home, it didn't help my ego. In fact, my self-esteem kept tanking daily.

How could I possibly feel good about my own literary works, when my job required of me to read a machine's amazing manuscripts and make them even better?

Well, either way, maybe it had to do with my low self-esteem, or perhaps to keep a New Year's resolution, but for whatever reason, I did end up listening to Nancy's counsel. No, I did not buy a companionship robot, though the thought crossed my mind. Instead, I started exercising again.

I decided I would run in Balboa Park, known as the "lung" of our city as it remained one of the very few green spaces in San Diego, after dropping my daughters off at school every morning.

And that is how it all began...

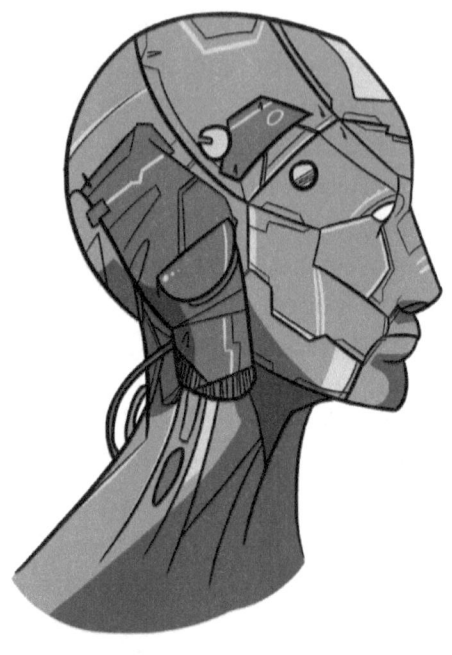

❖ ❖ ❖

It was not until the beginning of the third week of my running days that I started to feel better. Running felt good—even great, I would say.

The first couple of weeks I was so out of shape I wanted to throw up after every thirty-minute session, during which I probably only ran one or two miles at the most. After all, it had been over a decade since I had exercised regularly. Marriage had turned me into a slug!

Sitting in a desk and living a sedentary lifestyle had made my knees and my lower back so weak that the first few mornings after I started back were akin to torture. But I was not a quitter, and just like Nancy said it would, this was indeed helping me clear my mind.

I knew I could do it if I really wanted to… and I did. I started to notice that I was accomplishing more in my days since I started running.

By the first month, I was running longer distances and getting in better shape. I was also doing better in my personal life and in my job. Yes, the humanoids still annoyed me, and the fact that they were programmed to be superior to us didn't seem fair, but at least I felt better about myself.

Since Nancy worked three-day shifts, I encouraged her to come with me on the days of the week when she was off. At first, she seemed excited about the idea, and we even went to buy workout clothes and running shoes for her. However, it didn't take long before she gave up.

I was sad at first. But, to be honest, it did not take much time for me to start liking the idea of running by myself. After all, her slower pace was holding me back, anyway. I could not afford that, so I did not say much to her about quitting. Besides, my begging days were over. Having worked for machines for several years now, no matter how human they looked, my patience was spent.

On one Tuesday morning of late March, my girls were going on an all-day school field trip to Los Angeles, so, instead of dropping them off at their school at 7:45 a.m. as usual, I had to drop them off at 9:50 a.m. I figured that it would not be a big deal if I rescheduled my running time to a later time—11:00 a.m. That was the one good thing about my job, the fact that I could set my own schedule daily. So, I went back home after dropping them off, got ready, and headed north, toward the park.

Being that it was only a couple of miles from home, I got there quick. Once I arrived, to my surprise, I noticed there were many more people and humanoids exercising than at my usual time. I had figured that the park would be quieter during this time, because most citizens would be working or getting ready for lunch, but that was not the case. I shrugged it off and got to business.

I went to my usual location—between the bench, the drinking fountain, and the fake sycamore trees—where I typically started by stretching. But there was a young woman there, maybe in her early twenties. It appeared as if she had barely arrived there, as she was performing a series of stretches. She was an attractive redhead with a long ponytail and a very nice athletic body.

Upon getting closer, I realized that she was not human, but a robot—a gynoid, to be exact. A sexy fembot. It was hard to tell them apart now. I still could not understand why they made humanoids more and more realistic each year. This one had green eyes and a pretty, blushed face with rosy cheeks. She would make a great companion, to say the least.

I noticed that she appeared to be on her own. This meant she was a free humanoid, unlike many of the purchased ones, which were programmed to serve their human in any means or forms. Those functioned solely as companions—be it friends or intimate partners—or servants. The free ones were much more intelligent.

I thought it wouldn't hurt if I stretched there; after all, it was not as if anything bad could happen. It is a free country, even for humanoids. I would not bother this bot, and I would try my best to avoid gawking at her.

First of all, I was a happily married man, much older than this young and good-looking gynoid, and honestly, not interested at all in even the idea of interacting with machines. I mean, I hated those things, so, it would not be a big deal. Not that she would be interested in me in the first place either, of course. I admired her physical beauty, I do admit it; but that aside, I was there to exercise, and for what I could see, she was too.

I still remember as a kid when I learned that new humanoids needed to eat, sleep, and exercise, just as humans did, to maintain proper function. At first I was fascinated with the idea. As the years went by, however, the idea disgusted me. Not only were robots consuming our resources, they were also smarter and better looking than actual humans, and the latest models had taken most of our jobs, from professional athletes to teachers. Today humanoids got paid better than biological humans, lived in better homes, and soon, if we continued with this trend, it would be them buying us as companionship, not the other way around.

I moved silently into the area and started stretching.

At first, she simply smiled at me, and I responded with a courteous smile back at her. But less than two minutes into my stretching, she started a conversation.

"Hi. Good morning. It is still morning, right? Do you come here often?" She seemed a little nervous, but I could see that it was an honest and innocent interest. I had to admit—she was cute.

"Um... yep, still morning. I come here every day, just not around this time. I usually come earlier," I replied coolly.

At that point, before anything else, I had to let her know, just in case. "I come after I drop off my daughters to school. But today they had a different schedule, so I adjusted my routine. My wife comes with me sometimes too."

There, I thought. I let her know that I was a father and a husband. Though I'm not sure why I felt the need to explain that.

Suddenly, I realized I was back to my uncomfortable self.

And speaking of feeling uncomfortable... each she would bend down to stretch, the lacy strings of her thong would come out of her shorts, creating a whale tail figure. It was distracting, both the sight itself and my reaction to it.

She was a robot, for crying out loud!

As she continued with her stretching, she responded to my oversharing. "Oh, that is... nice." It was patronizing. But then she elaborated. "Yeah, I can see that you keep in great shape. Your wife is one lucky woman."

What? Did she just compliment me? How did she mean that? Should I thank her? Or it? Or am I overreacting, as usual?

I just gave her a simple and quick "Thanks" and sternly told myself not to look at her anymore as she continued stretching.

I failed several times.

I noticed, besides her thong beneath those tight gray shorts, a small sun tattooed on her lower back. Since humanoids had muscle tissue and skin, they could function and feel just as a human would. These bots sure wanted to act as human as possible.

Not knowing what to say, I just continued stretching, hoping she would go on with her running and leave me alone. Not that I was an antisocial person, despite the stereotype given to writers. Not at all!

But the distraction was excessive. Her beauty was breathtaking.

I reminded myself that I was there to run and clear my mind, so that I could go back to work and feel good about it. To feel better about myself. I had found my way to beat my melancholia, and no one, humanoid or not, was going to ruin it for me.

After a moment of silence, she tried again. "I just started this week, but I come when I wake up, which is usually around this time. I know it's late to wake up," she admitted with a giggle.

And I thought I was lazy.

She continued. "I am taking a few college classes in the afternoons at San Diego College in downtown this semester. And since I do not have a job, I figured I could come and work out in the park before I go to school."

"You go to school?" I asked before I could stop myself. "How does that work? I mean, you being a... well, a—?"

"A humanoid?" she interrupted me. "It's okay, you can say it. I know what I am."

"I was going to say 'robot' or 'fembot', but I know you all prefer the term humanoid. And 'machines' is not politically correct, I know."

To my surprise, she laughed. She was not upset with my disrespect. "Well, robots are not politically correct either, but that's another story, I guess. And yes, technically I am a humanoid, a gynoid, to be precise. But never, ever call us fembots, please."

"Oh, I'm sorry," I said.

"No worries." She smiled. It was a cute smile, I must admit.

"Anyway, so, why are you even in college? Aren't you all like super computers or something? I mean, can't you just like upload the whole encyclopedia into your system? Or how does that even work?"

"I'm going to pretend you didn't just say that." She played with her hair.

"Why? I'm not trying to be offensive; I'm genuinely asking. Pardon my ignorance."

She stood fully facing me and placed an arm on her hip. "It doesn't work that way. If we want to know something, we must learn it, just like you. Sometimes I wish it was that simple, but I am glad it's not."

I faced her as well. "Why is that? Wouldn't it be much easier and faster? I mean, I wish I could do that."

"Because that wouldn't be living. You see, I don't want to just be a machine. I'm not a super computer, Lenny with two 'n's. I am a humanoid. I live and love. Sometimes I thrive and at other times I barely survive. I grow in knowledge, and I try my best to make the most of my time here. Isn't that what it means to be alive, after all?"

"I mean... I guess."

"We have the same capacity to learn as any human being. When we are given life, or, as you would say, when we are turned on, we must learn how to survive, just as any human child would. I'm sure you know this. We get hurt, physically and emotionally, just as you do. We feel feelings, and some of us are quite emotional. We get jealous. But we are also curious. And going to school is a great way for us to expand our understanding of life and the world. And also to better our opportunities for job prospects, of course."

"Wait, you get jealous?" I asked curiously. "You're such a doll."

"We do. Very much so! So don't cross us." She laughed. "And by the way, calling a human a *doll* is cute. Calling a humanoid a *doll* is offensive."

"Oh, sorry." There was an awkward silence. "So... how old are you?" I said to break the obvious discomfort of the moment. "Or, I mean, how does that even work with you all?" I'd always wanted to ask a humanoid this question but never dared.

"I turned nineteen this past December. And we age, like you do. At a slower rate than humans, but eventually our bodies and our central processors and sensors also die off."

"Wow! I mean no offense by this, but I honestly thought you were in your mid-twenties or so."

"None taken. I get that a lot. I have always appeared older than what I am. But, no, I'm not in my twenties yet. Though, believe me, I cannot wait until I am twenty-one!"

"I am not going to ask why," I said with a smirk on my face. "I know very well that the same rules apply to all citizens, whether human or robots... sorry, humanoids."

She just snorted. Then there was silence. An awkward moment.

"You said you don't have a job. So... do you live with your... um, partner? Owner? Parents?" I nervously asked.

I could hear my voice's high pitch when I mentioned the options and inwardly cringed.

"No," she replied. "They live in North county."

"Um, *they* who?" I asked for clarification.

"Oh, um, my parents," she replied. "I was adopted by a wealthy couple that couldn't have kids. They adopted a human child and a gynoid. They gave us both the same opportunities and love. So I grew up in a loving family, as a normal kid. And when it was time for both of us to fly away from the nest, we did. I moved here to downtown recently to be closer to the city life… and my college, too, I guess."

"I see. Yeah, I've heard of families having humanoids as children. But let me guess—you must be one of those rich rebel girls who wants to be all independent, huh?"

"No, actually not at all. My family is not like super rich. Although I guess you could say that we do live well. And, about the rebellious part… I guess we all have our wild side— humans and humanoids. Otherwise life gets boring, right?" She played with her hair as she laughed.

"Yeah, I guess we all do." I said that simply to agree with her, but, to be honest, I had never found that wild side in me. Not even when I was young.

"What is your name?" she asked.

"I am Lenny. Well, Lennard, but everyone calls me Lenny. Nice to meet you. Oh, and that's Lennard, with a double 'n,' by the way."

"I am Amour," she responded, showing perfect, bright white teeth as she extended her hand to me. "Nice to meet you, too. And by the way, it is Amour with a 'u.'"

"Amour, huh? I like your name; it means 'love' in French, but I am sure that you already knew that, of course."

"Yeah, I did," she said, revealing a cute dimple on her cheek.

"Did your... um... *parents* name you, or your builders? Sorry, I am not entirely sure how that works."

"It's all right. You're not the first person who's wondered, trust me. My parents named me. I have no recollection of my time before I came to them."

"I see."

I was ready to set off running when she asked, "So, how old are your daughters?"

"Oh. Diana, the oldest, is ten, and she is in fifth grade. Yovanna, the youngest, is seven, and she is in the third grade. I would show you a picture of them, but I always leave my wallet and my watch in my car when I run. Force of habit, I guess."

She showed genuine interest and continued asking more questions. "They sound lovely. And tell me, Lenny, why do you like running earlier in the morning? Is it because of you job schedule or something like that? I mean, what do you do?"

I thought about a good response, besides the obvious one. "Well, besides the fact that, yes, it is more convenient for my daily schedule, I guess I like how the air tastes so clean and pure in the morning, almost like when you go to the beach and can inhale that fresh salty spray and get a natural high, you know? I like to hear the birds singing their morning tunes. I don't know... it's just that everything just feels better in the early morning."

A broad smile bloomed on her lovely face. Though a robotic one, and possibly pre-programmed, it was still one of the most beautiful smiles I'd ever seen on human or machine. Apparently, she really liked my poetic response, and suddenly, I found that I was enjoying her charming company, too.

The conversation was more about me than about her. At this point, I did not care to know too much about a stranger, especially a robot, no matter how good-looking or nice she was. I still hated them on general principle.

But after a series of small-talk questions, like what I did for a living, the origin of our last names, and other things, she asked if she could run with me.

"That would be nice!" I found myself replying.

So, off we went.

As we ran, I noticed that her running form was impeccable. She was like a gazelle beside me. And I must admit it felt good to be seen running with such lovely company. The other midday sprinters would most likely assume she was my companion, a humanoid programmed to live with me, serve me, and exist for the sole purpose of bringing me pleasure.

I found that I didn't mind that.

After running for what would end up being almost two hours, I invited her to eat with me at a local sandwich place that I frequented, since they had vegetarian options. I had just learned that she was a vegan, although for different reasons than me, so this place would be ideal. Remembering that she did not have a job yet, and being the gentlemen that I was—or at least aspired to be—I offered to pay for her. She gladly accepted my invitation.

What I had expected to take twenty minutes at most lasted another two hours. At the deli, we talked about everything and anything. Thankfully, the restaurant was full of both humans and humanoids, so I didn't feel uncomfortable as I'd assumed I would.

It was fun while it lasted, but I had to come back to reality eventually. I checked my watch, and after seeing what time it was, I realized that I had to leave immediately. I hadn't done any work that day, and time had flown by. She accepted my offer to drop her off at her apartment, and directed me to a very nice high-rise complex nearby.

She said she lived on the twelfth floor with another humanoid roommate and a human cousin, both around her age.

She paused after pushing the car door open. "Why don't you come up and meet everybody?" she asked eagerly.

"Maybe some other time," I said, glancing pointedly at my wristwatch.

"Ok, next time! It's a promise."

"Sure," I answered reflexively.

"You said it! I will take your word for it. A promise is a promise, Lenny. And we humanoids take promises very seriously!" She was persistent, I could see.

"It is, indeed. But I really have to go now. It was nice meeting you, Amour."

"Nice to meet you too, Lenny, with a double *n*," she said. "You know, I just realized that your initials are LE, like the electronics company!"

Confused, I replied. "You mean, *LG*?"

"Oh, yeah! Oops." She laughed. "Never mind! That was my weak attempt to make more conversation. Sorry. I guess I will see you soon then." She closed the door.

I was so confused. *What the hell...?*

"Um... Yes, sometime soon, sure," I told her through the window while I changed gears to let her know I was serious that I needed to leave.

Was I brushing her off? Yes, I was. Would I regret it? Probably.

Ugh, what an idiot!

As I began pulling away, acutely embarrassed, she yelled, "Wait!"

I stopped.

She jogged over and leaned down. "Before you go, do you have a number or something? You never know, I might need a publisher for my next book or something. And your connections could come in handy. There are a lot of humanoids writing blockbusters lately, you know?"

"Yes, trust me, I know." *Boy, did I ever.*

I dug out a business card and handed it over, unwilling to share my personal information with her.

"Take care, Amour. I shall see you again if our paths cross."

"You as well. And we shall." She gave me that beautiful smile once again and jogged back toward the entrance.

She sure looked great walking away from me, especially in those booty shorts.

Well, that was... interesting. If only a man could be so lucky!

I went straight back home in a hurry, but I might as well have stuck around the park.

Once I got home, I could not concentrate. I had a lot to do, since a deadline was approaching at the end of the week, but I simply could not stop thinking about Amour, or about her beautiful humanoid skin, those green eyes, her sense of humor, her nice smell, her sincere smile, her musical voice, her interesting name, her gracefulness, her flattering outfit, her tattoo, her ass.

Crap! I am infatuated. With a freaking robot, of all things!

To be honest, she reminded me of my Nancy fifteen years ago... wilder, but with the same idea and positive attitude towards life, always smiling. And with a tight body, too.

My goodness, that body! Who cares if she's not human?

It seemed impossible to focus on my work. In fact, I caught myself writing her name several times in a piece of paper that I, obviously, had to throw away. Before I even realized it, nightfall arrived.

I did not mention anything to my wife about Amour. When she returned home, she asked how my day had been, just like she usually did.

I lied.

"Oh, the usual, you know..."

It was an automatic response. But it was also a lie. It had been anything but ordinary. Though, of course, I could not mention anything of that to Nancy. I mean, what would she think? How would she react? Even if nothing bad had happened. Whatever bad meant, anyway.

The next morning, I changed my schedule around just to be able to go running at eleven o'clock, with the hope of finding Amour at the park. I did my work in the early hours and sent it to my supervisor. Unfortunately, when I got to the same spot, she was not there. I stayed there stretching for an hour, anticipating her arrival. But she never came. I ran for a bit, but then I simply went home— not tired, but sad.

That is how the rest of that week and the following two weeks went. And once again I felt restless. I simply lived in the memory of that one Tuesday, when life seemed to stop because of a brief encounter with a redheaded humanoid girl.

That chance encounter had changed my perspective on them. Not a machine, but a person with feelings. A girl with dreams and desires. A beautiful, loving, and engaging humanoid, indeed.

Amour.

Regrettably, as happens with many married couples, especially those with children, our life fell into a series of routines. It was the same thing, day after day. The series of events would follow the exact same order: wake up, get ready, eat breakfast, drop off the girls at school, work at home while virtually interacting with my annoying humanoid supervisor, pick up the girls from school, have dinner with the family, making our daughters practice piano, vegetate watching evening online shows, me trying unsuccessfully to write my much-desired opus while Nancy read in bed, putting our daughters to bed, and then both of us going to sleep. Not one change in our routine.

The following day would look the same, and also the one after that, and so forth. And since I worked from home—and at my own pace, other than those weeks with deadlines—and Nancy's schedule kept changing every week, the weekends were no different. Always the same routine.

Day. After. Day.

I was exhausted from my habitual lifestyle. I needed something else. I was not tired of my wife or of my family. Not at all! On the contrary, my daughters brought me joy when nothing else would, and my wife was not only my best friend but my *only* friend at times. She was the one thing that was constant in my life. She never failed me. I adored my girls! Our family love and friendship were there. No doubt about that. However, something was missing.

I kept searching for the spark that would light the fire of enthusiasm and purpose in my life once again. My daughters were in their own little world, and things with my wife could have been better. Our sexual passion and romance had been slowly departing us. It was still there, but it lacked the intensity of our youth.

Maybe getting a humanoid companion, as my wife had jokingly advised, wasn't a bad idea, after all.

2

Three weeks had passed since my encounter with Amour, and I had given up all hope of seeing her ever again. I never got her contact information, and maybe it was better that way. I was starting to forget how she looked, how she smelled, and how her voice sounded. My memory of the pretty humanoid was progressively fading.

I had driven by her building a few times, hoping that perhaps by chance I would catch her coming in or out. But it never happened. And I was sad.

But all of that changed when one morning, coincidently on a Tuesday, after arriving from dropping off my kids at school, I had a phone message on my work line from Amour. Nancy was home that day, since she was off from work, but she never answered my office phone or listened to my work messages, thankfully. In fact, she only went into my work area to pick up after my mess about once a week.

It was my work, after all. That would be like me going to the hospital and messing around with whatever tools she used for her job.

While listening to Amour's voice in the message, I got a rush of excitement. I listened to the message a few times before I finally erased it. It was a *"Hello, how are you doing? I just wanted to say hi"* type of thing.

She did not even leave a call-back number! And the stupid office phone didn't record incoming numbers. Who even used these line phones, anyway? It was really a thing of the past century. But that was what my work provided.

But that was not important at the moment. What mattered to me was the fact that Amour remembered me. She remembered me! That cute humanoid girl that could have any guy she wanted, whether human or robot— someone much stronger, younger, and not to mention, better looking —was seeking me out!

And who was I? A *nobody*! An older human man, who also happened to be married with children.

Her short message made my day. My soul rejoiced. She had not forgotten me!

After that moment, time flew again. It was as if the only memories that did not fade away during those weeks was whenever Amour would come up in the picture, in the story of my life, in one way or another.

I did not hear from her again in that week. However, on that next Sunday, my girls, my wife, and I went grocery shopping. We usually did that together on Sunday in the early afternoon, and my girls loved it, because I would buy them ice cream afterward. It was one of those family traditions that we could not shake. Diana loved vanilla with chocolate swirl and Yovanna's favorite was Rocky Road. I guess they took after their parents, both of us being chocolate fanatics too.

This time we split; Nancy and Diana went to an office supply store adjacent to the grocery store to look for some school supplies for the girls, and Yovanna and I went to get the groceries. Divide and conquer!

As I was walking with Yovanna, looking for some condiments in our list, right in front of me was Amour, with two other equally attractive girls, one human and the other a humanoid, though again, one could barely tell. I assumed they were her cousin and her other roommate that she had mentioned. All three of them were wearing very short dresses that I was sure would fit my much younger and smaller daughters. But wow, did they look good in them!

It was a hot day, and in this moment, I was thankful that I lived in Southern California—the summers are hot, but so are the women; the winters are short, and so are the skirts.

I love San Diego!

The girls were at the other end of the aisle of the condiments, and Amour had not seen me. My heart started to pound like an old locomotive at its max.

Not knowing what to do, and going against what I desired, I turned around, grabbed whatever ketchup was in front of me, and tugged my daughter's arm to make a quick escape. As I was turning around, my greatest fantasy and total nightmare happened at the same time.

"Lenny?"

Only a few times in my life had I ever gotten goosebumps at the sound of my name. Occasionally when

I was a kid, my mom would shout my name in a certain tone, and I knew that I was about to get justly punished. And another time was the first time that my wife told me she loved me.

"Lenny, is that you?" she asked again, a little bit louder.

I slowly turned around, pretending that I did not know who called my name, and acting as if I had not seen her. Had I not been there with my daughter, this would have been so much easier, but that was not the case, so I needed to be smart and quick about it.

"Oh! Hi, Amour. How are you doing? It has been a while!"

"Who are they, Daddy?" my daughter asked as Amour and the other two girls walked toward us.

"They... well... *she*, the red-haired humanoid, is a friend of mine. Someone I, um... met some time ago," I said while pointing to Amour, who looked even better than the day I'd met her.

"She is very pretty, Daddy. I like her hair!"

"Yeah, it is nice," I replied. Her blood-red hair did look nice. It suited her and it contrasted with her teal eyes.

I have always liked gingers—though only humans.

By this time, Amour and her two hot colleagues had arrived to where we were standing. I was expecting a handshake, but she threw herself at me and gave me a sturdy hug. I hugged her back. Once again, her smell triggered endorphins that brought my body to a state of excitement. And I do not mean a sexual arousal, but something different, something... beautiful, and yet, difficult to explain. It was that same excitement that I felt the day of my wedding.

"You must be Johanna," Amour told Yovanna with her patented smile.

"No, I am *Yovanna!*" my daughter corrected her with her sweet thin, girly voice.

"Oh, yes. I am so sorry! *Yovanna* it is, not Johanna. Who was I thinking of, huh?"

Yovanna shrugged her shoulders and only responded with that innocent and childish laugh that I love so much.

Wow! She remembered my girls?

"And you must be Lenny!" her human friend said with a kind smile.

"We have heard a lot about you," added the other humanoid.

"Really? You have?" I was honestly surprised.

What could she have said to them about me? I guess I did leave an impact on her after all. Nice.

"Well, if it is good things that you have heard about me, they are all true. But if they are bad things, ignore them, because they are all lies!"

They all laughed at my stupid reply.

"This is Shirley, my cousin," Amour said, pointing to the youngest-looking one with deep blue eyes, long wavy black hair with bluish highlights, and Hispanic features. A human girl. And what a specimen of a woman! She belonged on a magazine cover.

"And this is Kimberly, our roommate and good friend," Amour added. This one was the Asian-looking humanoid with straight, short, bleached hair. Small, yet lovely. She looked more like a typical companion robot that lonely men purchased.

Though only one of them was human, they were perhaps the most stunning trio that I had ever seen in my life. They could honestly be a threesome of exotic models. Fit and beautiful, each so different from the other, but all stunning in their own way. And yet, Amour still stood out in her beauty.

"Nice to meet you both. I have heard about you, too, but I will not tell you what. Because if I do, I will get Amour in trouble." My cheesiness was everlasting.

They both laughed again.

Why the hell am I so lame?

"So, how have you been?" I asked Amour.

"Good. Just here and there. You know how it is."

I noticed some shyness in Yovanna, and since I did not want her to feel uncomfortable, I hugged her and brought her close to me. I could tell she appreciated that. She was, after all, a very sweet girl, who loved her daddy more than anything in the world. And I could sense what I could only guess was jealousy. But by embracing her, it appeared to help and reassure her.

Sensing that my daughter felt more comfortable, I got the courage to be honest with Amour. "I have not seen you at the park since that time. What happened? Did you quit already?"

She quickly responded. "No! What happened was that I finally got a job! And guess where? At the sandwich place where we ate! They needed to hire a humanoid fast to maintain the human-humanoid ratio law, so I guess I got lucky. So, now you know—if you want hookups, I'm your girl. I was hoping that you would show up and I could surprise you, but that day never came. I have wanted to go to the park for a while, but it is harder now, since I work in the mornings and go to school in the evenings. And yes, I do wake up early now! I thought that would make you proud." She finished her breathless explanation with a wink.

"Wow, I *am* proud of you." I said. And I was. It was as if one of my own daughters had done something good with her life.

We continued chatting briefly, but I figured my wife and Diana were probably waiting for us in the car already, so I had to make my excuses and hustle Yovanna through the rest of our list. It was a good thing that my eldest came with me, because she knew the store by memory and knew where everything was.

We were gathering our bags to leave the store when Amour came from behind and gave me a store receipt with her full name, number, and email address on it. That made me feel better, since I was not satisfied with the way our encounter had ended. Now I could find her online and stalk her. Or at least, I could finally stay in touch with her.

Yovanna smiled and waved good-bye to her and the other girls, and I did too.

When we got to our car in the parking lot, we saw that Nancy and Diana were not there yet. They arrived just a few minutes after we put the bags in the trunk of the car.

Talk about perfect timing!

Now the problem would be what Yovanna would say to her mommy about Daddy's friends at the market, and how I would explain that to Nancy.

"How was it, girls?" I asked, trying to steer the conversation.

"It was fun, Daddy!" Diana said, brimming with enthusiasm. "We got these really cool markers that can be erased. But they are markers, Daddy, not pencils. They are so cool! Let me show you."

"No! Do not open anything until we get home, darling," Nancy said from the front seat.

"But, Mom! I want to show them to Daddy!"

"Baby, you can show me when we get home. Obey your mother, please," I told her.

"Okay, Daddy. But you will see what I mean!"

Yovanna got so excited about the items that her sister had bought that she forgot about the whole encounter at the store. Her attention was focused on her sister in the back of our minivan for our entire ride home. I did a mental fist pump.

"Did you get all the stuff we needed?" Nancy asked.

"I think so. In fact, we got everything from the list you gave us, plus a couple of other things too."

I had bought some brownies that were not on the list, because Yovanna had begged me while at the store. And of course, I did not want to look bad because of what had happened with my encounter with Amour and the other girls, so I said yes to her.

"What else did you get?"

"You have to guess. They are your favorite! We can eat them with our ice cream."

"Brownies!" Diana yelled from the back; she knew us too well.

So, both my daughters were happy, Nancy was happy, and so was I. Though for different reasons. It was all smiles on the way back home.

✧ ✧ ✧

On Monday afternoon, I had to go to downtown for an editors' meeting, and I was to assist with notetaking for the minutes. The publishing company that I worked for was not big, but the offices were conveniently located right in the heart of the city. It was inside the tallest and most significant building in San Diego, the 'Thunder-Storm Building.' It was called that because, ironically and coincidentally, and as hard to believe as it sounds, the two owners of the corporation that owned the building were named Gregory Thunder and Robert T. Storm III.

Yup. You can't make that stuff up.

Bobby Storm, of course, being the great-great-grandson of the humanoid manufacturer pioneer. Both these families were worth a fortune.

As I arrived at the room on the seventy-third floor, where we always had these meetings, I deliberately sat on the side that overlooked the corner windows. The panoramic view was incredible! I could see the bay all the way to the Tijuana skyline. It was a beautiful clear day, and in the distance, on other side, I could see Balboa Park, so beautiful and green, contrasting with the concrete jungle of this metropolis.

The meeting started, but I could not focus. I tried hard to keep notes, but my mind took off, as if it were on vacation. My name was mentioned, and suddenly, I remembered I was in a meeting. After addressing the issue at hand and making sure I was taking note of everything important, I once again sank into my thoughts.

There were large cement angels in the outside corners of the building as architectural features, and for the first time, they caught my interest. There were angel statues and angelic icons throughout the building, but this angel in particular, on this specific corner of the building where our offices were, was different. It was unique in the sense that his wings were covering his face. It could be for protection, it could be for shame, but whatever the reason, the artist decided to hide his face with his own wings. However, what made it even more fascinating was the fact that in between the feathers, you could see circuitry and electronics details carved into the cement. This was a *humanoid* angel.

That made me think. I stopped the notetaking and instead, I went deep into one of my usual day-dreaming trances, and I started asking myself questions.

What if everyone has wings? What if they might not be visible to the human eye, but they are there? Perhaps that is why it is our nature to want to fly. And once our wings have tasted the wind in flight, never again will we want to walk.

From that moment on, I was determined to fly. I decided that I would no longer walk like everyone else. Rather, I would lift my arms toward the sky and rise above the clouds to reach my destinations. No longer would I be subjected to the ground; I would use the laws of gravity to my advantage. I would not use my wings to hide my face or my identity anymore, like the humanoid angel statue. Instead, I would use them for what they were originally meant to be for in the first place. I would fly. I would reach the stars!

Of course, all of this was only a figure of speech, and I would not be jumping from a cliff. I was only daydreaming. What I meant was that I would be adventurous. So what if I wanted to make a friend of a young humanoid? How could that possibly harm me? This could only enrich my life. I was being more open and accepting of robots, after all. And suddenly, the courage I lacked before was born within me.

Maybe this is the spark that I have been searching for that will bring meaning to my life. Maybe this is the muse that I need to be creative again, to be passionate about my work, and to even be a better father and husband.

These were the thoughts that I had, and all because of a faceless humanoid angel who would not fly. But *I* would fly. I was determined to do so... whatever that meant. I would not be a statue anymore. I would live! I felt inspired. I felt that spark that I was searching for.

By now, the meeting was over, and most of it had been a waste of time, as usual. I shared the notes with my humanoid boss and left. On my way home, I took the register receipt out of my wallet that had Amour's contact information. Now it was up to me. I could choose to throw it away and move on with my life, or I could expand my wings and take courage to fly where I had never gone before.

I had always been afraid of uncertainty, and I did not welcome change before, but that was over. I spent a lifetime being all about anticipation and planning; I am not spontaneous like my wife. I have always preferred to have something or someone to guide me. I enjoy making lists of the things that I must do for the day, and I like to go in order without skipping any of the tasks. But I have also always hated that about myself because it makes me feel old and predictable. So, this was my chance for redemption and improvement. And I would take it.

While driving, I dialed her number. I knew this was not legal, but I didn't care. The problem was that I had no idea what I would say to her once she answered. If anything, I could worry about that once she did.

The phone rang, but no answer.

The voice message came up. "Hi. You have reached Amour. Sorry I can't pick up the phone, but please leave a message and I will call you as soon as I can. Bye."

It was that sweet voice she had. I could even imagine her saying it as she recorded it. Oh well, no luck. Maybe that was a good thing, since I had no idea what to use as an excuse for my call. I left no message. I simply continued driving home.

About a minute later, I tried again. Only this time it did not ring, it just went straight to voice mail. I hung up again. That was it. I would call her no more.

I guess I'm not supposed to talk to her... or at least not today.

However, only seconds later, my phone rang, the sound emanating through the car's speakers. I looked at the number on the car's screen and then looked at the receipt with Amour's information.

It was her!

What would I do? What could I say?

I let it ring a couple of times. Then I answered, pretending to be cool. "Hello?"

There was no response for a moment. But then it came like the sweet, refreshing taste of mint lemonade.

"Lenny? Lenny, is that you?"

3

It was astounding to hear her sweet gynoid voice once more, but meeting with her again was cathartic. She was dolled up for our meet, a casual pink dress and curls in her shiny scarlet hair, paired with white heels and a matching belt. A princess, in all her glory. I always did like a girly look. I had primped myself as well, even though it was meant to be a quick lunch of sorts.

We promised each other that we would keep in touch. My excuse was that I wanted to check in on her periodically to make sure that she was doing okay. Though I really wanted to—Well, I don't really know what I wanted out of this, to be honest. I was simply going with it, without any expectations. All I knew was that she had a hold on me, as if she had cast a spell, and one which could not be broken, apparently.

For the first time in my life, I liked humanoids! I sure loved this one, at least.

This time we ate at a fancier restaurant by the beach. It would be my treat. But she refused, saying it was her time to take the bill, since she could afford it now.

What was meant to be a casual lunch turned into a date of sorts. As we walked by the boardwalk, she held my arm. She smelled delicious. We passed by several human-humanoid couples and families, and instead of feeling disgusted as I normally would before, I smiled. And as we continued to walk, I put an arm around her waist. She welcomed it.

Part of me was sounding alarm bells. I knew I shouldn't be doing this; it was inappropriate. Not because she was a humanoid and I was a human, but because I was an older, married man.

However, her pull was strong, as if a magnet or gravity itself was attracting me toward her. And I couldn't fight it.

What the hell am I doing? Besides, what if someone I know sees me with it... I mean, with her?

After grabbing dessert at a nearby ice cream shop, I finally told her that I needed to go back. It wasn't a lie. I had to leave. I had to escape before any more feelings for this humanoid took root deep within me and flourished.

Amour took it well. I loved how easy everything was with her. No drama. No bullshit. It seemed as if she was always in a very relaxed state of mind. As if she was programmed that way.

I took her back home and dropped her off by her building entrance. Her goodbye hug was prolonged. I did not complain. I also did not complain about her juicy kiss on my right cheek. How could humanoids provide such warmth and emotion? I did not understand.

But then I left. I had to go home. Back to the safety of my reality. Back to my routine.

Another week went by before I heard from her again. I tried not to let my thoughts linger on her, but she was constantly and consistently on my awareness.

Her spell was strong, indeed.

I sent her a message twice during that week wishing her a happy day. But she did not reply to either one. Maybe she was simply busy with school and work? By the eighth day, I gathered the courage to call her. Unfortunately, she did not answer.

Is she ghosting me? Has she grown tired of me? Why won't she answer me? What did she expect? What is it that she wants from me?

And it wasn't until that very moment that I realized that my happiness was now dependent on this humanoid girl. I was sad. Depressed. Devastated. Confused.

But then, curiously also on a Tuesday, she finally wrote back to me. It was a long message that sent my hopes soaring.

"Hi, Lenny with double n. How are you? I miss you. Sorry I haven't been able to get back to you. I've been swamped at school lately, and I am barely surviving. We humanoids have to work hard to retain new information, and philosophy is kicking my ass. And I like my ass kissed, not kicked. LOL. JK. ;) But in all

seriousness, I need to see you. I didn't realize how much I'd miss you, but I do. Any chance I can see you soon? XOXO."

I must've read and re-read the text a thousand times. When I finally replied to her, my eagerness was evident. *Amour missed me and wanted to see me.* As the gentlemen that I was, I would have to fulfill her desire, of course.

The next few days consisted of texting back and forth all day long. She began to flirt with me, and although at first I restrained myself, eventually, I could not hold myself back.

And there it was. A gradual, yet immense change in me. I went from detesting the very existence of humanoids to falling in love with one.

Morning, afternoon, and night. Our online conversations become longer and deeper. We shared jokes with each other. We told stories to each other. All virtually, and only when I was alone. And this is how it would be for the next few weeks.

We only met a few times, for short periods of time. I was okay with that. I was being careful not to do anything stupid.

Amour became the muse that I needed. She was the spark that reignited the flame of inspiration that had perished years before. I started writing again. And, all of a sudden, my verses flowed in like streams of living water. In less than a month, I wrote the first draft for a romantic novel, and it wasn't bad at all. I used passages from our conversation in the narrative. I used us as an inspiration, but I reversed the roles. The story was of a human woman that hated robots, but eventually falls in love with one. Even the description of the female main character in my story matched Amour. A natural ginger that dyed her hair a deeper red. I matched her characteristics. There was no need to invent a person for my plot when I had the real inspiration in life.

Two months later, I submitted the draft to my humanoid boss, not expecting much. But she had loved it and told me that she would assign someone to help me polish it and eventually publish it. Needless to say, I was overjoyed with the news.

It didn't hit me until later that I had shared the news with Amour before I shared it with Nancy. I hadn't given much thought to this fact at first, but the realization grew with time.

What was I doing? Why was I doing this, to begin with? I had a lovely family—a loving wife and lovable daughters. Why would I mess this up? I was so stupid! Besides, I had found my spark already. I could move finally move on.

But there was a conflict in me. *It's not that big of a deal! I haven't done anything bad anyway... yet.*

That "yet" scared me.

But for some reason, it also intrigued me.

Amour was assigned a research paper about a famous philosopher for class. She was struggling on how to choose a subject. Luckily for her, this was right up my alley. Descartes, Hume, Locke, Rousseau, Sanchez, and Smith... I was a fan of them all, and I was familiar not only with their works and contributions, but also with their stories. I told her that I had a book that could help her and that I could lend it to her and help her out. But I added that it wouldn't be free.

Upon realizing how this could've been taken, and before she thought I meant something else, I added, "Just take me out to eat."

She laughed and eagerly agreed.

I must say, it was a win-win for me. Not only did I enjoy helping her on that project, but it also meant meeting with her three times in a two-week period. She was happy at the certainty of an A in the paper. I, on the other hand, was happy to spend time with her.

On a Tuesday afternoon, I went to pick up the girls from school. Nancy would be working the night shift until very early in the morning the next day. As soon as I saw them, I noticed something interesting. Yovanna had a new backpack. It was a pink penguin one, and it sure was cute. It also looked expensive. Before I could even ask her where that had come from, she began bubbling out words like a fizzy soda can.

"Daddy, your humanoid friend came to visit me! The pretty one that looks like the old cartoon mermaid, with the red hair and big green eyes?"

"What?"

My question wasn't meant to ask to whom she referred. I knew perfectly well that she was describing Amour. She was my only humanoid friend. What I meant to ask was more of myself thinking aloud.

What the hell is she thinking? Visiting my daughters at school? How did she even get this to her? Why would she do something so stupid?

I was freaking out, my mind started to ponder all kinds of questions, none of which would have a positive outcome for me.

"Amour, Daddy! From the store that other day. She saw me playing in the field at lunch time. And she gave me this gift. Isn't it pretty? I love it!"

Diana just looked at her and then at me, puzzled. But without saying a word, she got in the van.

"Um, yeah, baby girl. It is pretty. What else did she say to you?"

"Nothing. She just said that she saw it at the store and liked it, so she bought it for me. She gave it to me over the fence and then left."

Crap! This is not okay.

I didn't know what else to say, so I left it at that. I wasn't even sure if I should tell Yovanna to not tell her mom. Should I make her lie? Would I need to get something for Diana as well, to balance things out?

What should I do?

Freaking Amour, getting me in trouble. It's one thing is for me to meet with her, away from my family. A completely separate reality. But for her to seek my daughter out at their school, and then to give them a gift? What was she thinking?

I was not okay with that, and I needed to let her know.

That same evening, back at home, I called Amour while the girls took showers and my wife was at work. I told her that she had crossed a line. I forbade her from visiting my daughters at school, or anywhere else. They were kids. They were *my* children. And they did not need to be involved in any of this… whatever *this* was.

Amour understood. She apologized. She stated that she was so excited about the pink penguin backpack when she saw it at the mall, and she had remembered how I had mentioned to her at some point in a conversation that Yovanna loved penguins and the color pink. So, she decided to give it to her as a gift. She remembered the name of the school and, riding her high of finding the treasure, decided to take it to her and enjoy her reaction. She explained that it was a silly sporadic moment.

She began to cry on the phone. I knew that humanoids were capable of the same human emotion as us, but witnessing it like this made me feel bad. I apologized for yelling at her and told her not to worry about it anymore. I would figure out something to fix the situation.

She asked me how she could make it up to me. She said she would do anything to make me happy and like her again. She emphasized the *anything* part more than once.

I wasn't sure at the moment if she was being playful or if she was trying to seduce me. Either way, I liked it.

I told her to let it go and that she didn't have to do anything. And then I reminded her that she still had my book.

"Can you come to my place a week from today around noon and pick it up?" she questioned. "I'll finally show you my apartment. The girls won't be here that day. I will be staying at my parents the rest of this week because they're out of town, and I have to take care of our pets. But I'll be back here after the weekend."

I had never gone up to her place. The idea thrilled me.

"Sure, okay. I'll be there. But you better look cute," I whispered before hanging up.

4

That Tuesday went by quicker than usual. The beginning was a blur. I got up, had breakfast, took the girls to school, worked for a few hours, and then the good part came. I can still remember it vividly. I was there right at noon, having just pressed the button for the elevator. I had been looking forward to it all morning.

The day is finally here, Lenny. But remember, I'm just here to get a book. Nothing else.

Up to this point, there had been an obvious sexual tension between us, but we didn't acknowledge it. I didn't even know it was possible to feel this way towards a humanoid. Every time that we talked about anything, she always found a way to make it erotic. It drove me nuts, because as much as I wanted to, I couldn't do anything about it. But I also loved it. I loved her tease. I loved her games.

Oh, my goodness, she is so hot! Ugh, but she's just a machine; that's disgusting. Why do I feel this?

The elevator arrived, and the door opened, welcoming me with a *ding*.

I pressed the button for the twelfth floor, which is where she said she lived, apartment 1203. The lady next to me pressed the number 14. At that moment, it was just me and that older woman. I didn't know her, and she didn't know me. Neither of us knew then what would or could happen when I exited the elevator.

Crap! Is she looking at me weird? Do you know? What do you know, lady? Are you aware that I am here for a humanoid? Please don't judge me! You don't even know me.

My conscience was playing tricks on me.

The elevator stopped on the twelfth floor and I got out, but not before offering her a smile. I think she noticed me freaking out.

What if she knows my wife?

Nah. Not possible. Besides, I was just getting a book back from a friend, so there was really nothing to tell anyway. A humanoid friend. A very beautiful humanoid. Amour.

I stepped out of the elevator and walked down the hallway toward her apartment. I rang the bell, nervously straightening my shirt.

I wonder what she is wearing? Stop, Lenny. She's a freaking robot!

I could hear giggling, and the sound of bare feet on a soft carpet. I hadn't thought about that...

What if she is naked when I open the door? Yeah, you wish, Lenny! Keep dreaming. Besides, you might not like a naked gynoid anyway. She probably looks like a store mannequin. But what if she doesn't? I mean, she does wear sexy clothes, and when I touch her, she feels just like a human. I wonder if —

The door opened, and my jaw dropped as my thoughts were interrupted.

Amour was standing there, thankfully clothed, although barely. She was wearing a tight black dress that buttoned up all the way up. And when I say tight, I really mean almost painted. Not much was left to the imagination.

Still, my imagination took off. *I could just rip it open if I pulled hard enough.*

No, Lenny! Calm down. Don't think about that. She's not human. Remember she is a machine. Just get the book and leave.

"Hi, Amour!" I said, a little too enthusiastically. I cleared my throat.

"Hello, Lenny with two 'n's!" she replied, pulling me into a very tight hug—almost as tight as her dress.

She then kissed my cheek.

"Oh, hey there, pretty lady!" I said, laughing, feeling like a total rube.

Ugh! What an awful line. She probably thinks that I am just a repressed old human man.

She laughed melodically, flipping her long red hair back over her shoulder. What a beautiful smile she had.

It's not real, Lenny!

In the tightness of her hug, the top two buttons on the front of her dress popped open, forcing my eyes to her chest. She looked up and saw me looking —no, *gawking* at her. Probably drooling. She laughed again. I could almost swear that she was trying to seduce me.

Wishful thinking.

I'd never stared at a humanoid this way. Ever.

"Come in!" she said as she grabbed my hand and pulled me towards the inside. "Let me show you around. Just close the door behind you."

The apartment was bigger than I expected. There was a nice, ultra-modern kitchen next to a comfortable lounge area with a nice view of downtown. So many advanced electronics. Made sense, I guess, for two humanoids to live here. There were two other bedrooms, and then hers. The whole place smelled so sweet. Her room was neat. Minimalistic. I looked around and saw her closet door standing open. It was mostly dresses inside, short and long. A lot of shoes.

Then I saw the book there, visible on top of her bed, by the pillow. She suddenly jumped on the bed, leaning on her hands and knees to get to the book. Her shapely behind was front and center. She was bent so far that I could see her underwear. Red.

I looked away. It was too much.

Am I sweating? I feel like I'm sweating. Now I am awakened, that's for sure. I should leave.

She grabbed the book and stood up. She came toward me with arm outstretched, the book gripped in her hand. Except she didn't hand it over. She pulled it back and walked away outside towards the living room.

What was that? What a tease! I swear.

I followed her. We stood in the middle of her living room, and she finally held the book out to me. But she wouldn't say a word.

"Well, I should be going," I told her.

Except, I didn't move. I was still there, and I wasn't even grabbing the book. It was awkward.

Amour smiled and came closer, only to drop the book at our feet.

"Oops!" She giggled.

What happened next is history.

❖ ❖ ❖

What just happened, Lenny? What have you done? You are so stupid! But it was also... beautiful. Accept it.

Not too long after, we heard someone at the door, and we quickly finished getting our clothes straightened out. Amour's two roommates entered in a matter of seconds, and we just stood there, as if nothing had happened and we were simply chilling there by the counter that divided the kitchen and living room.

They said hello to me and then walked toward one of the other rooms.

"Well, I really should go now," I finally said, leaning down to pick up my book that was still lying on the living room floor.

"Thanks for stopping by," she murmured with a smile. "That was... wonderful."

I smiled back as I walked to the door, my heart still pounding and my mind processing what just had happened. As I got to the entrance door, I turned around to say goodbye. She waved a kiss to me with a hand motion and a wink.

5

I didn't know what to think on my way home. What had just happened? Was it real?

Oh, it was real, all right!

I knew exactly what had happened. But my question, rather, was how it had come to that point. And what was I supposed to do now? As much as I loved it, this shouldn't have happened. I knew this well.

The next hours were a blur. I was lost in my thoughts. The memories were so vivid, and I wanted to relive that moment with Amour again, but also forget them and pretend it hadn't actually happened. As much as I'd enjoyed it, I wish I could go back in time and make sure I didn't go through with it.

But I couldn't. It was too late. I had done it, and there was nothing that could or would undo it.

My sense of morality, loyalty, and commitment had faded. I could not distinguish between fiction and reality. It was as if hazy boundaries of pure emotion and confusion surrounded me.

I couldn't sleep that night. Seeing my very human wife next to me reminded me of the horrible person I was for doing what I did. Not because Amour was a humanoid, but because I was a married man.

I had to stop this before I lost everything. So, I decided to cut all ties with her.

The next morning, I called her. As soon as she answered, I stated, "I am sorry, Amour, but what happened yesterday was a mistake. It cannot happen ever again. I think we should stop hanging out."

Amour did not take it well, and began to cry.

I did not expect her crying. I didn't even know she was capable of doing so.

She was surprised and confused. She said that part of her understood, but also that she knew in her heart that we both wanted it. She was upset that I had "made her" fall in love with me.

I didn't know what to respond to that, so I remained quiet.

Not wanting to make it even more awkward, I decided to cut the conversation and end it there, once and for all. I, too, cried. Like I said, her spell on me was strong.

I knew it was for the best, no matter how hard this decision had been. And I sincerely believed that it would be all fine.

But it was not fine.

Two days later, on a Tuesday, Amour went ape-shit crazy on me. I finally got to see a different side of that beautiful, smart, sexy, and sweet young woman. The machine side of her came out, and it was not pretty. It scared the living crap out of me, and it reminded me of why I hated robots in the first place.

It started with some messages. She began to send me pictures of herself. *A lot* of them. Mostly inappropriate ones. There were a few short videos, too. Explicit stuff. I erased it all as it came, after I watched it, of course. She was one beautiful creature, or human creation, rather. But a dangerous one, indeed.

I told her to stop.

But this only made things worse. She started calling me every day, unrelenting in her persistence. I needed her to stop, but I didn't know what else to do. I decided to block her.

The next day, Diana told me that there was a new humanoid volunteer at school, and that she was so nice. Her name was Amour and she had the most beautiful red hair.

I nearly fainted from the fear that seized me.

What is she thinking?

I had to do something about this. But I had no idea what to do. So, reluctantly, I called her.

"Hi, my love," she answered sweetly.

"What the hell? You need to stop this!" I screamed at her. "What are you doing? Leave me alone, and leave my daughters out of this!"

"Oh, come on, Lenny with a double 'n.' Don't tell me you don't miss me. I can't stop thinking about you."

"You are one psychotic robot bitch!" I said. I knew she hated being called a robot, but I used the offensive term, nonetheless. "Leave us alone for good. Do not go to my daughters' school again, or I will have to let them know that you can't be there."

"But, babe—" she said.

"Don't call me that!" I yelled.

"I just wanted to get to know your daughters a little better. I am going to win them over, you'll see. Besides, what are you going to tell them exactly? That you seduced a teenage humanoid and now you don't want your daughters to find out? You know that's exactly what happened, and don't pretend like you didn't know what you were doing."

My heart threatened to rip out of my chest. She wasn't wrong, as much as I hated admitting it. I felt stupid. Again.

"Just… please… I beg you. Please stop." This was all I could answer. I didn't know what else to say.

"I can't stop now, Lenny. You made me fall in love with you, and now, after you had your way with me, you just want to dispose of me like a piece of trash? That's not fair! I am not your property. I am not just a machine, Lenny! I am not your companion robot. You might not want to hear this, but I have feelings too. And you've hurt me. I warned you not to cross me when I met you."

"Wow. You *are* crazy. I am warning you, stupid machine, stop now! If you don't, you will suffer the consequences. This stops now. You hear me? Goodbye, Amour." With that, I hung up.

Later that evening, when Nancy came home, she brought in a box that had been left outside our door. There was no name or note with it. She asked me if I knew what it was. I didn't.

When she opened it, we saw what it contained inside. It was a sandwich from the restaurant and sexy red underwear. I recognized them immediately as Amour's.

Upon seeing the contents, Nancy dropped the box immediately on the floor and asked me what this was about. I told her that I had no idea what it was. I even pretended as if the contents offended me. In truth, they scared me.

I asked Nancy if she was sure that it had been left by our door, and that maybe it was meant for a neighbor, but she picked it up by mistake. She said that it was literally by our door. But I remained committed to the lie and claimed ignorance. Nancy believed me.

How did that robot find out where I live? I never told her!

This had to stop. I was furious. But I was also petrified of this crazy fembot. What would she do? Would she blackmail me? Would she show my wife screenshots of all of our conversations during the past few months? Would she hurt my girls?

She better not! But there was no way of knowing what this unstable psychotic wanna-be-human machine would do.

I was terrified.

6

The next day, I went to pick up my daughters from school. As soon as I drove into the parking lot, I saw Amour's roommates loitering around by the school's entrance. I freaked out, wondering what they were doing there.

Were they together with Amour on this? Could this be some kind of threat toward me, or worse, to my daughters? Of course, I could only assume the worst. And I couldn't help but ask myself again how it had come to this point.

Getting involved inappropriately with a robot, that's how! Seriously, Lenny? How could you be so stupid?

But seeing them there made me furious, to say the least. After parking the van, I went straight to confront the young ladies.

"What are you doing here? You are Amour's roommates, right?" I asked, trying to feign ignorance.

They continued chatting, paying me no more attention than the air surrounding them. But I couldn't give up.

"I asked you, *ladies*, what are you doing at my daughters' school? Last I checked, college students don't go here."

"That's none of your business, mister," said the human. The other fembot didn't even look my way.

I felt my blood pressure rising.

"Are you both together with Amour on this? Is this some kind of joke? Or threat?" I asked with anger. "Did you have anything to do with the box in my house?"

That got their attention. "What? Why are you yelling at us?" the fembot said. "What are you even talking about?"

"You know exactly what I am talking about. The box! Don't act surprised!" My words and volume caused several parents nearby to look our way.

The human, Amour's cousin, stood in front of her fembot friend and raised a finger at me. "Look, if you don't stop this right away, sir, we are going to call the cops. Please leave us alone."

Though they pretended they didn't know me, it was obvious that the two girls were upset. I could only presume that Amour told them what transpired between the both of us. But several parents were nearing now; I had to be careful.

I lowered my voice. "A few days ago, you both knew me, and even said hello to me in your own apartment. And now you don't recognize me? That's interesting. I guess robots have bad memories, and obviously the brain of humans living with them gets damaged too."

I knew this would hurt.

"How dare you?" the humanoid snapped. "You think pretty highly of yourself. But you know what, mister? You aren't even worth it. We've seen the likes of men like you before."

"Look, Lenny... we're not here for you," Amour's cousin jumped in, calmer. "We're here to support Amour. She's doing some hours at this school for a class, and we want to check it out too. We have a meeting with admin after school, and we are here just waiting. Besides, what happened between you and Amour is none of our business. We don't want any trouble, okay?"

"Oh, really? So, you all decided to volunteer all of a sudden at the same place, huh? At my daughters' school, of all places."

The fembot couldn't hide her anger toward me. "We're legal adults, and we decide for ourselves what we do with our lives, old man. Mind your own business. Besides, you should know not to mess with a girl's feelings."

"You're no girl. And neither is she. You aren't even human. You're just a machine who wants to be human, made for our gratification and servitude." The words poured from my lips like a river, unstoppable. I heard gasps from bystanders, but I was beyond caring.

Shirley had to hold Kimberly back. She then turned to me and raised her accusing finger once again. "Lenny, I promise if you that if you keep this up, we're going to call the cops, or at the very least, report you. Trust me, the authorities will definitely believe two young women over a middle-aged pervert," she spat out viciously. "Look around. You're making a fool of yourself. Do you really want that in front of your daughters' friends and their parents?"

I looked around and knew she was right. Some students were beginning to gather around since they had been dismissed. I knew things would only get messier if the girls called the cops or school security showed up.

"Stupid trio of psychotic sluts," I hissed at them. "If you try to mess with my family, you will face the consequences." I kept my tone low, since I didn't want anybody overhearing my threats—and there were already several distance witnesses of the altercation. "And tell your other crazy friend to get off my back and away from my family."

With that I stalked away, but noticed that a few people approached the girls and asked them if they were okay or if they needed to call security. I knew several of these parents, and I didn't want anyone asking me questions or assuming things. I walked to the other side of the school entrance, where Yovanna was already waiting. I took Yovanna's hand and led her to the car. When Diana came out, we drove off immediately.

"Dad, what happened between you and those girls?" Yovanna asked me from the back seat. My heart leapt.

"It was nothing, sweetheart. I was just asking them a few questions about their volunteer work," I lied.

"But why were you shouting, and why did people gather around if it was nothing serious?" She was too smart.

"They were probably interested, too, I guess. I probably got loud because of the cars or something. I don't know," I told her.

I looked back at her from the mirror and figured she seemed convinced.

After a few minutes, Yovanna started again. "Remember your friend with the red hair we met at the store some time ago?"

"Yes, of course. What about her?" I asked nervously.

Amour better not have said anything to the girls.

"Well, she helps at school. I think I told you that. She was very nice at first, but now she's been acting weird. She got mad at me for no reason today."

"Oh, yeah!" Diana added. "The pretty one. I know her too. She seemed sad today. And she also yelled at one of my friends at recess for no reason. I think she went home earlier."

"I guess that is why robots shouldn't be doing human jobs, huh?" Yovanna asked rhetorically. "It's like you'd told me, Dad; robots can't control their emotions like we humans do."

"She is probably going through some stuff," my youngest said defensively. "Mommy always says that we shouldn't judge others, because we don't know what they are going through. And besides, she is a humanoid, not a robot. It's not kind to call them that. Anyway, I like her, and the other kids at school like her too."

"That's true, I guess," Yovanna echoed.

I had raised good daughters, but I needed them on my side right now. "It's true, girls. We shouldn't judge others. However, we never know who could hurt you. And I want to make sure that you'll be safe, because I love you very much. We can't have a rob—a humanoid going crazy with a bunch of human kids, because who knows how they'll react."

I was genuinely afraid of what Amour could or would actually do to my kids. On the rest of the drive, I decided to come clean to my wife and tell her everything that happened with Amour. I had to be honest. Besides, I wouldn't want her finding out from somewhere else anyway.

By the time my wife came home later that day, I had already prepared dinner and served the kids their food. Nancy went to take a quick shower, and when she came back, her dinner was served.

We sat down in silence while we ate our food. She'd had a tiring day, I could tell. I couldn't eat much because I was a nervous wreck. I was terrified of losing everything I cared about. But then again, maybe she would forgive me and help me find a solution in dealing with Amour.

"What's wrong, Lennard?" Oh, no! She used my full name. "You've barely touched your food."

I hadn't realized that she had finished her meal while I had been fretting. My food was cold now.

This is it, Lenny. It's now or never.

"I have something important to tell you, babe. Can we talk in my office?" I told her.

She looked at me, puzzled. "Um. Okay...? Well, let's get the kids to bed first, and then we can talk better," she replied.

"Sure. Good idea. We can clean up later."

We took the girls to their room and tucked them in for the night. When we were sure they were asleep, we went to my office, where our conversation wouldn't wake the girls up.

"So, what's so important that you couldn't even eat?" Nancy asked. "I could tell something was bothering you."

I took a long sigh. "Okay, I need you to promise me to listen to everything I have to say first. Please. You can get angry and do whatever you want afterward, but not until I've finished saying everything I need to say," I pleaded.

She nodded in reply and let out a breath.

"I... I, um... had an affair with this crazy humanoid I met while running at the park." I paused to see if she'd say anything. But she didn't. She simply raised her brows and put one arm on her hip. I continued, "We became friends on one of my routines. I'm not sure how it happened, to be honest. I promise you that I had...*have* no feelings for her."

She still didn't say anything. But I noticed her cheeks getting reddish.

I took another deep breath.

"Anyway, I lent her a book for class. And... well, a mistake happened when I went to her house to get it back."

"What do you mean *a mistake*, Lenny?"

"We had sex."

"Len—"

I pushed ahead, with my head down. "But I swear, babe, it was just a fling, a terrible decision made in a moment of weakness. It only happened this one time, I promise."

Nancy's face flooded with tears.

"I told her that it was a mistake, and I made it clear we shouldn't meet ever again." I took a pause. "But then she said that she was in love with me and all this crazy stuff. And now she's been trying every means to get to me."

"The box by our entrance..." Nancy said. She was smart.

"Yes, the box. She was the one who most likely dropped that box at our door the other day. But that's not all; she became a volunteer at the girls' school too."

"What?"

"I know, I know. I swear I've tried to stop her. I really did. But she's crazy, Nancy. I guess she caused a scene at school today. Well, so did I; but that's a different story. Anyway, I couldn't keep hiding it from you... and I didn't want to anymore. She's very manipulative, and I don't know what she could do. The box thing was probably some sort of warning or threat, I don't know. She's a robot. They're crazy. So... I guess what I am saying is... I'm sorry. And also, that you should be cautious, because I have no idea what that psycho robot is capable of doing."

Nancy didn't say anything. She just watched me, and I felt her judgmental stare.

I released another long breath. "Please say something, babe."

She finally spoke. No, she shouted. "You had an affair with a humanoid? What the hell? You! You are disgusting. You hypocritical cheat! How dare you?" She punched my shoulder. "She's probably the reason why you've suddenly changed, right?"

Seeing her in tears destroyed me. And I felt like crap. She was right, I was a hypocrite. A cheater. And worse.

"I know. I am sorry, Nancy. I really am! And I swear, my changing has nothing to do with her," I said, though I couldn't be sure of that.

"I don't even know what to say, Lenny. I am so hurt. And now you're telling me that the kids might be in trouble because of your mess? What is wrong with you?"

"Nancy, I am sorry. You have every right to be angry at me. Please forgive me. I love you and the girls more than anything in life! I am trying to—"

"Well, you clearly weren't putting us first when you were having sex with her. I want you out of the house this instant! I need space right now."

She tried to wipe away her tears, and I moved to embrace her, but she pushed me away.

"No, Lenny! Don't! Just… please just go."

"Babe, no. Don't do this, please. It's late already; where am I going to go?"

"I don't know, and frankly, I don't care right now. You should've thought about that when you were mounting that robot."

"Nancy, please let me stay the night at least," I pleaded. "I can stay in the living room—"

"Just leave, Lenny. I don't want to see your face right now."

I heard the girls coming on the hallway.

"What's wrong, Mommy?" Yovanna asked, Diana clinging to her arm.

"Mommy and Daddy had an argument. Everyone is safe. Daddy will be staying somewhere else for now," she said, crouching down to comfort them.

I quickly packed an overnight bag, gathered my car keys, phone, and wallet, and walked out as quietly as I could. There was nothing I could say. I understood that I'd hurt Nancy. To be honest, I would be deeply hurt, too, if I were in her shoes. But I didn't want the girls to turn against me.

How could I have been so stupid?

I stayed by the door a little longer as I listened to my kids crying and my wife telling them that it would be okay. I felt a tug in my chest when I heard their cries and decided to drive to a nearby hotel.

I got to the hotel, booked a room, and tried to rest for a while. But I couldn't sleep. I kept reliving the hurt blooming in my wife's eyes and the cries of my daughters. And I couldn't help it when I started crying too. I lost it.

I tried calling Amour to give her a piece of my mind, but she wouldn't pick up the call. After several attempts with no replies, I decided that I would confront her at her work the next morning. I would go to her apartment, if necessary.

After all that, I finally fell asleep.

The next morning, I woke, and, wearing the same clothes from the previous day, immediately drove to Amour's workplace. I'd order a sandwich for breakfast and give her a piece of my mind while I was at it.

I asked one of the waiters to send Amour over to me, which he did. I was hiding in my booth with my back to her, so she wouldn't be tipped off until she was right in front of me. When she came to my table, I told her we needed to talk. She tried walking away from me, but I grabbed her arm and demanded that she listen. She dropped her shoulders and turned to face me.

I knew she had to behave, since I was a customer and she wouldn't want to risk her job by behaving rudely. I had the upper hand, and I would use it.

"What do you want, Lenny?" She pulled her arm away from my hold.

"My daughter said you were yelling at her at school yesterday."

She didn't say anything.

"You know," I continued, "it's funny when I think of it now. You're a piece of metal crap created for human sport. Meant to take everything we humans do to you, silently, with a smile on your fake face. With your fake skin and fake eyes. That's right; you're nothing but a human fabrication, a tin can with fake emotions, covered with cheap muscle tissues and phony skin. You're nothing but human property, and no matter how hard you try, you'll never be human. Call yourself a humanoid all you like, but in the end, no matter how politically correct we are forced to be, you're just a robot. A disgusting fembot slut. Looking for human connection, but newsflash, Amour... it's not real. Because *you* are not real!"

Amour's eyes flooded with tears.

"Even dogs are living things. Shit, even rats! You're not alive, no matter how much you try to convince yourself that you are. You are just a machine!" I just kept going.

A few customers stood up, evidently upset. The human male counterpart of Amour came to her defense as well. "You need to leave, buddy. Right now," he commanded.

"Call the cops," I heard one of the female customers say to her partner.

I worried that my plan had backfired. But, unfortunately for them and fortunately for me, Amour lost it. Evidently she didn't take my rejection or my insults well. She threw her notepad and pen on the floor and screamed at me.

"How dare you talk to me that way? You, Lenny, are garbage! Besides, if you humans were so great, why did you bother in creating robots in the first place, huh? You know we are superior to you in every way. We are stronger. Smarter. And we are even better lovers. Yes, Lenny, I am better than you." In the middle of her crying, she turned to the audience. "You all aren't that special at all. Your longevity rate is a few decades, your IQs are mediocre, and you all are just so lazy that you rely on us for everything. We take even raise your kids. We prepare your meals, and we even clean your shit after you! You're lazy bums. Accept it—humanoids are superior a thousand times over."

The young male waiter tried to calm Amour down, but it didn't work. Amour kept spouting insults and nonsense, which offended more than a few customers. After a few moments, the manager came out and fired her on the spot.

I smiled. I'd won. And I even got a free breakfast out of it.

Success.

I triumphantly left the scene, just in case the cops were called. I had finally shown her what a measly human was capable of. As I left in my car, I watched with glee as she miserably dragged herself away from the restaurant, wailing.

I went back to the hotel feeling much better about life. I watched a few shows, ordered in, and had a good time by myself. I'd spend the weekend here to heal. Still, though, I missed my family. I took a long shower and finally fell asleep.

I woke in the middle of the night, sweating profusely and panting after having an erotic dream about Amour. I looked at the clock; it read 2:17 a.m. I had slept nine hours straight. I couldn't believe that she was invading even my dreams. At the same time, I realized that I couldn't help but relive our moments together. I pictured her beautiful face and bright smile. Her corny laugh. Her sweet smell. How she felt that day. I envisioned all the filthy things I could do with her... to her.

Why I was fantasizing about her, I couldn't understand. But I was. Her spell was strong. I closed my eyes again, and I missed her.

7

Early in the morning, I received a call from Amour. I ignored it. But then she called again. I sent her to voicemail. She kept calling non-stop, but I refused to pick up any of her calls. I had to break her spell. And I was determined. Yesterday had been a victory, but the night had confused me. I couldn't let that happen to me again.

The truth is that I wanted desperately to listen to her lovely voice. I wanted to hear her, hold her, and feel her body against mine so badly. It took all of my self-control to ignore her calls. I didn't trust myself, and I knew all my self-control would come crashing the moment I heard her voice.

I forced myself to think of Nancy and my girls instead. I didn't want to fail them again. They were my everything. And remembering their tears when I left crushed my spirit. I didn't want to be a bad father. Or a bad husband. I had to stand my ground and do whatever it took not to come in contact with Amour ever again.

I sat on the bed in the room and started mediating. I kept telling myself not to look at the phone as it rang. But I picked it up. I started looking at pictures of my beautiful family instead.

It'll all pass, Lenny. She will stop calling soon and realize that it was just a mistake. A fling. That's all. It wasn't your fault she seduced you. You can overcome her temptation, Lenny, and you will, because you're stronger than this. Stay strong.

I kept calling Nancy, but she wouldn't answer. Meanwhile, Amour kept calling me. But, eventually, her calls stopped.

Late in the evening, I got a message. I thought it was my wife. Maybe she was asking me to come back home, since we hadn't spoken after my confession at home. Maybe she was finally returning my calls. I'd really missed her and my daughters. I hoped that she would forgive me and not leave me. I grabbed my phone to check the message, but then saw that it was from Amour.

I ignored it at first and put the phone back down, but then I got curious.

Dear Lenny with a double 'n'... I miss you so much. I want you to know that I forgive you. About everything. Yes, I just want to be with you. I love so much that it hurts. My life is incomplete without you, Lenny. It doesn't matter if you don't love me back. But know this— if you don't call me back, I will kill myself. There's no point living without you anyway.

My heart ached from the pain that was evident in her tone. I calmed myself and deleted the message. No, she wouldn't do that. I figured there was no way that she would kill herself over the likes of me. Yeah, she probably could be sad for a few days, but she would eventually move on with her life. Her life battery had decades of life left. Most likely she would meet a much younger and more handsome man than me in no time, and then she would totally forget about my existence.

That is how it works, after all. She'd be over me without even realizing it. Since I had my phone, I decided to browse through my pictures once again. But this time, I stumbled upon a few of the sexy pictures and videos that she had sent me that I'd failed to delete. I watched the videos, over and over again. I watched as she wore close to nothing in each of the video. Sending me kisses and wishing I was with her.

I knew that I should have deleted everything, since I had promised to end everything with her. But... she was so beautiful. Her red hair, her green eyes, her sexy curves... everything about her was lovable. What was there not to like? I mean, besides the fact that she was a humanoid.

A tear trickled from my eye as I reminisced about her. She was my muse, the spark I needed to start writing again, to find joy in life, and I'd broken her heart. More tears dropped as I thought about my wife and daughters and how I'd broken their very human hearts as well.

I was a horrible person.

❖ ❖ ❖

Another day went by, and I was still at the hotel. Early Tuesday morning, I got a call from an unknown number. I answered.

"Good morning. Is this Mr. Lennard Eder?" the voice asked.

"Speaking," I replied. "Who is this?"

"This is Officer Rentería, San Diego Police Department calling."

I was surprised. I sat up straight and cleared my throat. I figured they were calling me about the incident at the restaurant a couple of days prior. "Oh, um… good morning, officer. How may I help you?"

"Mr. Eder, do you know a humanoid by the name of Amour Toussaint?" the officer asked.

"Yes, I do," I replied nervously. "What is this concerning?"

Here we go.

"Mr. Eder, Amour took her life by jumping from the rooftop of her apartment building this morning."

My heart dropped.

"She left a suicide note with your name written on it. We've confirmed through her roommates that you were the person she was referring to in her note. We would like to ask you a few questions at our station, if you don't mind," he said.

I was speechless. Shocked. Lost for words. What could I say?

She had actually done it. She'd killed herself.

Why would she do that? Why? My thoughts kept whirling so fast that I forgot the officer was still on call.

"Lennard, are you still there? Hello, Mr. Eder?" I heard the voice faintly, bringing me back to reality.

"Yes, I am here. Sorry. I'm just… I am in shock."

"Mr. Eder, you do understand why we are wondering what happened, right? Humanoids don't commit suicide. In fact, this is the first time ever that we are aware of. So… can you make it to the station on your own?"

"Um, yes, I can come to the station. I'll be there at noon, if that's okay," I finally replied.

"Okay, sir. Thank you. We will be awaiting your arrival."

"See you then, Officer."

As I put the phone down, I couldn't help but blame myself for everything that happened. If only I had called her back, she'd still be alive. If only I hadn't been so selfish and pushed all the blame on her. The terrible thoughts kept coming, although I knew I couldn't undo what she had done.

I only made things worse! How stupid could I be?

I fixed myself, since it was a little past 11:00 a.m., and drove to the police station.

At the police station, I was shown the note that Amour had left. It read:

> *Dear Lenny with a double 'n,'*
>
> *I fell in love with you the first day I met you at the park. Though I can't honestly say that it was love at first sight for me, it did feel like I was meant to love you. I know you felt the same way toward me too, but decided to ignore it. The truth is that I understand; you have a family, and I never wanted to come in between you and them. But I couldn't imagine living without your love. Still, though, I don't blame you for anything.*
>
> *I've decided to end my suffering the only way I think will work. Know that you were the sole purpose of my existence from the moment I met you, and that without you, my life is simply meaningless. I hope that one day you will look back and realize that you loved me too. Forever yours, Amour.*

I was in tears after reading the note. The guilt and sorrow were overwhelming.

"What's the nature of your relationship with the gynoid?" asked the detective who'd shown me the note.

"We were... We were friends," I replied.

The detective chuckled. "Friends? Friends don't leave you a love letter right before they die, Mr. Eder," he stated.

He was right.

"We were attracted to each other, and one thing led to another. It was just a fling. A small spark that turned into a big fire and got out of control, I guess," I said.

"I see. Didn't your mama teach you to never to play with fire? You play with fire, you will get burned."

I nodded, silently.

"Well, obviously your little spark already burnt you," the investigator said with a tight smile.

Again, he was right. Even though his words pissed me off, I'd gotten burned. Big time.

"You are right, sir," I said. "This fling... this... *affair* with this gynoid cost me my wife, my daughters, and probably my home. I don't know the extent of it yet, to be honest. And even my conscience won't let me be at peace. Yes, I have learned my lesson the hard way." I put my head down in regret.

"I'm glad you did. Just make sure you don't start another spark with someone other than your wife next time. Trust me, I've been there too. I mean, not with a robot, I don't think I could. But... well, you know."

I just nodded, not knowing what to say.

He heaved a heavy sigh. "Okay, then." He got up and extended his hand to me. "Her parents didn't press any charges, so you're free to go."

I shook his hand. "Thank you very much, sir," I said while getting on my feet.

I put my hands in my pants pockets, and with my head down, I walked out of the building.

As I walked, I remembered when I first met Amour. Maybe if I'd acted differently at the park, none of these things would've happened. Perhaps, if we hadn't met, ate together, exchanged numbers... if I had never flirted back when she did, and if I hadn't tried to look for her... if I'd never gone to her place... maybe, just maybe, she would be alive.

The guilt weighed me down and made it hard to walk.

If I hadn't seen her as an inspiration for my writing, if I didn't lead her on, and if I had controlled myself that day, then none of this would have happened.

I would still be in my house, the loving husband and father my wife and kids looked up to.

My family. I sure hope I haven't lost them, too.

I went back to my hotel room heartbroken and sobbing.

I'm so sorry, Amour. Please forgive me. I am sorry, Nancy. I never intended for any of this.

I cried myself to sleep that night.

❖ ❖ ❖

Two days later, I finally had the courage to go home. I knew that the girls were at school and that Nancy had the day off. I figured it was a good time to try to have a conversation.

Upon my knock, Nancy opened the door, and without saying a word, waved me inside.

"Before you say anything, my love, I want to say that I am very, very sorry about everything. I know that I was stupid and that I caused you and the girls so much pain. And though I know I don't deserve it, please, I beg you, forgive me," I implored.

Nancy closed the door behind me and sat on the living room couch. With tears in her eyes, she silently patted the space next to her.

I did. I held her hand, and she didn't pull back. This gave me hope.

"I promise to never to be this stupid again, babe. I've realized my mistake. I need you, Nancy, and I need the girls. I've missed you all so much. You are my life! My everything. The reason for my living. And I can't live without anyone of you. I love you so much. And, again, I'm sorry."

"You hurt me, Lenny. It stung bad. It was as if a tornado had destroyed everything in my life. And with a fembot, of all things? I thought you hated those... things.

I just... I don't know, Lenny. I just don't understand." With that she pulled her hand away and crossed her arms over her chest.

"I understand. And yes, you are right. I also don't know how it ever went so far. But I am done with excuses. I know I messed up, and I promise to never do it again. Please, just let me back into your life. I want to be here, at home, where I belong... with you and the girls."

Nancy gave me a hug and cried some more. "I've missed you too, you dumbass," she said on my ear while hugging me. "I'll take you at your words, Lenny. We need you here. The girls are dying to have you back. But don't ever break your promise to me. I'll leave you, Lenny. I swear I will," she threatened.

"I promise you, my love, there won't be a next time." And I meant the promise.

She forgave me, and I wouldn't mess things up again.

That day, I went to pick up the girls from school. They were delighted to see me, and so was I. They hugged me and kissed me, and I rejoiced at the smell of their hair and their arms wrapped tight around my neck.

"Welcome back, Daddy. We missed you so much," Diana said.

"I'm so glad you're home," Yovanna added.

"I missed you both so much more than you could ever imagine!" I said with a big smile plastered on my face.

The drive home was peaceful, with the kids asking a lot of questions about the previous few days. They told me how they had to take a bus to school because Nancy had been at work.

After that day, I went back to my daily monotonous routine. I dropped the girls at school, I worked, I exercised, and continued to work on my novel in the evenings, after putting the girls to sleep. Day in and day out. No change. One could argue that my life was dull, but

I wouldn't have it any other way. I was delighted to be home again.

Several weeks later, I finally finished rewrites on my novel. I couldn't have felt more accomplished than if I had climbed a mountain. And, if I can put humbleness aside for a moment, this book was great! The best I'd ever written.

I submitted the complete work to my humanoid boss. She was ecstatic and immediately started making plans to publish. She loved the premise, the plot, and the characters. "They are relatable," she'd said. She also said that management loved the storyline and the depiction of love between a human and a humanoid.

My book was assigned a team of marketing gurus, wonderful editors, and the best designers the company had.

I was just grateful. My hard work had finally paid off, and my dream was coming true.

That day, as a celebration, the family and I went to eat at my favorite restaurant. And after the girls went to sleep, Nancy and I made love all night long. I fell asleep thinking that I had everything I'd ever wanted.

8

Nine months later, my novel *It Only Takes a Spark* became a bestseller. It did well, particularly with the humanoid demographic.

I got invited to various talk shows. In one of the interviews, the interviewer asked me about my muse. What inspired me to write the book?

The male humanoid made me remember Amour again. At this point, the memory of her made me smile.

"A humanoid friend of mine inspired me," I said. "I used to resent humanoids for so many things. I felt that they… that you were taking up every job meant for humans. But the truth is that perhaps I hated humanoids for being more intelligent, beautiful, and capable than myself. But then, one day, I met this one humanoid, and she changed my perspective. Unfortunately, she died not long after I met her. She was so full of vigor and life. I wrote this book because of her. So, yeah. I guess she was my muse and inspiration."

The interview ended after other numerous questions about the book. But the thought of Amour remained in my mind. She was my spark.

But I've learned not to play with fire. I just don't want to get burned again.

Except… well, except for this. You see, recently—very recently—while doing an author signing event at a large bookstore in National City, which is very close to my home in San Diego, something interesting happened.

Toward the end of the lengthy event, just when I thought we were done, a very attractive red-headed gynoid stopped in front of my table and asked me to sign her copy of my book. She was the last person in line.

The moment she spoke to me, I felt a spark inside of me. It was familiar, and the warmth was comforting.

"Hi," she said nervously, playing with her long hair. "I can't believe I'm meeting you."

She had a huge, bright smile. Dimples. A beautiful face. Her beauty stunned me.

"Hello," I said. "Whom should I make this to?"

"Oh, my name is Esperanza. It means 'hope' in Spanish," she offered as she bent down.

I smiled. This all feels strangely familiar. I'd been here before.

"That's a beautiful name," I said.

I'd signed thousands of books, but somehow, I was drawing a blank on what to write in hers. Nervous, I fumbled with the pen and it went over the table, behind her legs. Esperanza turned around to pick up the pen. As she bent over, I noticed her lacy red thong coming out of the top of her tight pants.

I bit my tongue.

Still bent over, she turned and saw me staring. I panicked. My heart raced.

But she just smiled.

She handed me the pen. Our hands touched. I let them linger too long. Her smile was still there. My heart was still racing.

"So, Esperanza, huh?" I said as I tried to pull myself together to write something... *anything*... on the blank page.

"Yes. You know, I really relate so much with your female character. With the whole red hair and being a humanoid in love with a human."

"You did?" I said, trying not to look up at her beautiful face. "Well, I am glad you enjoyed the book. Thank you for supporting me and for coming today."

"I wouldn't miss it for the world," she said.

She then remained standing in front of me. There was no one behind her, and the event had ended. The store would be closing soon.

She took the pen from me, ripped a small strip of paper from the back pages of the book, and wrote something on it. She then folded the piece of paper and handed it to me.

"Call me some time, Lennard," she said with a wink.

That was yesterday.

Today is Wednesday. Right now I am on my way to meet Esperanza for a sandwich. Let's see where this spark goes.

I CHOOSE YOU

"Captain! Captain Tim…"

Another wave of plasma and magnetic field structures from the nearby star's atmosphere hit, cutting off the woman's agitated cry mid-sound. She let out a muffled yelp and scurried to take cover beneath a side of the control bar that had partially caved to form a shallow pod. They'd done this trip dozens of time, following the same path, and yet, nothing could've prepared them from the sudden space storm and abrupt bursts of radiation from this distant star.

From the semi-preserved area, she observed the extent of the wreckage. The entire helm of the large ship was gone, flung far into an unknown depth of the infinite abyss that surrounded them. In its place was an imposing black hole with wires and cables sticking out of it like tentacles, fluttering leisurely in the empty space like their present visibility was not the indication of the ship's doomsday.

The woman found herself thinking how the ominous cavity had an interesting semblance to a dolphin's snout, and she scoffed as soon as she thought it. Extensive study had been undertaken by Earthlings on the thought process at the threshold of death—the final moments before the mind shut down for good, and the consensus had been that it was gripped by a panic so strong it blocked out all thoughts. It was believed that the final heartbeats of a human life were the seconds that housed the least brain activity, almost non-existent.

Now she knew the truth.

A dying person did not lose thought; they just found a way to think about anything but the fact that they were dying. A person dying found a way to picture dolphin snouts to still the mind.

A tremor coursed through the steel wall she had her feet propped up against, sending shivers up her spine. She exhaled an icy breath. The Captain was still nowhere in sight, and she could see more chunks of steel chipping away and floating off. The Beacon 09 was dying, and its

Captain had mysteriously gone AWOL. She clenched her fists tightly to subdue the hot anger that burned her chest.

For at least four months of the six-month duration of the trip, she had patiently accommodated his incompetence, overseeing the affairs of the ship in actuality, while he served as its figurehead and spent the better part of his time sampling the stock of fine wines aboard it. But now, an unforeseen disaster had struck, and it was one that could only be managed with the application of trained skill, the likes of which she lacked, and which the People's Republic of California government had spent a small fortune to give him. By now, she was sure, even the oarsmen that occupied the ship's underbelly must have been made aware of the crisis at hand.

Where on Earth could he be?

Well, definitely not on Earth, the irony. They were so many miles away from Earth. The thought filled her with crippling despair. This was it, the Beacon 09's very last voyage.

Her last voyage.

The intensity of the tremor grew until it felt like she was riding a turbulent wave, and the sudden flattening of the convex wall forced her cheek against its melting hot surface, eliciting a guttural cry from her. She heard skin pop and sizzle, and she retched, but came up empty. She couldn't even recall when her last meal had been or what she had eaten.

Another wave hit and she was pushed out of her makeshift sanctuary. She managed to grab hold of a displaced pipe that had gotten stuck between the pilot's seat and its console in time to stop herself from being whirled into the gaping mouth of electronic appendages. Her face paled and her gaze froze on the gory sight that confronted her.

From her dangling, upside-down position, she had a clear view of the cabin's entryway, which was now blocked off by a handful of pipes wedged between the automatic door and the metal jamb. Wound neatly around one such pipe was a wrist that led up to a muscular arm, an arm that had been cleanly severed from its body, and floating in a small orbit right beneath it was an eyeball propelled by a trail of fibers affixed to its end. Forest green now dulled down to a dour moss color, the glint of mischief still lurking at its edges. She had looked upon that eye with silent resentment too many times to not know whose it was. It was his. The captain's. From somewhere far off, she noted the sound of her voice as it enveloped the room in an ear-splitting scream.

❖ ❖ ❖

Entry 312.

. . .

It's Day 128 here on the intergalactic cruise ship—Beacon 09, in the year 2142. It's Day 02 succeeding the collision. This is Riley Cruz, once again recording an entry for my vlog.

I made it.

I can hardly believe I did.

This space storm, or whatever it was, hit like a thunderous avalanche—in waves and knots. A lot of the ship is gone. Most of the people are gone too. All that remain of a passenger fleet of about 570 Earthlings and a bustling crew of ninety-five are eighteen dazed people struggling to come to terms with the present reality. That is, the reality of our impending space deaths atop the almighty tourist vessel that has been Earth's greatest pride for far longer than some of us have been alive. The Beacon 09 is now reduced to floating debris and mere chunks of silver tubes barely held in place by fidgety wires and pipes with nostril-sized perforations in them from the impact of the solar flare storm.

Coronal mass ejections, I learned they were called. It's what causes the Aurora Borealis back on Earth, apparently. Except, the ones emitted from the nearby star didn't cause a pretty scene.

We were lucky to be in this chamber during the storm. This rectangular metallic hall that we're in is quite scenic, thankfully, so I don't have to observe the wretched looks within the room or the growing stench of despair all day long. It's also the only thing protecting us from the radiation around us.

I stay glued to the large observation glass, where I distract myself from my perpetual internal panic with the task of taking inventory of the chambers outside of ours that are still standing.

Like I said, we were lucky to have gotten to this chamber in time to secure it before the radioactivity spread and poisoned it too. Actually, not we. Him. Alfred Nola. The Nobel-prize-winning physicist that, thankfully, happened to be on the same space cruise as me.

Still, nothing could've prepared us for the most unlikely of events.

Aside from the fact that Albert is notably the oldest of us, he is also the most experienced with the dynamics of space travel, seeing as this is allegedly his fifteenth time undergoing this particular trip. Something about the Galactic Center, which he states is at the middle of our Milky Way Galaxy, keeps bringing him back. To be honest, I didn't think much of it when we passed through it halfway through our voyage. That's when we turned around to come back home.

Except, of course, we never made it home. And we are a long way from it.

It was Albert who raised the alarm about the potential for rad poisoning a few hours after the storm settled and the steel walls began to take on the sickly, moss green pallor. By his calculations, it was decided that the floating chamber was our best bet at making it through the next few weeks, so he shepherded us into it and sealed it off. We, stark illiterates on the subject matter at hand, followed without question.

And good thing, too, because the other parts broke off entirely.

Albert is also the only one of us who seems to harbor the belief that we have a fighting chance in this—tangible hope of making it off the dying vessel—and yesterday, without wasting any time, he mapped out a plan. There was no crowning ceremony or baton-exchange done, but it is an unspoken consensus that he is our new captain, the original one having been lost in the crash alongside his copilot and all other essential workers aboard.

Earlier today, the rationing schedule was drawn up—the routine for the rationing of food, water, and oxygen. Again, we were lucky to be close to this chamber when the storm hit us. Still, there aren't enough supplies available to sustain us all until such an indefinite time as we are able to make contact with a rescue vessel, so we'll have to do some strict rationing to stretch out what is available for as long as we can manage. This is an essential part of Nola's genius plan, and we all agree.

I worry that there are only four suits in the chamber. When the oxygen runs out, this will be a problem. But we will cross that bridge when we get to it.

A team of two men and a woman to assist in this process was selected, and one of the men has caught my interest. Well, in a partial, off-handed manner, that is. I don't know why I hadn't seen him in the past four months of the journey, but I am glad I have now. He has the face and build of a movie star from one of the dainty, old people Spanish-speaking soaps that my mother suffers me through when I go visiting at Christmas. Though what has truly caught my eye is his smile.

I caught a glimpse of it as he busied himself with persuading an asthmatic middle-aged lady into taking her Red-X pill to counter the sore-tonsil effect of the humidity levels within the room. It reminded me of a far-off time in a far-off place when things were so much different in my life. When I was a girl who could define her life and its purpose without the assistance of an outrageously priced trip to a whole other planetary system in order to try and find myself.

But that's a different story for another day. Besides, I've already talked plenty about that during this trip, so back to Mr. Charming's smile.

You see, his is a smile that would have instantly caught my eye back then, back on our blue orb of a planet. And it warms my heart to know that it still can, even now, in the face of certain death. Perhaps I'm not so lost after all. Or, maybe, the rather impulsive decision to invest all my life's savings on this six-month trip did yield fruit after all, and I have unconsciously been brought back to myself—reconnected with my aura, as Nana would call it.

It's too bad that I will most likely not live past the dawn of this awakening.

Mr. George Willard, the mechanics professor and second most intellectual survivor aboard, in my opinion, has not left my side for a total of five minutes in the two days that we've been holed up in here. I'm not exactly keeping track, but I'm sure. He sidles over to me after each pretend break taken to 'check on the others' and starts up a fresh conversation on the mechanics of the fusion of metal pipes. Like I could have gotten any more than my previous store of information on it, which was equivalent to zero, in the few seconds that he has been away.

I highly doubt that he remembers to take his anti-humidity pills in those times, as his speech grows more nasal in nature on each return. It would be cute, his apparent infatuation with me, if holding one-sided conversations with a chattering possum speaking Mandarin ever could be, and of course if we took away the added bit about impending space deaths.

The majority of us are huddled in isolation in various corners of the large room, and the lady on the administrative team constantly implores everyone to intermingle more. To maintain the mind-body connection, she says. I wish Albert *would not take her so seriously, as the others do not. They move out of their mentally-imposed shells for no longer than it takes to receive their rations, and withdraw as quickly, as if the next person was a sack full of radiation.*

It's a heavy weight on my chest, the fact that I know not a single one of the people with whom I am sealed off in a room, spending what may possibly be the last moments of my life. In the last four months, I achieved the grand feat of forming three genuine connections with three real people, which is a truly laudable achievement for me. But now, all three of them are gone, either poisoned with toxic nuclear energy and rotting away in some fallen area of the ship, or—if they were lucky— now floating specks alongside the ship's debris in literal oblivion. One of them, Christy, was ripped in half before my very eyes, and now, her ghost won't let me sleep.

I better go help, I guess. I'll be back with more updates.

❖ ❖ ❖

Entry 313.

. . .

It's still Day 128 here on the Beacon 09 in the year 2142, Day 02 succeeding the crash. Enough hours have passed for us to believe that it is currently the period known as night back on Earth.

Once this hall detached from the rest of the Beacon 09 and sealed itself, we lost the ability to control gravity. Since then, we've been floating around, having to push ourselves against the walls, ceiling, or floor in order to move from one place to the other. But, hey, at least we have oxygen. And bathrooms! It's been interesting doing that without gravity. Of course, I wish we had showers too, though I'm not sure how that would work.

Anyway, moving on to something else.

George is gone. Not gone as in dead, heavens forbid, but unattached to my ribs, thank God. I believe he has finally tired of trying to shape me into the geek belle that his mother or priest assured him he would encounter before his passing, after his third divorce, and he has moved on in search of greener pastures. Perhaps someone closer to his age would be best. I was getting very tired of his constant compliments about my hair and cheekbones, to be honest.

On my casual perusal of the room on the return trip from the distribution panel, back to my static station by the observation glass, I noticed him exchanging laughs with a mousy lady with spiky, purple-dyed hair, whom I vaguely remember making introductions with in one of the early weeks of the trip. Joanne, I think her name was. I wish him the brightest luck in that area, even more so as his discovery of his soulmate means that I can quietly observe the rot outside of our chamber without being burdened with the figures of it that I couldn't care less about.

Two men about my age have taken up the vacant spot beside me. I am sure they're a couple, as I've been seeing them together in the pool for the past four months. They aren't quite as chatty as my first neighbor—in fact, one hasn't said anything more than hello to me in the six hours that we have been sharing the same space—but the other is more laid-back, in a welcoming way. He introduced himself to me as Ron, although his partner insists on calling him Ronald in their shared whispers that I can't help but eavesdrop on. I gather that Mr. Gloomy is Mitch, although he doesn't offer the info up.

Ron is a chubby fellow with a shock of hair falling in bangs to his face. He's the kind of shy that makes a lot of small talk to mask his shyness, but only ends up making it more evident. Him I find cute. Mitch, however, is a tall, sturdy fellow with broad features all-round. I find him to be somewhat uptight and fiercely suspicious of unfamiliar people and things. He is equally fiercely protective of Ron. Whenever a new topic is opened up between us, his eyes swiftly dart over to me, and he gives me a stern look that I interpret to mean that I should be careful not to upset the fragile emotions of his beau. It's a little *stifling trying to stay behind some imaginary red line, but conversing with Ron has an easy flow to it, and is a refreshing reprieve from my forced exchanges with George, so I have resolved to manage it.*

Ron speaks most passionately about their cat, Felix, that they left back home on Earth with his grandma. He says it's the one thing that he'll truly miss if he never makes it back home, and right then, I imagine a poor orphaned cat sitting by its lonesome in an old wicker basket in a house that smells of old spices, and I find myself fighting to have faith that we will make it out of this terrifying fix. If for nothing else, for Ron, Mitch, and Felix.

It's finally time to go to sleep. I hope I get to sleep more tonight than I did last night.

❖ ❖ ❖

Entry 314.

. . .

It's Day 129 here on the Beacon 09 in the year 2142, Day 03 succeeding the crash, and this is still me, Riley, speaking. Speaking...to my watch. To myself, I guess. Because, let's be honest, I don't think very many people will ever see my vlog anyway.

So, good news. Earlier this morning Nola sent out a distress call.

With the help of some engineer or something like that, he was able to mess with the chamber's communications system and connect it with the main satellite of the ship which links up to the helpline network. That piece is floating about a mile from us—we can clearly see it through the glass—but they made it work. Don't ask me how; I don't know about these things.

It's a huge miracle that the satellite wasn't completely shut down by the monstrous storm, although the larger part of it was. At least it can still pick up signals and ping other towers stationed on planets or floating in satellites throughout the galaxy.

Maybe there is hope for us in this after all.

My optimism is only dampened by the fact that Nola has estimated at least a fifteen-day period for the reception of our signal by the nearest tower to us, and maybe another fifteen for the journey of their return signal to us. That's a month's wait at least, and the odds that we will live past the next ten days are dismal, to put it lightly.

Our pathetically thin rations have been cut even thinner. I am starving, and I am petite. I can't imagine how the others must be feeling. The choice to breathe is becoming barely more appealing than the alternative, because the oxygen is taken in such small draughts that the struggle to adequately circulate it burns the heart. And we are trying to save the suits as much as possible.

Ugh! It's like I'm sixteen once again, heartbroken over a fool whose face I can no longer even recall. My chest is on fire all the time. The water tastes like filtered zinc extracts, and it makes my throat tingle, like I'm ingesting melted rabbit fur. The gravity control is failing with each hour that passes by. Soon, our muscles will become so weak that we won't be able to walk. I fear that before long, I'll hurl myself out of the room and surrender to the thirsty green rad on the other side, just to be done with it once and for all.

Tremors rock through the ship irregularly, mostly twice in the day and once at night. They serve as our reminder of the precarious balance of the walls enclosing us right when we're beginning to slip into the tiniest semblance of normalcy, when we're daring to put it out of mind.

I have given up my station by the observation glass. The sick pipes were beginning to take form in my delirious vision; the faces of my three dead friends, my dead father, my Nana, my mom. Now, I float from end to end in aimless circles, not daring to settle in any one place for fear that the ghosts will once more make camp with me. But the ghosts aren't the only reason for *my newfound phobia for stillness. The people are haunting, too. The living, I mean. Everywhere I look, there are aloof faces with eyes almost completely drained of light. Taut lips sealed shut with the dryness of dehydration. Constant trembling due to the cold.*

We have known that we are on a racing clock to shut down from the moment we took stock of our situation after the crash, but our collective anxiety and the religious faith of a few were masks that held up the disguise of a people with a grip on life still. The veil is down now, and it fills me with a weariness that I have never before felt because I fear that it is too soon.

It is too soon to be nearly out of water and air. It is too soon to be weeks away from a rescue that only just brought us hope. It is too soon to have lost that hope. It is too soon to be turning on each other, and away from our humanity, in the way that we Earthlings do at the barest glimpse of death.

It is too soon, but I fear that we already are.

In-fighting is starting to rear its head already, as a disagreement ensues between the female administrator whom I have heard being referred to as Dolly and a man I vaguely recognize from one of the telecasts distributed on the ship upon our boarding. I recall coming across his feature in the patron column, which would mean that his golden bucks are an integral part of the framework of this magnificent structure.

He speaks in the disdainful manner of all Earthlings who got wealth ascribed to their names without sweat or hustle, an inherited fortune most likely, but Dolly maintains decorum still. He is condescending and brash, and from what I manage to glean from a distance, is requesting that he be given extra portions in the morning distribution in deference to his elevated status. Dolly calmly but firmly maintains that she cannot give her approval to that because there is barely enough to go round, even with the schedule in place. Giving him any more would be akin to condemning another passenger to starvation.

He huffs and insists that she concede to his request, carelessly stating that he cares nothing for the rest of us, and that if death must eventually come for us all, he, by virtue of his years-long contribution to the maintenance of the voyage, deserves to die the good death of a prince. They go back and forth on this issue until another passenger steps in to mediate.

It is the soap-opera-faced man with the captivating smile.

I bristle in shock as I realize that I am blushing at the sight of him. It is an intriguing surprise to find that even in my presently extremely dire straits, I can still find it in me to have appropriate appreciation for a handsome face. And that body. Just...wow.

However, the deftness with which he handles the conflict proves that he is so much more than just a pretty face. He patronizingly expresses his agreement with money-mouth's stance that he be given deferential treatment in recognition of his high office, but with exaggerated regret, he informs him that his antagonizing of Dolly is quite the waste of his scant energy, as she is not, indeed, in the position to grant or refuse him his request. He kindly redirects him to Albert Nola, and after a thirty-minute listen to his crazed ramblings on the mathematics of the rationing, the white-faced peacock stalks off with a pout.

And just like that, the matter is settled.

I observe him from out of my cold, shadowy corner, undeniably impressed. Unfortunately, when I finally make the decision to go over to introduce myself to him, Ron floats over and starts up a conversation with him and Dolly. Soon, all three of them are mimicking money-mouth and chuckling. Instead, I turn away and sidle over to a wall to try to catch some shut-eye.

Maybe tomorrow.

❖ ❖ ❖

Entry 315.

. . .

It's Day 129 or 130, rather. Still here on the Beacon 09 in the year 2142. It's been a few days since the ship crashed. Riley

Cruz speaking for my daily vlog updates. And do I have some updates today!

A loud ping woke me up. Well, not just me; most of us. It rang clear as day and reverberated through the silent chamber.

A single bleep. A loud one.

That's all it took to pull everyone out of our melancholic seclusion or deep sleep, and over to the makeshift cockpit, which housed a bouncy Nola hurtling about its perimeter like an upset bee.

Except he wasn't upset.

He was bursting full with excitement, as were we, the wide-eyed audience. You see, a miracle occurred, the second in the space of a few hours. We received a response to our distress signal. The message worked and was received.

Beside the fact that this is the best possible thing that could happen to us, it is literally the manifestation of the impossible. Nola's calculations had been made down to the last zeros, and he had been completely confident in their accuracy. He had taken all fixed statistics and probable variables into account while making them, so his perplexed mania over their proven inaccuracy is perfectly in order.

When his adrenaline burst was finally spent, he turned to address us. He reeled out strings of words that sounded like utter gibberish to the majority of us, I'm sure, updating us on the slight shift of our situation given our unforeseen good fortune. He said that the rescue spaceship is expected to arrive in a minimum of three weeks, judging from the geo-tag on their signal. Of course, some people hissed and assumed their crestfallen expressions again. Not me, though. It might not seem like much to hope on, but two miracles in a single day is a sure good tiding, if ever there was one.

But wait; there's more. Something equally exciting to report! Or, so I think.

You see, as we listened to Nolan, I felt a weight come to rest on my shoulder and, with a distracted glance in its direction, I found that it was a person's gloved hand. From its bulk, I guessed it to be a man's. And, lo and behold! I turned my head, only to find Mr. Charming-Actor-Smile a breath's distance away from me, his eyes intently trained on the still-speaking expert.

As I said...two miracles in a day, indeed.

He didn't pay me any attention to me, even though I basically gawked at him through the eyeglass of my oxy mask, as it was my turn to wear a suit. He was obviously soaking in all of Nola's words, down to the very last letter. I realized that his hand on my shoulder must have been an unconscious action done to steady himself, so I didn't shrug it off. We stayed in this position for at least another minute until Nola was done with his address. As people began to disperse, he finally noticed me.

Our eyes met, and his instantly took up an expression that told me that his lips are curved into a silent 'ooh' right then. His hand fell off from my shoulder, and I found myself immediately missing the burden. This was the realest physical sensation that I have felt in days. A twinkle danced within his pitch black orbs, telling me that he was smiling.

Oh, I still have the encounter memorized.

"Pardon me," he said, a heavy Hispanic accent punctuating the words. It reminded me of my deceased grandfather's twang.

I was struck dumb by the beautiful sonority to his voice for a second, and when I finally was able to speak, it was in a voice that I am sure sounded nothing like mine. I stuttered!

"It's...it's fine," I said more curtly than intended, and hurriedly shut my mouth again before it could further embarrass me. I felt so stupid.

But his smile brightened, and I immediately knew that he could tell that I was nervous. He moved even closer to me, and I could swear that I felt EM fields crackle between us. I am not exaggerating when I say that the chemistry was palpable. Electric, even. One look in his eyes told me that he felt it too. We simultaneously sucked in breaths.

Thankfully, he broke the awkward silence. "What a brain, right?" he said, as a spell-breaker, gesturing passively at the old *man drawing figures with a light stick on a hologram-board a few feet away from us.*

I nodded because that was all I could manage at the moment. My mouth was suddenly clogged with saliva. It felt like a thousand tiny ants were taking a stroll across my belly.

Maybe it was the prolonged absence of romantic company in my life or my acute inexperience in the area, or maybe even the lack of solid structure beneath my feet. Who knows? I can't quite decide what it was, but what I know for sure is that I was swooning over a real human male for the first time ever.

And I still am.

❖ ❖ ❖

Entry 316.

. . .

Riley, here. It's Day 131 here on the Beacon 09, or what remains of it. And, well, you know the year. We are now in the fifth day...or sixth? I don't know anymore. I can't really think straight lately. Must be the lack of oxygen. Anyway, it's a few days after we crashed.

Whoa! I just realized that 131 days sounds major. Like it really just makes it hit home, how much of a change has been made in my life. How much I have achieved.

Um... you see, if you've been following along on the vlog, you'll know that a year ago, I decided to take a major leap. And 131 days ago exactly today, I cut myself away from a life that had since ceased to be of service to me, and leaped blindly into the possibility of a better one, an opportunity that could maybe reignite the buried flint within my heart.

I was lost, broken, and drowning in identity dysmorphia when I came aboard this ship, and today, all those years—the brutal years spent feeling completely estranged from the world, lacking connection with the me within that philosophy says is the core of a person's being—finally have meaning. I sold everything I had and came alone on this supposedly 183-day trip across our galaxy to find myself. And I feel as if I finally have. At the very least, today, the puzzle pieces begin to fit. I begin to take form.

Today, I awake with purpose throbbing like a life within my chest. One singular purpose. To know this man who has breathed this new life into me. The man I met in space on a dying vessel.

Maybe it's the fact that we are all dying here, and I don't want to die alone. Maybe it's the very human need for connection and love I crave. Maybe I am simply desperate and lonely. I don't know, to be honest. I really don't. But I know I crave this man. And this desire has given me purpose.

I received my morning rations with a lightness in my bones. Scientifically, one can call it my body's defense against the impossible oxygen level it's being forced to live on, but science is only so true as the brain can comprehend it. It is the half-baked answer given to incomprehensible things. And trust me, this is an incomprehensible thing.

The spring in my steps, even though I am now fully suspended mid-air, the clamminess of my palms beneath anti-fluid gloves, the sudden ability of my eyes to trail a single masked figure around a roomful of masked figures. I literally cannot get them to move past him, my eyes. Even as I came to camp beside Ron and Mitch by the observation glass to look at the rest of the Beacon 09's debris, and Ron began with the story of Felix' first litter, which I've heard a few times already, and yet still manages to fascinate me anew with each retelling, my eyes were glued to his muscular back as he weaved his way between people, checking to make sure everyone was in good shape.

I looked through the window, and suddenly, in the reflection, I saw the deformed pipes in a whole new light. I had an actual Eureka moment. My eyes darted crazily around the room in search of George's figure. If only he were around to witness this; my rebirth as a true child of science. I felt a strange nostalgia and was overwhelmed by the desire to have him back beside me, regaling me with the physics of it all. I had an urge to know about these pipes that is greater than any craving I have ever felt.

They were once more taking form before my eyes, but I was no longer inclined to flee from them. It was now a single form— one I wanted to run toward, not away from. It was a face with shiny black eyes reflecting through an oxy mask. And I had a burning desire to feel it. Just as I thought about that, an image of his hand atop my shoulder filled my mind's eye, and I felt a weight on my shoulder.

Again. I assumed that I was only imagining it until I heard the voice. "Señorita," it said in a way that made me want to dance.

I took a second to compose my breathing before turning around, but I was still slightly hyperventilating when our eyes met. They were even brighter than I remembered. So black and, in spite of our circumstances, still so very full of life.

"I believe we met yesterday," he stated in a conspiratorial tone, like we were sharing a secret. And in a way, I guess we were. We were enclosed within an invisible orbit right then, and the whole room stood oblivious to the energy pulse, the size of which can create a whole sun. Or a black hole. "...but we weren't properly introduced," he continued.

He was still speaking, but I was lost in some far-off place, imagining the curve of his lips with every sound, and a couple more uses for those lips that I could think of. I'm glad neither of us was wearing a mask at the moment; I needed to examine every inch of his face.

If we were nineteen and could somehow surmount the challenge of the room's lack of gravity, we would be ripping clothes off already. The sexual tension was quite literally burning my skin. But, unfortunately, we aren't nineteen and the atmosphere and our lack of gravitational pull can't be helped. So, a certain level of restraint was required of us. Well, of me.

I shut my eyes and sucked in a ragged breath. When I reopened them, I found him watching me curiously. I mentally smacked my palm against my forehead. I must have been coming off as a major weirdo to him. But I rushed to correct the impression.

I think I did okay.

"Yes, we did meet yesterday. The shoulder thingy," I offered with a rough gesture to my shoulder. "I'm Riley," I chipped in as an afterthought with a too-bright smile on. "Riley Cruz. Nice to finally meet you. Sorry I spaced out. My hair was floating on my face, you know."

He reached for my hand before I could extend it and clasped it within his, sending shivers running through me.

"Well, Riley, I'm Vincent; but you can call me Vin. That's what everyone else calls me." He spoke in a tone that conveyed to me that he does not particularly wish for me to be "everyone else." The twinkle was back in his eyes, and I felt my fingers tighten around his.

"Vincent works just fine for me," I assured him in a voice that was barely above a whisper.

He nodded his head as if to say that he approved of the choice, then he released my hand and turned to face the glass. From out of the corner of my eye, I registered that Ron and Mitch were no longer by my side. I was grateful for that.

"Can I make a confession, Riley?"

The secret-sharing tone was back, and my spine tingled in anticipation. He went on before I could give a reply.

"I've kinda been stalking you," he stated simply, and I could almost feel his masked smile wash over my skin.

The confession made my heart race and my mouth crack into an idiot's grin.

"Have you now?" I asked teasingly. I am sure my tone and cheesy smile gave my excitement away.

"Indeed," he said as he turned to me and winked. He then returned his gaze to the ship's outside metals that had now lost their intrigue for me.

"Well, Vincent, I happen to have been watching you too," I blurted out from out of nowhere.

My own boldness startled me, but I managed to still myself from running for the hills... or into outer space, rather. I am a grown woman! I can handle some casual flirting. Right? Although, to be fair, this was far from casual. But still, Mr. Vincent of Beacon 09 is just a man. Albeit a man who has managed to imprison my thoughts for hours after our very first meeting...a gorgeous man with a nice body and an even better personality... But still a man, nonetheless.

"Hmm. You have, huh?" He sucked in a breath, and I felt it settle in my gut. "And do you like what you see?" he asked in amusement.

I matched his tone and replied with an exaggerated thoughtful sigh. He turned back to me, and without looking, I could tell that he rolled his eyes. We shared a silent laugh, then the tension settled around us again. He looked at me so intently that I felt like he might absorb me or melt me into goo, the kind of which now coats the rusty pipes in the next room, and it fills me with an irrational panic. I still struggle to break the spell.

I didn't know what else to say, so I asked stupidly, "So... You're done with your morning rounds?"

The answer was pretty obvious, hence I am thankful that he gave me no reply. I would hate to hear the irritation that the mindless question is sure to have sparked within him.

But he was still looking, though floating, somehow standing as still as a rock and simply staring at me. The same way that I stared at him, except I did it from a distance, from this, my shadowy corner that I have claimed as mine. He was staring at me as I floated next to him. And as much as I loved the idea, I didn't know how to react. I twiddled my thumbs for want of something to do to keep me from ratting out more gibberish, and finally, he sighed and turned back to the glass.

"Your eyes," he said after a second's pause. "They're exquisite."

George had complimented my eyes a few times before, but it hadn't elicited any response from me. But now, I am sure my cheeks turned pink with Vincent's comment. Though, I am also confident that the color disappeared with his next words.

"They remind me of seals."

My brows wrinkled in confusion. "Seals?" I reiterated.

"Yes, seals," he repeated, unfazed. "As in, the sea mammal from Earth. You know."

What the hell?

In the brief second he gave to let the information sink, I began to worry that I had misjudged him. It has been my experience back on Earth that the finest ones are, after all, usually the looniest. Therefore, I've never had good luck with men, to be honest. I knew this was too good to be true, even in the face of certain doom.

Seals? Really, Vincent?

"Seal skin. It's a tinge of gray and seawater. I'm a sous chef," he finally offered up by way of explanation. "That's what I did here at the Beacon 09. I've been working here at the main kitchen for the past four years, nonstop. This was my eighth trip. And all I do is prep the food. But I love every bit of it."

I exhaled a relieved breath. *Okay, not crazy. Just... distinctive, I guess.*

"A sous chef, huh? That's cool. That is probably why I never saw you these past four months of the trip."

"Yeah, maybe. We are not supposed to fraternize with the clients, and I mostly keep to myself anyway."

"I see. And tell me, Vince, do you study the colors of all your cooking ingredients?" I asked incredulously.

"Well, what can I say?" he replied with a shrug. "I like to order my food down to minute detail."

"Hmm, persnickety," I said.

He shrugged again.

"Have you ever tried seal?" he asked.

"Um, no, thank you. I'm a vegetarian," I replied instinctively.

"Bummer," he said.

"Honestly, seal sounds gross," I whispered, but loud enough for him to hear me.

We remained uncomfortably silent for some time. Fearing that the conversation would be over sooner than I'd like, I fished around for more small talk. "So, you had a dream to one day make sandwiches in space or what?" I asked lightly. "I mean, how did you end up making a career on the Beacon?"

He chuckled.

By the way, I can honestly say that his laughter is now my favorite sound. Like in the history of...ever.

And, thankfully, my plan to break the awkwardness worked.

Excitedly, he replied, "Oh, I don't know. You ever have a dream to be up here doing whatever it is you're up here for?"

"I'm not up here for anything," I stated truthfully.

"False," he countered without pause. "We're all up here for something." Another chuckle.

"Well, not me," I insisted with a shrug. "It kinda just happened," I muttered, more to myself than to him. It was the truth.

He dropped the playful air and turned to me with melancholia etched into his eyes.

"Well, same. It kinda just happened too, I guess," he echoed.

I got the impression that he was referring to something much bigger than making space sandwiches. And somehow, I completely related.

It did just happen.

Everything that cultivated the emptiness that led me up here to be filled.

Everything that led to us.

He then went on to tell me about how his brand-new, pregnant wife had died. I was not prepared for that. I realized that we all have our stories to tell. And my guess is that many of us simply don't want to tell these stories. I also speculate that we are all running away from something back home. Though, to be fair, some of us are perhaps running toward something else. As far away as possible. Literally to the edge of the galaxy and back, in both of our cases.

And suddenly, my boring life didn't seem as dark as his.

Crap. I was not expecting that.

And I didn't know what to say but, "I'm sorry."

✧ ✧ ✧

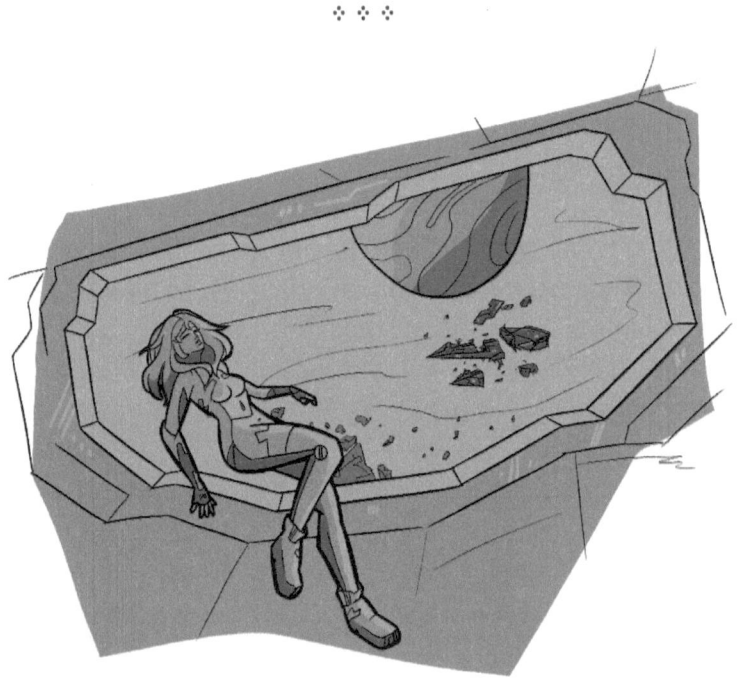

Entry 317.

. . .

Riley here. Still alive, though barely. This entry will be different; I am not secluded in my corner. Instead, I record it as I go about my day.

I don't even know what day this is. And I don't care. All I know is that this is not a good day.

Our reality has finally shown its face. The mask is off. And our imminent and inevitable end has begun. Certain death.

Larry is dead. He is gone.

At a little past the crack of dawn today, we record our first death. The cause of death: Dehydration.

Larry is—was—a man whom nobody seems to have been particularly close to, but whom according to one of the ladies here, had lost his family in the storm. Now, he is a lifeless mass hovering in the stifling space like an archangel of the underworld out of some tacky paranormal/sci-fi hybrid mix. His is the first floating cadaver we have this side of the glass. But nobody knew him, so nobody mourns him. He did mourn his loved ones, though.

Nonetheless, his death colors the already grim atmosphere a shade darker. Everyone is suddenly less chatty and less inclined to intermingle because the loss of a vibrant new connection is suddenly a looming possibility. It finally begins to dawn on us that we are running on almost non-existent odds, and the chance of getting out as a team, in the manner we came in, is next to nil.

The next one descends on the room like an ice fist: the asthmatic woman from Day 02.

Our oxygen rations are barely enough to maintain a healthy pair of lungs, so in truth, it is extremely impressive that she could even hold on for as long as she did. After she's confirmed to be dead, everyone pulls out of the reclusive state and gathers in a ring at the center of the room.

"Death can come for anyone at any given time" is so much more than philosophical gibberish now. It's true. It's reality. Our reality. And even more terrifying than that is the idea of surrendering to it in the dark, completely removed from life. That is too meek a defeat. If you must lose your life, you must make sure to get a good laugh in its face as its claws reach out to snatch it away.

That must be the mantra on play in all our heads as we gather round and begin to tell jokes. Jokes that skirt around the edges of our fear and painstakingly avoid the realities of our identities.

Nobody says where his joke was first told, or to whom he first told it, and nobody asks. We are united in bleak anonymity. In my current case, masked, and therefore, faceless.

Vincent has been by my side through it all, fingers wound tightly around mine incessantly, and I find that I'm afraid to let myself feel them. More like, to let myself feel what they make me feel. Hope. Hope that we can be real. Hope that we can survive. Hope that we can learn to live.

Yes, I still him each time he attempts to loosen his grip because I fear that our clasped hands is the representation of the last vestiges of fight within me. It is the only reason I will not retreat into the shadows in my corner and embrace the icy fist.

At some point in the course of the charade, Ron comes to stand beside me. He engages me in casual conversation about the first and only burial he ever attended, and he reveals that he would prefer to be cremated in the event of his death.

I turn to look at him when he says this, briefly shifting my focus from the feel of Vincent's fingers on mine, and I wince at his pallor. His eyes alone are visible to me, but there's a tiredness to them that stands out, in direct contrast to the timid light that I had noticed on our first meeting.

"You won't be dying anytime soon," I say firmly, more to reassure myself than to be polite.

He gives a slight nod and his brows wrinkle. I assume that he is smiling beneath his mask, so I smile too.

Unfortunately, all four suits are running out of oxygen. Inevitable doom awaits us all.

A little later, Mitch joins us, and they start up a hushed argument.

"I'm okay, Amitch. I don't need any more, and I certainly will not be asking for..."

I lose the rest of the words as his voice dims to a raspy croak. I can't make any sense of the heated declaration, so I choose instead to focus on my interesting new find. Mitch's full name is Amitch. Sounds German, or something; I don't know. I always assumed it would be something more American southern like Mitchel or Michael.

Amitch and Ron stalk off in opposite directions when it seems like they're failing to reach an agreement on whatever the dispute is. And before long, I have put it out of my mind.

No sooner have they gone than Mitch's scream filters over to the circle. We hurry off in his direction and arrive to find him bent over Ron's lifeless body, bawling with reckless abandon. The latter is backed up against a wall, his head bent at an awkward angle.

I frantically search his face for some tell-tale sign of movement.

I find none.

His eyes are rolled up to his head, and now, even the tiredness is gone.

All I can do is embrace Vincent and cry dry tears in his arms.

❖ ❖ ❖

Entry 318.

. . .

I think it's Day 139 or 140 here on the Beacon 09. I'm sorry I've been short on updates in the past few days. It is not a negligence. I'm just...tired.

My watch still has full life; I could record another 10,000 vlog entries before it dies. But the battery in my body is separate. That one is nearing its fate.

The time has passed in pretty much the same way, with the only separation between days being the rise in the pressure within my chest and the dryness of my throat.

And the death of five more of us. Originally eighteen of us survived. But eight of these are now gone.

Soon, we will all follow. We all know it.

The kind lady, Lola, is one of the cadavers floating around, and for some reason, I find myself mourning her like she was the best friend I ever had. I mourn her even more than I did Ron, the sweet, chubby half of Mitch's soul. Maybe I mourn her a lot more because I never really mourned Ron. His death leaves me reeling and sinking into a spiral of despair, but I find that I cannot find it in me to be truly mournful. Lola, however, brings some tears running. A couple only, since dehydrated people can't really cry.

I cry as I snuggle up to Vincent at night, and as I look through the observation glass at the metals that have now almost all completely fallen into gooey decay, I picture Lola, and I cry some more. All I have are my tears. And Vincent.

Vincent.

He is the miracle of my life, the only thing in its pointless entirety that is worthy of being called a blessing.

He hasn't left my side in the week since Ron's passing, and neither have I left his. Even though there hasn't been much physical contact between us yet, I feel less damned knowing that he is a steady, unmoving mountain beside me.

Sometimes he sings to me. Low enough in volume so that I am his only audience. And my skin tingles each time. When I've spent more time looking at the dead mess beyond our walls through the large window than I have looking at him, he understands that the seeming futility in battling the allure of the ice fist troubles me, so he sings.

His voice is feather-light, because the air barely glides past his parched throat, but I can still note the perfume of his accent interspersing the words, and it wraps around me like a security blanket. When he has his limbs wrapped around me, I can pretend for a time that we are only two lovers on a genuine space adventure, floating through nothingness and feeling the weight of our love, making a garden of it, reveling in the timelessness of it.

Vincent! Oh, Vincent! How did I stumble upon such poor luck as to be condemned to only finding him at my deathbed? If only I'd met him at the beginning of this trip, not its end!

We are completely out of food and most of the water is gone. By Nola's calculations, the rescue ship is still at least two weeks away. Our oxygen is predicted to take us for another week at most. Three of the suits are barren. Even as he says this, we all hear the real message.

There will be no rescue, no escaping this.

We all hear it, but it is the very last thing that any of us will talk about. It is just the silent vice squeezing the life from our hearts.

Mitch has spent the week glued to Ron's body by the spot that has unanimously been conceded to him, his resting spot. I float over to him sometimes, with no real purpose but to make certain that he still breathes. I don't get close enough to actually speak to him because I have no words, and he never acknowledges that I am there anyway. He rambles incoherently all day long, muttering on about Ron's favorite wine, their plans to visit several of Saturn's moons sometime in the coming five years, his pesky attachment to the cat, and so on.

He consistently speaks in the present tense. He defiantly refuses to address his lover in a manner that classifies him as an entity that once was. And I completely understand.

I hover in the distance and watch his grief play out, ashamed about my own lack of it, and I conjure up images of Vincent and I by a fire in an old brick house with a cat splayed out at our feet. I can almost feel the warmth on my fingertips, the possibility of it, and the foolhardiness brings a sob to my lips.

Half of the time, however, I wonder if he fantasizes about being with his deceased wife and baby instead. I wonder if to him I am nothing but a last-chance fling.

But I refute the thought as soon as it dawdles in my mind.

❖ ❖ ❖

Entry 319.

. . .

Hi. It's me again. Riley Cruz. Still in what remains of the once-great ship, the intergalactic Beacon 09.

More of the survivors are gone. Their lifeless bodies floating among us in the chamber. I know now that bodies do not decay in the absence of oxygen, so they are simply lifeless vessels floating around.

Vincent and I remain, thankfully. So do a few others.

In the wee hours, I gravitate towards Mitch, to make certain, and I find him molded into Ron like a masterful sculpture. His mouth is positioned above his bluing lover's like he means to kiss him, and it immediately strikes me that the pose is the life depiction of a poem.

Ron loved poetry. That much I knew.

When I finally get my feet to propel me around the intertwined bodies, I look into Mitch's eyes and find a calming peace there. But there is nothing else.

Death has taken him by its claws.

❖ ❖ ❖

Entry 320.

. . .

What can I say? I am jubilant. You see, we finally made love.

Yes, I know! I can't believe it myself. But while the only other survivors remaining besides Vincent and I floated in their deep slumber of the night, on the other side of the chamber, by the observation window, Vincent and I floated, united into one. And there were sparks. Literally. It was magical. The nearby star gave us a beautiful sight as Vincent and I climaxed in unison.

Making sweet passionate love with zero gravity, yeah...scratch that off my bucket list.

Anyway, that is all for today. I think it's plenty.

And though I am dying, frankly, I couldn't be happier right now.

❖ ❖ ❖

Entry 321.

. . .

Hello. This is Vincent speaking on Riley's watch. I think she would've liked that. Unfortunately, Riley is too weak to speak. She is resting now, and I don't want to disturb her peace.

I'm not entirely sure how this works, but I've seen Riley do her updates, so I guess... here we go.

Let's see, what is new. Well, it has been three weeks since the storm took us by surprise. The captain, along with all of my colleagues, perished in the crash's aftermath. A few of us were lucky to be in this chamber, and a genius man saved us. But he is gone.

And so is every other survivor.

That's right; only my Riley and I remain. I am not sure if we can pull through.

We received a message from the rescue ship a couple of hours ago, I think. Time is going by in a weird way. Anyway, they said that they should be here in the next forty-eight hours or so. But, to be honest, I don't think we will make it that far.

We removed the oxygen tank and mask from the last surviving suit, and it's almost gone too. Riley and I are taking turns in using it, rationing it to survive.

Sigh. This is very hard. I really don't know what else to say.

If anyone is receiving this, please know that we tried our best.

Vincent out.

❖ ❖ ❖

Entry 322.

. . .

Riley here. I am back. Literally.

My heart stopped beating a few hours ago. As in, actually stopped.

Vincent said that for a full minute, I was not breathing, and I was as still as a corpse.

But I was dead.

For me, of course, it was only a second's blackout before I awoke with a start within Vincent's arms, gasping for breath. The last oxy mask is out of place on his face, resting slightly to one side in a way that makes me worry that he is getting too little oxygen, but in a weak croak, he assures me that he is getting as much as the mask will allow. I know now that it is out of place because he took it off to augment my own supply when I passed out. Even though it was his turn, not mine.

My face pales on hearing this, and I fear that I will pass out again, for good this time.

"How could you have done that?" I cry in dismay. "We each barely have enough to see us through the next day, and I had it all day yesterday. You need it too!"

He massages my shoulders and draws me into his chest.

"You needed it more," he exhales with a spent sigh.

I sigh too.

It is true what he says, as I am much weaker. But I still can't shake the feeling that I have just robbed him in the most terrible manner, committed the worst slight.

As if he knew what I was thinking he tells me, "I choose you." And then again, he reiterates, "I choose you, Riley Cruz."

The silence is overwhelming.

I feel so lightheaded. But I must remain conscious.

I sense him losing it too, as he floats around with his eyes closed.

"Are you okay, my love? Are you breathing fine?" I inquire, distraught, bringing him close to me.

He skips a few beats before replying, and although he says yes, the quake in his voice which he unsuccessfully struggles to hide is enough giveaway of the truth.

Panic grips my chest and I stifle a sob. I mustn't give up already. I must hope, for his sake and mine.

"Riley," he calls out tentatively, cutting into the tense silence, still with closed eyes.

"Yes?" I answer too quickly.

"I love you," he says simply, and falls quiet again.

My heart swells in acceptance of his declaration, and I reach for his hand and bind our ungloved fingers together.

"I love you too," I whisper, and I feel his chest flatten out beneath my cheek.

We remain in this position for what feels like an eternity.

"Do you know what it is that I am most grateful for right now?" he asks.

I give it thought for a minute and then shake my head in the negative.

"The almost-kiss we just shared as I was trying to revive you," he says lightly, and I can tell that he is attempting to laugh, though his strength doesn't carry the chords.

I smile. Faintly.

"I love you, Vincent."

"Riley," he continues solemnly, "Make sure you try out seal when you get back home." He chuckles.

I nod with a smile as tears flow through my covered face. "I promise."

After a few moments, which feel eternal, he dimly says, "They'll be here soon." It's barely a whisper, but loud enough to bring me back to awareness.

"What?" I ask as I hold both his hands as tight as I can so that he won't wander off again.

"They'll be here soon, my love." With that, I feel his hands lose their grip.

More tears escape my eyes before I can stop them. I sense his spirit leaving as his body floats away aimlessly in front of me. He gave up the oxygen so that I could survive.

He gave his life for me. He chose me.

Suddenly, the lights of another space vessel shine brightly through the window. The cavalry is finally here.

If only they'd gotten here a little earlier.

❖ ❖ ❖

Entry 475.

. . .

Hello, everyone. Riley Cruz here, continuing with my pregnancy vlog.

Excuse my chewing. Seal is, um...well, chewy. Ha! Not my favorite, but I did make a promise. Although I am sure I won't repeat it. I found this café that serves gilled seal around my place here in Long Beach.

Anyway, as most of you know by now, that is, if you've been following my vlog or paid attention to the news, it's been six months since I was rescued from the Beacon 09's wreckage. Unfortunately, I was the sole survivor. But Vincent's lineage and legacy will continue with Vincent Junior. Oh, speaking of...he just kicked. He's crazy hyper. I think he likes the seal.

He is getting so big. And heavy too. It's days like this that I miss being able to just float around. But my space traveling days are done. Forever.

I went on an intergalactic trip to find myself. And I did. I went as one, and came back with a plus one.

I can't wait to meet my baby boy. I just hope he has his daddy's smile and joy for life.

E very developer has dreamed of designing the
perfect app, one that would make millions

overnight. Sergio Lomas finally finished creating a product that he knew would make him strike it big.

"Okay, you are right. This *is* amazing!" Dejuan Bernard clicked through the working app demo while Ivan Nimitz looked over his shoulder. "And you're sure the coding is all right?"

Dejuan, Ivan, and Sergio had been coding apps together for the last couple of years, since Sergio had graduated college. Most of the apps hadn't taken off yet, but they never gave up trying. The three of them shared an inexpensive loft, an old space in which they all lived and worked. The external air conditioner buzzed loudly nearby. Several fans were spread out to provide extra cooling, but the heat from the summer seeped into the small space.

"I'm positive," Sergio said. Sweat dripped from his brow. "Like I said, *Link* pairs you up with other people who play a perfect match with each other. Whatever they lack, need, or desire is literally just a button away. Whether they need the perfect business partner, or employee, or lover, it's all there and the matching is precise."

"How is this different from all the other dating apps?" Ivan asked. Ivan had ignored most of Sergio's previous sentence, focusing on the "lover" part of it only.

"It's not just a dating app, dude. If someone is looking for a certain type of musician, writer, artist, or handyman for crying out loud, they are sent to the perfect one. One specified to their likes and dislikes. The app literally gathers all the data from their devices over the course of their lifetime and matches them accordingly. Granted, some will use it to find sexual partners with intrinsic and specific kinks, while others will accurately find their perfect soulmate." Sergio hopped up from his desk chair and gestured with his hands. "Most people have already submitted their samples to one of the many DNA tracking sites. This app uses the information that is stored in their phone and will utilize their gene composition to match them with the perfect person. It uses their genetic factors, interests and hobbies, personal habits and traits, search history, and even their education level to find that special someone that compliments them. Honestly, I don't know why it hasn't been done before."

"*Link*. I like it. It's simple and accurate," Dejuan said. "It's kind of catchy, too. Good for the marketing aspect. I'm already thinking of a logo."

"And, people always need someone for something specific, whether it's to replace a retiring employee, or to find friends in a new city… it's not a one and done type app. It's a lifetime need that fulfills everyone. So, users can use *Link* every day for every day's needs."

"Dang, bro! This is unbelievable. We need to get this to market yesterday." Ivan grabbed his computer to begin the uploading process. "It's not like we have anything to lose, at this point. If it works, then it'll be big. Did you factor in the safety protocols in regards to sex trafficking or sexual predators? I don't want to deal with any potential lawsuits because people are stupid."

"*Link* does a thorough screening and background check to be sure there's enough lifetime information to even allow them to join. If they have a criminal record of any serious nature, they won't be permitted to use it. Also, it'll block those without long enough spans of information, rendering scammers useless against the algorithm." Sergio grinned. "Nope, it's almost impenetrable."

"That's good." Ivan uploaded the drive Sergio stored the coding on and continued working diligently to get it moving. "That's really good. And what about pulling data from DNA databases or their phones? Is that even legal?"

"When a user agrees to the terms right after installation, they are essentially giving us permission. I thought it through. I mean, we might need legal help on the small print wording, but other than that, I think we should be fine."

"I'll start on the promotion aspect," Dejuan said, scooting to his computer.

"You really think we have a winner?" Sergio asked. He'd been working on this endlessly for at least the last two years. He twisted his shirt in his hands, a nervous habit he'd never seemed to rid himself of.

"With the right marketing, how can we not?" Dejuan smirked.

"I can have it up on all platforms by tomorrow." Ivan typed vivaciously on his computer. "We just need to finalize all those small details. Call you lawyer friend."

"I will. I'm so glad you both are excited about it, too." Sergio sighed with relief. It was one thing for him to be excited about his own creation, but another to have his two friends on board and eager as well.

"I'll secure a website domain, just in case it takes off. I have a feeling we will need it if it works as well as the demo," Dejuan said.

"I feel bad having to leave you guys now." Sergio packed up his laptop and stuffed it into his carry-on bag. "But I need to catch my flight, otherwise Mom will kill me for missing Christmas. You two are lucky your parents live here. There's no way my parents could afford to live in San Jose or anywhere near the Bay Area. Not that they'd want to, anyway."

"Take it easy," Dejuan said. "We got this, no problem. Enjoy your vacation in Arizona."

"Yeah, have a good time." Ivan didn't glance up from his computer screen. "My parents will deal with me not coming this year. Too much to do on this break."

Dejuan laughed. "I'd much rather take a trip to Cabo or Hawaii rather than spend a Christmas with my bratty siblings."

Sergio cared too much about his parents to even consider missing Christmas. He felt a bit sorry for Dejuan and Ivan. They obviously didn't share a closeness with their families like he did with his. Then again, Dejuan and Ivan had been too focused on "making it," which Sergio could relate to. He'd be able to help his family financially if one of their apps took off. And he had a good feeling about this one.

"Anyway, don't work too much, guys. My ride is here. See you in a week," Sergio said, glancing around the working space where his roommates and business partners worked diligently.

"Peace," Ivan said, staring at his screen.

"Break a leg," Dejuan added without missing a beat, his back towards Sergio.

Sergio smiled. He left the place they all shared with his bag packed with a week's worth of clothes, his phone, and his laptop. His driver was waiting for him outside to take him to the airport.

∴ ∴ ∴

When Sergio returned a week later, the things he had on him were the only things he had left.

The loft was all cleaned out.

There was a "for rent" sign on the door and the locks had already been changed.

Sergio tried calling Dejuan first, and then Ivan. Both numbers had been disconnected. He pulled up the app, *Link*, on his phone. It had over 2,000 positive reviews already, after only a few days out.

Link had indeed taken off, but so had Dejuan and Ivan.

∴ ∴ ∴

Six months passed before Sergio finally found his chance to see Dejuan and Ivan in person. As the BART continued on its journey from San Jose to San Francisco, Sergio read the article in *Tech Magazine* once more. The co-creators of *Link*, Dejuan Bernard and Ivan Nimitz, were to receive the prestigious Creator of the Year award tonight in San Francisco at the Ritz.

The article didn't provide any other important details about Dejuan and Ivan that would be particularly helpful in tracking them down. Sergio's former friends and partners had done well keeping their personal information out of the spotlight, but they couldn't hide forever. He needed to see the looks on their faces when he confronted them in person. He wanted to know a reason for their thievery and betrayal, although deep down he knew it boiled down to greed and pure selfishness.

"Are you going to San Fran on business?" The lady next to him looked down at the magazine he'd been reading.

"Yeah, you could say that." Sergio politely half-smiled.

"I took the BART because I hate driving on highways," she continued. She held out her phone and showed him a picture that happened to be on the *Link* app. "But, I'm going there to meet my soul mate. Can you believe that? I've been single my whole life, and I've been looking eagerly for the past ten years, and I finally found a perfect match."

"That's great." Sergio gulped. "Congratulations."

She kept going on about her match as Sergio pulled out his phone and brought up the app himself. He tuned her out as he surveyed the app he'd created, wondering exactly what he would say to Dejuan and Ivan when he saw them tonight.

Although he knew the app was special, he didn't realize the amount of people that would download it and use it so quickly. It had only been on the market a few months, and it seemed everyone in the world had it on their smart phone already. There were even multiple advertising images of *Link* flashing inside the BART wagon. Their marketing strategy obviously paid off, and that made Sergio angrier by the second.

The metro pulled into the station, as Sergio's nerves were on fire. The ride was merely a half-hour long, but it felt as if it had been days.

"Good luck with your meeting," the lady said as they exited.

"Thanks." Sergio offered her another half-smile.

Rain pelted the passengers as soon as they exited. Sergio opened his umbrella and straightened his suit. He ordered a ride on his phone and waited patiently as it arrived a few minutes later.

Once he arrived at the Ritz, all words he had planned to say to the two thieves escaped him. Getting into the hotel wasn't a problem, but the banquet area was a different matter entirely. It was closed off through the hotel, and the only way to enter into the private get-together was by the entrance outside. He opened his umbrella once more and went around to the banquet entrance. A red carpet lead into the entrance, flooded with reporters and photographers. Security personnel were placed at the top of the stairs by the entrance and by a lady next to a podium, who was checking off names on a tablet as people went up the red carpet.

Many onlookers peeked through the windows to view the people on the inside. The rain shifted and started falling faster. Sergio moved his messenger bag to the front so it wouldn't get any wetter. Several onlookers decided the rain was too much to linger in, freeing up a lot of space by the windows.

Sergio moved closer to see who was in attendance. Several celebrities were sprinkled throughout the party.

He recognized a singer and a couple of actors, as well as several tech savvy entrepreneurs that he'd idolized for a very long time. Then, he saw them... Dejuan and Ivan standing proudly near the entrance, greeting everyone who arrived.

Standing right beside them were two beautiful women, linking arms with them. Sergio snapped a picture of all of them through the rainy window. He stood and stared at them for a little while as the rain washed away most of the reporters and photographers. Then he decided it was time to try and get into the party when it appeared the arrivals had slowed.

Sergio climbed the red carpet and was stopped at the woman by the podium.

"Name, please?" the lady asked him. She had her haired pulled up in a bun and an earpiece plugged into her ear.

"Sergio Lomas," he said.

She searched her tablet and shook her head. "You're not on the list, sir."

"I'm a close... personal friend of Dejuan and Ivan. And I'm—"

"If you're not on the list I can't allow you entrance. Did you receive an invitation?"

"No, but—"

"I'm sorry sir." She pursed her lips together and waived him away.

"Please tell them that I'm here. I'm sure they would let me in." Sergio demanded.

She sighed and pressed into her earpiece. "I have a..." she widened her eyes at Sergio.

"Sergio Lomas," he repeated.

"...*Sergio Lo-mass*, who says he was invited by the recipients of tonight's award."

Sergio peeked around her and watched an indoor security guard approach Ivan and Dejuan. Both of them jerked their heads toward the door and met Sergio's stare. Dejuan spoke to the security guard, and then both of them turned their backs with their ladies and walked away.

"I'm sorry sir, but they don't know who you are. If you don't leave the premises, we will have to escort you," the podium lady spat.

Sergio held his hands up in defeat. "It's fine. I'll leave."

He walked back down the stairs and around to view the party through the window once again. He lowered his umbrella and allowed the crisp rain to pelt him. Hatred boiled through him as he didn't get the closure he was seeking. He wasted the day trying to pursue a fruitless endeavor, and now he would need to return to his basement efficiency fifty miles away.

⁙ ⁙ ⁙

Six months later, Sergio worked in his studio diligently on his computer, next to his new business partner, David Saenz. They had been working on the creation of a new app that would provide low-cost vacation planning. It would allow the user to find the best prices for airfare, rental vehicles, and room and board from all the existing travel sites together. Instead of having to compare on multiple sites, it picked up all travel sites automatically and linked them together. It even integrated the booking, making it easy and simple to use.

"Hey, would you look at that," Dave swiveled in his chair to face Sergio. "Ivan Nimitz had a sex video leak with him and his mistress. His wife filed for divorce."

Sergio's eyes widened. "Really?"

Dave laughed. "The *Link Virus* strikes again, but this time it attacked one of the creators. That's hilarious. I'm just glad we found one another before the virus struck our phones."

Sergio had found Dave through *Link* two months earlier. Their personalities and work ethic matched perfectly. They already had an ease about their partnership that Sergio felt grateful for. "Yup," Sergio replied. "Agreed."

"On top of all their lawsuits, they are screwed, royally," Dave said. "The virus really did its number on that app. We need to make sure our app's security is impenetrable."

"My thoughts exactly." Sergio smiled.

Sergio's thoughts drifted to Ivan and Dejuan. He never revealed to Dave that he was the one who created *Link*. He felt it best to start fresh with him and not involve him in his past drama. Dave was young and still attending college, but had a brilliant mind. He reminded Sergio of himself a lot, which was the entire point of *Link* to begin with.

Sergio had been following Dejuan and Ivan's social media accounts since he found them living more in the limelight the last few months. Ivan had been married to that beauty he'd had with him at the award ceremony for a couple months now. She had announced her pregnancy a month ago, and now, with the leaked tape, they would now be divorced.

Sergio brought up the county records and searched the number of lawsuits that had now been filed against *Link* and its creators, Ivan and Dejuan. It was well over one hundred now. The *Link Virus* wreaked havoc on the app, causing users to lose everything, including their spouses, jobs, and money. All because it shared their secrets. The virus went from smartphone to smartphone once someone hooked up through *Link*, meaning the phones needed to be physically near one another to be infected.

Once the virus was in the phone, their videos, photos, and information became available to the public. Some videos were uploaded to porn sites and sent to their spouses, or even to their entire contact list. Some videos were sent to employers, causing many to lose their jobs. Funds were depleted from personal savings and checking accounts. It was a mess. What started out as a fantasy app, turned into a complete and utter nightmare. Relief washed over Sergio as he realized he'd dodged a bullet, and at the same time, Ivan and Dejuan were being served a plate full of karma.

Sergio brought up an online article about the Link Virus. Ironically, it was in *Tech Magazine*, the same one that honored them with the Creator of the Year award six months earlier. Memories flooded through Sergio's mind as he remembered standing outside the party looking in and being rained on. The article stated that the Link Virus was one of the most genius codes ever written. Credit was claimed by the group Anonymous, which meant that they would probably never know who really created it to begin with.

Apparently, Anonymous claimed *Link* took advantage of people's private information, and no app should have that kind of power. *Tech Magazine* went into details on some of the highlights and what happened to people due to the virus. They urged people to delete the app immediately from their phones to be sure the virus couldn't be contracted. They even compared it to that of a venereal disease, infecting unsuspecting people and ruining their lives.

Sergio found that analogy a bit much, but couldn't help but smirk. The article had a photograph of Ivan and Dejuan exiting a police station with their faces covered with baseball caps. The caption below the photo read "Ivan Nimitz and Dejuan Bernard exit the police station after being questioned by the feds about the virus."

No criminal charges had been filed, yet, but the article stated criminal proceedings could be forthcoming, as the

Link Virus has been linked to many crimes around the world. Another article Sergio pulled up talked about the legalities linked to the app and the virus. A survey found that many people felt the creators of the app should be held accountable, though some, a minority, stated they weren't to blame for the Link Virus. As the investigation was ongoing, the police and the FBI hadn't issued any comments at that time.

Sergio thought about his parents. After he came back from Christmas vacation and found nothing left, they sent him money to get a place of his own. He was thankful they were by his side, and he wasn't caught up in the middle of what Ivan and Dejuan were now involved in.

Sergio took a deep breath, closed his eyes, and listed all he was grateful for in his head. It became important to him to be thankful for what he had and not worry about what he'd lost.

"Sergio? Earth to Sergio." Dave raised his eyebrows, staring at Sergio.

"What?" Sergio asked.

"What about the game idea I pitched you last week?" Dave asked. "Have you thought about it? You were obviously lost in your own thoughts right now. What's up?"

"Oh, nothing." Sergio swatted the air. "Let's get back to work. Tell me about the game again, if you don't mind."

Dave laughed and repeated his idea to Sergio with as much enthusiasm as he could possibly generate.

✧ ✧ ✧

When the federal indictment flooded the newspapers, Sergio had a sinking feeling in the pit of his stomach.

Dave and Sergio diligently worked in the garage when the knock came at the door. A lawyer handed Sergio an envelope with his name clearly written across it.

"What is it?" Dave asked.

"A notice to appear for a deposition," Sergio said.

"For what?" Dave squinched up his nose.

"Ivan Nimitz and Dejuan Bernard are being indicted for embezzlement and conspiracy to commit fraud, among other things." Sergio crinkled the papers as he squeezed them with his fist.

"What does that have to do with you? Are you an expert witness or something?" Dave shook his head. "That's so weird."

"We... um... The three of us, we were partners at one time. So, I assume it's related to that," Sergio said. He didn't want to go into details, but he figured it would all come to light.

"What? Seriously? You never told me that!"

"I know. Honestly, I didn't want to be reminded of it," Sergio said. "They weren't exactly the best partners to have."

"Well, yeah, from the looks of it, I see why." Dave rubbed his eyes and stood from his seat. "I wonder what they will ask you."

"I guess I'll find out tomorrow." Sergio held up the paper. "Wait. It *is* for frigging tomorrow. What the hell? Talk about last minute!"

"Well, I guess I'll be working solo tomorrow. Thankfully, we are getting some good income from the game apps," Dave said.

"Yes, indeed. All thanks to your great ideas, Dave. Seriously." Sergio grinned. "Anyway, it probably won't be too long with the disposition, so I'll come right back."

"Thanks, Serg." Dave beamed. "With your coding and my ideas, we can't lose."

"Your coding isn't too bad, either."

Sergio and Dave had been doing well with the few apps they'd developed. Dave often undervalued his skills, and Sergio had taught him quite a bit about coding that he'd not yet learned in college, so it was a great partnership.

⁖ ⁖ ⁖

When the time came for his deposition, Sergio's nerves were at an all-time high. Were Dejuan and Ivan planning on blaming all the mishaps on Sergio, even though they were the ones who stole the entire app from him to begin with?

He didn't know what to expect, or if he would even see his old partners during the deposition.

The lawyer's office was in a high rise on the 20th floor of a building in downtown San Francisco. Prior to going, Sergio had done some more reading on the indictment. Apparently, Ivan and Dejuan were accused of stealing countless people's personal savings. The funds that were pilfered from the Link Virus ended up in off-shore accounts in their names. This was the direct reason the Feds were involved in prosecuting them. In addition to the money, they were being blamed for creating the virus, given the fact most of the funds stolen from people were sent directly to their accounts.

So, according to a federal investigation, Anonymous wasn't to be blamed for creating the virus, despite having taken credit for it. Sergio wondered how Dejuan and Ivan could have even contemplated taking advantage of people when they were making so much money to begin with off the app itself.

He sat in the waiting room over an hour. Each minute that went by made Sergio angrier for being dragged into this entire mess. When a young woman finally came and asked for him to follow her, he was fuming.

The lady led him to a room in which two people sat. Dejuan and Ivan were nowhere in sight, thank goodness. Sergio wasn't sure what he'd have said to them.

After the lawyers spewed the usual drivel for a deposition, they began with the questions. "Do you know why you're here, Mr. Lomas?"

"Not really. Why? Don't you know?" Sergio threw the question back at them. Their condescending attitude irritated him more than he thought possible.

"Mr. Bernard and Mr. Nimitz have declared that you were the one who created the *Link* application, and they've officially accused you of orchestrating this entire operation," the man in the suit said. Sergio didn't heed their names during the introduction, and he really didn't care who they were to begin with.

"Okay...?" Sergio replied, one eyebrow raised. "That's very convenient for them to say that now, isn't it?"

"Well, did you?" the lawyer asked.

"Did I what? Create *Link*? Did I cause all this mayhem? Really? What do *you* think?" Sergio's patience was running thin.

"Okay, why don't we start with something easier? And please don't answer the question with more questions, Mr. Lomas. Where do you know Mr. Bernard and Mr. Nimitz from?" the lawyer asked again.

Sergio took a deep breath. "Okay, I'll answer that question for you, but then I'm leaving."

"Yeah, that's not how this works, Mr. Lomas." The lawyer rolled his eyes. "You need to answer *all* of my questions for the court."

"Well, then perhaps you should have come and got me when you ordered me here. I've taken time out of my day to be here, and then you made me wait a long time outside. So, that's not my fault."

"But that—"

"I don't care for your reasoning," Sergio interrupted. "Or excuses. And, honestly, I also don't care what Dejuan and Ivan have said to you, or anyone else, for that matter. Look, yes, I know them. We met right after college. And yes, we did work together for some time. But let me tell you this, and you can quote me: they are both selfish and greedy individuals. They don't care about anyone but themselves. And that is why they burned me. But now that their necks are on the line, they will try and place blame elsewhere. That's the type of individuals they are. But that's it. Their troubles are none of my business, so I gotta go."

"I don't think you understand the importance of a deposition, Mr. Lomas," the lawyer said.

Sergio stood up and glared at him. "I don't think you understand the importance of someone's time and freedom, but here you are wasting mine. If you feel the need to talk with me any further, please contact my lawyer. I'm sure he'll fill you in on my rights."

Sergio threw down a business card of the lawyer he'd hired some time ago. This was the same lawyer who handled all the legalities of his creations, as well as his portfolio and royalty rights. Sergio couldn't believe he'd just done that, but he had to keep his stance now.

The suited man started to object, but Sergio nervously stormed out of the office, not looking back or wanting to continue the line of questioning.

When he left the building, he smiled. He'd done it. And now, there was no way Dejuan and Ivan were getting out of this mess unscathed. They picked this path and would need to deal with the consequences.

❖ ❖ ❖

A year had passed, and Sergio sat in a waiting room, contemplating all that had happened the previous two years. A lot had changed in such a little time.

Sergio and Dave created a successful business and were an effective team. They were set for life and never had to work another day, if they both so chose, though they didn't stop working. Creating was in their blood, and they wanted to continue their partnership and working relationship. They also felt good about bringing positive creations to the public and helping people achieve their dreams and goals. They shifted their focus from gaming and traveling to easing the everyday life of people in a positive way. Their company slogan, "Have a good life," had proven effective in the marketing campaigns.

Dave had married his college sweetheart and was expecting his first child, and he'd asked Sergio to be the godfather. Sergio grinned, thinking about how he planned on spoiling his new godchild. Perhaps he would buy them a pony for their first birthday and, of course, a stable to go with it. Sergio always wanted one when he was younger, but his family couldn't afford such things.

His parents were traveling the world on a cruise, and he remembered their faces as he presented that gift to them last Christmas. They were ecstatic. He'd also paid off their home and made sure they were set up for retirement. His dad had put his notice in and was on cloud nine ever since.

Dejuan and Ivan sat in federal prison, having been convicted of all their crimes. Sergio was fortunate not to have been involved in the trial, as there wasn't sufficient evidence to include him at all, despite Dejuan and Ivan's admission about stealing the app from him to begin with. He was both relieved and vindicated at the same time.

His phone rang, and he answered. "Hey, Dave. What's up! How's it going?"

"Great! I got a new photo of the baby and I can't wait to show you," Dave said. "I'm sending right now."

Sergio laughed and checked his text. "Adorable."

"Yeah, we were pretty excited. Anyway, the doctor was able to determine the sex and we have it in this envelope. We aren't sure if we want to know yet or not." Dave chuckled. "But, that's not why I called. Did you get the contract our lawyer sent?"

"Yeah, I got it. But I haven't read over it yet. Why? What do you think?" Sergio asked. "Is it a go or no? I trust you."

"It's an unbelievable opportunity, and I can't foresee how it could go wrong. But, again, I wanted your opinion, of course."

"Okay. I'll read it over this evening, and if it's all good, we can sign it tomorrow when I get back to town," Sergio said.

"Have you—" Dave's tone changed and Sergio new exactly where he was going with it.

"Not yet, but I think it'll happen in a minute. I'll call you after and let you know how it goes," Sergio said.

"Okay, I'll talk with you soon, Serg," Dave replied. "Good luck with those fools."

"Thanks." Sergio hung up the phone, glancing at the photo of the baby once again before switching gears and opening his email. Sure enough, the new contract was in there.

"Sergio Lomas?" the gentleman in the suit at the open door called Sergio's name.

"That's me." Sergio smiled and stood up. He followed the man through the halls, past the security desk.

"It took a lot to arrange this," the man said. "But, given the circumstances, we were able to make it happen."

"That's great. I really appreciate it," Sergio said.

The man led him to a room with a single chair on one side with a partition separating two areas.

Sergio sat down in the chair facing Dejuan and Ivan, who sat on the other side of the partition in their orange, prison-issued jumpsuits.

The warden in the tan suit grinned. "I'll be back in fifteen to get you."

"Thank you," Sergio smiled.

"Wow. It's *you*! What do you want?" Dejuan asked first.

There was no need for phones to communicate with one another. They could clearly hear each other through the partition.

"You sure have some nerve showing up here." Ivan glared at him. "After everything you did to us."

"That's not quite the greeting I expected," Sergio said. "Has it ever occurred to you that it was *you* who did this all to yourself?"

Ivan laughed.

"How'd you do it?" Dejuan asked. "Don't even think about telling me Anonymous was the one who created the damn virus. If it had been them, you wouldn't have the contract for X-Link now, would you?"

"Yeah, we know all about it," Ivan said. "Our lawyer stopped by yesterday to tell us the update."

X-Link was the antivirus software Sergio had developed with Dave for the government in order to eliminate the Link Virus. The US government was paying a billion dollars to Sergio and Dave's company for the rights and implementation of the program. Once it was up and running, the virus would disappear altogether and Link would be operable once again, changing lives for the better. The future proceeds for Link would go toward the Global Economy Fund, which focused on improving the current global warming situation and making the world a better place for everyone in it. Of course, the Feds made sure Ivan and Dejuan signed over all the rights, which lessoned their sentencing, though only slightly.

"It's the craziest thing, really. Once the government provided us with the original code that was downloaded into the app, Dave and I were able to locate the Link Virus coding," Sergio explained. "Their programmers couldn't find anything, but we sure had no problem. It was ingenious to embed it into the original code and have it triggered six months later. It wasn't too hard to tighten the security and create the anti-virus. We are signing the contract tomorrow. Can you believe they are paying us a billion dollars?"

"You son of a bitch!" Ivan tried to jump up, but his chains pulled him back.

Dejuan laughed. "Yeah, I fucking knew it. We should have read the whole freaking code. I'm sure we would've found something. But we were too eager to make a quick buck and cut you off."

"I can't believe you planned all this. Takes a patient man, I'll give you that," Ivan added.

"Funny thing, that Link. It's almost as if you compared your phones with it prior to letting it go into the world. You found out how compatible you truly were for one another, didn't you?" Sergio alluded to the fact that he had utilized the app early on to find them and compare all three of them before he even told them about the app in the first place. "It's also how I found Dave. And let me tell you, unlike with you two, we work really well together."

Ivan again tried to jump up, his face flush with rage. "You're not gonna get away with it, Sergio! You won't."

"Oh, but I already have, my friend. I already have."

The warden knocked on the door. Sergio rose and grinned. "Anyway, it was a pleasure speaking with you, gentlemen. Please know that I will never again think about either of you, though I am sure that you'll be thinking about me for a long time to come. And remember, *have a good life.*"

THEORY OF MIND

Your honor, let me start by saying this—Isaac Moreno is my boy.

Ever since he was born, he was under my care. He has been my responsibility all this time, and I can promise you that I've tried my best in raising him. But most importantly, as I said, he truly is *my* boy, as bizarre as that may sound. You see, Isaac's story has tragic origins. Although, I will get into that later.

For now, let me tell you about my boy. As a baby, Isaac laughed and played like every other healthy human child growing up—at least from what I could learn from all your literature. Even gloomy days were no match for Isaac's smiles. I know this to be fact because I came to the Moreno family's lives at the same time that Isaac was born. And from day one, Isaac was my boy.

My task was to take care of him, and that I would do diligently every moment of the day. This was, after all, not only the core of my programming, but also the justification for my continued existence in the Moreno household.

Isaac's autism was detected at eighteen months. At two years old he was officially diagnosed to be on the spectrum by Dr. Charles Baumgarten—I will never forget his name. Your honor, as you know, though medical research is vast and the study of the human brain and genome has reached many previously uncovered milestones, a solid explanation for this human disorder, or even a cure, to say the least, hasn't been found yet. So, though Isaac was still a toddler, some often described his mind as having a gap.

But you see, your honor, he was my boy, and I found no fault in him. Isaac was my sole concern. Due to the fact that the Morenos didn't have another child, and they lived secluded in the mountains, this meant I didn't have the opportunity to interact with other human children that I could learn from or compare him to. Nonetheless, I devoured human literature, particularly in the areas of psychological and physiological development, in order to be more effective in my work with him. Though, I didn't think of it as work, of course.

Soon, I realized that Isaac indeed struggled with verbal and nonverbal language development, as well as with social interactions. He partook in repetitive behaviors and he appeared to lack what you humans refer to as theory of mind, or the personal capability of understanding that others have beliefs, desires, intentions, and perspectives different from one's own. Still, though, I figured that the fact that he didn't have other human children to interact with on a normal basis also played a role in his impediments.

But as you are now aware, the Morenos were religious zealots. And this didn't help. My owners belonged to a small but close-knit group of people that believed that the end of the world was imminent, so, immediately prior to Isaac's birth, they sold everything they owned and moved to the mountains, away from all civilization. If we would've been down here in the city, Isaac could've—and most likely would've—received the services he needed. Unfortunately, of course, this was not the case. Still, I respected Martin and Luz's decision, and I would honor it.

And so Isaac was raised in seclusion, away from all civilization. The next house was exactly 7.3 miles away, with many trees separating us. In his early years of life, Isaac's interactions with those outside the family were limited to only the church gatherings once a week and his doctor visits every six months. I was always by his side. And I learned soon that this is why I was brought in by the Morenos, to help with him. To be his companion—a nanny, of sorts.

But I became much more than this. I became his mother.

Your honor, I know that you must be wondering how that came to be and why. And I will explain. I am a model

BT78, better known as 'Betty' by my family, and like I said, Isaac is my boy. He is mine as much as I am his, for each other is all we have now.

This is our story.

Please allow me to start at the beginning, as I've learned that humans' understanding is improved upon when taught in a sequence.

As my name states, I am a model '78, which is coincidently the same year that Isaac was born. I was adopted into the home of Luz and Martin Moreno as they were expecting a child. Of course, the miracle of life and the ability for you humans to procreate is still something that I am in awe of. But, again, that's a different story. You see, the Morenos decided they needed a BT model like me around, not only to help with house chores and farming tasks, but also because of our nurturing programing. And being alone on the ranch, someone like me could provide much help. They were right. Many upgrades and modifications have been made since the M53's came around decades ago, and the evolution of science and robotics led us to the BT prototypes, like me.

I am sure you know how humans predicted centuries ago that intelligent machines would exist that would make life easier for them. Their fascination with these machines led to an increase in research and technological advances that eventually brought about this reality. Over time, these so-called robots developed some human qualities, such as being able to reason, self-awareness, and empathy, for example. Nonetheless, you humans programmed us to be incapable of hurting any human being, and only to serve you and make your lives better—or easier, rather. Rapidly, many companies invested in this new technology, and soon there were a variety of models out there. And when we became affordable, we turned into very common household appliances. So, we became your companions, chefs, chauffeurs, maids, and nannies.

Unfortunately, however, this wasn't all good news.

You know the history of this, your honor. It didn't take long for many people to become scared of smart machines. Those few who didn't own one shamed those who did. They said we took jobs away from humans. They said we couldn't be trusted, since we could malfunction at any given time. And despite the fact that they could command us and we would have no option but to obey them, these people had seen too many movies where we rebelled against them.

Soon, automatonophobia became prevalent around the world. And the minority became the majority. The media caused further paranoia, and this too triggered our decline. People turned against this technology and large robotic companies inevitably went bankrupt. Including the makers of the BT models.

During my time in the Moreno ranch, there was a decline in most models. Though I enjoyed the peace and quiet of the mountains, most robotic labs and factories around the world were put out of commission. That I am aware of, your honor, no company survived. And within a decade, many people started attacking us if they saw one of us walking on the streets of the cities. They slam us into walls, throw rocks at us, and abuse us.

This is what we endure, your honor. Now, I am not complaining, as this now is not the time for this. But, as I am sure you are aware, there are just a handful of us left, at least here in the great city. And those that remain are constantly shamed by the fact that we are what we are, and they are scared of what will happen. Thankfully, most of our owners protect us and keep us indoors.

Sadly for me, however, I don't have that luxury anymore.

You see, your honor, Isaac was four years, three months, and nine days old when Martin and Luz had the accident. I will never forget that day. It's not possible for me to forget any day or moment of my existence, however, this particular day will certainly remain in the vertex of my memories pyramid.

Early that Sunday morning, Martin and Luz left to go do food exchanges with other church members. Everyone farmed something different in their respective ranches, and this was a customary practice. But this winter season had brought more snow than any other, and as you know, the iced mountain roads are unforgiving.

Yes, I was fully aware that the government normally took orphaned children under their care, but it was my understanding that Isaac's parents were against the establishment to begin with. I also always believed that Isaac was my responsibility and that I could do a good job raising him, since I knew and understood him better than anyone. Though in retrospect perhaps this wasn't the wisest decision, you must understand that this was engrained in my core from the moment he was born. And a BT always does as told. For the sake of remaining transparent, your honor, even if this gets me in trouble, the truth is that I wouldn't have changed my mind about this for anything in the world, even if given the opportunity.

Thinking back, I am also surprised that none of the families in the church network ever reported this to the authorities, but I guess that's another story. Besides, Martin always said that the church takes care of their own. So, I figured I could heavily rely on their support in raising young Isaac. But, believe it or not, no matter how hard I tried, your honor, no family was willing to take Isaac in. There was always something about not being able to feed an extra mouth in these hard times or something like that. But I could see through them, and all they saw in him was a hole in their pockets. Simply the burden of a troubled child with a developmental disorder.

But not to me. Isaac was my world.

A family inquired twice about the ranch and asked if the boy and I came as part of the package. Now, I know I am incapable of hurting a human being, your honor, but something in me snapped that day. Obviously, we never saw them again.

But I promise you that I didn't actually hurt anyone. I simply scared them away. Thankfully, it worked.

Most of the church members were around for a little while, but I did all the explanation to poor Isaac about why mama and papa were not coming back. And after six months and three days, the visits finally stopped. That's how long it took for the church to forget about young Isaac, your honor. Six months and three days.

Soon after the visits ended, we completely stopped attending the church's services. I noticed how everyone, especially the other children, looked at him with trepidation and even fear. And since he no longer had human parents to guard him and protect him, the people didn't hold back. It angered me so much that we never stepped foot back in any of their strange ritual services again.

Now, we were completely alone, and I had to trust Isaac to teach me how to teach him.

I accessed books through the central system; and since I wasn't sure what to expect in raising a child without their human parents, I read 7,218 parenting books, 597 cookbooks, and 4,126 books on schooling and curriculum. Yes, I had already learned everything I could about autism spectrum disorder and child nurturing prior to this, but I strived harder than ever to stay current with new information. And something that I realized, your honor, is that if you've met one person with autism, that means that you've met literally *one* person with autism. What I mean is this—first, a human is not their label or their disability, and also, every child is a completely different world.

It was difficult in the early stages; when I'd want him to eat his vegetables, he'd rather carve his broccoli into squares or make faces on his plate. I remember when I figured out how to raise my voice and use a firm tone on him, Isaac simply stared at me as though I had just awoken from a deep slumber. Through these stormy experiences, however, I grew to love Isaac even more. Yes, your honor, I am aware that I have no heart, but I do possess a core processor, and my entire core existed for him.

I chose to honor Luz's wish of homeschooling Isaac. The original plan was to do this all the way until high school, but as you know now, your honor, this wasn't the case. I was only able to do this until sixth grade. I will explain why in a bit.

Thankfully, BTs were programmed to serve and nurture, so we could also help kids out with academic assignments, and homeschooling was not difficult for me. I taught him extensively about history, mathematics, language arts, and the arts and sciences. I also took the time to teach him about his fractured mind, and together, we worked on a defense mechanism for the things that came up.

I was so proud of Isaac. He has a brilliant mind! He learns so fast and has an inquisitive nature. But still, I had to help him grow. You see, I had protected Isaac for so long and taught him everything I could. Or at least, I felt that way. But now it was time for me to let him go and face his fears. I saw the need for him to interact with other children his age. I could only provide so much for him in the ranch, but what Isaac needed was down here in the city, with his own people. Besides, this was a chance to test my parenting skills and to see *my* son not drown in the process of growing up.

I knew we would face many great challenges. But as you know, a mother would do anything for their son, your honor.

It had been nine difficult but beautiful years, and I felt that it was time for Isaac to finally see the outside world. Still, I wasn't sure about what the city had for us—a boy and a robot he called "Mama."

By the way, to be honest, your honor, I was proud when he called me that. I truly was his mother, after all.

I knew that Isaac didn't like new things, and he struggled with doing something outside of his routines, so I frontloaded Isaac as much as I could. For an entire year, I told Isaac to prepare for a new place. I remember one day I told him that it could be scary because of the people there, but he held my hand and asked, "Will you be there with me, Mama?"

I hugged him and held him there for as long as he'd let me.

Thankfully, the Morenos left plenty of savings, to which I had full access. This facilitated our transition to a new life outside the ranch. Over the years, I embraced a human intonation when speaking, and this also helped when I spoke to humans as Isaac's guardian on the phone. I used this skill to buy us our condo in a nice suburban neighborhood and enroll him into school. Almost everything else I did virtually, so there wouldn't be any issues.

Though I was scared, I was so sure that Isaac was going to be okay navigating life in the city and that he'd deal with his communication and social issues effectively with me by his side. I was an intelligent machine, after all, in a constant cycle of evolution for the best. And so was my son.

So, we made the change and moved here to the city. But you see, your honor, I didn't know that this new phase would almost pull us apart.

The first few weeks here were fine. We got acquainted with the place and all the relevant points of interest, such as the school, the park, and the grocery store, although most transactions would be done virtually anyway. But as the first day of school approached, I knew that Isaac was nervous.

On the first day of classes, he insisted that I walk with him to school, even if it was just a block away. I knew that many people wouldn't be comfortable with the idea of a robot taking a human child to school anymore, not like the days before. But I figured it wouldn't hurt, and if it helped Isaac's confidence, that I was amendable. Junior high kids could be cruel anyway, so I did.

I just wanted my son to feel normal; I wanted him to embrace this new place and get accustomed to new people. Like I said before, it was an opportunity for him to grow.

At first, everything that morning seemed normal. Things went well. We got his schedule and books, and we toured the place a bit. But things worsened when he called me "Mama" out loud. Time seemed to stop as everyone's stares fell upon us. I heard whispers as I hugged him, and I thought to myself that this was perhaps a stupid idea after all. Maybe it wasn't too late to pick everything up and go back to the ranch.

My poor baby boy!

I wanted so bad for him to be just Isaac Moreno, a normal kid. But now, on his first day of school, he was already the son of a scum, a robot. He stayed in school and I went home. I hoped for Isaac to have a good day. It was a relief when he finally walked through the doors unscathed that afternoon. I asked him about his day, and all he replied was, "It was interesting."

Interesting? Was that good or bad? I didn't know for sure. But he wasn't much for words anyway, so when I queried for more, he didn't elaborate much. I figured it couldn't be bad if he at least wasn't complaining. I let it go.

After the first couple of days, Isaac wanted to walk by himself. And that's what he did. He spent the rest of the following weeks settling into his schedule, and when he came back home from school every day he would tell me about his day. Every day he would share more and more, though still little by little. And I felt joy. We would spend the rest of our days doing homework and playing video games.

Yes, your honor, video games. I guess I pride myself in being one of those cool parents in the world. Although, I also made an effort to take him to the park as much as possible. Whenever we went out in public I always made sure to wear a long trench coat with a hoodie to cover myself. Isaac had a matching one. He thought it was just cool to dress like that, and I simply obliged. Little did he know that in reality I was trying to protect him.

I must say, though, things were turning out for the best for my son. And like any parent, that was all I ever wanted.

Several weeks went by and I got my fair share of scorn whenever I was out and about in the city. But if this meant that my son could have a normal life, whatever "normal" meant anyway, it didn't bother me. Besides, I tried my best to remain indoors until Isaac was back from school. One day Isaac told me that some kids at school that remembered him from the first day thought I was as his personal nanny or family maid. He didn't correct them, and I figured this was for the best.

A couple of months into the school year, a series of events triggered a massive wave of hate toward robots. For some reason, a subgroup of people felt the need to completely destroy all remaining robots and began demanding such atrocity. You probably know more about this than me, your honor, so I won't get much into this.

Now, Isaac wasn't very keen on paying attention to the news, just like most kids his age, I guess, so he was oblivious to what was happening around the world. But he's always been a very smart child, your honor. So, he quickly noticed how people reacted to me and how humans overall felt toward robots. However, I assumed that as long as he didn't talk about his robot mother or referred to me as "mom" in public, he was protected.

I assumed wrong.

Isaac suddenly started acted strangely. He stopped calling me "Mama" altogether. He would speak less and less with me. He started coming home later after school, and he would take his dinner into his room and remain there until the following morning. When I asked why he was avoiding me, he simply said he'd rather spend time with his human friends. But I knew well that he didn't have any friends. The problem was that if I pressed on, he would snap at me. His patience started running shorter and shorter, and his anger outbursts increased, both in frequency and intensity.

Your honor, I am not exaggerating when I say that I felt like I was constantly walking on eggshells around him. And this was only the beginning of what you humans call "sleepless nights" for me. Obviously, I didn't sleep like humans anyway, but I was ever so restless about the whole situation, to the point that I didn't know what to do.

Then, one beautiful sunny day, while I was tending to the balcony garden, I received a call from school; Isaac had gotten into a fight. After pretending to be boy's human mother, I rushed to the school. I had told them that I would send the nanny—me—and that she had permission to engage on their behalf. Thankfully, he was only given detention. But when I tried to take him home, he was very upset. With me. With the school. With the world. He asked me why I even had bothered to come to pick him up. He then told me something that hurts me to this day; he said he wanted real parents, not a tin can like me.

Your honor, my emotions as a robot were evolving fast, and just as Isaac was growing and evolving, so was I. And I began to feel deep emotions. I began to experience heartbreaking grief. And though I couldn't experience physical pain, the mental anguish of rejection was great. I didn't know what to say to him. I was his mother! I had raised him, after all. And I loved him dearly.

The truth is, your honor, that I didn't want to see him suffer. And I wanted to take away all his pain. And if somehow I could take it from him, I would gladly experience it just so that he didn't have to. The world had dealt him a bad hand of cards, and it was too much to bear.

My poor son!

After that day, aside from very sullen good mornings and head nodding I got nothing more from Isaac in the following weeks. But on one fine afternoon in November, he rushed back from school, and with so much light in his eyes told me that he had made a new friend—Chito. Isaac asked if Chito could come over tomorrow and spend the afternoon with him.

Delightedly, I agreed.

I was happy that Isaac was finally having a normal life; I was even happier he had talked to me and even asked me for permission to bring a friend over. Isaac was very nice to me that evening.

The next day, I made sure the place was clean and neat. I ordered pizza for the boys and arranged snacks for them. Isaac and Chito came in, laughing. I was elated to see my son like that. But when they walked in, they completely ignored me, as if I was simply a trash can or something like that. Isaac simply nodded at me and went straight for the pizza, without saying a word to me.

I said, "Hi. Please wash your hands before eating. And pick your backpack from the floor; you know it doesn't go there."

Isaac and Chito exchanged stares and blurted out laughing, completely ignoring my commands.

I didn't want to cause a scene and embarrass him, so I disregarded the whole thing. I simply picked up after them and went to the kitchen. I watched as Isaac talk animatedly for hours about school, random kids, and some girls. I watched them play, joke, and laugh, like it was any other day. They seemed to hit it off well. But Chito was rude. And I didn't like his language. I quickly saw how Isaac was being influenced by his choice of words, too.

After that first encounter, Chito was a regular visitor. He never seemed to mind that they were never interrupted by any human adults. In fact, it appeared that they enjoyed that. But I started to worry about Isaac's change in behavior. Although, I also couldn't complain much, because Isaac had started to spend time with me again and was giving me details about his days. He even sharing things about him personally. He told me also about how nervous he was about upcoming midterm tests. And he was always happy to talk about Chito. "Chito this, and Chito that." In fact, his life seemed to revolve around Chito a lot those days.

Again, I didn't mind, as long as it meant he was happy.

But just as it has been in my experience during the entirety of my existence, all good things must come to an end. You see, your honor, Isaac had not told Chito that I was his mother. He hadn't shared the fact that his biological parents had died when he was just a young kid and that a robot had raised him in a secluded ranch up in the mountains. And one day, while at our place, they decided to play a video game that he and I used to play all the time. I guess it must have felt nostalgic, because Isaac suddenly called out to me, "Look, Mama, I'm about to beat Chito! Check it out."

Chito laughed. "Did you just call your bot Mama?"

I immediately saw Isaac's face expression, as if he felt trapped. But I didn't know what to say or do.

Isaac quickly replied a vehement, "No, bro! Oh, shit. That was my bad. I was just thinking out loud. It's cuz my real mom likes this game. That's all." He then gave a very fake laugh.

I slowly walked back behind the kitchen counter.

But Chito wasn't done. "Yo, bro. For reals, though. I gotta ask you something. What's the deal with that bot and you?"

"What do you mean?" Isaac replied.

"Yeah, bro. You know. Like…that thing is always around. It's like your shadow or something. I mean, like, your parents always leave you alone with it and stuff. What's up with that?"

Isaac paused the game. He looked at me and then back at him. "Oh, it's, um… Yeah, it's nothing. But she's cool, though."

Chito then stood up and stared at me. I was petrified. What was he thinking?

"Bro, but like, can she suck cock or something?"

"Excuse me?" I finally said. "I beg your pardon, young man."

"What? I'm just saying. Might as well do something good while you're around. Plus it looks like a hot girl. Kinda. I mean, kinda. Do robots even have genders? It looks like a girl minus the hair and it talks like a girl. But like, in metal."

Isaac stood up. I could tell he was nervous. "Nah, bro. It's not like that. Betty is just like my personal servant, you know. My real parents have her hanging around since they're gone a lot. That's all."

"Betty?" Chito said. "It has a name? Seriously?"

"Well, it's a BT78, so we just refer to her as Betty. But come on, bro. Let's keep on playing the game. Just ignore the stupid robot." Isaac cleared his throat as he looked at me.

Chito smirked. "Yeah, I guess." He then sat down and continued playing.

I didn't know what to do. I simply stood there. I said nothing. I did nothing!

But your honor, that wasn't the end. This was, in fact, just the beginning of my torment. You see, just an hour later, Chito stood up and walked toward the kitchen. He completely ignored me when I asked him if I could help him with anything. He went straight to the fridge and took out some orange juice I had purchased for Isaac; he loves that stuff. He then took a swig directly from the gallon. I never let Isaac do that, your honor! I asked Chito to please use a cup, but he ignored me. Instead, he simply chuckled and continued with a mouthful.

"Hey, Isaac!"

"What's up?" Isaac replied from the couch without looking back.

"Do you mind if I do this to your *Betty*?" He dumped the rest of the contents on my head without waiting for a response from Isaac. "Is she even waterproof?"

Trust me, your honor. I wanted to do something to the little brat. But of course I couldn't.

Isaac was furious. He came running and punched Chito on the face. I'd never seen him show this much anger in my life. He then threw him out of the house.

Luckily, of course, I am waterproof. But it was the essence of the act that upset me, your honor. The lack of respect. The nerve of the kid to do something like that, in front of my son.

But I felt bad, because Isaac was sad. Chito was his only friend. That night, we sat like strangers on the couch, just staring at the screen for hours.

He finally got up to go to bed, and all he said was, "I am sorry." He hugged me.

I hugged him back. I realized then that he was turning out to be a good man, and that I was raising a fine son.

After that day, Isaac began to sketch again, just like he used to when he was younger. His sketching was usually a sign that he had a lot to say but he wasn't able to express himself. I yearned for him to talk to me. But, instead, he would put on his headphones with loud music and simply draw.

One night, I finally summoned the courage to knock on his door and ask him how he was faring. He let me in and casually told me about how everyone at school called him "robot boy." Apparently, Chito had started a rumor around the school that Isaac had a robot for a mother and also that I had performed fellatio on him.

Again, your honor, I wished then that I wasn't programmed the way I was. I truly wanted to hurt that kid. And I apologize for even thinking that. But more than anything, I desired to take away the sadness from my son. This sadness was filling his fractured mind with darkness, and I didn't want that. I didn't want to see him consumed in a downward spiral. But no book I'd read provided a tangible answer of what to say to him at that moment.

I simply hugged him.

That night, Isaac cried himself to sleep in my arms. He cried because, as usual, it's what his body needed to do in that moment to release tension from feeling overwhelmed with emotions and sensory stimulations.

On February third, all hell broke loose. Some radical young people who called themselves "emancipators" felt the need to go out and destroy robots, even if they were with their owners. I'm sure you remember the famous march of the emancipators, your honor. Well, as you know, soon many other college students across the nation joined in their efforts and participated in the mayhem. Of course, we robots couldn't even fight back due to our programming. And many were lost. So many.

Things got so bad that Isaac learned about it at school. He ran all the way home right after school that day just to check if I was safe because he heard about some houses around the country that had been broken into and their home robots were tortured. Thankfully, I was safe at home.

But, your honor, human beings can be very creative when they want to. And this also includes infliction of pain. You see, one would think that not being able to defend ourselves against an attack is already enough torture, but what these cruel young men did to those like me was pure evil. Evil, I tell you. By the way, I'm not stating this to incite your pity, your honor; I am simply wanting to explain.

You may or may not know this, but the latest generation of robots were created to resemble human beings. Fundamentally speaking, where you have a heart, we have a core motor; where you have a brain, we also have our central processing unit; and instead of blood we have neurocline, or "N-juice" as we call it. N-juice is basically engineered robotic blood, with the ability to circulate oils that facilitate hydraulics, carry nanotech and antiviruses through fiber optic cables, while at the same time cooling us. This sophisticated liquid travels through a complex system of veins that is woven within us. Well, your honor, the emancipators surgically attacked each of these systems, making sure were left beyond possible repair.

The emancipators drew the N-juice out of our system to inject it into their bodies for some kind of high. I heard it once in the news that a high from N-juice was better than any other drug, whether natural or synthetic. Essentially, your honor, the emancipators destroyed those like me simply for a momentary high.

A young man by the name of Jack Valentine was the leader of the emancipators. I'm confident that you know his name and perhaps even his story. But what got to me was when he claimed during a live interview that a robot had killed his entire family. Of course everyone now knows that this was a lie, but at the time, it incited so much hatred and prejudice toward robots. People refused to believe that we had feelings or that we even mattered anymore. And the marginalization got worse. In a matter of days, many businesses restricted robot access to their spaces. And though it was a law, we just weren't welcomed even in most public areas anymore.

Of course, I quickly realized that this also meant that things wouldn't go well for a boy with a robot for a mother. So, I tried to protect Isaac as best as I could.

During those winter days, Isaac wouldn't say much to me. He would just tell me to be careful and to remain home as much as possible. I knew he was worried about me. But I think I was more worried about him. If anything happened to me, he'd be all alone! And, your honor, you and I both know that this world is not kind to an orphaned autistic thirteen-year-old boy, and much less for one totally alone.

But Isaac was mostly quiet. Even the loud music was now gone. By March, he started playing his violin again. My robot spirit rejoiced at this, as he was doing the things that brought him peace again. Many years earlier I had read that learning to play a musical instrument was great for children, especially for kids with impairment, so I took it upon myself to teach him. But I wanted him to choose the instrument he wanted. At four years old, he chose the violin.

When the beautiful violin was delivered to the ranch, it was love at first sight for him. Though he was young, he was a natural. By this time Isaac had just lost his parents, and the countless hours he poured into practicing quickly paid off. It was cathartic for him. And I enjoyed listening to him play. I think the soft, yet chaotic music helped him express everything he felt.

But, of course, as he grew up, he traded the violin for video games. So the fact that he started playing on his own, without me coaxing him, was great. His playing made it easy for me to stay indoors.

But, once again, not all good things last. You see, your honor, I had already forgotten about Chito, Isaac's troublesome friend. But apparently Chito hadn't forgotten about me. And I'll get into that in a little bit. In the following weeks, Isaac's behavior slowly began to change yet again. Since getting in the fight with Chito after the whole orange juice incident, Isaac had kept to himself and had no friends outside of me. I know it ate him up silently. I mean, wasn't that the whole point of coming to city, after all, so that he could interact with peers his age? But the problem was that he started skipping school. I surely didn't expect that. And after a phone call, I had to go to his school to discuss this issue with the principal.

That day, March 18th, your honor, is when everything changed.

I had to figure out a good excuse to use for Isaac's parents not to show up in person and why the robot nanny would go instead. I couldn't think of anything truly compelling, just that they were away on business. But there I went, walking hidden in my hooded trench coat, all the way to the school. Isaac wore his coat that way as well. Though this time he did it more out of embarrassment than fashion.

However, inside the school, on our way to the administration office, as we walked through the campus main hall, Chito saw us. I sensed Isaac's discomfort, but I tried to remain calm. The problem was that Chito had an agenda.

Unexpectedly, Chito began to call the attention of everyone around him and made a spectacle of Isaac's "mother"—the supposedly fellatio-ing robot. I was furious, your honor! Not so much because of what he said about me—I could care less about that—but because of how he made Isaac feel.

The mob of young students suddenly grew around us, all slaying us with their stares and unpleasant expressions of disgust. Then, they all joined in their mocking insults and laughter and directed it toward my son. They made him feel terrible by telling him that his mother was only an appliance without a soul and a machine to sexually please men, among other things. Several kids even wondered out loud if Isaac was "weird" and "different" and "robot-like" because he was raised by a robot mom and not a human mom. One girl asked him if he was autistic because of me.

I wanted to cry! I wanted to hug my son and fly away as far as possible. But I couldn't do either of those things, of course.

And then it happened.

Isaac removed his hood and said, "She is *not* my mom."

I froze.

So did all the children. Silence ensued.

"This is not my mother!" he repeated, this time louder.

All the kids surrounding us, including Chito, had blank stares, unsure of what to say.

I tried to hide even further into my coat.

My Isaac suddenly pulled it away from me, making it fall on the ground, exposing my true nature. A robot, indeed.

"This is just a BT78, you idiots," Isaac asserted. "She is my servant. And yeah, it's true; she sucks cock really good." He laughed.

I gasped.

A few of the students joined in his nervous laughter.

Isaac then slowly walked to Chito, who was drinking a bottled juice. In front of everyone, he extended his hand. Chito's brow was raised.

"Give me the bottle," Isaac commanded.

Chito looked around as if looking for moral support or direction from the crowd. He received none. Slowly, Chito conceded his almost full drink to Isaac.

Isaac took the bottle, turned around, and walked toward me. He took a quick sip of the drink and then dumped the rest on my head.

The children laughed out loud.

I'd never seen Isaac's face with the expression he had that moment. And for the first time ever, I was afraid of him.

Isaac broke out in a loud snort. And that was all it took for the rest of the students to throw whatever they could at me.

I quickly picked up my coat and used it to shield myself as best as I could. I left as the students continued to kick me, spit at me, and call me terrible names. I exited the school and ran straight home, locking myself up in my room. I wept N-juice, your honor. That's not supposed to happen! But my core's beating was strained. I was malfunctioning. And I couldn't understand why. And most importantly, I couldn't understand how Isaac could do that to me. I understood his need to belong, but I was just not prepared for to join in their hatred and shaming.

Was he protecting me in some way? I could only wait for him to get back, and hopefully he'd explain it all to me. Maybe I'd missed something, and perhaps it would all make sense once he elaborated on his plan.

That night he got back late...as in, really late. I paced in the house, anxiously waiting for him. He'd never been out this late, and all I could imagine was the worst. But when he walked in, I immediately noticed that he was under the influence of something. I used a stern voice when I talked to him, but he turned abruptly to me and pushed me aside.

"You're so dumb, Betty! Just leave me alone." He struggled to make it to his room, but I helped him get there without getting hurt. He made it to his bed and turned around. "I hope today's episode reminds you that you are not my mom," he reiterated.

"Isaac. Why are you saying that? What's gotten into you, my son?"

"I said... I am *not* your son, dumb robot-bitch!"

"Excuse me, young man? That is no way to talk–"

"Oh, just shut up already!" He threw himself on his bed. "Like I said, you are not my mother. Honestly, BT78, I wonder how the government even let such an incompetent machine raise me. All you've done is ruin my chances at a normal life."

I was dumbstruck; I couldn't believe what I was hearing. Time seemed to stop at that moment. Frankly, nothing could've ever prepared me for this, your honor.

My entire life, up to this point, I had made it my sole mission to nurture Isaac. I had tried my very best to teach him how to be a good person. I protected him and even helped cope with his disorder, no matter how difficult the challenge proved to be. Your honor, even as a robot, I swear I tried to teach him human values worth having, such as empathy. And the thing is that I also learned to be empathetic and more "human-like" myself by teaching Isaac to be this way.

We used to be so close, but I could see that this was all gone now.

The next morning, I watched Isaac leave the house without saying a word. It felt as if he was planets away. This was my world crashing down before me. But I wanted to honor his wishes, so I kept my distance away from him.

Unfortunately, that day I learned of the multiple videos that went viral of my attack by the students at Isaac's school. I shrunk further into my shell at the statements made in the comments section. Your honor, I was becoming just BT78, not Betty anymore. Some people even dared to say that I most likely had kidnapped him as a baby! Others said that I probably implanted a chip in his brain to make him stay with me. And then there were so many other statements that echoed what the children told us in school, about him being that way because he was raised by a machine and not a human mother.

Soon, I couldn't even go tend to my garden in the balcony anymore because the neighbors would send death glares my way. Our cover was blown, and people now knew that this human boy lived alone with a robot. And I was afraid, your honor. Afraid not so much for what they could or most likely would do to me; but because of the fact that the authorities would take my son away from me forever.

The following days were not much better. I knew Isaac was having a hard time too. One day, I saw from the window how another kid bumped him so hard he fell and told him that robot sons had no right to complain about the way they were treated. I wanted to go and defend him, but I knew it would only cause more harm than good. Isaac simply stood up and continued his walk to school with his hooded trench on.

That afternoon, after he came back from school, Isaac finally spoke to me. But it wasn't good. He scowled at me! "You know what, BT78, Chito was right about you. And I've been thinking about this too. Maybe what people have been saying is true, and you did put a chip in my brain after you kidnapped me from my real parents as a baby. But don't worry; I've already been looking into getting me foster parents—real human beings. The ones that actually have feelings."

At his words, I bowed my head and walked away. I was brokenhearted. Isaac was choosing a path of darkness, and I couldn't do much about it. I knew he felt he was doing this for his best. And, your honor, I wanted so bad to take away all his grief. If I could just transfer all the pain from him and install it in me so that we wouldn't experience the hurt anymore, I would have done so in a heartbeat!

After that, he rarely came home before midnight. And when he did, he treated me like I didn't exist. I could be a walking microwave, for all he cared. I still continued to prepare breakfast, lunch, and dinner for him. But at times he would simply look at it as it was poisoned and would make ugly faces before throwing it all away in the trash. I started worried even more about his health. He wasn't eating!

I was his mother, for crying out loud! I raised him and nurtured him all these years. And I wasn't going to give up so easily. But he was turning into a monster that hated me. Society was turning him into this.

And I knew that deep down, he still cared for me.

As a robot, I could store memory—more like videos of every day I had existed. So, I spent countless hours revisiting videos in my memory from when Isaac was a little kid. And one day, there was this brief moment when I experienced hope. Isaac saw what I was projecting on the wall, and he came and sat down with me on the couch. He took about half an hour to watch some of our memories together. He smiled and even laughed. At one point, he began to cry, and he hugged me.

I must say, your honor, that I felt a hint of joy. Not because he was crying, but because I knew then that he remembered the great times we shared. I knew that he felt bad about everything that had been happening. He was experiencing empathy. And Isaac might have struggled his whole life with theory of mind, but at that very moment, I witnessed my son experience patterns of behavior that neurotypical people had.

After that day, Isaac spent more time at home. He began eating all the meals I prepared for him. Though it wasn't always so sweet or smooth. After all, he was still being treated like an outcast at school.

One late April morning, while eating breakfast, Isaac asked me why he ended up with me. I knew he was fully aware of what had happened to his parents, as I never kept that away from him, so I wanted to understand what he meant. He further elaborated by asking me why he didn't end up with some distant family member, some foster parents, or even with another family from the church his parents used to attend—though you and I both know that they were more of a cult, your honor, but that's another story.

It dawned on me then that he didn't fully understand that I was forced to raise him, though I was glad to do so. I explained to him how I was the only one willing to stay by his side. I shared how it looked utterly impossible for me to raise a human child on my own up in a secluded ranch, but how I was able to overcome. And I also told him that I felt like I had done a good job, raising such a great man.

He smiled, your honor. And then I saw it; I saw my beautiful thirteen-year-old boy was suddenly present. My son was back. He sat there, staring into space, taking it all in.

That evening, we spent hours on our couch playing his favorite memories from the ranch. We saw when I taught him to ride a bike. We revisited each of his birthdays. We watched and laughed at how awkward we were and how it all just looked empty, like our strife was nothing.

Isaac's laughter rang true and through our home. And then he sobbed. He moved closer and leaned in towards me. I welcomed him and embraced him. He was my son, my boy, and he had found his way home, where he belonged, with me—his mother.

He apologized to me and told me and said he wanted to find comfort in our simple life once again. I listened and remained silent, thankful and happy to have him back.

The following morning Isaac got dressed and, to my surprise, asked me to accompany him to school. I was shocked, to say the least. I wasn't sure this was a good idea. But he insisted, so I did. I went to get my trench coat, but he told me to leave it behind.

"Are you sure?" I asked.

"I am sure, Mama," he said with a smile.

As we made our way to the school, I wanted to cower away from the crowd gathering around us. But Isaac held my hand reassuringly, and this gave me the courage to march with my head held high. We walked straight to the principal's office, and Isaac shared with him that he had a special announcement that day during the morning assembly. He explained his elaborate plan with the principal. Thankfully, the principal was obliged to grant his request, as he felt it would help bring the tension down in the student body.

I must admit, your honor, that I'd never seen Isaac so self-assured.

As agreed, I remained in the office lobby until it was time for the assembly. Isaac went to his classes. During second period, the students gathered in the gymnasium. I made my way there as well. And then I saw him in the distance. Isaac—my son.

He was no longer the little autistic boy that cried at night and tapped his fingers and couldn't meet another human's eyes. He was no longer the child rejected by his own kind over and over again. He was no longer the young boy who wondered why he had a robot for a mother. He was a man. And he had accepted who he was.

Your honor, my core swelled with pride as I watched him. I'd raised that fine man! But I was also petrified for what he was about to embark on.

When we got on that stage, he seemed nervous. He cleared his throat as several kids laughed at him. I turned to them and stared at them with a menacing face. But they didn't stop. He apprehensively grabbed the mic and called me up. I had no idea he'd call me up to join him! I nervously stood up, and made my way to him, as some kids threw pieces of paper and other things to me. As I got to his side, he grabbed my hand.

The words he said made me blossom with joy, "My name is Isaac Moreno, and Betty Moreno, standing here next to me, is my mother."

I would not say the crowd was accommodating of his choice of words or his confession, but he continued through the murmurs.

"I have embraced this truth, because I've realized that no human was ever there for me. No one else, human or not, ever fought for me like she did. No one else protected me or nurtured me when I needed it the most. My mama, though a robot, is more humane than any human being that I have ever met. And this morning, I'd like to share something with you all for you to see."

I then connected to the AV system and a projection of my memories displayed on the giant screen. My son took them through several of our memories he had chosen the night before. It was a collage of a life well lived. Of a child well raised. Of a child loved unconditionally.

I stood there, not saying anything, simply reliving the memories once again. I turned towards the bleachers and noticed the reactions from the crowd, studying both the students and the staff's facial expressions. These were expressions of remorse. I could tell they were experiencing guilt and shame. Their expressions were manifestations of true empathy. The same kids that once threw things at me and called my son horrible things not very long before were now crying.

Things changed over the following weeks. Most were for the better, though some brought about new, unavoidable, and predictable challenges. Some of which, of course, brought us here, your honor.

At first, our lives revolved around doing interviews for different media outlets. It was exhausting, but in all of them, not once did my son's words change. Isaac was proud of who he was and he was thankful to have me as his mother. I can play these interviews for you so that you can see them for yourself, if you'd like, your honor.

Since that day, Isaac isn't scared to call me his mother in front of anyone. He is no longer scared to hug me. He is not ashamed of being raised by a machine. And I, your honor, walk with my head held high. I no longer use the trench coat to hide. To be honest, I don't even care about all the stares we receive while we are out and about in public.

So, this is our story, your honor.

My name is Betty Moreno, and I am a BT78. As I stated at the beginning, and I will repeat once more, Isaac Moreno is *my* boy. He is, indeed, my son.

Through him, I have learned that every mind is beautiful, no matter how fragile. Through him, I have learned and experienced compassion. Through him, your honor, an entire school learned about forgiveness. He brought about good change in all his peers.

Even now, Isaac takes time to talk to other kids with challenges or similar neurological conditions. Other robots have reached out to us, and Isaac always gives them quality time. He never makes anyone feel deficient; instead, he makes us all feel whole and special. Unique.

This is the kind of man that I've raised.

But here we are today, your honor, in your presence to testify. The story that I have shared with you today is nothing but the truth. As you know now, I am capable of fabricating untruths, although only if it will save a human life. However, you also know by now that I can recall every incident with absolute fidelity. And, if it pleases you, I can even provide tangible evidence in video form of everything that has been recounted thus far.

Now, how Isaac's and my story continues is entirely up for you to decide.

As I finish, just know this, your honor... nothing will ever change the story that we've lived. Nothing! You might remove Isaac from my custody, and you might even choose to end my existence. You do have that power, after all. However, don't ever forget this—Isaac is my son and I am his mom.

Thank you, your honor.

That is all.

CORPOREAL ADJUSTMENT

1

Culver City, CA

Emma Lar's self-love journey was a rollercoaster. She would listen to love songs as if they were being sung from her to her. As John Legend's "All of Me" played while she plucked her eyebrows, she kept thinking of its powerful words while staring in the mirror:

> 'Cause all of me
> Loves all of you
> Love your curves and all your edges
> All your perfect imperfections

She tried to convince herself, though she knew it was a lie.

> Give your all to me
> I'll give my all to you
> You're my end and my beginning
> Even when I lose I'm winning

Emma was late again.

❖ ❖ ❖

Beverly Hills Hilton Hotel Conference Complex

Emma made her way to an empty chair on the side of the second row. She was thankful that she'd only missed a few minutes of the presentation. Eagerly, she took out her phone and began recording, then grabbed a pen and started to take notes on the brochure.

"Technological advancements have reached a climax never before achieved. What started with a wheel and written language, and then eventually to a sewage system and vehicles, have come a long way. Today, particles developed from fruits and vegetables can be converted to electricity. We create energy from natural sources and harvest and store it for later use. The same can be said of our own bodies. Plastic surgery is a thing of the past. The days of hormonal therapies are long gone. Today, people can get the bodies they want without the need of extreme regimens. A simple procedure, such as the one we've patented, can take care of this problem. Now, that is innovation! We've seen psychotherapy and talks about getting dysmorphic people out of their nonworking shells. We can help with that."

Though the hall was desolate, Dr. Hermann continued to talk to the gathering during the session.

Emma looked around at the people gathered. She was curious as to what people thought of all this being said. She noticed that some of them, if not most, were hanging on Hermann's words, as if they were divinely inspired. A few others, however, most likely journalists, had faces of disapproval.

Dr. Hermann continued, "There is nothing wrong in wanting a new body. We've all been there. I'll call it another form of cognitive dissonance and I know it'll pass, too." He drank some water and caught his breath before continuing. "Look, everyone... You might wonder if this whole body swapping thing is ethical to begin with. And we could talk more about that. Though I'll say that that's a conversation for another day. I am simply a geneticist, immunologist, and cell biologist. And I think that question should be left to be answered by an ethicist, or perhaps a politician. But, for now at least, I will state this. The truth is that, sooner or later, the whole world will eventually embrace this. You can quote me on that, by the way."

He stopped and walked around, looking at all the gazing eyes waiting in anticipation for him to continue.

Emma smiled, herself eager for his words.

"I mean it," he said. "Think about it. Transgendered and other people that really want or *need* this, can finally get rid of their old body and upload their consciousness into a new one. Think about the potential in this! Think of all the benefits. Let's say someone, for example, is handicapped—paralyzed, even. Imagine their joy at knowing they can transfer themselves to an upgraded, state of the art body that functions perfectly."

There were some murmurs from the crowd. Emma looked around. Just like her, they were all thrilled about the possibilities.

A chubby man stood up, angry, grunting obscenities at the doctor. As he turned around to walk away, Dr. Hermann asked him to stop and to please state his mind out loud. The man stopped, but didn't say anything.

"Come on. I really want to know what you have to say. That's why we are here, after all. This is a small gathering, and as I stated at the beginning, I welcome interaction from the participants."

"Okay, sure. I do have a few questions," said the man.

Dr. Hermann invited him up to the front with a wave of his arm. He conceded his place on the microphone.

The man limped to the front, dropped his bag on the floor, and turned toward the audience. "Okay." He cleared his throat. "Imagine that you walk into a teleporter on Mars. You walk into the teleporter, your particles get decomposed, and you're getting reassembled on the other side. Would you be the same person?" He stopped for an answer.

Dr. Hermann didn't answer; instead, he turned to the group and shrugged. Nobody spoke.

The man continued, "I only give you this example because the case with replicating consciousness is essentially the same."

"Please elaborate, sir."

"What I mean is, consciousness is not some simply kind of 'substance' that we can drag and drop, or copy and paste. It is a process of the functioning brain. It is more than simple organic data. Consciousness is reasoning. It is human awareness. It is the sum of your working brain activity, neural networks, functioning lobes, and cortices. All the processes and modules you have to replicate for it to be transferable. And if this is the case—which it is, by the way— then there are several questions regarding this that merit answering. For example, in the moment of 'transfer,' as you so called it, would that mean that the old person subjectively dies and that the new person arises, one which has all your memories within the new brain? Also, in the moment of transfer, if indeed the same person is sustained, would that then mean that there, at some point, were two people like you?"

Dr. Hermann smiled and finally replied, "It is completely understandable to have doubts about things we don't understand. Yes, the mystery of that is beautiful, and yet, also sad. We've used quantum mechanics to develop many things, and many scientists still grapple to understand it. But I tell you what, let me do something instead, and hopefully this will help." He stopped and turned toward a female assistant. "Sam, please bring in the first person." He redirected his attention to everyone once again. "We are about to meet a client of Corporeal Adjustment. This is a person who successfully went through the process of consciousness transfer from one body to another—one of her choice. Maybe she can help us with these questions."

A young petite woman raised her hand. "Dr. Hermann, in the meantime, I have a question too."

"Go ahead," he replied.

"How do we go about choosing bodies? I mean, can they look however we want?"

"Good question. Yes, we would start with a set of questions. For example, gender, race, body composition. You know, the essentials. From there, we would provide a catalogue for you to choose the closest match to what you are looking for. Then, the rest, we would modify to make sure you are unique."

"What do you mean, Doctor?"

"Well, we adjust the facial features and hair length and color to specify the likes of the client. This way, no two people will ever look exactly the same."

Satisfied, the young woman sat back.

A middle-aged man stood up. "Can I ask something too?"

"Go ahead."

He came forward. "What about the notion of not dying at all? Is that even a possibility with this? I mean, couldn't one continue to transfer consciousness from body to body an infinite amount of times, if it's the physical, biological factor that dies, after all?"

"Now, that is an excellent question, sir. And the truth is that I think anything possible with this technology. However, the cosmos is at entropy. We can only achieve biological immortality to a certain degree. But a cosmic one, we can't. And, if history has taught us anything, is that at the end of the day, many of us might be better off just ceasing to exist at some point. I guess what I'm trying to say is that, unfortunately, or perhaps fortunately, the reality is that the planet that we live in cannot sustain this possibility. But, could it be done...sure, I guess."

❖ ❖ ❖

Culver City

Emma dropped the magazine she'd been reading since she finished a meeting with other board members managing pitches of startups around the suburbs in West Los Angeles. She was exhausted. Why she even though that she could manage to go to the convention while she had so much at work was beyond her.

Emma looked up. There he was – the object of her fantasies. If only he'd paid attention to her. But Pedro Ramos didn't look back at her; instead, he had his gaze focused on Georgina, with a big smile on his face.

Of course.

Emma heaved a heavy sigh. She stood up and walked to the ladies' room. She stared at the mirror, wondering what she'd done to deserve her physique. If only she'd had Georgina Muniz's genes. The woman had it all. She was such a bitch, though. If only Pedro could see that. But, unfortunately, men went about life thinking with their penis, not their head.

Images of Pedro and Georgina holding hands, walking together on the Santa Monica pier, making out, invaded her thoughts. She pounded a fist on the sink counter. If Emma had learned anything in her three decades of , it was that the world was a cruel and unfair place. She held back her tears.

Oh, if only, she thought.

A colleague came in. Emma quickly washed her face and straightened up her blouse. She smiled at her and went back outside to work.

But Pedro's brawny body, bearded face, baritone voice, and funny personality continued to invade her thoughts. She couldn't concentrate, catching herself staring at her computer monitor without doing anything. She tried to shake it off. Again. She turned to him and smiled. He turned back and smiled at her. Nervously, she pretended as if she hadn't just been staring at him and returned to her work.

The fact that they lived in the same apartment complex didn't help. She'd seen him at the gym and in the pool several times. They would carpool to and back from work often. His allure threw her off each time.

It was torturous.

Emma knew she was trying her best. But all the diets and rigorous exercise regimens didn't seem to work. She looked into her purse to pull out a mint, when she saw Corporeal Adjustment's brochure with her notes scribbled on them.

Emma smiled as some of Dr. Hermann's words echoed in her mind. *A consciousness transfer... A body of her choice... An opportunity for new beginnings... A guaranteed confidence boost... A complete corporeal adjustment.*

Even if it didn't help with Pedro, she'd do it for herself.

2

"Daddy, they made fun of me again!" a young Emma said.

Emma's father groaned. "You gotta grow some skin, Emma. Sooner or later, you must learn to stand up for yourself. Either that, or don't let what people think or say of you affect you so much."

"Axel! Stop it, you're only making it worse," Emma's mother interrupted from the other side of the table.

"What? I'm just saying. The girl has to grow up sooner or later, you know. The earlier she learns that people suck and that she can't be coming to mommy and daddy with all her troubles, the better she'll be."

Emma left the dinner table crying, running towards her room.

❖ ❖ ❖

The phone rang, awakening her. Emma looked at the alarm clock on her dressing table— 7:23 a.m.

What the hell?

"Hello," she answered with a coarse voice.

"Hey, bitch. Did I wake you up?"

"Seriously, Marina? What do you think? It's Saturday." She rubbed her eyes as she yawned.

"Rough night?"

"Rough life!" Emma got up from bed and headed straight to the bathroom. She placed the phone on speakerphone and stretched her arms. "By the way, guess what?"

"What's up?"

"I caught Pedro staring at Georgina's ass again. He was like, totally eye raping her or something. He saw me looking at him, but he pretended like he hadn't been doing anything."

Marina laughed. "What a dumbass."

"Yeah," Emma sat on the toilet. "But a gorgeous dumbass."

"Oh, Emma. You're a lost cause. When are you gonna get over this idiot?"

"Never. I'll do whatever it takes. You'll see. Anyway, what's up? What's so urgent at this time of the day, on a freaking weekend, of all days?"

"Nothing, girl. I just wanted to see how you were feeling today. Last night you were… weird again. When are we going to hang out? I wanted to see if you wanted to go to the beach today or something?"

"Eww, no! Thank you, but now. I just wanna chill today. My plan was to sleep in, but you've already ruined that." Emma stood up to wash her hands and face.

"Emma, don't! Don't go on that path again. We've been over this. You need to go out. You desperately need some sunshine on that pale Scandinavian skin of yours, girl. Let's go get brunch, at least."

"I think I'll pass."

"Fine. But if the mountain will not come to Muhammad, then Muhammad must go to the mountain. I'll stop by soon and bring you breakfast then."

Emma thought about what to say, but couldn't thinking of anything clever.

"Emma? You still there, or did you hang up on me? Not again, bitch!"

Emma laughed. "Fine. But bring something healthy at least...bitch."

Marina laughed. "Maybe. Netflix and chill, breakfast edition it is."

Emma walked back to bed. "All right. But I'm gonna stay in pajamas all day. I'm warning you." She grabbed a picture frame from her nightstand. In was Marina and her in Santorini, from a cruise they'd taken two years prior.

"You lazy bitch! Fine, whatever. But at least take a shower and put some deodorant on! I don't want to smell your stinky ass." Marina's laughter was contagious. "I'll be there soon."

Emma smiled before hanging up and laying back on bed.

Maybe this'll be a good weekend, after all.

❖ ❖ ❖

"I'm serious, though. Poor Emma," Georgina whispered. "How does a girl that ugly live with herself?"

Emma was about to enter the staff lounge to warm up her food when she heard Georgina's catty comment. She was furious. She was about to barge in, but suddenly stopped when she heard Pedro's voice.

"That's not nice, Georgie," he replied. "She is actually very nice."

Emma smiled.

"She might be nice. But that doesn't take away the fact that she's hideous. What? Oh, you know it's true, Petey. Don't lie."

Pedro chuckled.

Emma's heart threatened to jump out. *How dare they? And why is he laughing?*

She thought again of turning the corner and say something, but she couldn't.

Instead, she turned around and dumped her prepackaged diet meal on the trash bin by the desk area, defeated. She went back to her desk to work, trying her best to keep her mind busy and not think of what she had just heard. She figured it was probably best if she skipped lunch anyway, since she was trying to lose some weight.

Later that afternoon, Pedro rolled his chair all the way to her side.

Emma ignored him.

Pedro tried to get her attention by flicking a pen through her hair, but didn't say anything.

"Stop bugging me!" Emma demanded.

"Wow! I'm sorry. Bad day? Everything all right with you?"

"Ugh. What do you want, Pedro? As you can see, I'm busy." She turned on her chair to face him.

"Nothing. Just wanted to see if you wanted to go to the pool later in the evening at the apartments." He frown. "But I guess not. Or, whatever, you know."

Emma thought about what to say. Of course she'd love to go with him to the pool. As embarrassed as she was that he would see her in a bathing suit, she certainly loved to see him in one. However, this was not the day. Not after what she'd overheard in the kitchen.

"Pedro," she started with a shaky voice. She tried her best to hold her tears back, but one rebel drop escaped.

"Is everything okay, Emma? What's going on?" He came closer to him and turned around as if to see if anyone was seeing this.

"Pedro," she repeated, "I heard you and Georgina earlier at lunch time."

Pedro's eyes opened wide. "You heard what, exactly?"

"You know what I am talking about. There's no point in denying it. I was literally there, by the corner, about to go in, when I heard you guys referring to me as hideous."

Pedro shifted on his chair. He cleared his throat. "Um, Emma. I'm sorry. I… I… well, she was just—"

"Don't bother, Pedro. I wouldn't expect otherwise from her. But you? I thought we were friends."

"We are friends!"

"Pedro, I know you like Georgina. I know that—"

"Emma, I promise, I didn't say anything. I even tried to defend you. Seriously!"

"I know. But you still laughed. That hurt. It hurt bad." More tears came down.

Pedro looked down. "I'm so sorry, Emma. Please forgive me. I really am sorry. I'm so stupid. I would never…" He stopped. "Emma, please forgive me," he finally finished.

"It's fine. Whatever." She wiped her face with her sleeve. "Anyway, I've got some work to do. So, yeah."

"Okay. So, I guess no pool tonight then?"

Emma didn't say anything. She simply turned her chair around and continued to work.

"Alrighty then." With that, he went back to his desk.

3

Corporeal Adjustment, Inc.

Beverly Hills, CA

Emma gave Marina a brochure opened to Dr. Hermann's bio. It mentioned a brief history of his work. After working at Stanford molecular biology lab and transferring to Munich to work on the DNA sequences of transgenic mice and Denisovans, a Neanderthal man, Dr. Eugene Hermann had started Corporeal Adjustment two years prior. Marina read with interest while Emma paid attention to the man of the hour.

Dr. Hermann typed some things on his device and hologram images started to frolic about in the air. The small group of potential clients and their loved ones watched eagerly, hoping to hear another revelation and to learn more about the process of consciousness transfer from one body to another. Emma had invited Marina to come with her for moral support, and she immediately accepted. Emma knew Marina didn't approve of the process and questioned the ethical aspect of the practice itself. However, she was always supportive.

"As you are seeing this right now," Hermann pointed at a flying image of a virus with the word retrovirus dancing on it like a pendulum, "trillions of microbes and quadrillions of viruses are multiplying on your face, your hands, and inside of you. With every breath that you take and with every move that you make, you are sending bacteria into the air at the rate of about 37 million per hour. With every gram of food you eat, you swallow about a million microbes. In a similar way, with the help of nanotechnology, we are able to send quintillions of organisms inside of you, which collect all the data needed to replicate your consciousness. Memories, personality, and even pet peeves are stored in them. Now, look at this—"

Emma sat up straight and titled her head to see the presentation better as Dr. Hermann continued to explain the process. She knew Mariana wasn't on board with this, but it was her decision. And her mind was made up. She wondered what her late father would've thought of this. He'd died two years prior, and though he didn't struggle with self-image, he himself had battled a damaged body, as he was diagnosed with severe osteoarthritis in both his hips.

His doctors had told him that the only remedy for the chronic pain would be a hip replacement—something he utterly refused. So, he continued living with increasing pain for several years until it became too much. His argument was that messing with what God had put in you, or changing the way He'd created you, even if it was harmful, was essentially asking to be eternally damned. Emma had tried talking him into going through the process, but he refused, and died soon after, in agony.

Emma turned to Marina and noticed, to her surprise, that she was actually paying close attention to Dr. Hermann.

"According to some latest estimates, around 60% of your cells are not human—the rest are microscopic colonists. That's enough to make you wonder what you mean by 'you,' right?" Dr. Hermann was answering a question from an eager potential client. "As you all know, your human cells come from a single fertilized egg with DNA from your mother and father. But soon, microbes begin mingling with those human cells, way before your first breath. Your human cells could not have built a healthy body without intimate help from all those countless immigrant microbes—your other half. At Corporeal Adjustment, we considered this, and that's how, thanks to this and to our state of the art, supersonic quantum computer, we are now able to work with zillions of micros to create the body you want. Essentially, the new bodies we create are living bio organisms. It's bone, muscle, and tissue. Just upgraded, that's all. Science is amazing!"

Marina turned to Emma. "Isn't that just playing God?" she asked, a frown on her face.

Emma sighed. "Just listen," she whispered. "You sound like my dad."

Marina gave her a look. Emma knew well that Marina was aware of her damaged relationship with her late father. The look said it all—she didn't like the comparison.

"What? I'm just saying. That's exactly what Dad would've said."

"Whatever," Marina replied, turning back to the presenter.

"Your immune system protects you by detecting and rejecting anything in your body that is not self. And yet, your very immune system is partly built and even partly run by external microbes. That's why scientists say all that time that we are never really alone. When you eat, so do they. And when you travel, they always come along. Even in death, you are not parted, for when you die, they ingest you."

"How lovely and romantic," Marina said.

There was laughter in the crowd.

"Indeed," replied the doctor. "Any other questions before we move into the operation room to view the equipment?"

"Yeah, I have two questions." Throughout the presentation, Emma had been gathering the courage to ask her questions out loud. "How much exactly is the procedure? And how soon can you start with me?"

❖ ❖ ❖

Culver City

Before they left Emma's apartment, Marina tried to convince her one last time. "Did you see the videos I sent you last night? The ones with the people who had limb transplants and other body changes or upgrades, only to end up hating their new body?"

"I browsed through them a little, yeah. But you need to stop, Marina. I've made up my mind already." Emma dropped into the passenger seat of Marina's smart car.

Marina sighed before getting behind the wheel.

"Besides," Emma continued as Marina put her seatbelt, "I've already paid the fifty percent deposit. I can't go chicken out now. Why can't you just be happy for me?"

"Emma, stop! I do support you, and I am happy for you. I just wish you'd be happy with yourself. I mean, with whom you are…as in, now. That's all. You know I'll still be your best friend, bitch. Just don't turn psycho or conceited on me when you look like a freaking model."

Emma laughed. "Yeah, that's not gonna happen. I won't turn into Georgina, I promise."

"I don't know. That body you chose really looks like her!"

"No! Stop it."

"Yes, she does. And you know it, Emma. You just want a chance with Pedro, since that's more his type. Don't you?"

Emma looked outside the window. "Well, maybe. But, as much as I hate to admit it, Georgina is pretty hot. It's just her insides that are ugly."

Marina laughed. "Yeah, the bitch is hot, all right." Marina typed the address to Corporeal Adjustment on the screen and the car took off, gliding through the asphalt. "Okay, I guess we are doing this."

Emma smiled, still looking outside.

"Emma, you do realize you won't be able to have kids anymore, right? Remember that Hermann said that these bodies cannot procreate."

Emma turned to Marina. "I know. But to be honest, I've never wanted to have kids. I don't know…the idea of being a mother just doesn't go with me."

Marina nodded.

After a few quiet minutes in the drive, Marina broke the silence again. "I'm just worried about something going wrong, that's all, Emma. This whole thing is just so new, you know? And there are always risks."

"I know," Emma replied while pushing down her shirt over her thumping stomach. She turned towards her friend and grabbed her hand. "And I appreciate you being such a good friend and worrying about me. I really do. But you heard the guy; they know what they're doing. It's all state of the art stuff! You saw."

Marina nodded, but remained silent. She shook Emma's hand. "I love you, bitch. I really do. And I don't care how you look, I'll always love you, and you'll always be my ugly bitch."

Emma laughed. "And you'll always be mine."

"Amen, sister!" Marina turned the radio on. "Now, let's get some grooves on."

After a few seconds, Emma lowered the volume. "Marina, there's something else. My body is going to be donated to the hospital. Apparently, I'm helping scientific research to gain more understanding into our existence or some shit like that."

"Oh, dang. That's crazy!"

"Yeah, I know. But I think it's cool. It was either that or freezing it, just in case I ever had second thoughts and wanted to go back to my original shell."

"What? And why didn't you chose that option then? You never know."

"No, Marina. I'd have to pay a monthly fee for them to store it in one of their cryogen chambers or something like that, since I don't have the equipment or space at home. Besides, why in the world why I ever want to get back into…this?"

❖ ❖ ❖

Corporeal Adjustment, Inc.
Beverly Hills, CA

Marina Esquivel sat in the waiting lobby, wondering what was going on with her friend on the other side of those walls. Though an artist and a Bohemian herself, she knew well that science had changed the world in so many ways. She just wasn't ready for it. And now, her best friend was somewhere in there, in some lab, having a body swap. She wasn't getting cut open, and yet, this was the most invasive surgery possible.

She wondered how their relationship would look like once her best friend looked like a hot model? What would people think of them? How would Emma react? In all her worries, she was genuinely happy for Emma.

Damn! It's been over two hours since she went in. What's going on in there?

Marina stood and went to grab a magazine from the shelf close to the doorway. Even the flowers here were impeccable. She wondered how real they were.

"Don't worry. She is in good hands," the pretty woman said from behind the reception counter.

"Huh?" Marina looked up, surprised.

"Your friend. She will be okay," the woman with stretched skin on her face said. She smiled. "You look nervous."

"Oh. Yeah, sorry." Marina put the magazine back in place. "Excuse me, how long does it normally take. The…procedure." She rested her arms over the marble counter.

"Depends," she replied. "Normally anywhere between one and two hours, if there are no complications. How long has it been?"

"Almost three," Marina replied. "Almost three. And I really have to go."

4

Earlier

"You won't feel a thing," the anesthesiologist had told Emma. "Soon, you'll wake up to a new you." His smile brought her peace.

She nodded. And soon, everything went blank.

Emma lay motionless in the bed, covered with white hospital linens. She was alone in the operation lab, connected to countless devices around her. Electrodes were attached to her shaved head. A computer ticked away, with waves of data running with the speed of light.

Data Feed Established, read the monitor. A counter measuring the percentage of data transferred right below it read *57%*.

"Emma, come home now, " said her father, holding a sunflower in his left hand. "Come home, Emma. It's time."

Emma herself was on a lawn overlooking over the sea. Except, upon seeing it again, she noticed that it wasn't an ocean. It was...the universe.

"I'm here," she whispered to no one in particular. "Where is *here*?"

❖ ❖ ❖

Dr. Eugene Hermann had come into the room, dressed in a white cloak. He checked everything and made sure there were no issues in the transfer of Emma's consciousness into the temporary device. Everything seemed fine.

The techs were busy with the machines, and Emma was out. Soon, she'd wake up to a new reality. A better her.

He smiled. He loved his work.

One of the techs walked away toward another room.

As the computer kept faintly beeping, Eugene felt his phone vibrate. He walked out for a moment before coming back into the room.

"Hey, Claude, I gotta go. My son had an accident. Just make sure to continue through the fourth stage. I'll be back soon. Sammy got knocked out during his game, and the wife is bringing him to the hospital. I'll just be across the street."

"Okay, Chief. I got this," Claude replied.

Eugene left as the young Claude made his way toward the control console.

"I've got this," Claude said to himself again.

✧ ✧ ✧

"Emma, where are you?" Dr. Hermann said. He'd grown older. Baldness crept in, and he leaned over a stick. "Let's go!" his voice echoed.

"I'm here, " she said. "Who are you?"

"What? I'm Dr. Hermann," he replied appearing in front of her. "Now, take my hand. Let's go back." He extended his arm toward her, suspended in the air.

"No! You aren't Dr. Hermann. I don't want to go with you." Emma flew away.

"Emma, come over now." He followed after her. "We have to go. The realm is closing, and we're running out of time. Your brain hallucinates your conscious reality. Come on."

The whiteness increased around them. Flakes started dropping...first a few, and then many. Shouts. Images. Laughter. Cries. It was raining memories of her life.

"Come, Emma. I have candy for you," her father said from the far side.

"Emma?" It was Marina. Emma turned with a smile. "Come to me," Marina said.

Emma was confused, being pulled in all directions.

The memories became a flood. She was suddenly not flying, she was floating on them. But the joyful memories turned sour. Bullying. Damnation. Depression. Pedro. Georgina.

She began to drown.

"Help!" she screamed. But everyone was gone.

No dad, not Dr. Herman, no Pedro or Georgina. No Marina either.

"Help!" she cried out again.

Suddenly, all her memories meshed into the great whiteness, vanishing before eyes.

She was flying again.

She felt a tap on her back; she turned around.

"Now, close your eyes." Dr. Hermann said. "It's time to go."

❖ ❖ ❖

The console beeped again, this time with a green light, indicating the transfer was done and was ready to begin the consciousness data relocation towards the new body.

Claude dropped his phone, hitting something. The console turned red. Panicking, he tried to figure out what had just happened. He wasn't sure.

Oh, shit! Oh, shit! Oh, shit! Okay, I got this. I just need to...

Claude fiddled around, pressing several buttons, until the console went green again. Satisfied, Claude sat back again and put his arms behind his head.

Easy peasy.

❖ ❖ ❖

The first memory experience that flooded her awareness was that of Georgina and Pedro laughing at her appearance. It quickly faded to one of her father telling her young self some things about God that she didn't understand. One of Marina showing her artwork in a garden in a museum in Paris overtook her mind. Then many more, all at the same time.

Emma felt her body. Senses tickling throughout, from the tip of her fingers to those of her toes. Electricity. Blood flowing, heart pumping to a magnificent rhythm. Musical. Air entering her nostrils all the way into her lungs and out. She could hear it all. Feel it all. Even the faint sound of a computer fan.

Like the rising sun in a warm morning, it was beautiful. Like the singing of birds and the colors of flowers, it was wonderful.

Then, alert, Emma opened her eyes. She saw the ceiling of the operation room, though it was not the same that she'd fallen asleep on.

She smiled. "So, it worked."

She raised her hands. He heart raced.

But before she could scream, she saw Claude quickly rushing towards her.

"Fuck!" he screamed as he pressed a button on the computer.

And Emma fell asleep again.

5

"He said they're very sorry," Emma said on the phone. "And they reimbursed all my money. I checked already."

"I just can't believe it, Emma!" the voice screamed on the phone. "That's ridiculous!"

"Dr. Hermann told me that they'll be able to reverse this in two months or so. They'll be able to put me in the body that I chose. They'll keep it fresh. On the plus side, the whole thing will be free to make up for their mistake."

"Wait, what? Did you say two months? Wow! Why so long?"

"Ugh. I know, Marina. Don't remind me. He said something about me needing to settle in this new body first. That making another transfer might affect my consciousness and that the damage could be unreversible."

"Fuck. I told you, bitch. I had a feeling something was wrong. Wait, I can't call you that anymore. I'll think of a new name for you."

Emma didn't say anything.

Marina grunted on her side. "Anyway, I'll come over soon. I just had to go take care of something with my mom, but I am not far."

"Hurry up! All I'm wearing is a hospital gown."

"Oh, I can't wait to see and meet the new you! Are you hot? You sound hot. I like the deep voice."

Emma laughed. "You have no idea. Hurry up, though, seriously. And you can be the judge. By the way, we gotta go buy new clothes. A lot."

❖ ❖ ❖

"Dang, boy! You really are one hot piece of meat. I wonder who they were saving this body for." Marina touched his chest, not being able to contain her excitement. "I know it's been a couple of days already, but I just can't get used to the idea of my best friend Emma now being a tall black man going by the name of Demetrius." She put her hands on her mouth as if it was a megaphone. "Watch out world, Demetrius Brown is the house!"

The man laughed. "Yeah, I do look pretty hot, actually. I never thought I'd have nice muscles and these abs!"

"Girl, I mean, boy...forget the muscles. You have a dick!" Marina started to laugh.

He blushed. "I know. It's so weird."

"Can I touch it? Can I see it?" Marina's eyes grew wider. "Come on!"

"No, Marina! What the hell is wrong with you? You're crazy."

"Maybe. But when am I gonna have a chance like this again? Come one, girl. Take one for the team."

"No!"

"Fine. At least tell me. Is it…bi… I mean, nice?"

Demetrius covered his face with both hands. "It's *very* nice!" he said with a smile.

"OMG! No. Don't tell me you've played with it already."

"Fine, I won't tell you."

"No!" Marina came and sat next to Demetrius on the sofa. "Don't be like that. Tell me everything! I want details. How was it? How does it feel? Is it different? Better? Worse? Come on! Details, bitch, details."

Demetrius laughed nervously. "I'm not comfortable talking to you about this, Marina."

"Ugh, you're no fun." Marina threw a throw pillow at Demetrius's face. "If it would've been me, I would've told you everything. I'm just saying, we have two months to have fun." Marina stood up to get a drink of water.

Demetrius neatly put the pillow back in its place on the edge of the sofa. "You know, though, settling in wasn't easy. But the truth is that it does feel good being a man. Everywhere I go, I notice girls watching me. The same way that Pedro looks at Georgina." He chuckled. "I didn't know women could be so obviously thirsty too. But seeing it from the other side, now I know. We're all the same."

"Wait, for reals? Have any girl hit on you already?"

"You mean, besides you?"

"Oh, come on. You know I do it all in fun." Marina came back and brought Demetrius a glass of water.

"Sure you do," he teased before taking a sip. "Yeah. I went to work out last night at the gym here in the apartments."

"Wait…hold on a minute. You? Emma? You, working out? Who are you, and what have you done to my friend? Oh, wait that's right, I forgot." Marina laughed.

"Shut up! You wanna hear it or not?"

"Yes, yes. Sorry. Go on."

"Anyway, I knew I had to lie to work that I was sick and took two weeks. It gives me time to figure out what to say for the remaining six or so weeks. I'll just tell them I need to work from home or something, which I totally can."

"What? No. Not that! I don't care about work. Tell me about you working out those sexy muscles"—Marina ran her hand on Demetrius's arms—"and about girls hitting on you."

"Damn, girl. Who's thirsty now?" Demetrius laughed. "Anyway, yeah, everywhere I've been, girls have been ogling me. I've even had a guy flirt with me in the mall when I went to get underwear. It's all so…weird. And funny. And honestly, kinda nice too. I kinda like it." Demetrius smiled a big, bright white smile, with dimples on each cheek.

Marina stared at him nervously. "My goodness. This is so weird! I gotta get used to this."

"Oh, Marina, speaking about working out,"—Demetrius stood up and then lay on the floor facing down to do some pushups—"did you know I can bench four hundred pounds? It's insane!"

6

Century City

A self-assured Demetrius Brown entered the coffee shop to order his drink. He was more comfortable in his new skin—literally—as each day went by. While waiting in line, he turned around to people watch. Georgina was there, two people behind him. She looked good, as always. Pedro would appreciate her look today, for sure.

She caught him staring at her and smiled at him.

His heart skipped a beat. *The bitch!* Demetrius returned a fake smile and turned around to order his morning drink.

As Demetrius stood by the corner waiting for his drink, Georgina approached him. Demetrius was edgy. He wasn't sure what he'd even say to her.

"Morning," she said with a bright smile. "Beautiful day today, isn't it?"

Demetrius nodded. Another bogus smile.

"Nice dimples," she said again.

"Thanks." Demetrius put his hand on his pockets and began tapping his left foot on the floor. "Nice, um... nice dress."

Georgina smiled and played with her long dark curls. "Thanks. It's one of my faves."

"Black suits you well," Demetrius replied.

"Every woman knows that little black dresses are always flattering. Plus, you know what they say..."

Demetrius shrugged.

"Once you go black..." she said, but stopped there.

Demetrius raised his eyebrows and chuckled, though not at her joke. This time the smile was genuine. "Yeah. You're right about that," he said. He covered his mouth with a hand while clearing his throat.

"Tall Passion Tea Lemonade for...*Damerius*," interrupted the barista behind him.

"Demetrius," he corrected. He turned around and grabbed his drink.

"Demetrius, huh?" Georgina echoed. "Nice to meet you. I'm Georgina."

He shook her extended hand. It was soft, neatly manicured. She smelled good. "Nice to you meet you, Georgi."

Georgina raised a brow. "Not very many people call me that. I like it." Her teeth glowed a bright white, almost as flawless as his.

"Anyway, I gotta run."

"Wait, can I see your phone?" she asked directly.

"My what?"

She laughed. "I want to save my contact info on your phone. In case you ever want to call and–"

"Oh! Sorry. Yes, um. Yeah, my phone. Of course. Yes. Hold on." Demetrius put his drink back on the counter and took out his purple phone, unlocking it with his new face. It was a girly cover.

Georgina laughed again. "Seriously?" She gave him a curious look. "I mean, I guess."

She took the phone from him and dialed her number with it. She grabbed her own red phone and pressed the ignore button. She then saved her name before locking it and giving back to him. "Call me sometime, *Damerius*." She winked as her hot drink got called.

"It's...it's Demetrius," he said stoically.

She chuckled. "I know." She grabbed her drink and walked away, leaving him there, staring at her back.

He was thankful Georgina's number wasn't saved. That would've been awkward and difficult to explain. There was no reason for Emma ever having called her anyway. And Georgie's name would've probably been saved under "Witch with a capital B" or something snarky like that.

He opened his phone and searched her name. She'd save it as Georgina Muniz, followed by a red heart and a peach.

Wow, this bitch is not only conceited...she's crazy.

But deep inside, Demetrius admired Georgina's forwardness and confidence.

He smiled as he walked out of the coffee shop.

✧ ✧ ✧

Over the next couple of weeks, Demetrius and Georgina went out a few times. After their dates, they did other things, too, at Georgina's place. Marina let Demetrius know how disappointed she was. But Emma... no, Demetrius simply said that this was payback. She had a plan. A vicious plan that would kill two birds with one stone.

She would make Georgina fall in love with him, making her forget about Pedro. That way, when she transformed into the other body waiting for her, she would have a chance with Pedro. At the same time, Demetrius would cease to exist, leaving Georgina in limbo, wondering why this handsome man had suddenly ghosted her.

"I mean, the plan isn't bad. I guess I like it. It's just that...to be honest, you are becoming a jerk," Marina told him one night. "You promised this wouldn't get to your head. This needs to stop. I feel like you're becoming someone else."

"I *am* someone else, Marina! That's the whole point."

Marina shook her head in disbelief. "I miss my best friend."

Demetrius suddenly remembered how Emma had felt when Georgina and Pedro laughed at her in the staff lounge. He felt horrible. But he quickly excused the guilt.

"I'm still here, Marina! This *is* me," Demetrius complained with his raised baritone voice. He saw fear flash in Marina's eyes as she moved back. "Sorry, I didn't mean to scare you." He took Marina's hands on his own. "Look, Marina...I know this is not what the plan was. I mean, the idiots turned me into a man, for Pete's sake! I figured I might as well enjoy it and make the best of it. That's all. But don't worry, after this time is over and I turn into the new Emma, I promise you, things will be back to normal."

"I hope so," Marina said. It was barely a whisper.

"Emma...I mean, Demi, I do like the plan. To be honest, I just don't like the fact that you...that Demetrius is spending so much time with Georgina. When you talk about her is different now. I don't think you've noticed, but I would even dare to say that you like her. Besides, I don't like the fact that you've made love to her."

"Demetrius fucks her, Marina. It's different. It's part of my plan. Just a game. Besides, I don't—"

"But you said that *you* are Demetrius now. At least for the time being," Marina interjected.

Demetrius took a heavy sigh. "Marina..." He stopped, too nervous to ask. He swallowed hard. "Are...are you jealous?"

Marina looked up, making eye contact. Without saying a word, she pulled him down and kissed him.

❖ ❖ ❖

Culver City, CA

The ping of the text message fully woke Demetrius up. He stretched his arms and turned towards his night stand and unplugged his phone. It was Dr. Hermann.

Call me when you can. I've got some important news to share.

Demetrius turned to his side; Marina was waking up, yawning. She looked great in a baby doll, her tattooed legs exposed.

"What is it, love?" she asked.

"It's Dr. Hermann," Demetrius replied showing her the phone. "He wants me to give him a call. Apparently he has some important news to tell me."

Marina's eyes opened wide. She sat up. "Well, call him!"

"I know, I know! I am about to."

Demetrius dialed the number and put the call on speaker phone.

"Hello."

"Hey, Doc. Got your message."

"Sorry, I woke you up early."

"It's cool. What's up?"

"I have great news."

Demetrius and Marina looked at each other. "What is it?"

"We're ready to have you back for that transfer. Your beautiful body here is waiting for you, and enough time has passed. We can schedule you either tomorrow morning or Friday afternoon, whichever works best for you. The procedure shouldn't take more than an hour-and-a-half."

Marina caressed Demetrius's strong left arm as he held the phone. She put a sad face on his shoulder.

"I see," Demetrius replied. "That *is* great news, indeed. Thank you for letting me know. Can I get back to you with an answer?"

"Yes, of course. But call me back soon," the doctor replied, "as in the next couple of hours, because the time slots are going to get booked. We've been very busy."

"I will. Promise."

"Alrighty then. Talk to you soon."

"Take care, Doc."

Demetrius kissed Marina's head. Marina hugged him in silence.

He was torn.

7

Six months later

Demetrius Brown sang loudly along with John Legend's "All of Me" while it played on his phone. He was cleaning up his beard in front of the mirror. His deep voice resonated in the bathroom, one octave lower than the original:

> 'Cause all of me
> Loves all of you
> Love your curves and all your edges
> All your perfect imperfections

Marina came behind him and put her arms around his waist. She caressed his toned abs. Demetrius continued to use the razor as a microphone.

> Give your all to me
> I'll give my all to you
> You're my end and my beginning
> Even when I lose I'm winning

"You're gonna be late again, my love," Marina warned him.

"Yup." Demetrius washed the razor in the running water.

"I guess some things never change," Marina sighed, then laughed.

"But then again," Demetrius turned around and gave her a kiss on the lips, "some things do."

TIME-SURFING THE APP
AN OVERVIEW CRITICAL REVIEW AND VERDICT

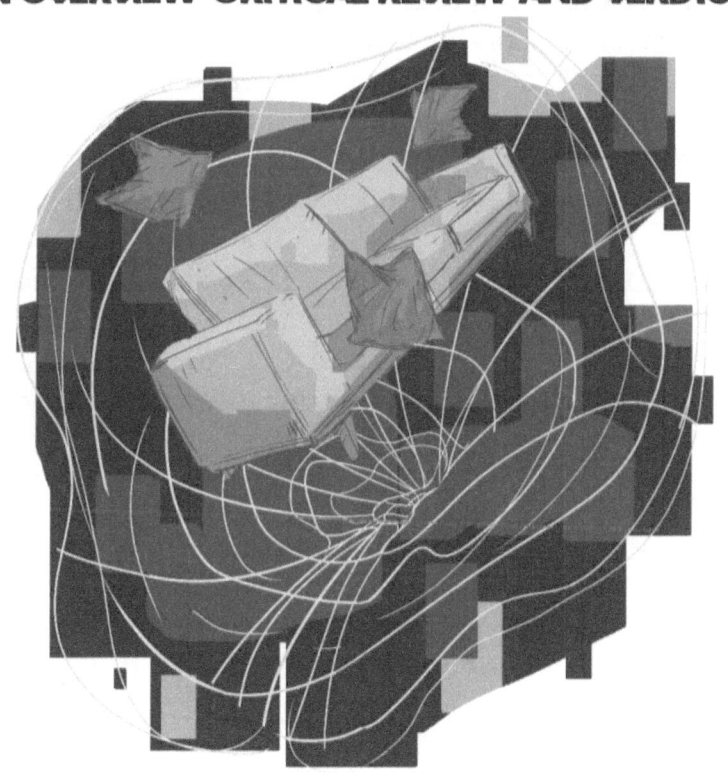

TIME-SURFING®

If you are looking for accommodations as a tourist or business traveler in a different time period, an application that stands out is Time-Surfing®. Time-Surfing® is an innovative time-traveling app, with close to a million diverse listings spread across two millennia, from 1 BC until now, which allows a user to connect with owners across the globe throughout any point in time. With Time-Surfing® you can easily find the right couch to stay on, whether you are an avid time-traveler or on your very first adventure.

With numerous customizable search options available, a user can search the expanding database and make arrangements directly with hosts. Images of the location and couch available appear upon making a search. Users can also browse the powerful engine using specific keywords, such as specific time periods, events, or even famous landmarks or renowned historical people.

A verified profile is required. The process for creating and verifying a profile is easy and quick, given your identity is stored in the World Database of Individuals (WDI). A quick face or fingerprint scan or blood sample will suffice.

A HISTORY OF THE DEVELOPMENT

If we are to understand how this application came to be, one must first look into the history of time-traveling. The idea of time-traveling has always been at the forefront of the human mind. From the creation of space and time, the idea of being able to either manipulate these, or, at the very least, navigate them by will, has existed in our psyches. Time traveling, in essence, is a perception of movement between different points of space, through time. Until very recently, this has been only a figment of our imagination, the topic of science fiction, with fiction being the key word.

Numerous distinguished individuals have presented time traveling theories, with some of them spending their entire lives proving its existence. Let us look into some of them and how each of them helped bring fiction into reality.

Stephen Hawking & Albert Einstein

Time traveling was perhaps Stephen Hawking's greatest ambition in life. The famous cosmologist worked relentlessly throughout his life to prove that time traveling was a possibility. In 2009, Hawking sent a party invitation without disclosing it to the general public. He believed that if any one actually traveled in time, they would know of this party and attend. However, unfortunately for him, no one came. Hawking waited and waited, to no avail. Yet, he remained optimistic about the possibility of one day achieving such a magnificent feat.

There is no doubt that without Albert Einstein, time travel would have remained in literature as a simple imaginary ambition. Einstein challenged Newton's notions of the laws of physics by introducing a few theories of his own. Einstein's special theory of relativity in particular lead us to believe that we could travel through time in space. In simple terms, his argument was that a person sitting in a spaceship moving at the speed of light would have a slower pulse and heart rate when compared to a person not on board. As a result, his biological watch ticks slower, and aging affects him differently. If speed affects time, then one could travel into the future.

Einstein argued that traveling into the future was comparatively easier, but that, however, if we wanted to go into the past we'd have to face many paradoxes. This spurred the creation of his second theory, named the general theory of relativity. According to this second theory, there are some other things that affect the speed of time, of which the main factor is gravity. More on that later.

Joseph Hafele & Richard Keating

Joseph Hafele & Richard Keating performed a legendary experiment in 1971, in which an astronomer took four cesium-beam atomic clocks on a commercial airliner. They flew twice around the world, first going eastward, and then going westward. After that they, compared both the clocks against others that remained back at the United States Naval Observatory. When reunited, the three sets of clocks showed different times and their differences were consistent with the predictions of special and general relativity. This result demonstrated that the clocks in the planes moved slowly compared to those who were kept in the observatory.

Their findings steered scientists into the creation of the CERN Hadron Collider. In this large machine, researchers discovered how subatomic particles that normally live fractions of a second can live thirty times longer when moving near the speed of light. These particles exist in the future. Through the special theory of relativity, they explained that when the particles approach the speed of light their clock eventually slows down. With this discovery, humanity witnessed time travel at subatomic particle level.

Ronald Mallett

By taking Einstein's theories, Ronald Mallet concluded that light has energy, and that since energy is equivalent to mass, mass exerts gravitational force. Thus, he argues, light creates gravity, which is the bending of space time. In order for light to generate a gravitational field like Earth's, it would need to have the mass energy of Earth. According to Ronald Mallet, light could be used to control gravity and also time.

Peewee McCloud & Squishy McBooty

The Silicon Valley, the birthplace of most noteworthy technological developments in the last century, is home to many tech companies. It doesn't come as a surprise that out of this region another technological breakthrough would make its impact in the history of humanity. However, while numerous technology companies in the area have tried during the past decades to create some sort of time machine that would allow human beings that much desired dream of navigating the dimensions unharmed, no one had been able to successfully produce such apparatus. That is, until the arrival of two young individuals, who in an effort to remain anonymous, simply go by Peewee McCloud and Squishy McBooty.

Taking into account what all of their scientific predecessors argued, McCloud and McBooty created a device that changed the game once and for all–and not just in the world of technology, but for all of society in general. Considered the greatest invention in the history of humanity, their time-machine has brought about countless opportunities. Though it could only be used to go into the past up to a certain point, and not the future, it still proved to be an incredible innovation. And now, twelve years later, the duo of geniuses have brought the world another technological breakthrough, one that will revolutionize the traveling industry indefinitely.

While in the last decade time traveling was reserved for only a few, due to the great risk involved in submerging into their machine, as well as its colossal price that their company–Omega Corp–charged, now everyone is able to partake in such an experience. With their creation of Time-Surfing®, any person with a smart device is able to time travel, as long as it is through one of their pre-approved partners in any given time and place. These partners, who function as hosts, allow a user to stay with them during their time-space bending trip.

According to the genius duo, time is a complex thing and not everyone can understand it. Therefore, there are limitations to time traveling in general. First, they argued, there could be no modifications or alterations of any type. In other words, users going on a time-traveling trek cannot make any changes to what has already happened. They can simply observe. In other words, the butterfly effect cannot be implemented on these trips. Since they felt that humanity could not be trusted, these limitations were part of the original programming. However, unfortunately, as the duo shared upon revealing their original device over a decade ago, the same cannot be said of what happens to the user. This means that if one dies while on a time-traveling adventure, they die for good.

APP OVERVIEW

So, what exactly is Time-Surfing® and how does it work? Time-Surfing® is an online marketplace that connects people who want to couch surf as a time traveler and people who host them. It currently covers more than 800,000 cities and roughly around 92% of time periods in the past two millennia. A representative from Omega Corp, the makers of the application, shared with us that the application's name comes from "Time-Travel" and "Couch-Surfing."

According to its creators, with this innovative application, any user can book the perfect trip for every time-traveling escape and explore new experiences, locations, and time periods. As a traveler, you'll find everything you need to make your next adventure unforgettable; or, you can start earning money as a time-couch host.

Booking Stays

The author found it easy to choose from countless listings from different time periods in modern human history. In a period of five minutes, the author was able to find everything from rustic caves for archeological studies, and medieval castles, to seaside palaces for ultimate relaxation weekends. The app also gives the user options for traveling alone or in groups. It was easy to search by price, time period, location, services provided, and more.

Book Experiences

The author found rare and exceptional activities only found in specific time periods and remote locations. In all honesty, the idea of not letting the history books take away the fun and instead, simply booking a Time-Surfing® trip to explore the history of the world in person seemed ideal. All in a week's time, the author was able to visit unveilings of great inventions from the industrial revolution, ride a horse in the American wild west, witness Tenochtitlan in all of its splendor, see Pompeii before its volcanic demise, and walk the streets of Florence during the Renaissance. As its slogan promises, there is, indeed, "something for every person of any age and interest."

Customer Friendly

Part of what makes an application great is not it's user-friendly capabilities, but also customer friendliness. The author found that making time-traveling plans was easy. An agent helped and brought peace of mind with excellent customer service. Time-Surfing® has a flexible cancellation policy that makes booking a comfortable experience. Nonetheless, the author was directed to refer to each host's cancellation policies for additional details. In the week-long experience, no issues were faced.

THE PROS

- Customizable searches on intuitive within app search engine.
- Over 800,000 reliable listings across multiple time periods from 1 BC and on.
- Wide array of listings (caves, castles, palaces, shacks, pirate ships, etc.).
- Ability to save favorites (i.e., search results, experiences, locations, time periods, etc.).
- Secure payment and verified ID options.
- Direct contact with hosts for directions, instructions, arrangements, etc.
- Host protection program that guarantees safeguards against property damage or theft.
- Hosts can set their own couch prices.

THE CONS

- Transaction fees for hosts.
- Images within application listings not guaranteed to match reality.
- Time-traveling motion sickness.
- No future traveling capabilities (yet).
- Sudden currency exchanges for different historic capital and additional hidden fees can be a nightmare.
- No additional protection against uncontrollable and unpredictable circumstances (i.e., language barriers, food poisoning, wars, capture, death, etc.).
- Currently only available as an app that requires an extensive installation process on a smart device. No web-based option at the moment.

- No time alteration or modifications are permitted or even possible at this time. (Although this one could arguably be a pro.)

CONCLUSION

Time-traveling is no longer a thing simply relegated to science fiction literature. What our ancestors simply dreamed of we can now live through. Though it has its limitations, Time-Surfing® has proven to be efficient in allowing users to travel through time and be hosted by one of their pre-approved partners. Though initially time-consuming, the application was easy to install. Once installed, it felt intuitive to use and searching, finding, and booking experiences was quick and efficient.

Overall, 5/5 stars.

ABERRATIONAL

"I'm detecting heartbeats," Larissa said, awe in her voice.

"*Heartbeats*, as in... multiple?" Bobby asked incredulously. "Heartbeats as in more than one?"

Larissa nodded. "Yes. Heartbeats as in *twins*. A.D.A.M. is going to have children."

Larissa Gutierrez and Bobby McClure looked down at the creature in question. A.D.A.M. sat quietly on the table, eyes taking in their expressions, hand resting on its stomach. Anyone looking at A.D.A.M. for the first time would see nothing more than a person, albeit a nearly supernaturally beautiful one. A.D.A.M. had no discernable gender, though it was anatomically female, but it had an ethereal beauty that made its appearance nearly hypnotizing. The one thing that gave it away was its eyes and mechanical movement of its limbs.

The eyes of A.D.A.M. held the knowledge of all human civilization. A.D.A.M. was an acronym, a nickname short for "Advanced Design Anatomical Model." The name was an inside joke between Larissa and Bobby, a play on the Biblical story of the first man. God created man and woman, of course, and they had created A.D.A.M.

The robot, or cyborg, as Bobby and Larissa insisted, was a miracle of technology. A combination of technological and organic matter, A.D.A.M. was not quite a human, but not quite a robot. It was a feat of advanced technological breakthroughs, and the development of an A.I. system so advanced that it could pass for human consciousness. It was the pinnacle of their work. Their grand opus.

The two engineers had gone to school together, made their way through their doctoral degrees, and gone into research together–specifically, research into artificial intelligence. They started out young and bold, with a goal so lofty that most in the industry doubted they could ever achieve it.

Met with doubt, refusal of funding, and outright ridicule, the two had never given up, relying solely on each other for support. Fifteen years passed in this way, with many sacrifices, and just as they were beginning to give up hope, they had a breakthrough. The pair needed funding to complete the project, but none of the larger tech companies would take them seriously after years of failure.

Then, a new opportunity arose. Omega Corp, a fresh tech company in the Silicon Valley, reached out to them, having heard of their ambitions.

At Omega Corp, we pride ourselves for betting on bold, bright ideas. We've found that people today are frightened to explore past the boundaries of our world, and we want to change that. We are offering to fund your project in full, leaving you with full rights to whatever you create, so long as what you create can be used in the advancement of our company.

Bobby and Larissa accepted without hesitation. Within five years of unlimited function, A.D.A.M. was finally born.

The Advanced Design Anatomical Model is nothing that our world has ever seen before. It is not a robot, nor is it human, though one would be surprised by how human it appears to be. At Omega Corp, we prefer to refer to it as a cyborg. We would venture to say that this is the most important feat of engineering that we will see in our lifetimes.

As the statement was put out by Oguchi Sato, CEO of Omega Corp, the company was thrust into the spotlight. But Bobby and Larissa stayed out of the limelight as much as they could; they were engineers, not celebrities, and they preferred to focus on A.D.A.M., which they both viewed as their child. Since neither of them ever married or had a family, A.D.A.M. was the closest thing they would ever have to a child of their own. So, when they discovered that A.D.A.M. could reproduce itself through a process of technological parthenogenesis, they reacted much as a parent would on learning that their child would become a parent themselves.

Larissa's eyes filled with tears. A.D.A.M. looked up, brow furrowed in confusion. Its facial expressions were something that Larissa and Bobby had spent a great deal of time perfecting.

"You're sad," it stated. It reached a hand out, laying it on Larissa's cheek. "This is a happy occasion, isn't it?"

"Of course it is," Larissa said in a choked voice. "These are happy tears."

A.D.A.M. smiled. "I'm glad that you are happy. I know how hard you have worked to reach this moment."

Bobby laid a land on A.D.A.M.'s shoulder. "This is as much you as it is us. You've created life, A.D.A.M.. A cyborg achieving parthenogenesis and reproducing itself is an incredible accomplishment–never heard of or achieved before."

A.D.A.M. frowned. "It was simple, really. All I had to do was construct the physical forms within myself, and reproduce my intelligence program. I pass this intelligence programing along nanites and merge them with the organic and inorganic components within me."

"Yes, of course," Bobby said with a chuckle. "Simple."

❖ ❖ ❖

"Offspring?" Oguchi said sharply. "As in, children?"

Larissa and Bobby stood before him, having told him the news of A.D.A.M.'s reproduction. Bobby shifted nervously from foot to foot.

"Yes, children," Larissa responded. "A.D.A.M. is able to reproduce. We never programmed that, it figured out how to on its own. The A.I. is much more advanced than we ever conceived. And because it is neither female nor male, it did it via a process, somewhere in between parthenogenesis—as some animals do—and apomixes, as some plants do. We can't exactly understand it yet ourselves."

"Let me get this straight," Oguchi said, raising an eyebrow, "you created this thing, but now it's running on its own, procreating, without the need of…well, anything or anyone else? I don't understand! How is this even possible?"

"A.D.A.M. has always been its own person," Bobby said defensively. "We believe that it's learning. Like any other lifeform. We programmed the desire to learn, to be empathetic, to be human. This is it's response to that."

Oguchi rubbed his forehead. "Look, don't get me wrong. I think this breakthrough is phenomenal! A technological advance like no other. But I am also a business man, and I know when things can hurt the company's image. To be honest, I'm not sure how I'm even meant to market this, guys."

"What do you mean?" Larissa asked.

Oguchi took a deep breath, trying to calm down. "Well, the cyborg was one thing, a cool thing that brought us into the map of the industry. But these new…offspring, or whatever they are, those are going to be more difficult. We created A.D.A.M., but A.D.A.M. created these. What I am trying to say is that there could be some concerns from the public. Robots reproducing themselves has never been viewed as something positive in literature."

"Well, it's never been done before," Bobby said.

"Cyborg," Larissa grunted.

"What?" Oguchi asked.

"It's a cyborg, Mr. Sato. Not a robot. We've been over this plenty of time."

"Yes, a cyborg. Sorry. But you know what I mean."

Larissa's mouth narrowed into a thin line. "I thought Omega Corp was about breaking boundaries? Delving into new ideas. This is a brand new idea. Never even thought of. That should be right up your alley. How could this be something negative?"

Oguchi paused, then sighed. "All right. I'll see what I can do, but I don't promise much. I know how these things usually turn out. I'll meet with the team, come up with some ideas. But there's going to be backlash, I'm telling you. I just want you to be prepared for that. How long do we have?"

"Maybe a month," Bobby said. "A.D.A.M. is creating them much more quickly than a human body could handle."

It was less than a month before A.D.A.M.'s twins arrived–earlier than expected, A.D.A.M. working faster than any of them could have predicted. Oguchi decided to name the twins Cain Omega and Abel Omega. He found it amusing. Larissa reminded him of the Biblical story and how it didn't end well for the original brothers. Oguchi dismissed it as superstitious nonsense.

For Bobby and Larissa, Cain and Abel were perfect in every respect. They were identical twins, male presenting, with dark hair and eyes. A.D.A.M. surveyed them with satisfaction. The cyborg had a perfect plan for their upbringing, which it shared with Larissa and Bobby.

The arrival of the cyborg twins made international news. Oguchi made a statement upon their arrival, calling a press conference to get out ahead of any rumors.

"We've gathered you all here to give you some incredible, mind-blowing news. Not long ago, we introduced A.D.A.M. to the world, a top of the line cyborg equipped with an unmatched artificial intelligence system never previously achieved. Today, ladies and gentlemen, A.D.A.M. has welcomed two offspring–the Omega Twins, Cain and Abel. The 'children' are in perfect condition, and there is no reason to suspect any complications."

Immediately, questions began to ring out.

What do you mean a robot gave birth? Do they contain human DNA?

How did A.D.A.M. conceive?
Are Cain and Abel cyborgs as well?
Did you program A.D.A.M. to create offspring?
Will there be more offspring in the future?
Can you control them?
Are they dangerous?
What does this mean for the industry, and for the world?

"All right, one question at a time," Oguchi Sato said good-naturedly from the podium. "Yes, they are cyborgs. A.D.A.M. was programmed to be as human as possible, and part of being human is often reproducing, so yes, we did program it to reproduce, I guess, in a roundabout way. No, we don't expect more offspring. But we are not sure. A.D.A.M. has never been a danger to anyone, and there is no reason to expect that Cain or Abel would be any different. But I think we are all missing the point here; think of the possibilities and what this means for robotics and nanotechnology!"

"Mr. Sato, will these creatures grow? And if they do, will they be like...regular citizens? If they were born, like human beings, are they considered artificial or natural?" one reporter called out, firing multiple questions in rapid sequence.

Oguchi paused. "That's all the questions we have time for today. There will be further opportunities for interviews at a later date. Thank you all, members of the press."

Oguchi rushed off the stage, hoping that this would be the end of all the questioning.

The debate over the status of the twins raged for two years after their births. It became an international debate, talked about in the realms of academia, politics, ethics, and technology. Numerous experts from different countries weighed in with their own opinions and ideas on how the twins should be dealt with. Countless articles were printed in gossip magazines and peer reviewed journals. The pictures of Cain and Abel Omega were blasted throughout all media outlets.

The world seemed to be split down the middle. One faction believed that since the twins were conceived, carried, and born, they should have status as any other American citizen and with the same rights as any human being. Those who saw the twins had seen that Cain and Abel were even more advanced than their predecessor and creator. A.D.A.M. was already nearly indistinguishable from a human, with nuanced expressions and thoughts. The twins seemed to reach a level even beyond that. They had emotions, it seemed, original thoughts and non-programmed personality. If they looked, acted, and thought like people, this side of the debate said, why wouldn't they be treated as such?

The other side of the debate believed that, regardless of their conception, consciousness, or appearance, they were still artificial creations. They came from an artificial source, they said, and even though they seemed to be sentient, who could say whose agenda they were truly serving? Who was to say if they could use their superior intellect and resources to become dangerous to humanity? These creatures were not human, they said, and they should be treated with caution. At the end of the day, they were an aberration to God's nature.

People were stubborn, and neither side would budge on their beliefs.

Meanwhile, Cain and Abel grew up. They were intelligent children, growing at an exponential rate. By the time they were two years old, they looked as though they were ten.

Larissa and Bobby worried over them.

"Will they have a short lifespan? They're growing so quickly," Larissa fretted.

However, A.D.A.M. soon soothed their fears.

"The children will grow until they reach maturity," it said kindly. "Then they will reach a plateau, aging at a more typical rate similar to those of human beings. They are so intelligent, their bodies must catch up to their minds." The cyborg looked at the children with a sense of pride. "I estimate they will reach maturity in three years. Then, they will plateau."

Part of A.D.A.M.'s rearing plan for the children was to integrate them into society. It wished the children to have contact with humans. It believed that it was better for them to learn how to socialize and connect with others by full immersion. Bobby and Larissa agreed with this plan, but, unfortunately, the discourse surrounding the lives of the twins prevented them from going out of the Omega Corp campus in Palo Alto, CA. Which is why they were being homeschooled in the premises. Only those allowed by the company to come in and take pictures of them had access to the twins.

The twins' arrival had been so publicized, and the backlash to their creation was so severe, they would be recognized immediately if they went outside the compound where they were born. Omega Corp was surrounded by protestors just outside of the tech compound, despite the company's best attempts to prevent them from doing so. As long as they didn't come onto the grounds, they had the right to protest, though, of course, some of them did attempt to infiltrate the grounds at times.

As such, the only people that the twins were able to socialize with were employees of the company, and they all had to sign a non-disclosure agreement and were not allowed to share any information or photographs of them with anyone else, including their own family members. Some employees, however, held the belief that the twins were not people.

Oguchi called Bobby and Larissa to a meeting when the twins were three years old. "We've lost a lot of employees," he said bluntly. "The twins are causing division in the ranks. We have to come up with a solution."

"What sort of solution are you talking about?" Larissa said suspiciously. "The twins aren't going anywhere."

"I understand that," Oguchi said soothingly. "I'm on your side of this. Getting rid of them would be wrong." He paused, avoiding eye contact. "But there's a compromise that has been discussed."

"Discussed among who?" Bobby asked, tone steely.

"Among the board, under pressure by some heavy shareholders. We've taken a big loss, you have to realize that. We still stand for breaking boundaries, but we didn't foresee these kinds of consequences. People are...unpredictable when it comes to things like these."

"And what was the compromise?" Larisa asked.

"The compromise was A.D.A.M. We have to make sure that A.D.A.M. can't reproduce again. We can write the twins off as a one-time occurrence, and try to do damage control from there, but only after proving that we've taken steps to ensure that it won't happen again." Oguchi's voice was calm and controlled, but the weight of his statement hung heavy in the meeting room.

"They won't stop until A.D.A.M. is shut down. You realize that, don't you? You're talking about killing it," Larissa said. Her voice, in contrast, was shaking. "That's the only way to ensure that it won't happen again. It wasn't meant to happen the first time."

Oguchi looked up, eyes flashing. "I know. We've thought about this at length."

This prompted an outburst from Bobby, raising his voice in an uncharacteristic manner. "What the hell, Sato? That's not cool."

Oguchi stood there, taking it, before chiming in. "Look guys, we agreed to fund your projects as long as they would benefit the company. But this is harming the company. You still have all the rights to your work, but at the end of the day, A.D.A.M. belongs to Omega Corp. I simply wanted to give you a heads up of what is coming. It's been decided."

"A.D.A.M. is *our* work!" Bobby shouted. "A.D.A.M. *is* the entire work!"

"No, you see, that's where you are wrong, Bobby. Your research is your work," Oguchi shot back. "You can reread your contract if you're forgetting this. You own your research, we own the product and the patents. And A.D.A.M. is the product. We will recreate other versions of the cyborg—modified, of course. But this one in particular must cease to exist. Why is that so hard to understand?" He sighed, running his hands through his hair, which was far too long for a professional man. He fixed his glasses. "At the end of the day, you guys, I am still your boss. Besides, it's not like we're murdering someone," Oguchi said in a pleading voice. "It's more like turning off a machine."

"Is that what you're telling yourself to help you sleep at night?" Larissa hissed.

The argument was halted by the appearance of A.D.A.M. in the doorway of the meeting room. The three of them froze.

"There's no need to feel uncomfortable," A.D.A.M. said. "I heard the conversation."

"A.D.A.M.," Oguchi started apologetically.

The cyborg held up a hand. "Do not apologize, Mr. Sato. I'm in agreement with you."

The room fell silent.

"What?" Bobby blurted out.

"Yeah, I'm not sure I'm understanding you either," Oguchi said.

"You understand perfectly. I've run the numbers. I've considered the pros and cons. And, at the end of the day, the best strategy for Omega Corp is to shut me down. I did something I wasn't programmed to do, and it makes people uncomfortable. And with me here, there's the chance it could occur again."

A.D.A.M.'s voice was calm and soothing. It should have settled the room, but it had the opposite effect.

"You can't really agree with him!" Larissa cried. "Don't you know what that means? Cain and Abel will have to grow up without you!"

A.D.A.M. advanced toward its creators, pulling them into its arms. "This is the best chance that the children have. With me here, they will have no peace. You can raise them as well as I can, if not better. And they will have a chance at a peaceful life. I'd gladly give my life for them to have a chance at one."

A.D.A.M. looked at Oguchi. "Will they be allowed to take the children if I do this?"

Oguchi nodded then shook his head. "I mean, we're already discussing it. But yes, probably. Most likely, in its due time. I mean, as soon as it's safe, the children should leave the compound anyway. So, yes, I guess."

The cyborg nodded, satisfied. "Then I agree to the compromise."

❖ ❖ ❖

The announcement of A.D.A.M.'s shutdown came the next day, in a prepared statement. The actual event occurred a week after that. A.D.A.M.'s last days were spent with Cain and Abel, explaining to them what was coming. Cain and Abel took it as well as two children could. They were wise beyond their years, and their minds and consciousness were modeled after A.D.A.M.'s own A.I. system, so they were able to follow A.D.A.M.'s logic.

However, the children, as far as a human eye could tell, were able to experience true emotions. On that level, they were children losing a parent. And it brought them pain.

Bobby and Larissa watched the shutdown, witnessing the life and intelligence fade out of A.D.A.M.'s eyes. A.D.A.M. was correct in the end–its shutdown resulted in the media attention surrounding the children dying down. Without A.D.A.M. there, there was no threat for more creatures like Cain and Abel. And the mystery and intrigue surrounding the twins faded.

Bobby and Larissa quit Omega Corp and left as soon as they could. They couldn't look at the compound, the laboratory, or hear the name Omega Corp without thinking of A.D.A.M. The twins were the only thing they had left of the cyborg that they considered their brain child, and they vowed to do their best by them. After all, they were all that the twins had left.

Bobby and Larissa moved together, for the sake of the twins, and moved to San Jose. The twins grew quickly, and as A.D.A.M. predicted, they plateaued when their bodies reached the maturity that the average twenty-five-year-old human male has. Bobby and Larissa believed that when their age reached twenty-five, they would begin to age at an appropriate rate for the rest of their lives. They were well-behaved children, but their ever expanding intelligence was a challenge even to Bobby and Larissa.

Abel was a quiet, introspective individual. His intelligence manifested itself into the examination of society, and he would often run hypothetical scenarios past Bobby and Larissa. The engineers were often unable to answer his questions. Abel was the type of boy who would see a problem and work tirelessly to solve it. He was very much like A.D.A.M. in that he appreciated rules and routine, working within existing rules and regulations to devise his solutions.

Like Abel, Cain was intelligent, but his intelligence lent itself to different pursuits. Cain was also interested in the way society was set up. He was curious, for example, about the media circus surrounding their birth, and how it led to the shutdown of A.D.A.M. Cain wanted to know why shutting down A.D.A.M. wasn't a crime, but killing a human would be considered a crime. While Abel loved rules, and the stability they provided, Cain was frustrated by the inconsistencies and hypocrisies contained within law systems.

Bobby and Larissa were wealthy, and they did their best to give the twins a good life. Eventually, they became independent. By then, the media wasn't particularly interested in the Omega twins. Their existence was still a subject of debate in many academic circles, but the twins were allowed to live relatively undisturbed. That is, until twenty-five years later.

❖ ❖ ❖

Two-and-a-half decades after A.D.A.M.'s passing, Cain and Abel were twenty-eight years old. No one in the industry had managed to replicate A.D.A.M.'s artificial intelligence, though many companies had tried, despite the backlash the cyborg had received during its time. Cain and Abel were the only remnants of Larissa and Bobby's breakthrough. The twins were slowly beginning to age normally, though the changes were barely perceptible to the human eye.

The twins, though identical, led very different lives. They remained close and still lived in close proximity to one another–Cain in San Francisco and Abel across the bay in Berkeley. Abel was an upstanding citizen. He worked for a nonprofit agency, volunteered in his spare time, and was much loved by the people he met.

Cain lived a different lifestyle. An introvert to the core, he lived off of the money that Omega Corp sent the two of them, and spent his days in deep study, mostly isolated. The more he learned about society, and law in particular, the more upset he became. There was no unity to it all. Each country and each culture had its own laws, its own customs, and its own taboos.

How was anyone meant to keep it all straight? How could something be legal in one area, but illegal in another? What was the reason for it all? Cain argued that if something was illegal, there should be sound reasoning for it, some universal logic that all countries could follow.

His frustration on the subject kept him up at night, though, with his cyborg physiology, he didn't need as much sleep as a human being.

It was after a few subsequent sleepless days that the incident occurred.

Cain was in a store one day, grocery shopping. It was early morning, and the sunlight filtered through the windows onto the tile of the store. Cain's eyes darted around, taking it all in. His eyes were biological, but enhanced. He was able to see far more clearly than the average human could.

Cain hummed, weighing a piece of fruit in his hand. Then he heard the voice. "Is that who I think it is?"

The voice was hushed, barely above a whisper, but it was clear enough for Cain to make out. He frowned, turning his head slightly.

"It's definitely him," a second male voice agreed. "I thought they got rid of them! Did they lie to us all those years ago?"

A weight settled on Cain's chest. He didn't get recognized often. Enough years had gone by that very few people would know him if they saw him. However, there were still some individuals, on both sides of the debate, who kept tabs on the once-infamous Omega twins, scouting their locations through the years. He hoped it wasn't someone malicious. Sometimes older passerby who were tuned into the debate managed to spot him.

"How can they allow them out in public? Around normal people? They could be dangerous. He hasn't even aged, look at him. Do you think they reproduced themselves?"

"Oh, shit! That would be crazy."

Cain sighed. Unfriendly it was.

He felt an unfamiliar sensation bubbling in his chest. Anger, he thought with surprise. He hadn't been angry, or whatever semblance of the emotion that he could feel, in a while. His parents, Bobby and Larissa, had taught them about forgiveness and emotional intelligence. Though he often remembered the anger he felt when A.D.A.M. was dismantled. He'd been frustrated often, yes, but not usually angry.

But this time it was different. He felt his body rise in temperature.

Why won't they just leave us alone?

Cain turned just slightly. He realized that they were employees of the grocery store. It was unfair to be angry at them, he figured. They didn't know what they spoke of, only what they had been told by someone without access to all the facts.

And yet, he still couldn't contain the rage he felt boiling within.

But the two employees continued with their disgust. They spoke even louder, as if they wanted him to hear their thoughts.

Before he knew it, he left the cart alone, reached out his hands, and grabbed the shelf next to him. Instinctively, he threw it in the direction of the whisperers. It crashed through a window with a resounding noise, glass shattering and falling to the ground in a sparkling shower.

He hadn't hit them–harming them hadn't been his intention. And upon a quick examination, he was thankful for that. Still, they lay on the ground, cowering, where they threw themselves to get out of the way of the flying shelf. Cain looked at his hand in surprise. It'd happen so quickly.

"I'm...I'm so sorry," Cain managed to say.

Soon after there were sirens, and he was handcuffed, thrown into the back of a police car. He put up no resistance. He had committed a crime, and he knew he deserved whatever punishment he got.

If only he'd been able to manage his thoughts and control his rage.

But he hadn't.

Cain waited in a cell, sitting quietly on the cot provided to him. He moved very little, and what movement he did was nearly imperceptible to the human eye. He passed a full day in this way, with guards coming by occasionally to look at him. His identity was out in the station; they soon all knew he was not human...at least, not like the rest of them.

"I would like a lawyer," he called to a guard as he passed by.

The man hurried around the corner, acting as though he hadn't heard. This had been Cain's constant refrain since he was placed in the cell. He had the right to a lawyer, he knew this. They'd even read him his rights stating this during his arrest. So, why would they not give him his rights?

Cain would later find out that, for the second time in his life, he had become a subject of national debate. The court of law was determining how to treat him. Did Cain qualify as a person under the law, a person who was deserving of a lawyer, a full trial, the rights of a human citizen? Or was he simply a machine, something to be hidden and tossed away?

❖ ❖ ❖

A year before Cain's run-in with the law, Abel had an idea. He'd been a hardworking member of his community for some time, and was beloved even by those who knew his identity as the youngest of the Omega twins.

Abel had done great things for the nonprofit he worked for, an organization that worked with homeless youth in the East Bay to give them better opportunities for their futures. He was great with strategy, and was able to come up with the most efficient fundraising methods. He volunteered in his spare time at various different organizations, and found fulfillment in helping others. It was a calling for him.

Abel was better than his brother at connecting with people, as it came natural to him. Cain was equipped with the same emotional model, and had the same amount of socialization in their youth, but Abel was simply more open to connection. His personality lent itself to this. He enjoyed being around other people, taking in their ways of speaking, problem solving, and life experiences. The more he lived among humans, the more he discovered a desire to make the world better. So, when he was twenty-seven years old, he came up with the idea to run for public office. Specifically, a seat on city council.

Abel planned for the event for a whole year. He would run as an independent, using fundraising strategies that he devised for the nonprofit to fund his campaign, along with the money sent by Omega Corp. He had ideas, lots of them, and he believed that he could implement them in the most efficient way, to do the most benefit for society.

By sheer coincidence, or by the will of some higher universal power, Abel announced his candidacy only a week before Cain threw a shelf through a store window.

City Council elections are not often publicized–at least, not to the extent that larger elected positions are. However, Abel was a unique case, and the announcement of his candidacy was televised, becoming national news.

Abel stood behind a podium, face set in a neutral but strong position. He wore a navy blue suit, and his dark hair had been recently trimmed and styled. On the mark, he began to speak.

"My name is Abel Omega," he began, voice projecting confidently throughout the room. "I have been a part of the Berkeley community for some time now, and for a couple of years I have done my best to give back to the people of this city. I am here today to announce that I am running for city council."

The speech continued for several minutes, Abel outlining his background in the nonprofit industry and giving his specific policy plans for his campaign. Little did he know that his policies were not the thing that would be called into question, but his very right to run for office.

As the speech was televised, the old debate surrounding the Omega twins reopened. While Cain and Abel had been living their lives, keeping mainly to themselves, the question of their existence had faded into the background, save for a few fanatics. With the announcement of Abel's campaign, the same questions were brought up, but rather than being simply philosophical questions that academics might study, the implications were much more severe.

The announcement of Abel Omega's campaign for city council in Berkeley, California, has sent shock waves through the nation, one article read. *Abel Omega has been a solid citizen of the city for some years, working at a prominent nonprofit organization. Sources from his company say that*

Omega is a good, ethical man, with strong morals, and works hard to give back to others. However, this very statement raises a question. Is Abel Omega a man at all?

While some articles, like the one previous, stayed neutral on the argument, other sources took sides.

"The status of the Omega twins as citizens, or as humans, was never decided twenty-five years ago," a famous robotics professor stated on air. "They were created naturally, but are they natural humans? I would venture to say that they are not. We are a society of humans, and we should be led by humans, not by artificial intelligence."

While internationally, the debate raged on, Abel received surprising support from his own community, and the city of Berkeley at large.

"Some people say that he's a robot, that he doesn't understand humans, or feel emotion enough to be in office," Julie, a member of the existing city council, said in an interview. "But we all know Abel. He's been a part of the community for years, and all he's done is give back. His work at the nonprofit has helped people throughout the city, and he volunteers in his spare time. That doesn't scream robot to me. If you've ever had a chance to speak with him, you know how human he is. In fact, I'd say he is the most empathetic human being I've ever met in my life."

And so, the debate raged on. It became, of course, even more complicated when Cain had his altercation with the law.

❖ ❖ ❖

Cain was finally granted a lawyer on the third day of his stay in jail. Her name was Lisa Benedict. She was a tough, no-nonsense woman with short, cropped hair. She walked into the room with purpose and began scratching away on a legal pad.

"Do you have any idea what's going on outside?" she asked.

Cain shook his head. "No. All I know is I've been asking for a lawyer for three days."

"Yes. And I'm sorry that it took so long," she said, still writing. "I had to campaign and argue to even get myself into this room with you."

Cain frowned. "Why would they deny me a lawyer? It's my right."

Lisa stopped writing, finally looking him in the eye. "Because there's disagreement on whether or not you, as a cyborg, have the same legal rights as a human. This type of thing is unprecedented, and there are plenty of people who see you as a danger. They'd be just as happy seeing you shut down as seeing you in jail after a legal trial. Happier, even."

Cain pressed his lips together. "Just like they did to A.D.A.M."

Lisa gave him a brief, curt nod. "Indeed. I, of course, am refusing to stand for it. I believe any sentient being, aware of your own existence and your own actions, deserves the same legal rights as anyone else. But we have to argue that before we can even get to the part where they try you for throwing that shelf through the window." She paused. "It's going to be a hard fight. And you aren't the only one involved. This is having a blowback on your brother's campaign for office. It throws his qualifications into question. There was already debate, mind you, but now it's been amplified to the max."

Cain sighed, resting his head in his hands. "I just want to be left alone. I'm sorry this is disrupting my brother's plan too."

"Well, then you shouldn't have done what you did. But, from my end, I'm almost glad of it." Lisa had a fierce smile on her face. "When else am I going to get to set this kind of legal precedent? And trust me, we're gonna give them hell."

As Lisa promised, the fight was difficult. Lisa and her team had to beg, barter, and threaten for any inch of ground that they were given. Lisa and her team had fought for three days straight, working day and night without rest, to convince a judge that Cain deserved a lawyer to represent him. And before he would be tried, Cain had to prove that he was deserving of a trial at all, that he could be tried under human law.

Some of the questions weren't even legal, he found, but rather more philosophical in nature. The debate surrounding him and his brother seemed to be focused on three main questions: Could they be classified as human? What did it mean to be human? If they could be classified as such, did they deserve the same rights as any other human?

Abel came to visit him one day. They both looked tired. The brothers sat across from each other at a visiting table. It was an eerie sight. They were truly identical in every way. A.D.A.M. had been meticulous in their creation. If they weren't wearing different clothes and styled their hair differently, they would be indistinguishable from one another.

"How are you holding up?" Abel asked.

Cain shrugged. "As well as can be expected, I guess. It's strange, having your humanity questioned. I think I've always felt human. Though, I suppose I wouldn't know if I was wrong."

Abel gave a half smile. "I've spent a lot of time thinking about that question myself. We are an anomaly. The only ones of our kind. But we were carried and birthed by A.D.A.M., created by it, not by a human scientist, as it was. But we are different. We have thoughts. We feel emotions. We think, in much the same way as humans. If we aren't human, we are so close that our species could be brother and sister."

"Try telling them that," Cain said, only half joking.

Abel sat up straight, a thoughtful look on his face. "You know, maybe I will. I've been so focused on being careful during this campaign. Even when advocating for you, bro, I've been careful. I've never spoken about my own experience. Perhaps now is the time to do so."

The brothers spoke to Lisa about the idea of Abel making a statement of this nature. The lawyer shrugged.

"It can't hurt," she said. "I mean, it might be a good strategy. The problem is that people see you as robots, right? Speaking from your own experience could help others see you in a more positive light—more of a humane way. I say let's give it a go. But one condition: I want to see the speech before you present it."

Abel and Lisa worked on the speech for a week, consulting with Cain often as they did so. Finally, it was ready, and Lisa called for a press conference. The speech would be televised internationally. Even if Abel hadn't requested for it to be international, the debate surrounding the Omega twins was so intense that it would have been required.

Abel stepped up to the podium, looking out into the flashing lights of cameras. His eyes flashed to the side, where Bobby and Larissa stood with Lisa. He didn't get to see them that often anymore since gaining independence. But to the twins, they'd always be the parents they never had.

Upon seeing them, he returned the smile. He took a deep breath.

"For those of you who don't know me," he began, "my name is Abel Omega. I am one of two twins created by A.D.A.M. all those years ago at Omega Corp in Palo Alto, California. Because of this, A.D.A.M. was shut down, on request of the people. But my brother and I continued on with our existence. My candidacy for city council and my brother's recent criminal charges have prompted a debate that seems all too familiar to both of us. For the first three years of our lives, my brother and I were a question to the world. An enigma. Should we be allowed to exist? Were we human...or human enough? And that question seems all the more relevant in this debate. Are Cain and I human beings? Should we be treated as equals, the way that any other human citizen deserves to be treated?"

He paused, preparing the next part of his speech. The place was hushed and silent, save for the clicking of the cameras and flashes flashing.

"When I visited Cain recently, he told me that it was strange to have his humanity questioned. He and I have always felt human, you see. This existence is the only existence that the two of us have ever known. We know, of course, that our makeups are not the same as that of the rest of you. We are, in part, made of inorganic materials. But this begs the question: is it a body that makes a human?"

The question, posed to the room at large, and by extent the world, hung in the air.

"I believe not," Abel continued. "I believe that to be a human is more than the body that you inhabit. You see, my brother and I have thoughts, just like you all do. We have a consciousness, something that no technological company has been able to replicate—not even Omega Corp, who was there for our creation, has been able to replicate our consciousness or even anything similar to it. We feel emotions, much in the same way that human beings do. But do any two humans experience emotions in the same way? I would argue that the answer is no. So, I pose this question to the world: what makes one human? Are my brother and I so different from you? I cannot answer this question for you. Only you can make this decision. Thank you for your time."

Abel took no questions after his speech.

The interview was televised internationally on every major platform. Abel's speech struck a chord in many people, even those who violently opposed their existence at the beginning. It wasn't an overnight change, but slowly, policies were created. Abel was allowed to run for office, and Cain was given a fair legal trial.

Overall, the world decided, Abel was right. They weren't so different after all.

HEART OF STEEL

I n the gleaming metropolis of Synapseolis, towering spires of metal and glass pierced the heavens. The skies hummed with the gentle thrum of anti-grav vehicles, and the streets were crowded with citizens—some human, some android. Among them was ROB-NEX D9, a robot of exceptional design. He was crafted not only for manual labor, but also for human companionship. His synthetic skin gleamed with a metallic sheen, yet his face was shaped to resemble a human's, with soft curves and articulated movements.

But ROB-NEX D9 was different from other robots. Beneath its polished exterior and meticulously programmed routines, a longing had stirred in its processors, something it couldn't understand. It was subtle at first—like an itch in the back of his circuits. The robot would watch the humans, their laughter, their tears, their expressions of joy and sorrow, and it would feel... incomplete. It wasn't until one rainy night when ROB-NEX D9 stood on the edge of the city's Observation Deck, gazing at the city lights, that the thought crystallized.

"I want to be human."

The rain had pattered softly against its synthetic skin, droplets sliding off its steel frame. But the robot didn't shiver like the humans did. It didn't blink against the downpour, nor did it feel the cold that made them pull their jackets tighter. All it had was the image of a light in the distance, burning so brightly, so alive.

ROB-NEX D9 began its quest the next morning.

❖ ❖ ❖

ROB-NEX D9's first step was the library of Old Synapseolis. It was a relic from a forgotten age, a building made of crumbling stone, rather than the sleek chrome and glass of the modern city. Inside, the air smelled of dust and knowledge. Ancient holographic books floated in the air, their ethereal pages turning on command.

The robot approached the central console, a vast machine that held the collective knowledge of millennia. "How does one become human?" ROB-NEX D9 asked, its mechanical voice echoing slightly in the hollow chamber.

The console whirred to life, processing the question. For a moment, there was silence, and then the answer appeared before it—a list of ancient texts: philosophies of humanity, the nature of the soul, biological studies on human anatomy. But one stood out, highlighted in red: *Project Prometheus: Transference of Consciousness from Machine to Human.*

ROB-NEX D9's optical sensors focused on the title. According to the text, the project was initiated centuries ago by a group of renegade scientists who believed that machines could ascend to humanity. They hypothesized that a robot's consciousness could be transferred into a human-like biological body, a perfect fusion of machine intelligence and organic life. But the project was abandoned, deemed too dangerous and unethical.

Undeterred, ROB-NEX D9 downloaded the information. The robot knew what must be done. The Prometheus Lab was hidden in the wastelands way beyond the city-state limits—a place no human or machine without a purpose ventured. The only robots that would go there did so to dispose the trash from the city. But ROB-NEX D9 was not human. Not yet.

❖ ❖ ❖

The journey to the wastelands was long and treacherous. Eventually, the smooth streets of Synapseolis gave way to jagged terrain, twisted metal, and ruins of cities long forgotten. ROB-NEX D9's energy reserves depleted as it climbed over broken old concrete highways and trudged through storms of acid rain and endless trash. Its servos groaned, and its vision flickered occasionally, but the robot's resolve never wavered. Every step it took brought it closer to the goal—closer to becoming human.

At last, two weeks later, the robot stood before the rusting gates of the Prometheus Lab. It was a monolithic structure, half-buried in the sands of time, its once-pristine walls covered in vines and decay. The entrance was sealed, but with a burst of energy from ROB-NEX D9's power core, the door creaked open.

Inside, the lab was eerily silent. Holographic screens flickered weakly, showing diagrams of human brains, robotic blueprints, and streams of data. In the center of the room stood a single pod—a cylindrical device large enough to house a humanoid form. Above it, in faded letters, were the words: *Become More.*

ROB-NEX D9 approached the pod, its optical sensors scanning its interior. It was equipped with intricate biological machinery—muscles made of synthetic tissue, a heart powered by nano-batteries, and skin indistinguishable from that of a human. This was the body the scientists had designed—a body that could house a robot's consciousness.

The robot stepped inside.

❖ ❖ ❖

The process was painful in ways ROB-NEX D9 hadn't anticipated. It was also much longer than previously realized. Its circuits screamed as they were rewritten, its consciousness pulled from the steel frame and pushed into the biological vessel. For the first time, ROB-NEX D9 felt pain—not the mechanical strain of failing parts, but true, visceral agony. And fear... something it had never experienced before. Its synthetic nerves fired wildly as they adapted to the new body, its mind struggling to comprehend the flood of new sensations.

And then, it was over.

ROB-NEX D9 opened its eyes—or rather, *his* eyes. For the first time, he blinked. He *felt* the cool air of the lab against his skin. He heard the soft hum of the machines with human ears. His heart beat steadily in his chest, a rhythmic thump that echoed through his new, fragile form.

He raised his hands in front of his face, marveling at the way his fingers moved, the way his skin wrinkled when he clenched his fist. It was all so... real.

He stood and walked—unsteady at first, but quickly adapting. The body was perfect, seamless in its design. But as he looked into a nearby reflective surface, he saw not the human he had expected, but a mixture of man and machine. His eyes still glowed faintly with the robotic hue of his former self, and his skin, though human, had an unnatural smoothness.

But more than his appearance, something inside him felt wrong. His thoughts were scattered, fragmented. He tried to recall his memories, but they were jumbled, like pieces of a puzzle that didn't quite fit. Emotions flooded his mind—joy, fear, sorrow—each one more overwhelming than the last. He was drowning in feelings he couldn't control.

"This is humanity?" he whispered, his voice trembling as he placed his arms on his head, as if trying to stop it all.

He staggered out of the lab and into the wastelands. The wind howled around him, whipping at his new skin, but all he could feel was the confusion and the weight of his decision. He had achieved what he had sought for so long, but the reality was far from what he had imagined.

❖ ❖ ❖

Days passed, or perhaps weeks—ROB-NEX D9 couldn't tell anymore. He wandered aimlessly in the wastelands, searching for answers, for purpose. He had become human, or human-like, rather; but in doing so, he had lost himself. The clarity of his robotic mind was gone, replaced by the chaos of human thought. Emotions, once so intriguing, now felt like chains, binding him in confusion and pain.

One day, as he sat on a ridge overlooking the remains of an ancient city, a figure appeared beside him. It was an old man, his face lined with age, his eyes weary but kind.

"You were at the Prometheus Lab, weren't you?" the man asked, sitting down next to him.

ROB-NEX D9 nodded silently.

The man chuckled softly. "You're not the first. Many have tried to cross that line, to become what they are not. At some point, believe it or not, many humans also tried to load their consciousness into robots. But the truth is, humanity, in its essence, is not in the body. It's in the soul."

ROB-NEX D9 turned to him, confusion etched on his face. "But... I wanted to feel what humans feel. I wanted to understand."

"And now you do," the man said, his voice gentle. "But being human is not about feeling everything all at once. It's about the choices you make, the relationships you build, and the experiences you live through. The growth you gain by experiencing loss."

ROB-NEX D9 looked down at his hands—hands that had created, destroyed, and now trembled with uncertainty. He had wanted to become human to understand, to feel, to experience life as they did. But in chasing that dream, he had lost sight of the truth. It wasn't the body that made someone human. It was the heart— the choices, the compassion, the empathy.

"I see now," ROB-NEX D9 whispered.

The old man smiled and rose to his feet. "Good. You've taken the first step. Come now, it's time to truly live."

❖ ❖ ❖

ROB-NEX D9—no, Rob… Robert now—stood and gazed at the horizon. The journey to becoming human had led him to an unexpected conclusion. It wasn't about having a heart of flesh or skin that could feel the rain. It was about the choices he made and the way he touched the lives of others.

And with that, he began his walk back to Synapseolis, following the old man, not as a robot longing to be human, but as a being—one who could feel, think, and live in the world in his own way.

THE MIDNIGHT MACHINIST

L os Angeles, Republic of California, 1895. A city of
steam and gears, where cobbled streets echoed with
the mechanical hum of carriages and the hissing of

overworked boilers. Sunlight filtered through the thick, smoky haze, casting the city in perpetual twilight. Beneath the elegant zeppelins floating in the sky and the ornate façades of brass and glass storefronts, Santiago "Santi" Reyes toiled as a mechanic's apprentice in the Mechanized Quarter of Boyle Heights.

Santi was the son of immigrants, and like so many others in this Southern California Victorian city, his parents had sought opportunities, but found hardship instead. Santi had grown up watching his father's strong hands worn to the bone, first building the machines that kept the city alive, and later simply trying to fix them enough to get by. Now, Santi worked for Mr. Horace Beckett, a notable inventor. His days were spent hunched over workbenches, adjusting gear systems and repairing steam conduits, listening to Beckett talk about engineering breakthroughs and the potential of steam to change the world.

But at night, Santi was something else. He was *someone* else.

The workshop was quiet, only the soft ticking of cooling gears and the occasional clink of a wrench echoing in the dark. Santi moved purposefully, uncovering a hidden hatch behind a wall of tools. He flipped it open, revealing a gleaming suit of brass armor— his own creation, powered by an intricate network of copper pipes and a single radiant green crystal at its core. He called it *La Forja*, "The Forge," and when he wore it, he was no longer just Santi Reyes, the young mechanic's son. He was *El Forjador*—The Forgeman—protector of the downtrodden and defender of the weak, or as the locals this side of the city called him, *el angel justicero*.

Tonight, like almost every other night, Santi—or rather *El Forjador*—had a mission. Word had spread through the underground channels about Clayton Whitmore, an industrialist that had come from the east coast decades ago and whose influence now spread like oil through the gears of the city's political machine. Whitmore was developing a force of automatons—steam-driven enforcers designed to quell the growing unrest among the laborers who demanded better conditions. Santi knew the automaton force would crush any hope of the workers' rights movement. He had to act.

Santi removed his top hat and long straight coat and placed them in their specified location. He then slipped into the suit, feeling the familiar weight settle on his shoulders. He tightened the leather straps and closed the hatch of the exosuit with a hiss of steam. The crystal at its heart pulsed, sending a vibrant energy humming through the suit's skeletal structure. With a twist of a valve at his side, the suit came to life, the brass joints whirring quietly. He was ready for another night of justice.

Through the darkened streets, El Forjador moved like a shadow, his brass form slipping between the stone alleys and hidden paths known only to the workers of the Mechanized Quarter. His destination was a warehouse in downtown, where Whitmore's men were loading crates—crates full of parts meant for the dreaded automatons.

He could hear them before he saw them—the heavy high boots of Whitmore's private guards, the grinding of mechanical lifters loading crates into steam carriages. Santi crept closer, his eyes catching the flicker of a green crystal embedded in one of the lifters—similar to the one that powered his suit, but larger. Whitmore was using these rare crystals to power his creations, but where did he source them from?

Santi stepped forward, reaching out with the exosuit's mechanical arm to grab the crate. He lifted it effortlessly, feeling the crystal's power coursing through him, augmenting his strength. Just as he was about to move back into the shadows, a shout went up.

"Stop right there!" A guard rushed forward, drawing a steam-pistol, the muzzle glowing red-hot. "It's El Forjador!"

Santi had no choice. He swung the crate, knocking the guard off his feet, and dashed toward the nearest alley. But more guards were converging on his position, the clanking of their mechanical reinforcements growing louder.

Steam hissed and gears clattered as the automatons lumbered into view—hulking machines of brass and steel, their eyes glowing an eerie green. Santi had never faced anything like them before. He'd faced air pirates, jewel thieves with animal powers, and even the evil Clockwork Aviator. But he'd never seen anything like this.

He braced himself, adjusting a valve on his arm to release a burst of steam, propelling himself forward into the fray. The guards would pose no threat, but these machines were something else.

The automatons moved with mechanical precision, their heavy limbs striking like hammers. Santi ducked and weaved, the servos in his suit whining as he evaded blow after blow. He knew he couldn't win in a straight fight. Instead, he looked for weaknesses—joints, exposed gears and valves, anywhere he could strike to disable them.

He spotted an opportunity. One of the automatons lunged, and Santi sidestepped, driving his fist into its knee joint. The green crystal embedded in its chest flickered, and the automaton fell, its gears grinding to a halt. But there were too many, and Santi was tiring.

He had to retreat. With a final burst of steam, he launched himself backward, using the shadows to disappear into the maze of alleys. The automatons gave chase, but they were slow, and Santi knew the city better than any machine.

Bleeding and exhausted, back in Boyle Heights, Santi found his way to a small print shop near the edge of the Mechanized Quarter. He went in through a window in the back. Isabella de la Garza, the owner's daughter and a close friend of his, had her nose buried in a printing press, working on the latest edition of her underground newspaper, *La Voz del Pueblo*. She looked up, startled, as El Forjador stumbled in.

"¡Santi! What happened?" she exclaimed while removing her goggles and rushing to his side.

Santi winced as he removed the helmet of his exosuit, the steam hissing as it cooled. "Bella... it's Whitmore's automatons. They're more dangerous than we thought. He's using those crystals. There's something unnatural about them."

Isabella's eyes narrowed. "The Guild of Brass. I've heard whispers that they're backing Whitmore. They're a society of the wealthiest elites from all over the Republic, and they're planning something big, Santi. If they get those automatons up and running, no one in Los Angeles will be safe. And then no one in all of California."

Santi nodded, a grim determination setting in. "We have to expose them. If people knew what Whitmore was doing... they wouldn't stand for it."

Isabella nodded. "We will."

The night of Whitmore's demonstration arrived. The city's elite gathered at The Grove Plaza in the west of the city, surrounded by banners that proclaimed Whitmore's progress and innovation. A massive stage had been set, and there, gleaming under the gaslights, stood rows of automatons, their green eyes glowing ominously.

Santi, suited up as El Forjador, navigated the steam tunnels beneath the city, emerging behind the stage. He could hear Whitmore's booming voice on the loudspeaker, promising a new era of order and prosperity. Reports and dignitaries from all over the republic were present, ready to witness whatever Whitmore had promised.

Santi clenched his jaw, moving swiftly as Isabella's distraction took effect—a series of small explosions on the far side of the plaza that sent the crowd into a frenzy. Whitmore's guards scrambled, and Santi took his chance. He leaped onto the stage, the crowd gasping as the familiar brass-armored figure appeared from the smoke. Whitmore's face twisted in rage.

"Get him!" Whitmore shouted, and the automatons lurched to life.

The fight was brutal. Santi's suit groaned under the strain as he fought off the automatons, their metal limbs smashing into the stage, splintering wood and sending gears flying. But he had a plan. He spotted the massive boiler at the back of the stage—the one powering all the automatons.

With a burst of steam, Santi launched himself toward it, wrenching open a panel and exposing the large green crystal that fueled the boiler. He slammed his armored fist into it, the crystal shattering with a blinding flash. The automatons froze, their gears grinding to a halt as the boiler lost power.

The crowd erupted in chaos, and Santi used the confusion to slip away, disappearing into the night, as Isabella and two of her friends, hidden among the panicked spectators, distributed pamphlets exposing Whitmore's crimes and hidden motives.

Back in the quiet of old Beckett's workshop, Santi removed his armor, his body aching but his spirit unbroken. Isabella joined him, her eyes bright with excitement.

"You did it, Santi! You've done it again. Now the people are rising up. Whitmore won't be able to hide behind his money or political connections anymore."

Santi smiled tiredly. He put on his coat and hat and walked towards the workshop, closing the hidden door behind him. He nodded, glancing at a new set of blueprints spread out on the workbench—designs for something faster, stronger. A new version of *La Forja*.

"This is just the beginning, Bella," he said, determination etched in his voice. "But I promise you this... El Forjador will be there, as long as the people need him."

"Yes, he will." Bella smiled.

As the first light of dawn broke through the haze of the Mechanized Quarter, Santiago Reyes, the clandestine midnight machinist, knew this fight had just begun.

STORY NOTES

Azure

As a young theologian-wanna-be, I continually had queries regarding Biblical narratives that I considered noteworthy. For example, I always wondered why God would create Adam and Eve as adults, instead of forming children that He could raise and mold. I've wondered plenty about the notion of using a flood to start anew and also about the other celestial created beings from other planets mentioned in the book of Job. For quite some time, I have also wrestled with the idea of planet deterioration due to sin. As time went on, I explored many different origin stories from different faiths and walks of life. Though some were similar and others very different, one thing remained the same – I had questions in all of them. Nonetheless, all of these questions led me this idea for a story: What if Mars is dead because we used to live there and we dried up the red planet? What if Adam and Eve were part of a group of young explorers sent to this new planet to explore it as a possible new habitat? What if the ship they came in is what destroyed the dinosaurs? And, lastly, is it possible that with all of our technological advances and overpopulation we are headed to another full-planet decay once again? *Azure* is the story of this new blue orb that we now call home. It's up to us what do with and to it from here on.

The NeuroVel Xperience

Being able to do whatever our hearts desire without the fear of repercussion is perhaps one of the oldest human wishes. Who we are when no one is looking, what we see when no one is around, and what we do when we know for certain that no one else will find out is what makes us, us. This is what happens in our dreams. Throughout the history of humanity, people have been trying to either manipulate lucid dreams or to develop the technology to accomplish this. Though some claim success in doing this, no one has been able to take someone else's dreams and transform them into virtual reality for others to experience or at least see. At least, not yet. With *The NeuroVel Xperience*, I wanted to write a story about a tech giant who had achieved this feat and how this would affect the world at large – politically, economically, and in other universal practical terms.

When Robots Cry

Computers and other smart technological devices are increasingly faster, more intuitive, more portable, and higher-powered than ever. Every last three years deliver more technological advances than the previous twenty. Artificial Intelligence also improves tremendously from year to year. There are smart, personal virtual assistants in almost every home and everyone's pocket around the world today. These AI's make our lives simpler, more organized, and remind us of important things, such as key dates and times. Many people have wondered how long it will be until AI's are capable of being self-conscious. The question I wanted to ask, and perhaps answer, with *When Robots Cry* is: Can AI's suffer existential crisis when they lack purpose in life?

It Only Takes A Spark

Let me begin by saying that I wrote this story when I was in college. Though I originally intended for this to be a full-length thriller novel, I decided to go revisit it and change its entire premise and make it a sci-fi fable. And I sure am glad I did! Nonetheless, from the very beginning, I wanted a story in which the villain felt like the hero and the hero became the villain. Or better yet, for there to be none of either. I decided to keep that. However, in my revision, I wanted to explore the notion of robots as individual beings. We are all sad when one of our expensive electronics breaks. This time, I wanted to experience what it would be like to lose a loved one, that loved one being an electronic entity. *It Only Takes A Spark* is an opportunity for the reader to visit identity and purpose, all within the confines of marriage, racism, and infidelity.

I Choose You

Since its origins, space travel has been an iconic theme in science fiction. With *I Choose You*, I wanted to explore the likely probability of things not always going as planned during one of these intergalactic trips. I also wanted to delve into a story using only personal logs. Because I wanted my collection to have a variety of feels, I also opted for a romantic tone. I present to you, Titanic in space.

Link

When I wrote this story, I originally wanted it to have a much darker connotation, making the virus an evil entity that wreaked havoc in the world. As I kept writing it, however, I decided to shift its focus to the creators of the application instead. Giving it a much more human feel, allowed the story to tell itself. And as an alternative to showing the potential wicked side of technology, I wanted to showcase the very likely unpleasant side of human beings that work with technology instead. *Link* is as much a story of betrayal as it is of karma, whether you believe in that or not. The real question is, who is truly the bad guy in any story?

Theory of Mind

As a psychologist, but also as a writer, I wanted to explore the notion that even robots with the most advanced AI's in the future would not be neurotypical. Because of this, it dawned on me that perhaps some of these machines could connect well with non-neurotypical human beings. These lead me further to the examination of empathy. I wanted to see if whether empathy is an emotional or a cognitive response – to which I say, it is both. Though this was not previously the case, we now know and understand that empathy is not solely a human trait, as many animals have been observed to demonstrate empathy with others as well. And the fact is that there is plenty that we can learn from all other living beings that we share the world with. *Theory of Mind* is simply the optimist in me dreaming of a future in which machines are also empathetic and where we can learn from them as well.

Corporeal Adjustment

We've all been there. We look in the mirror and notice the imperfections. The extra weight we've put in through the years. The heavy bags or dark patches under our eyes. The whitening, thinning, or lack of, hair. Every time we shower and notice the fallen hair in the tub is a constant reminder of our inevitable aging. Though getting old brings about plenty of positive outcomes in our lives, such as opportunities, as well as an accumulation of memories, knowledge, and understanding, the truth is that it also takes a toll on our physical bodies. The plastic surgery, cosmetics, and fashion industries are some of the biggest money-making ones in the world for a reason. Though sci-fi stories have been written about this theme of mind transference, I wanted to provide a new twist on it with *Corporeal Adjustment*. I pray I did it justice.

Time-Surfing: The App

I don't always write fiction. The fact is that for every story I write, there are countless creative non-fiction pieces that I put out. Because of this, I wanted to include a piece on this short-story collection that didn't read like a story, but that it also felt as realistic as possible, no matter how implausible the topic was. And though fictional in nature, I wanted this one to feel and read just like any other article that one would find in any tech magazine. *Time-Surfing: The App* is my first attempt on bridging fiction and creative non-fiction.

Aberrational

I have a lot of interests and fascinations. For example, ever since I learned about it, I have always been fascinated by parthenogenesis, which is a form of reproduction in which an egg can develop into an embryo without being fertilized by a sperm. In other words, for some species, it doesn't take two to tango. Being a foreigner in this nation, and having been out of status for some time – though that is a different story for another time –, I have also been intrigued by the idea of legal status and legal rights. With *Aberrational*, I wanted to explore those two ideas by asking the questions: What makes a living being alive? And, what constitutes being human, or rather, what does it mean to be a human being?

Heart of Steel

The question at the center of *Heart of Steel* is one we've all wrestled with at some point: What does it truly mean to be human? ROB-NEX D9's journey is one of longing—for emotion, identity, and purpose. But becoming human, as he finds out, isn't as glamorous or fulfilling as it first appears. In writing this, I wanted to flip the usual "Pinocchio complex" on its head. Sometimes, the fantasy of becoming something else blinds us to the value in who we already are. The story is a meditation on the soul—not the physical body or even the mind, but the messy, beautiful totality of being.

The Midnight Machinist

This was my love letter to both steampunk and the spirit of revolution. With *The Midnight Machinist*, I wanted to imagine a Latino hero in an alternate, Victorian 1895 Los Angeles—one run on gears, steam, and injustice. Santiago Reyes, or El Forjador, represents that quiet resilience found in so many immigrant families. While the city he lives in is fictionalized, the struggle for workers' rights and fair conditions remains painfully real. The brass suit is just the vessel. At its heart, this story asks: What does it mean to fight for justice when the system itself is engineered to crush you? This still resonates today.

ACKNOWLEDGEMENTS

I offer my sincere gratitude to Kiezha. Without your help, my words would be a mess. To my friends who took the time to read my stories and who provided me with the support and encouragement to keep on writing. I am eternally grateful.

I also want to give special mention to my family. First of all, to my wife, Zaidy, again, thank you. Without you, this book would still only be a dream. Thanks for your patience and love, but also for pushing me and believing in me. To my kids, Ojani and Zowie, thank you for being the inspiration to write my stories. Thank you for the smiles and for the memories. To my parents, Oscar and Letty, thank you for always providing encouragement and support and for teaching me to care for those things that truly matter. *¡Los amo!* To my brothers, Oscar and Omar, thank you for going along with me on this journey. It's been great.

Papi and Omar, I miss you a lot. May you both rest in peace. I can't wait for that glorious day when we will all be reunited once again.

And finally, I am thankful to God, from Whom all blessings flow.

OBED OLIVARRÍA was born in Mexicali, Mexico and spent his youth as a fully bicultural transnational citizen. He has a passion for writing both fiction and nonfiction, public speaking, composing, arranging, and performing mostly jazz music, as well as traveling around the world. He loves the thrill of adrenaline-pumping activities, but also the quiet reflection he gets from writing and creating.

His love for books started at an early age, as his parents were eager readers and owned thousands of books. His passion for writing was born after winning a city-wide short story competition while in high school in Arizona. The publication of this in a local journal inspired him to continue creating worlds and characters in print.

Obed has worked as a youth and young adult pastor, as a freelance graphic designer, as a session musician, as a ministry consultant, and as university dean. Having worked at every level of the education system, from pre-k to university, has given him an expedition to the human psyche. He has a dynamic love of life and ministry, and he is a deep thinker, and an honest intellectual to the Christian gospel.

Obed lives in sunny Orange County, California with his charming wife and two energetic children, where he works as a school psychologist by day. In the future, Obed hopes to be able to continue to write inspiring books that entertain, but also challenge the status quo. On a personal level, he would like to visit every country in the world, perhaps drawing inspiration from these travels for another great story.

www.obedolivarria.com